CRITICS RAVE FOR PEARL AWARD WINNER PATTI O'SHEA!

THROUGH A CRIMSON VEIL

"This adventurous thriller is searing hot and filled with passion, treachery and danger. It's paranormal adventure at its ultimate! O'Shea has definitely found her calling."

—*RT BOOKclub* (Top Pick)

"[A]nother thrilling and dangerous walk in Crimson City.... Danger is around every corner; demons and otherworldly creatures lurk in the darkness, and passion comes alive in Patti O'Shea's *Through a Crimson Veil*."

—*ws Today*

"I got so inv_____ I could not put it do_____ ____dertones of the futuris_____ ____a's] character develo_____ ____first-rate and believable, her dialogue is crisp and snappy, and her narrative is vivid and spellbinding."

—Fresh Fiction

"You will love the spin Patti O'Shea puts on this paranormal keeper. It's exciting, fun, dangerous, and sexy! ...Action-packed, scary, romantic and laugh-out-loud funny, *Through a Crimson Veil* makes for a book that is hard to put down."

—Romance Reader at Heart (Top Pick)

"*Through a Crimson Veil* is a fantastic paranormal romantic suspense thriller that never slows down.... The story line is action-packed.... Patti O'Shea spins a jewel of a Crimson City tale."

—The Best Reviews

MORE RAVES FOR PATTI O'SHEA!

THE POWER OF TWO

"Fabulous action sequences, an engaging and believable romance, and some of the most well-written lovemaking scenes of the year make the fourth entry in this exciting futuristic series terrific escapist reading."

—*Booklist*

"Patti O'Shea pens a gripping tale that certainly lives up to the high standards set by the other authors in the 2176 series. Witty dialogue and an engrossing plot make *The Power of Two* a must read."

—*Romance Reviews Today*

"Make sure to fasten your seatbelt for this wild ride!"

—*RT BOOKclub*

"Ms. O'Shea has done a splendid job of furthering this series and I give *The Power of Two* my highest recommendation. Grab a copy today."

—A Romance Review

RAVYN'S FLIGHT

"Danger, fast action, and alpha males and females create a nonstop futuristic keeper with a touch of alien mystery."

—*RT BOOKclub*

"Intelligent, admirable, and appealing…. There is a new star in the paranormal and futuristic heavens—Patti O'Shea."

—*Romance Reviews Today*

"*Ravyn's Flight* is a strong military science fiction romance that once the plot goes into gear never leaves hyperspeed until the final pages are finished."

—*The Midwest Book Review*

A NARROW ESCAPE

Wyatt stood facing the gap in the wall, pistol drawn, prepared to fire if the secret door didn't shut in time. Kendall's eyes were glued on the corner, waiting for those smugglers to round it.

The gap continued to narrow, and Wyatt shifted, keeping his weapon trained into the hall until, with a nearly inaudible scraping sound, they were entombed.

"Where'd they go?" The voice was muffled.

"They gotta be hiding around here somewhere," the other man said. "We'll find them."

Her adrenaline began to ebb, and Kendall swayed as lightheadedness replaced it. Before she could catch her balance, Wyatt's arms were around her and he held her against him. For some stupid reason, she felt emotion slam into her. He always took care of her, protected her. He'd been willing to stand in front of her and shield her from the bullets as long as he could.

She reached out and hugged him back. One or both of them could have died—her mind circled back to that fact repeatedly. She might have gone to her grave without feeling his body over hers, inside hers, and that loss suddenly was more than she could bear.

Eternal Nights

PATTI O'SHEA

LOVE SPELL

LOVE
SPELL

NEW YORK CITY

LOVE SPELL®

August 2006

Published by

Dorchester Publishing Co., Inc.
200 Madison Avenue
New York, NY 10016

ISBN 0-505-52660-3

The name "Love Spell" and its logo are trademarks of Dorchester Publishing Co., Inc.

Printed in the United States of America.

Visit us on the web at www.dorchesterpub.com.

Eternal Nights is dedicated to the men and women of the United States Army—especially to the men in Special Forces—as a tribute to their sacrifice, courage, honor and willingness to defend their country. Most Americans will never know their names, but these are our real heroes and heroines.

Thanks to:

SSgt. Brian Jensen, SMSgt. Kennith Mazac and Lt. Jason Hull of the Minnesota Air National Guard for patiently answering my many questions. Any mistakes or alterations are mine.

Melissa Lynn Copeland and Theresa Monsey, my writing buddies. Yes, Mel, Wyatt belongs to you, I promise.

Kate Seaver, Leah Hultenschmidt and Lucienne Diver for their roles in bringing this book to life.

And a special thank you to all the people who contacted me after reading *Ravyn's Flight* and asked for more. This story is for you.

Eternal Nights

"True love is friendship set on fire."
—French proverb

Prologue

After hours of relentless searching, Wyatt found Jim "Catfish" Hunter in one of the many parks inside the Old City. His buddy was lying on his back with his hands behind his head, stargazing, and Wyatt hesitated before closing the distance between them. "You're a hard man to track down," he said.

"Not hard enough." Hunter's gaze returned to the sky. "Nothing is familiar in the heavens here. Take a look and tell me what you see."

Since Wyatt planned to ask for a favor, he obliged. He squinted, trying to get a better view, but it didn't do much good. "Sorry, Catfish. I can pick out a few of the extra bright stars, but the energy field around the Old City makes it hard to see much more than that."

There was a long silence, then, "So you're one of the handful of people who can see the field, huh? What's it look like?"

Wyatt hesitated, shrugged. "It's orange right now, but that changes depending on the time of day."

The quiet dragged out again before Hunter asked, "So what's up, Marsh? There must be a reason you came searching for me."

Wyatt took a deep breath. "I need a favor."

"What?"

"Watch out for Kendall while I'm gone, will you?"

"Sure," Hunter agreed easily. "What's going on?"

"I don't know, but something's bothering her."

"Did you ask what it was?"

"Yeah. She said there's nothing to talk about yet, but she'd tell me if and when there was." That cryptic statement made him nervous, but he hadn't been able to get any more out of her. Kendall could be damn stubborn when she wanted to be.

"Well, at least it can't be another man after her. The only person stationed on Jarved Nine who doesn't realize you've staked your claim is the lady herself."

"That's supposed to make me feel better? She's driving me insane." And she was. As long as he stayed firmly in the "friend" category, everything was fine, but if he took one step outside that box, he felt as if he were walking on eggshells.

"I'd suggest you find someone else, but it's much too late for you, Marsh. She has you hogtied." Catfish laughed. "And the best part is that she doesn't know it."

"Some buddy you are."

"Come on, you can't blame me for enjoying this. What's that thing called? You know, what goes around comes around?"

"Karma," he said glumly.

"Yeah, that's it. Karma. The rest of us endured some rocky love affairs, while you escaped unscathed. Now you're the one suffering. It's only fair."

Wyatt wasn't in the mood for jokes.

"So," Catfish said a bit too heartily, sensing his friend's

concern, "are you going to inform Kendall that I'm on the job or is this a covert mission?"

"I'm going to tell her. I want her to know she can count on you if she needs someone." Wyatt wasn't sure why he was worried. There were only a little more than six hundred troops and consultants stationed on Jarved Nine and plenty of MPs to keep order. The few problems he'd heard about were some minor fights, but he never discounted his instincts, and they were turning cartwheels. "In fact, I should head for her quarters—she has early morning duty tomorrow. You want to come along?"

"Nah, I'll let you mess this up on your own." Jim reclined on the grass again. "I'm going to do some more stargazing."

Wyatt took a few steps, then stopped. "Catfish? Thanks, man. I owe you."

"No, you don't." Hunter didn't look away from the sky.

After a brief hesitation, Wyatt walked away. Smart money said Kendall would be furious that he'd arranged for someone to look out for her, but he'd handle it. And maybe, while she was spitting fire, he could provoke her into telling him what was gnawing at her.

He heard the wind chime as soon as he turned onto the street she lived on. Since there was no breeze inside the Old City—the protective shield kept out all the elements—someone had to be making it sing. As he grew closer, he saw Kendall's shadowy outline sitting on the railing, her fingers toying with the dangling rectangles of glass.

In daylight, it was an incredible piece—the sun would send prisms of color shooting around the porch. The corners of his lips tipped up in a small smile. Kendall was saving every cent for grad school and owned nothing that could be labeled frivolous. Except for the wind chime. The musical tones stilled and he put aside the contemplation. She sat on the balustrade, one arm wrapped around her knees, her fingers tangled in the chime.

"I was wondering if you'd come by tonight." She released the ends and the tinkling music resumed, but softer than it had been, and it continued to lessen as the movement slowed.

"Hey, Bug." He climbed the two shallow, slate steps and leaned his hip against the stone railing near her bare feet. "I didn't expect you to be outside this late."

Wyatt wanted to take her in his arms, but instead he curled a hand around her ankle and rubbed his thumb across the bone. Even this innocent touch sent a thrill through his body. He ached to wrap his arms around her, kiss her, love her, but the reserve in her eyes held him back.

Damn, he wished she could recall their past life here—the life when his name had been Berkant and she'd been called Zolianna—but like most people, Kendall had no memory of any other incarnation. He didn't know why he remembered, just that he'd always been aware of it.

She'd left the lights off on the porch, but he saw her clearly despite the shadows. Kendall had pulled her light brown hair back into a loose braid and his fingers itched to free it—he had wet dreams about her long tresses grazing his naked body as they made love. With a silent sigh, Wyatt settled for trailing a finger down the blond streak near her temple. Wariness filled her jungle-green eyes. Regretfully, he withdrew his hand from her face and stopped caressing her ankle.

"What time are you leaving tomorrow?" she asked quietly. Bug wasn't meeting his gaze and he didn't know how to read that.

"First light—allegedly—but I'll believe that when I see it. Civilians," he added with a grin. She smiled up at him and he lost his breath for a moment. He had to clear his throat before he could resume speaking. "We're supposed to be gone for two weeks, but it seems the geologists always find something they want to investigate more closely. My team will probably be out there baby-sitting them longer than what we're scheduled for."

Kendall bit her lower lip, her lightness gone. "More than two weeks? Really?" Her gaze dropped to her knees, but not before he saw the concern flit through her eyes.

Wyatt took her chin between his thumb and forefinger and tipped her face to his. "What's wrong, Bug?" he asked. "I can't help fix it if you don't tell me."

"If I were ready to tell anyone, you'd be the one." She gently brushed his fingers from her face, but she didn't let go of him. "It's nothing concrete, you know, and I'd feel really stupid if I was jumping to conclusions."

"Don't you understand?" Every instinct told him to gather her close, but he fought it. The fact that she'd linked her fingers with his was a hell of a big step for her, and if he pushed, he'd lose this tiny bit of ground. "You can tell me anything and not worry about feeling stupid later."

"You're a good friend," Kendall said with an overly bright grin. She freed her hand from his, swung her feet to the ground and crossed the porch, putting space between them.

He wanted to curse, but swallowed the words. She always did this, always pulled away whenever things started to get intimate, and he hated it. When he regained control, he said, "I talked to Catfish. He's going to check on you while I'm gone." Wyatt threw that out like a gauntlet.

"Okay, thanks."

Bug was feisty, fiery and independent to a fault; he'd expected her to tear into him, but she didn't, and that made him even more uneasy. "For God's sake, Kendall, if whatever you're stewing over starts coming to a head while I'm away, go to him. He'll take care of you till I get back."

For a minute, he thought she was going to deny it was

anything serious and that would have pissed him off big time. He knew her too well to buy that bullshit. Instead she nodded and said, "I will. Promise."

Wyatt had been in Spec Ops long enough that it took one hell of a lot to leave him terrified, but with three words, Bug managed to turn his blood to ice. If she wasn't fighting him on this, it meant she was scared. "Kendall?"

She turned and gave him another too-bright smile. "It's late and I need to get up early tomorrow. So do you if you have to report before first light. Have a safe trip."

Bug held out her hand. She held out her *hand* as if he were some stranger she'd just been introduced to. The gesture infuriated him—and it pierced him to the very core of his soul. He struggled to keep his tone neutral. "Friends hug good-bye."

"What?"

"You heard me." He stared until she lowered her arm. He wasn't willing to make it easy for her. Not this time.

Slowly, she studied him, her head tilted a shade to the left. "I'm sorry," she said at last. Kendall closed the space between them, and shocking the hell out of him, she wrapped her arms around his waist. He'd never expected her to actually do it. "You *are* my best friend; I don't want to hurt you."

"Aw, damn, Bug, you're my best friend too." She'd taken the heat out of him that easily. Wyatt returned the embrace, but kept his hold loose since he knew how uncomfortable she was with such close contact. Her eyes never wavered from his, and in the darkened porch, the communion seemed more intimate than a kiss. At the thought, his gaze dropped to her lips. They were slightly parted, moist, and he wanted a taste so damn bad he nearly shook with need.

She swayed toward him. Her breasts pressed into his chest as her face tipped up to his and Wyatt felt his heart skip a beat. Finally, he was going to kiss Kendall.

But he miscalculated. He started to lower his head to

meet her and that one motion broke the spell. She stepped back from him so fast, he didn't have time to react, and before he could blink, Kendall reached her front door.

"Take care of yourself, Wyatt."

"You too, darlin'," he said quietly, but she'd already disappeared inside the house and didn't hear him.

Chapter One

She had them. She had them!

Well, kind of. She had *one* name. Maybe. If it wasn't co-incidence. Dr. Charles B. George. Kendall took a deep breath and tried to quiet her trembling hands. She had to stay calm and not call attention to herself. Not now.

Surreptitiously, she peered around the room, but no one appeared interested in her. Still, she couldn't take any chances. Not when she had no idea how many people were involved or whom she could trust.

She'd stumbled on the thefts by accident. One of her jobs was to clean up the notes made in the field by the archeologists, so she viewed the raw data almost daily and she also read the reports that the research team sent back to the Western Alliance. It had been a little over three weeks ago that she noticed some of the digital sketches seemed to have been altered and artifacts erased. At first, she'd been sure it was her memory—after all, she pro-cessed a lot of information—but she still felt uneasy.

The relics she thought were missing were valuable, but

not so unusual that their absence would be noted. That made them perfect to be stolen. Kendall took another quick glance around the room and keyed in a search command for Dr. George's ID code. She wanted to see every file he'd changed.

Most everyone was unaware there were two programs that recorded who made data changes. One loaded up front and some had discovered a way around it, but the screener that ran in the background was a different story. It was this program that she was scanning through for evidence.

The computer beeped and she jerked. Her station was at the back of the room and in the corner—no one could see what she was doing—but she had to stay cool or she'd give herself away. She ran her clammy palms over the thighs of her camouflage fatigue pants and started paging through the records.

There were a lot of them. Most, no doubt, were legitimate, since Dr. George was the head of one of the archeological teams, but surely all of them couldn't be. What she needed was definitive proof. Something she could take to the officer in charge of planet security.

Kendall wasn't easily daunted, but Lieutenant Colonel Alexander Sullivan intimidated the hell out of her. He was a hard-ass from the word go, and if she approached him with nothing more than anecdotal evidence and gut instinct, he'd blow her out of the water. She knew it.

But she'd had to tell someone, and when Wyatt hadn't returned from his mission on schedule, she'd finally gone to his friend, Catfish. She'd been too scared to wait any longer once she was certain she wasn't misreading the situation. Catfish had promised her he'd look into it and told her not to do anything, but how could she sit back and let thieves loot the Old City? She was familiar with the systems that the project team used and could discover things Hunter couldn't.

Wait a second. Kendall stopped paging through the records and tabbed back a few screens. Something had looked wrong.

Nothing there. She went back another screen to a sketch of the temple's receiving room. As she studied the digital image, she knew something was off, but couldn't figure out what bothered her. Her eyes widened as she figured it out.

The antiquity missing in the drawing hadn't been stolen yet!

At least it hadn't been a few hours ago. She knew because she'd been in that very room during her lunch break and had seen the sculpture with her own eyes.

She finally, *finally* had something she could take to Sullivan. Of course, this file with the missing relic wasn't irrefutable. It would be easy for Dr. George—or anyone else, for that matter—to claim it was an oversight. That the statue in question had been inadvertently left off the room sketch. But it would be enough to cause security to investigate, and once they started, they'd surely find all kinds of evidence.

Kendall forced herself to take a deep breath and then another. She had to stay calm, had to think. First, she needed pictures that clearly showed the carving had been in this chamber of the temple, and the shots would need to be dated. That wouldn't be too hard. She'd get the digicam from her quarters, sneak over to the pyramid while everyone was in the mess hall, and then she'd head straight for the colonel's office. Sullivan had a rep for working long hours, and he'd likely still be there. If not, she knew where he lived. She couldn't let this go one more night, not when it looked like one of the most beautiful pieces of art inside the temple was slated to be stolen.

When she realized she was tensing up again, Kendall made herself take it down a few notches. The artifact wasn't gone yet. She could save it as long as she played it smart.

She needed a copy of this sketch for sure. After keying in a command, she strolled to the printer with as much nonchalance as she could manage and retrieved the page. As she turned, she caught sight of Dr. George. Kendall felt her knees sag and she locked them, but there was nothing she could do about the wild pounding of her heart.

Act normal.

She had to act normal. She had to breathe. He didn't know what she'd printed, didn't know what she suspected, and he didn't know that she was on to him.

Oh, my God!

Kendall's eyes widened with horror. She was an idiot. A complete moron. She'd left the file with the evidence up on her screen for *anyone* to see while she was away from her desk.

Her first instinct was to run to her station, but she couldn't. That would definitely bring unwanted attention her direction and everyone would wonder what was up with her.

A very young, very eager second lieutenant stopped the archeologist and Kendall sighed with relief. Keep him talking, she thought, but the doctor put the man in his place—George was without question the biggest jerk on Jarved Nine—and continued down the aisle. What were the odds he was coming to see her? He mostly ignored her unless it was to say something snide, and as far as she knew, she hadn't done anything that would put her on his radar. But Kendall had a bad feeling about this.

Just in case, she eyed the distance to her desk. Her route there was shorter than George's, but he was moving faster.

The lieutenant didn't give up easily. He called the doctor's name and hurried after him. Kendall picked up her pace. Not enough to be noticeable, but every second counted. She rounded the corner of her desk and resumed her seat as George the Jerk blasted the man a second time.

With a few clicks, she closed the telltale file and pulled up the database in which she was supposed to be working.

But she couldn't breathe easy yet.

Now she had to unobtrusively get rid of the paper she was holding. That was as damning as the info on her screen had been. Her hands fumbled as she tried to pick up a memo about adhering to scheduled break times. It started to flutter to the floor, but she caught it in time, crumpling one side with her grip.

George was one row away.

With as much casualness as possible, she put the memo on top of her printout and rested both on the left corner of her desk, opposite the side the archeologist was approaching from. Relief flooded through her body, and she slumped back in her seat.

Dr. George stopped at her desk and cleared his throat. Kendall quickly sat upright as a new shot of adrenaline surged through her.

Before she could say anything, a sheaf of papers dropped onto the station in front of her. For a moment, she frowned, and then she recognized the report she'd written on the crystals of the Old City. This method of returning it to her could only mean one thing—she was about to receive a scathing commentary on her effort. She had a moment to wonder how George had gotten his hands on it. Kendall had turned her paper in to Dr. Hudson, the head honcho on the archeological project team.

"Miss Thomas, would you care to explain why you thought you could waste Dr. Hudson's time on *that?*" His twang grated on her nerves, though that same Texas accent sounded appealing—all right, let's be honest, sexy—coming from Wyatt.

"*Captain* Thomas," Kendall corrected stiffly. Not that her rank would impress him, but she had to behave normally and she never let him call her *Miss* without straightening him out.

"Perhaps you believed you were writing for some half-baked New Age Web site," he continued, raising his voice so everyone in the room could hear him lambaste her. "This, however, is a scholarly endeavor, one comprised of the brightest minds in the Western Alliance. If you want to invent stories about irrational things like the energetic meaning of crystals, I suggest you join a commune."

Her face went hot. Thank goodness she hadn't put her more controversial speculation on the crystals in the document. It took effort to keep her voice even. "If you had read my report carefully instead of jumping to conclusions, you'd know that I was theorizing about what the people who lived in the Old City believed about the gemstones, not what I believed."

She met Dr. George's angry stare without flinching. If he reported her, and he might, she knew Colonel McNamara would be understanding. It was no secret that the commander of Jarved Nine didn't like this pompous windbag either. Besides, if Kendall was right and he was involved in the smuggling of antiquities, her lack of respect would be the least of his worries.

"The curriculum of Introduction to Anthropology must be much more rigorous than I recall from my days as an undergraduate," he said. "In the near future, we must arrange for you to pass along your vast store of knowledge to the *doctors* on this team. After all, it's not every day we have an opportunity to receive instruction from a cheerleader."

Her hands clenched in her lap, and she pressed her lips together to contain the torrent of words. Four years in the army had taught her to be silent, but she didn't like it.

"Nothing to say?" George's smile was smug, contemptuous. "What a pity when we could have gleaned so much from you."

She fisted her hands tighter, struggling to remain quiet, until with a nod of superiority, Dr. George walked away.

When he left, Kendall slowly relaxed her grip. There were red indentations where her nails had pressed into her skin, and she rubbed one hand with the other as she looked around. Everyone seemed to be concentrating on their jobs, but she knew that wasn't true.

A rhythmic flash brought her attention back to the screen, and after pushing a loose tress off her face, she entered the correction with shaking hands. Once the program resumed its comparison scanning, she retrieved her drawing, and, putting it on her lap, slid closer to her desk. Quietly, she folded it into a small square and slipped it inside her pocket.

Taking a shaky breath, she resumed her job. She'd barely processed the first scan when about a dozen wrist alarms went off, startling her. End of duty shift, she realized, and tried to calm her racing heart.

Kendall picked up her report and looked ruefully at it for a moment as she took some deep breaths. She'd written it in the hope that Dr. Hudson would be impressed enough to offer her a field assistant's job. What a mistake. She grabbed her bag out of her lower drawer, jammed the paper into it, and headed for her house.

Jarved Nine was a planet light years from Earth, but this place felt more like home to her than anywhere she'd lived in the U.S. Kendall wished she knew why this world had been abandoned. It seemed as if the residents had just walked away and could return any minute. The lack of deterioration had a good deal to do with this perception— the field of energy encapsulating the city had preserved everything perfectly—but according to the tests the archeologists had done, the walled compound had been deserted nearly three thousand years ago.

The stone buildings lining the streets seemed to glow in the early evening sun, and as she walked, it relaxed her. Kendall was almost home when she was blinded by a beam of sunlight reflecting off the capstone of the pyramid at the center of the Old City. She brought up a hand to block the glare before memory slammed into her.

Damn. She'd forgotten. Forgotten the dream had awoken her again in the dead of night. Forgotten how frightened she'd been as she'd curled up in the middle of her bed and tried not to fall back asleep. Forgotten the way her heart had pounded and her lungs had strained for air. Kendall *hated* the dream.

Despite everything she'd tried, she couldn't remember what it was about, no more than a few stray details—like the shaft of light hitting her eyes in almost this exact manner.

And the blood. So much blood.

If she could recall what happened, she could look up the elements in her dream dictionary and analyze them. Her mom had always told her that every vision had a message, and considering how many times Kendall had replayed this nightmare lately, it must be a pretty important one.

God, she wished Wyatt were here. Not that she'd tell him about her night terrors, but somehow they didn't feel as horrific after she saw him. Shaking her head, she started walking again.

She wished he were here for another reason. As much as she liked Catfish, she wanted Wyatt working with her on the thefts. Kendall turned another corner, and the light was blocked. She lowered her hand and bit her lip.

What if the dream was a warning not to involve him in her investigation? She'd never been precognitive, but the nightmare had started four months ago, immediately after she'd met Wyatt. That had to mean something, right? What if he got hurt because he was helping her? Kendall sucked in a sharp breath and turned onto her street.

What if he got *killed* helping her?

She dropped her head back and blinked hard a couple of times. He'd already known something was bothering her before he left the city. Since she'd only been maybe ten percent sure at that point that something more than a memory lapse was going on, she hadn't felt she could say anything. Now, however, she was ninety percent sure, and she had to tell him as soon as he returned. If she didn't, Catfish sure as hell would.

Feeling as if the weight of the world rested on her shoulders, Kendall climbed the two stone steps to her front porch. As she passed her wind chime, she put out her index finger and set the rectangles of patterned glass dancing.

Instead of entering her quarters, she sank onto one of the chairs she kept outside, leaned back and listened. The tinkling tones soothed her, but it was more than that. The chime was one of the most beautiful things Kendall had ever seen, and the instant she'd laid eyes on it, she'd known she had to buy it.

Growing up, she hadn't had much, and as an adult, Kendall still didn't accumulate things. But she'd taken this wind chime with her to every post she'd been assigned to for the last four years.

With no breeze, the music didn't last long. Too lazy to get up, she turned her gaze to what she could view from her seat. Since the temple was not only the biggest, but also the tallest structure in the Old City, she could see it over the roofs of the other buildings. Before she'd arrived on J Nine, the teams had performed about a gazillion different measurements and learned it was larger than the Great Pyramid in Egypt. Much larger.

It didn't make sense to her. Why build such an enormous pyramid and put only a few rooms in it? But she'd perused the data on the temple more carefully than any other structure in the Old City, and according to everything she'd read, the interior was solid stone. That felt wrong.

The capstone continued to shine. With a loud exhale, she put aside her thoughts and checked her watch. A few more minutes, then most people would be at mess and she could make it to the pyramid without worrying too much about being spotted. Kendall bit her lower lip. Maybe she should look for Catfish and ask him to go with her. Except she had no clue where he was. She could waste hours searching for him, hours she didn't have, since she needed to have her mission accomplished before dinner ended.

Besides, once she got to the temple, she'd probably be safe. Almost everyone avoided it as if there were DANGER: KEEP OUT signs surrounding it. They all spoke of feeling as if someone had walked over their graves while they were inside, usually adding an embarrassed smile at their foolishness. She'd never had that sense. To her, it was peaceful. Perfect. Hers.

Kendall reached for the fasteners keeping her hair up and yanked them free. She opened a pocket on the front of her bag and stowed the clips, then went inside to retrieve her digicam. It was time.

Once she reemerged, she took a careful look around, and when she didn't see anyone, set off. Her nerves strung tighter as she hurried through neighborhood after neighborhood of alien houses. Time seemed to stand still, but she was taking a roundabout path to the pyramid to improve the odds that she wouldn't see anyone.

Her luck ran out in a side plaza filled with shops. Kendall couldn't stop the gasp of dismay as she saw a man striding toward her at full speed. She didn't recognize him until he was about twenty yards away from where she was standing. Colonel Sullivan.

Maybe she should tell him right now what was going on and bring him to the temple with her. She wouldn't have to worry whether she was spotted if he were accompanying her—no one would mess with the colonel.

She waited for him to reach her, but he didn't pause, didn't even acknowledge her despite her salute. Kendall watched his back for a minute, then gathered her courage and chased after him. "Colonel Sullivan," she said as she pulled even with him, "I need to talk to you."

He glared at her. "Not now."

"But sir, it's important." She was practically running to keep up with his long strides.

"Captain, I said not now. Which word was over your head?"

Her bravery was flooding away from her but she grasped one small portion of it and said, "Sir, please—"

"Make an appointment, Captain, and that's an order."

"Yes, sir," she said quietly and drew to a halt. He left her behind and she was sure he'd already forgotten her existence. Well, she'd planned to go to the pyramid alone anyway; she'd just return to her original idea and hunt him down later.

Once she had proof, he wouldn't brusquely blow her off.

Alex was pissed.

Damned kids. These officers seemed to get younger every day and they had less common sense than ever. Any fool could see that now wasn't a good time to bother him, but had that stopped the girl? Hell, no. She'd hounded him like a reporter after a disgraced politician. Shit. He put her out of his mind. Alex had more important things to worry about than some idiot captain.

In the time there'd been army personnel on Jarved Nine, he'd never had to deal with a major crime. A few fights, some petty larceny, nothing too big. Now it looked as if he'd be facing his first huge problem.

Murder.

He hoped to God the MPs who'd found the body were wrong, that it was some kind of accident, but he was too pragmatic to believe that. He'd known it was only a matter of time until something like this happened. A small post where people ran into the same faces day after day—

sooner or later someone was bound to enrage another person enough to want them dead.

Or maybe it was a crime of passion. Stacey and Ravyn would both rip him up one side and down the other if he were stupid enough to say it aloud, but having women stationed here was asking for trouble. The troops had started pairing off almost from the beginning and the affairs didn't always end cleanly. At least if this were the case, it would be fairly easy to find the guilty party and McNamara would have his—or her—ass confined so fast, he'd have imprints from the bars on his backside.

McNamara. He'd been butting heads with the woman from day one; she'd be all over him to solve this thing ASAP. Like he wouldn't be working as hard as he could to come up with answers. He forced his fists to unclench as he reached the square where the body had been found. At first, he didn't see anyone; then a head popped up.

Oh, this was great. His MP was puking his guts out. But the sarcasm covered fear. Three years ago, there had been no one on this planet except a Colonization Assessment Team and nineteen of the twenty members had been slaughtered by an alien ritual killer. The Special Operations team that responded to the emergency signal hadn't fared much better, losing six out of seven men to the same murderer. Alex had led the rescue team from Earth and he could still remember the sick feeling that had swamped him when he'd seen the mutilated bodies.

"Where?" Alex asked, raising his voice to be heard over the dry heaving. The MP attempted to stand, gave it up as another spasm went through him, and settled for saluting while bent over. Alex bit back a curse and repeated himself. "Where?"

The kid managed to point, and Alex left him to see firsthand what was going on. What a mess. Too many people on his military police force didn't have real seasoning and hadn't acquired any while on Jarved Nine. He had his Spec Ops soldiers—no one could say they were green—but now half of them had been ordered to return to Earth. If this body had anything close to the type of wounds he'd found on the CAT, there was no way in hell he was letting Special Forces get on that transport.

Alex located the second MP and was relieved to see the woman noting details about the crime scene. Thank God for sergeants who had a few years under their belts.

The noncom met him at the mouth of the alley and went through the formalities before filling him in. She was thorough, but Alex was impatient to see the victim. "Why don't you keep talking while I take a closer look," he suggested.

"Sir . . ."

"What, Sergeant?" he prompted when the woman didn't immediately spit it out.

"He's one of ours."

Alex didn't wait to hear more. He went down the alley and took a look for himself. As he stood, gazing down at one of his men, he decided there was good news and bad news.

The good news was that the murder was definitely committed by a human and not some alien. It was a simple knife across the throat. Ugly—the puking kid said it all—but not as gruesome as what he'd seen when he'd come to J Nine on that rescue mission.

The bad news, however, went beyond the fact that he'd lost a man. First, the victim was a Special Operations officer, one of Alex's best. That someone had managed to take him out meant they had a serious threat inside the Old City. Second, it wasn't going to be an easy crime to solve. Not when no likely motive sprang to mind.

Captain James Hunter didn't drink, didn't get into brawls, didn't gamble, and since he was still mourning the death of his wife, he didn't play around. He was quiet and easygoing, making it unlikely that he'd just plain pissed someone off.

So with all the simple reasons gone, why the hell had anyone murdered Catfish?

Chapter Two

Wyatt pulled his olive T-shirt over his head and reached for his jungle camo fatigue pants. He tucked, then zipped before taking one last look in the mirror. Bug would know immediately that he'd showered and shaved before seeing her, but maybe she'd assume it was because he was ripe from three weeks in the field. It wasn't true, but if she jumped to that conclusion, he wouldn't straighten her out. As skittish as she was, it would set him back a few steps if she thought he'd spiffed up for her, especially since they'd nearly kissed.

For that same reason, he wasn't going to her quarters. Instead, he planned to casually bump into her in the mess hall. It would be natural then to join her for supper and maybe spend some time together afterward.

The thought made him smile and he left the bathing chamber—he couldn't think of the elaborate marble expanse as a bathroom—and tugged on his socks and boots. This alien house was a bit ornate for his taste, but he liked the privacy it afforded over the prefab barracks. Of course, it helped that he was one of the small number of people who could turn on the water and lights. It took some practice to learn to draw energy from the planet and aim it with his mind to manipulate basic household functions, but it was kind of cool once he got the hang of it. Bug was the one who'd shared the secret of how to manage the power.

And maybe now she'd be ready to share more with him. Like what the hell had been bothering her before he'd left the Old City. If not, he'd hunt down Catfish after he escorted Bug home and find out if anything had gone down while he'd been away.

Whistling under his breath, he headed toward the front of the house. In a few minutes, he'd see Kendall again. He'd missed her like hell.

Wyatt paused; instinct and experience told him someone was in the shadows of his porch before he walked out the door. "So much for privacy," he drawled as his executive officer unfolded himself from his chair.

"No one likes a smart-mouthed kid," Flare shot back.

"Haven't we spent enough time together, Chief Cantore?"

"Don't worry, I won't be here long. I have plans."

Wyatt hitched his thumbs through his belt loops and leaned back against the front of the building. "What's up?"

"Word is The Big Chill called you and the other Spec Ops officers in for a meeting tomorrow morning," his XO said. "You have any idea what it's about?"

Hell, he should have figured Flare knew about that. The noncoms had a grapevine that would make Hollywood gossip mavens green with envy, and his warrant officer was plugged in good and tight. "No. The message didn't say. What do you know?"

Flare looked grim. "From what I heard, it sounds like a formal declaration of hostilities with the coalition is coming sooner rather than later and about half the Spec Ops teams are being rotated home in preparation." His chief leaned against the stone railing. "I was hoping the rumor was wrong."

Muttering a curse, Wyatt rubbed both hands over his face. "Are we one of the teams going?"

"No clue about that. Could be, although the others have been here longer."

"We both know that won't mean jack shit."

His second-in-command nodded and they fell silent. Damn, he wasn't ready to go back to Earth. If he left and Bug stayed here, he'd lose the ground he'd gained with her, and God knew, forward progress had occurred one agonizing inch at a time. He thought of how close he'd come to finally tasting her. He wanted more than that almost-kiss. A lot more.

Wyatt put thoughts of Kendall aside. That was personal, and he had to consider his men now. "You get a time frame on how soon it'll be before we're officially at war?" They'd been fighting *un*officially for a while. Prior to being assigned to J Nine, his team had spent nearly three months solid out in the field.

Shrugging one shoulder, Flare said, "You know as much as I do. A week till the transport is scheduled to leave for Earth. Two weeks for the teams to report home and another week or so for them to get into position. Unless some event sparks it sooner, I'd say we're looking at about five, maybe six weeks max."

With another curse, Wyatt sat in the chair his chief had vacated. He didn't doubt Cantore. The man might look like some surf bum—hell, he'd *been* a surf bum before joining the army—but he was the sharpest damn soldier Wyatt had ever met. He'd trust the chief with his life, but more important, he'd trust Flare with *Bug's* life and Wyatt would never risk her.

Flare took the other seat. "This isn't a surprise."

"No, but I was wishing . . ." He let his voice trail off. After a moment, Wyatt said, "You know that I'll tell you and the men as much as I can as soon as I can."

"I know." Flare paused, and when he continued, it was clear he was attempting to break the somber mood. "We can't go home yet. I haven't made it to the ocean here or caught any waves." He studied Wyatt. "Maybe you should try to stay on The Chill's good side. Might make him more amenable to keeping us around. You officers are always good at ass-kissing."

Wyatt flipped off his XO and ignored the chuckle. Leaning back in his chair, he looked out on the Old City. If the team was sent back to Earth, he'd have come up with some new strategy to win Kendall. No way was he starting over at square one with her, not after everything he'd already done.

There were times Bug frustrated the hell out of him, times he wondered why he went to so much effort for her. But then she'd smile at him, and he knew she was worth every sleepless night, every cold shower. Wyatt blew out a harsh breath. Besides, he might be worrying for nothing. There was a fifty-fifty chance that he and the team would be staying.

"Is there anything else we need to talk about? I want to catch up with Kendall in time to eat with her."

"I saw her hurrying by about twenty minutes before you came out of the house, but she wasn't headed for the mess hall."

"Which way was she going?"

Wyatt followed Flare's pointed finger. "Oh, shit," he said under his breath. The pyramid was that way, and she was obsessed with that damn pile of rock. He knew why she was attracted to it, and he didn't like it. But it was just some stone hallways and a few rooms filled with relics, nothing to worry about now.

To be safe, though, he'd better find her and keep her

out of trouble. He put his hands on his chair arms to push to his feet. Flare called after him, but Wyatt ignored his XO. Nothing mattered except finding Kendall.

Kendall. What the hell was she up to? He had a bad feeling about this. Very bad.

Almost involuntarily, he glanced up at the pyramid. The capstone was glowing bloodred. Shit. Wyatt started running, not sure why he thought the color was a sign of trouble. All he knew was he had to find Bug. Now.

Kendall carefully scanned the area near the temple from the recessed doorway of an adjacent structure. Though she'd made it here without running into anyone except Colonel Sullivan, she was erring on the side of caution. She couldn't risk being seen, not at this odd hour of the day. If word reached the wrong ears . . . well, she didn't want to think about it.

After pushing her hair off her face, she wiped her clammy palms off on the seat of her fatigue pants. She wasn't sure why she was so nervous. How many times before had she entered without anyone knowing? A hundred? Two hundred? Really, this was simply one more excursion.

Five minutes. That was all she needed to get to the room, grab a few pictures, and get back out. But she didn't move.

She never tired of looking at the temple. Its color seemed to change on a whim, and the capstone was even more mercurial. How could she not be fascinated?

Shifting her attention, she glanced at the small square to her left. For an instant, her abdomen clenched, and she felt dizzy. A sense of aversion filled her body. Kendall blinked to clear her head. Damn, maybe she shouldn't have skipped lunch today.

Unsettled, she looked in the other direction and took in the enormous plaza stretching away from the opposite

side of the pyramid. Steps rose in the square, starting at
the base and ascending three quarters of the distance to
the peak. Along the way, there were two altars—at least
that's what she called them—one at the top of the stairs,
and the other much lower.

She was stalling. Kendall knew it, but her stomach was
tied in knots. Every time she thought about entering the
temple, her heart rate increased and a feeling of dread settled in her chest. She wanted to leave. Wanted to forget
about the pictures.

Except running wasn't an option.

Not unless she wanted to watch another priceless artifact disappear. Not unless she wanted to live with the
knowledge that her cowardice had aided the criminals.

There was no reason for her to be reacting like this, and
Kendall forced herself to move. By the time she reached
the temple, her legs were trembling as if she'd run a klick
full-out instead of walking a few hundred feet. Even her
hands were shaking. Why the hell was she so scared?

A burnished metal ring about five inches in diameter
was at waist height. Without allowing herself time to
think, she reached for it and pulled. Like everything else
in the Old City, the large portal was in pristine condition.
Despite its size and weight, it opened easily and without a
creak.

She stared at the passageway in front of her. It was well
lit, the glow seeming to come from everywhere and yet
nowhere. The experts were still trying to reverse engineer
the technology, but no one had figured out the system of
illumination yet.

Kendall paused after closing the door behind her, and
couldn't move any farther. It was as if some essential piece
of her balked; she didn't understand it. Why now and not
the many times she'd come here in the past?

The longer she delayed, the more dangerous this mission became. She *had* to deliver the evidence to Sullivan

before dinner ended. Kendall couldn't have anyone asking questions, and besides, time was critical. The smugglers could come to steal the statuette at any time.

The realization was enough to propel her forward.

Although the hall was wide enough that she couldn't touch both sides if she stood in the center and extended her arms, she felt as if the walls were pressing in on her. She'd never been claustrophobic, but when she rounded the corner and lost sight of the door, her lungs seemed to seize up, and she gasped for air.

The room wasn't too deep inside the temple, but it seemed to take forever to reach it. Her eyes zeroed in on the figurine and her knees sagged with relief. It was still here.

Kendall pulled out her digicam and carefully framed the shots. She knew she had to show where the statue was located or the pictures were worthless for her cause. After a quick review to ensure the images had turned out, she slid the camera back in her pocket and headed for the door.

She was about halfway down the seemingly endless corridor when she heard voices.

Damn, damn, damn! Wildly, she looked around, searching for somewhere to hide, but the hall was solid. No shadowy nooks or crannies would offer concealment. It was sheer luck that she glanced up and saw the ledge in the corner of the passageway.

Though it was ten feet off the ground, it was directly above another rock projection, one that might give her enough of a boost to gain the top tier. She had to try. There were no other options, not that she could get to in time.

Scrambling onto the first shelf, she reached for the one over it and began to pull herself up. Thanks to working out with Wyatt, her upper-body strength was better than it had been three months ago, but even so, her arms started to ache as she struggled to draw herself atop the ledge.

The voices grew closer. Maybe it was adrenaline that gave her the extra impetus, but she made it up and flat-

tened herself against the wall. Kendall checked her bag
and adjusted it until it rested against her back. The ridge
of rock was narrow—her body just fit—and if anyone
looked up, she'd be seen.

With her cheek pressed against the smooth stone, she
kept watch on the passageway. The two men who came
into view were dressed like she was, in camouflage pants
and olive T-shirts, the uniform of choice on J Nine. No one
was authorized to be in the pyramid tonight, but she
couldn't assume these men were part of the smuggling
ring. The temple, after all, wasn't off-limits.

From her perch, she was unable to see their faces, and
she didn't recognize either voice. If she could glimpse the
rank insignia on the left breast of their tees, she'd at least
narrow the possibilities, but Kendall couldn't see that either. She noted that both wore sidearms, and her hope
that this was an innocent visit died.

Only on-duty members of the security team were allowed to carry weapons inside the Old City. The MPs
didn't dress this casually when they were working and it
wasn't any of the Spec Ops guys.

She continued eavesdropping, hoping she'd figure out
who they were. The men were talking about the upcoming
All-Star game and arguing over whether the American or
National League would win. It was barely discernable, but
both guys had a note of unease in their voices. She'd lay
money that the nerves came from whatever it was that
made people feel creeped out in here.

They were out of sight, but not out of hearing range,
when an odd scraping noise made her frown. What the
hell was that? They hadn't gone far enough to reach any
of the rooms, let alone the chamber with the figurine, but
it sounded as if they'd dragged something across the stone
floor. The conversation was muffled now, but she could
still pick up every word.

A lull came and Kendall hoped that meant they were taking care of whatever they'd come here to do. She wanted them to leave so she could escape unnoticed. Sneaking out while they were so near wasn't an option. If she could hear them, they'd hear her if she made any noise, and the way her luck was running today, she'd probably start a rock slide if she jumped down now.

"He's going to keep us waiting again," one of them griped.

"He always does," the second man said, but he didn't sound as irritated as the other guy.

Despite her earlier apprehension, right now she was cool, calm, and clearheaded. If another person were coming, Kendall needed to be able to act without some stupid anxiety attack getting in her way.

When the two soldiers went back to talking sports, she listened with only one ear. The rest of her was focused on the impending arrival of the mystery man. She had to be ready in case he glanced up. She couldn't let him take her by surprise.

She discerned the sound of footsteps before a figure turned into the corridor. Kendall didn't dare blink as the man walked beneath her position. When she saw the bald spot on the back of his head, she felt certain it was Dr. George.

"Gentlemen, I see you've accomplished nothing this evening." The obnoxious superiority and the twang confirmed the ID she'd made. "The transport leaves in one week and these vases and urns need to be properly packaged."

Realization dawned. The temple was the ideal place for the looters to set up their headquarters; she should have guessed that. It was the one structure in the entire city that was universally avoided. She was probably the sole exception.

"I don't think it's a good idea to put anything on this

transport," the more patient man said. "Word is that at least half the Spec Ops teams are being shipped home on that flight and it's not easy to get much past those guys."

Leaving? Wyatt was leaving? Her stomach sank, but she pushed her dismay aside and concentrated on the men.

"It's not your job to think," George said. "Your job is to follow orders. These items need to be aboard and they will be. There are buyers waiting."

"The buyers will be waiting for a long time if the goods are confiscated," the edgier man argued.

"I can't believe you're frightened of a few Special Operations soldiers. These men were picked for their ability to kill, not their brains. They'll never know anything is wrong."

Kendall started shaking in fury. She'd been angry over the stealing of the relics, but to hear that *ass* disparage Spec Ops left her royally pissed. Wyatt, and men like him, risked their lives to keep idiots like George the Jerk safe. They routinely pulled missions that were incredibly dangerous, accomplished ops others deemed impossible. And that parasite had the nerve to insult their intelligence? She'd like to see him survive behind enemy lines with nothing except his wits to keep him alive.

But then he'd never make it through Spec Ops training. He'd weenie out before the first day was over.

George cut off his two accomplices when they started to disagree with him. "Let's not waste my time. The decision's been made. It's your job to ensure that these pieces make the deadline." There was more grumbling, but he talked over the top of the two stooges. "Did you want your share of the proceeds to go to others more willing to obey?"

Dead silence.

"Will there be any problem finishing this tonight?"

"No," came the grudging reply. "A couple more men are meeting us here to help with the packing."

"Good," the doctor said. "Now I have one more assignment. Someone has put in an order for a specific item and it will be up to you to acquire it."

"What item?" It was the patient man again.

"The pyramid. It must be stolen, readied for the trip to Earth and put onboard the transport."

The pyramid? Was he nuts?

"The pyramid? Sir, no ship could take off from the surface with even one of the smaller blocks on board. There's no way to send any of it back to Earth."

"Not *this* pyramid." George didn't add, *you imbecile,* but his tone implied it. "In the master suite of the royal residence there are four obelisks that create a pyramid of light inside the bedroom. Each is a different color and approximately one foot in height. Weight is around fifteen pounds per stone and they're positioned in the corners of the room on niches near the ceiling. Are there any other details you need to complete this task?"

There was another silence; then with obvious hesitance, one of the men said, "I don't think this has been thought through, sir. Not only is the royal residence situated in the middle of the section where we all live and work, but Major Brody and his wife live there. It's going to be difficult to snatch those stones from their bedroom with two adults and a toddler to contend with, and just as hard to get away unnoticed."

"And Brody is former Spec Ops," the other soldier added.

Dr. George sighed loudly. "Don't start that again. You'll retrieve the obelisks before the ship leaves Jarved Nine, no matter what action you need to take to guarantee the procurement. This buyer, gentlemen, is someone you don't want to disappoint."

Kendall's eyes widened. Who the hell was this customer? As soon as she got out of here, she'd go straight to Colonel Sullivan and tell him what she'd heard. He wouldn't brush her off this time. Major Brody's wife was the colonel's sister, and Kendall knew Sullivan would move heaven and earth to protect his family.

"Sir, not to be the voice of doom, but this is a lot of merchandise to transport at once. We normally send a few items at a crack. Look around, we've got ten times more than usual for this trip. It's going to be noticed, and when that pyramid goes missing, all hell is going to break loose even if we can grab it without hurting anyone."

The man definitely had a point. Part of the reason she hadn't been able to prove anything was the minuscule amount pilfered, but maybe avarice was leading them to take bigger risks than usual.

"There is no concealing the disappearance of the pyramid, but not to worry," Dr. George said smoothly. "We have the perfect patsy: a snoopy cheerleader who's been poking her nose into things that don't concern her."

Kendall caught her breath. As far as she knew, George didn't refer to anyone else as a *cheerleader*. Then the words sank in. He knew about her investigation? Had he seen something this afternoon, or had she done something earlier that tipped him off?

"A few token deposits in her bank account," the jerk continued, "and no one will have any doubt that she sold artifacts to finance her doctorate in anthropology."

He was going to pin this on her! Bastard!

Beyond furious, Kendall lowered herself until she could drop to the floor. She wasn't going to let him get away with this! Hands fisted, she rounded a curve in the corridor, ready to face off with the thieves. Until she spotted an opening in the wall where she'd never seen one before.

The sight drove some sense into her head. If she charged into a secret passage to confront them, they'd kill her. And she'd deserve to die for being so stupid. She needed to get the MPs and Sullivan.

Cautiously, she backed away, but when she turned the corner into the final hallway, her messenger bag scraped loudly against the stone. Damn.

Kendall stopped being careful. She turned and ran.

The large door to the temple gaped in front of her, but it seemed a million miles away. She heard them behind her and peeked over her shoulder as she bolted through the exit. Once outside, she saw it was closer to night than dusk and hoped the dimness helped conceal her.

Heart in her throat, she scurried across the open ground. There was yelling, and though she couldn't discern the words, the urgent tone made one thing clear— they'd seen her.

Kendall ran full-out. She knew this sector around the temple better than most—that gave her an advantage, *if* she could hit the clusters of buildings before they caught her.

They sounded nearer and she looked back, trying to gauge the distance. The grayness of the sky made it difficult for her to judge accurately, but it was too close for comfort. She faced forward again as she reached the residential area and turned one corner, then another at full speed.

But what should have been an open walkway, wasn't.

The impact drove the air from her lungs and knocked her off balance. Two strong arms wrapped around her, locking her own arms at her sides. Damn it. She'd forgotten about the men who were coming to help the first two stooges pack antiquities.

Just her luck to run smack dab into another rotten thief.

Chapter Three

Though her position gave her very few counterstrike options, Kendall fought anyway. His arms tightened and she couldn't break loose. Like hell. No way would they get away with looting the Old City. She was going to bring them down. She'd grown up in some rough neighborhoods, and now Kendall fell back on her street-brawler roots. With rage fueling her, she jerked up her knee.

Her captor got clear in time to avoid the blow to his groin. Angry that she'd missed, she stomped on his foot, but his grip didn't lessen. She twisted, trying to free herself.

"Damn it, Bug, settle down. It's me."

"Wyatt?" She immediately went still. Her long hair fell into her face, obstructing her view. "Why the hell are you pinning my arms?"

"I'm not trying to pin your arms." His hold changed, became a hug, not restraint. "At first I was trying to keep you from falling, then I was trying to stop you from hitting me." His voice deepened as he said, "I didn't mean to scare you."

Kendall pushed her hair out of the way. Although it was too dark to really see his navy eyes, she felt a clutching in her chest. Now she wasn't only responsible for herself; she needed to protect Wyatt as well. "We have to get out of here." She stepped back and took his hand. "Come on!"

Maybe her urgency got through, because she saw an intensity settle over him. It wasn't as pronounced as it had been when he'd first arrived on Jarved Nine, but she recognized the look. Warrior mode.

As they started to run, she didn't hear anything behind them. She hadn't had an enormous lead when she'd plowed into Wyatt. Where were her pursuers?

That question was answered before they reached the next intersection. The two men from the temple stepped in front of them, pistols drawn, and Kendall came to an abrupt stop. Wyatt pulled his hand from her clasp and only then did she realize how much comfort she'd taken from his callused touch.

She wasn't sure what to do now. Did they try to run for it? The bad guys only needed to squeeze the trigger to take them down. The Old City had a dampening effect on noise and they were far enough away from the rest of the troops that it was likely no one would hear gunshots.

Damn it! She hated that now Wyatt was in danger too. What the hell was he doing here anyway?

"Sometimes simple plans are the best."

Dr. George's voice came from behind her and she took satisfaction in the fact that he sounded winded. Slowly, she turned to face the biggest threat. While the other men might be holding the weapons, she knew who would give the order to fire.

The jerk wasn't alone. Somewhere along the way, he'd acquired another pair of enforcers and they flanked him, their pistols also aimed at her and Wyatt. This situation appeared grimmer by the minute. The newcomers shifted their weight from foot to foot, looking unsure of them-

selves. This might put her and Wyatt at higher risk. She'd
read somewhere that amateurs were more dangerous than
professionals. That had to apply to soldiers-turned-
antiquity thieves too.

"Montgomery," George said, still slightly out of breath,
"I didn't realize you were back in the city. Good work
holding her until we could arrive in force."

Kendall went rigid. She realized immediately the doctor
was attempting a divide-and-conquer scheme. If she mis-
trusted Wyatt, she might not support him if he tried something. Might not run with him if he managed to create an
opening for them. She wasn't falling for it.

"If you think you can fool me into believing for even a
half second that Wyatt has anything to do with your band
of looters, you better think again." Her voice came out
low. "He has more honesty and integrity than anyone else
I've ever met."

George studied her. Perhaps gauging how adamant she
was in her belief, perhaps looking for something else. "Put
your hands where we can see them. Both of you."

"Do it," Wyatt said under his breath when she hesitated.

"Search them," the doctor ordered.

The man who stepped up to frisk her took her bag
away, and the way he jerked it over her head left her hiss-
ing with pain as the strap caught her chin. He hesitated
before the pat-down, though, which made her think he
wasn't well versed in this type of procedure. She wondered what kind of training these guys had, what their
normal assignments were. It couldn't be security, not with
this lack of confidence in a routine inspection.

Since she wasn't carrying a weapon, it didn't take long
to finish with her, and the guy moved to Wyatt. It didn't
surprise her one bit when, from the corner of her eye, she
saw the goon pull a knife from Wyatt's boot. Her friend
remained stoic, but she didn't know if that meant he had

another weapon stashed somewhere or if the unresponsiveness was part of his warrior persona.

"Well, well, look at that," Dr. George said with mock dismay. "Mr. All-American is disobeying a direct decree from the post commander. I'm appalled."

Wyatt didn't react. Not so much as a blink.

"Nothing to say?" When no reply was forthcoming, the doctor shrugged, then folded his arms over his chest. "At least the cheerleader has some intelligence, questionable though it may be; perhaps it's for the best that you let her do the talking."

Kendall snarled and took a step forward.

"Bug, cool it," he said just loud enough for her to hear him. "This is the response he wants, don't give it to him."

She went still at once, and, taking a deep breath, attempted to force aside the temper. As some of the rage ebbed, she noticed the two sidekicks in front of her were rattled by her actions. Damn. That made them unpredictable. Wyatt was right; she needed to keep cool. He was right about George too. The doctor was trying to get Wyatt steamed so that he couldn't think; it would diminish the threat he posed. Luckily, he'd kept his head, even if she hadn't.

And Wyatt *was* the one they were worried about. His skills had been honed to a sharp edge while she had nothing beyond required training. He'd been in combat situations, while she'd manned a desk. Yeah, the doctor was aware of who was the bigger danger, but he must also know that if she got riled and did something stupid, Wyatt would try to save her. That realization iced over her remaining anger.

The sky finally darkened enough to activate the lighting in the Old City, and it cast a glow along the streets, giving Kendall her first clear view of the men. It didn't reassure her. The two stooges in front of her looked more anxious than she'd realized, and sweat beaded their faces. One slip of a finger and the gun could go off. If Wyatt got hurt, it would be her fault.

"The cheerleader and the quarterback," George the Jerk said scornfully; it dragged her attention back to him. "Don't they make a cute couple?"

Now that she understood the game, Kendall found the comment laughable. She didn't realize she'd smirked till George unfolded his arms and asked, "You find this amusing, Miss Thomas?"

This time she opted not to correct him about her title. She did, however, clear the expression off her face and stand a little straighter. "No, of course not."

For an endless moment, the doctor did nothing but stare at her, and Kendall's heart started to pound in double time. He was angry over her perceived disrespect. Very angry. Don't let him take it out on Wyatt, she pleaded silently, and released a silent sigh when some of his pique appeared to subside.

"Let's take this gathering back to the pyramid, shall we?"

They couldn't let themselves be moved. As unlikely as it was that anyone would stumble across them here, the odds were greater if they returned to the temple. She shifted, balancing her weight evenly. When Wyatt took action, she was fighting with him. Kendall wouldn't run while he battled four armed men.

She sensed someone approach from behind, but before she guessed what he was up to, he grabbed her. One arm went around her throat, the other over her raised arms, lowering them and pinning them at her waist. His hold was secure, giving her fewer options than Wyatt had left her. She kicked backward anyway.

Though she was largely ineffectual, the man tightened his grip, cutting off her air. She didn't stop struggling, not until the roaring in her ears blocked all other sound and blackness encroached on her vision. Passing out wouldn't help, and Kendall quieted. The hold eased enough for her to breathe, and when her eyes cleared, she saw they'd moved a few steps away from Wyatt.

Apparently, the stooges weren't quite as untrained as she'd believed. Though she was far from expert herself, she could identify the wise choices they'd made—separating her from Wyatt for one, and using her for leverage to keep him in line, for another. Then there was the way the two who'd flanked Dr. George stayed out of Wyatt's reach. He wouldn't be able to disarm them, not easily and not in time to keep the guy who was holding her from snapping her neck.

Kendall had the feeling she'd missed a few things while she'd been gasping for oxygen. They seemed to have decided on how they'd proceed to the pyramid. She thought about dragging her feet when they began moving, but didn't. Wyatt was ahead of her, his hands on the back of his head, and since he was cooperating, she followed his lead.

The distance between them increased even more as they neared the temple. Dr. George opened the carved door and the man she'd thought of as being the impatient one went in first. Wyatt was held back—she'd bet until the man got into position—then ordered inside. Kendall took a step forward as he disappeared and was jerked back by the arm at her throat.

"Watch it!" she rasped.

"I'll tell you when to move," her captor growled.

Wyatt had been out of view for what felt like forever before she was walked inside the pyramid. With the cautions the goon squad was taking, it was a while before she and Wyatt were reunited. This wasn't a secret passage, she realized, looking around, but a secret room. And there were dozens of alien relics scattered around. Damned thieves.

She was still about eight feet away from where Wyatt stood in the square stone room when she was released. Though they ordered her to raise her hands again when she was beside him, Kendall only half obeyed. She put one arm in the air, and rubbed her throat with her other hand.

When she noticed Wyatt had turned his head to study her, she looked up—and caught a glimpse of raw fury in his eyes. She quickly stopped kneading and raised that arm as well. Darn it, she should have followed instructions. Now he was pissed off because she'd been hurt and God knew what he'd do. "Marsh," she breathed, using the nickname his men had for him, "cool it."

Unfortunately, the gray rock walls made her voice carry despite the fact it hadn't even been a whisper.

"Yes, *Marsh*," George said, disdain in his voice, "cool it. We wouldn't want you to do anything rash."

Wyatt had his blank mask firmly in place again before he faced the doctor. "You realize," he said, addressing George the Jerk for the first time, "that this is a losing proposition, don't you? Capturing us is the beginning of the end."

"Unlikely," George disagreed. "Once you're out of the way, no one will be any wiser."

Out of the way? That didn't sound good. She eyed the only exit from the room, but the five men stood between them and the corridor. Odds were pretty low on overcoming them and escaping. Then there was the ricochet factor if one or more fired their guns. With stone everywhere, bullets would bounce around like pinballs.

"If Kendall and I turn up missing, someone will notice and investigate," Wyatt argued calmly.

"Oh, I'm sure your absences will be remarked upon, but I doubt there will be much investigation. Two lovers going AWOL so they can spend more time together. What is there to look into?"

The doctor's plan could possibly work. Maybe. A lot of people who knew them casually assumed her relationship with Wyatt was sexual. The few who were bold enough to say something to her face had been quickly straightened out, but she doubted they'd believed her. This was one of those times that being on a post with a small population was a drawback. Not only did everyone know everyone else's business, but they gossiped about it too.

George's scheme wasn't a long-term solution, though. Not on a planet that was deserted except for the members of their group. People might believe they were off having sex for a few days, but after that there would be questions. Where could they go? There was only one gate in the walls surrounding the Old City that hadn't been permanently blocked, and it was always guarded. Even if a member of the security force claimed he'd allowed them to leave, a long absence would raise questions about their well-being. Maybe the doctor hadn't thought of that.

"No one who knows us will buy the AWOL story." Wyatt's deep drawl almost made her jump.

"It's human nature to believe the worst of others." The confident smile on Dr. George's face sent a shiver down her spine. "While a few might proclaim your innocence, they won't sway the masses." To the guy on his left, he said softly, "Get a popper so we can finish this."

With a nod, the stooge disappeared from view. Kendall didn't know whether to be alarmed or relieved. Poppers had been around about forty years, created to quell war protesters without causing injury. They delivered individual doses of a knockout drug, taking down the person fired at, but leaving bystanders clear. It was used in crowds where not everyone was a dissenter.

But she didn't know what amount they'd load in the popper or what kind of drug they'd use. If it was too heavy, or too toxic, it could still cause death.

The errand boy was back in almost no time, making Kendall wonder where the thing had been stashed. He didn't hesitate, not for a split second, before aiming at Wyatt and firing. The popper caught Wyatt midstride and she figured he'd been trying to disarm the guy. In her peripheral vision, she saw Wyatt go down face first and knew it was her turn to act, her turn to protect.

Kendall dropped and rolled. The popper discharged, but missed her. She came to her feet and made a dive for the goons. The second blast delivered the drug dead on. Trying not to inhale, she kept moving, but it was too late. The floor rushed up to meet her, and as she felt her consciousness fading, she reached out a hand toward Wyatt.

Shit, his head hurt.

Wyatt would have cursed aloud, but he didn't have the strength for that. What the hell had hit him? A laser cannon? As he tried to figure it out, he felt himself start to drift.

He didn't know how long it took him to regain awareness, but his head didn't feel any better this time. His thoughts, however, were clearer. Wherever he was, the ground was hard as hell. Without moving, he listened carefully, trying to pick up whether there was any threat present, but it was quiet.

Good thing. He hadn't felt this weak since he'd taken a bullet two years ago. His front side ached—probably because of what he was lying on, rather than any injury—and his head throbbed like mad. Everything else, though, seemed to be pain-free and in working order. Slowly, he brought a hand up to his skull, but he didn't find any blood or other sign of trauma.

Okay, now he needed to open his eyes and discover what was going on. Simple. But the thought of light made the pounding in his head increase in intensity. Come on, Marsh, he told himself, gotta check out what's happening. Barely suppressing a groan, he forced his eyelids apart. It was pitch black, and he couldn't see a damn thing. Where in the hell was he?

Again he listened, and again he heard nothing that concerned him. As he breathed deeply, trying to work up some interest in moving, he detected the faintest hint of some spicy, sexy scent. Bug, he thought, his lips curving.

Bug!

Memory came back in a merciless wave and he pushed himself from his belly to a sitting position. The pain reached a crescendo, as if rockets were being launched inside his brain, but he ignored it. It was Bug who was important. "Kendall?" His voice came out thick, raspy, almost unrecognizable and close to inaudible. He cleared his throat and tried again. "Kendall?"

No response.

Damn it, he needed some lights!

Lights. The pyramid had to have the same system of illumination as the other buildings, right? The pounding in his head slowed him down, but at last, he managed to raise a soft glow.

Frantically, he scanned the room. He saw her bag in the middle of the floor and figured they'd tossed it in here to prevent anyone from finding it. His gaze kept moving until he spotted Bug's procumbent form. Wyatt ran his eyes over her, searching for some sign of injury, but she appeared unharmed. A second, longer look showed her arm was extended toward him and that made his heart stutter. Maybe that was how she'd fallen after taking a blast from the popper, but he wanted to think it was significant. Particularly after the way she'd ardently expressed her belief in him.

When he'd heard that lie about detaining her, he'd expected Bug to think the worst—and it *had* looked bad, even he could see that—but she hadn't bought that bullshit for an instant. Hell, he still felt heat warm the center of his chest when he thought about how she'd jumped in to declare her faith in his integrity.

He moved next to her and pushed her long brown hair off her face. The small frown between her brows made him smile. That was his Bug, ferocious even while unconscious.

"Come on, Kendall, you need to wake up."

She didn't so much as twitch. Okay, she was smaller than he was—if she'd been hit with the same amount of drug, she would be out longer. But he wanted her eyes open, wanted to see she was for sure all right. If anything happened to Kendall, he'd kill each one of those sons of bitches and he'd do it real slow.

Carefully, tenderly, Wyatt moved her so she'd be more comfortable. He held her on his lap because that made *him* feel more comfortable. Her soft breath puffed against his throat and he swallowed hard. "Damn, darlin', you don't have a clue what you do to me, do you?" Moving slowly, he cuddled her against his chest. "Probably a good thing," he continued softly. "You'd run so hard and so fast, I might not be able to catch you."

Leaning forward, he shifted her in order to press his lips to her forehead. Wyatt watched her face, waiting for her to wake, and stroked her hair. He knew she hated her wholesome look. How many times had he heard her complain about her girl-next-door appearance? She always used that phrase and he supposed it fit.

But there was a lot more to her than that.

At her heart, Bug was a warrior. He doubted she realized it herself, but she didn't back down from much, and when it came to friends, she was fiercely loyal. A man could count on a woman like this. If he could pin her down long enough to make her his.

He smiled again, but ruefully this time. Wyatt had never thought it would be this hard—he'd thought she would know him the same way he'd known her—but he wasn't giving up. The soft, warm weight of Kendall in his arms filled him with such contentment, such a sense of rightness, that he knew the work was worth it. His hand stilled mid-stroke and he let his fingers stay tangled in her hair. Her eyes were open, but unfocused.

"Kendall, are you okay?" He kept his voice low, sure her head hurt as bad as his had when he first awoke.

Her green gaze sharpened, zoomed in on him, and he let out a quiet sigh of relief. The awareness had to be a good sign.

"Why'd you let me drink so much?" Her voice was a croak, but he made out the words.

"You didn't drink anything, I promise."

Kendall's brow scrunched up. "If I'm not hungover, why does my head feel like someone used it as a bowling ball?"

Wyatt laughed, he couldn't help it, and when she glared at him, he laughed harder. It wasn't until she reached up and gave his bicep a hard pinch, that he forced himself to sober, but he couldn't quite banish the smile. Especially when he realized she was making no effort to get off his lap.

"Your memory will come back in a few minutes and then you'll know why your head hurts." His lips twitched again and he got another pinch. "Sorry. I'm laughing from relief, I swear. You've been out for a while and I was worrying, that's all."

She scowled at him for a moment more, then it eased. "You must be concerned—your drawl is thicker."

It didn't surprise him that she knew him that well. They'd spent a lot of time together since meeting—he'd made sure of that—and if Kendall thought they were nothing more than friends . . . well, whatever the hell worked. For now.

He went back to stroking her hair.

Her hand curled around his bicep and the feel of her fingers pressing into his muscle made him feel connected to her. It wasn't only him hanging on to her any longer—she was holding on to him too.

He knew he should be doing at least half a dozen other

things right now, but he didn't care. They weren't in immediate danger and he had Bug in his arms. The rest of the world could go to hell. But far too soon, he felt her stiffen and saw her eyes were clearing.

"They had a popper," she said.

"Yep. Told you it wasn't anything fun like a night out partying."

She tightened her hold on him, using his body as leverage to sit up with a groan. "Why aren't you hurting?"

"I was—I am—but I'm getting past it now. You gotta remember, I was awake before you and I outweigh you by at least seventy pounds. Not only is the drug going to hit you harder, but it'll take you longer to recover too."

Wrapping her other arm around him, she rested her forehead against his shoulder. "We need to get out of here," she said, voice muffled against him. "Warn them."

"Warn who, Bug?"

"Major Brody and his wife. They're going after the obelisks in their rooms and those thieves don't care if they have to hurt them or their son to get the stones. I heard them talking before they knew I was there."

Wyatt digested that. Though she hadn't filled him in on anything yet, he'd seen enough to make an informed guess about what kind of mess she'd run across. Leave it to Kendall to find a smuggling ring. But from what she'd just told him, it sounded like the bastards were upping the ante, and he knew exactly which obelisks they were targeting.

He and Brody were on friendly enough terms that he'd received an invitation into his home. He'd been waiting for the major in the sitting room when an odd glow had drawn him forward. Even knowing how rude it was, he hadn't been able to resist pushing open the door. He'd been so fascinated by what he'd seen that he hadn't realized he'd barged into the man's bedroom until Ravyn

Brody had called him on it. Luckily, the woman had a sense of humor.

"The light pyramid," he said, half statement, half question.

"You know about that?" Kendall straightened and he missed the feel of her against him.

"Uh, yeah," he said cautiously, unsure what had put the edge in her voice.

"And you never told me about it?"

His lips twitched again. "Sorry, it slipped my mind."

"It slipped your mind?" She surged to her feet, froze for a moment as if steadying herself, and then rounded on him. "You know how interested I am in this kind of thing."

He stood up himself, felt his head start to throb harder, and guessed Kendall had gotten the pain worse than he had. "Sorry," he repeated. "It won't happen again, I swear."

"It better not," she grumbled, but he knew she wasn't mad anymore. Moving carefully, she retrieved her bag and hitched it on her shoulder. "How do we get out of here?"

Wyatt looked around, but didn't know for sure. The room was perfectly square, each wall identical. The boxes of alien goods were gone and the place was barren. "I think the entrance is to my left." At least the opening had been on his left when he'd taken the hit. If they'd moved him after he'd gone down, then all bets were off.

Hours later, after feeling around the wall, trying to find some gizmo to open the damn thing, Wyatt conceded he could be wrong. Maybe it wasn't this wall. Or maybe the only trigger was on the outside. He slammed the heel of his hand against the stone in lieu of cursing.

Kendall was on her knees to his right, patting around near the floor, and she stood when she heard the slap of skin against rock. She smiled at him and he felt his frustration melt away.

"Maybe we'll be stuck in here for a while," she said,

sounding like the bubbly cheerleader she'd been accused of being, "but we'll get out in time to sound the alert, and at least we won't have to worry about hunger or thirst. Not right away. I still have my lunch and some water in my bag."

"Food and water aren't the top two items on my list of concerns." He'd tried to keep the grimness out of his voice, but when he saw her smile fade, he knew he hadn't succeeded.

"What are the top two worries?"

For an instant, he thought about lying. But Bug was tough enough to handle the truth. "My number one concern is they'll realize how stupid it was not to kill us and come back to finish the job."

"And your number two worry?"

"That they won't." She looked confused and he moved to pull her into his arms. "I'm beginning to wonder if the room is airtight. If it is, they don't have to return. The lack of oxygen will kill us without leaving any evidence of foul play."

Chapter Four

Although Alex hadn't managed to catch more than a couple hours of sleep last night, he wasn't tired. Anger was pumping adrenaline through his system. He'd been worried when Montgomery hadn't shown up for the morning briefing. With another Spec Ops captain found murdered the evening before, he couldn't help wondering whether the kid was in trouble—or dead himself.

Then he'd received word that Captain Kendall Thomas was AWOL too, and Alex's temper had gone through the roof. He might not be able to put a face to that name, but he knew who she was. He kept track of what went on in his command and he was aware that Montgomery had been taking shit for months about the woman. The entire Spec Ops contingent thought it was hilarious that he'd been chasing her and getting nowhere.

Looked like the kid had finally caught her.

Impatiently, he checked his computer, but Thomas's file hadn't arrived yet. He cursed beneath his breath. Wasn't technology supposed to speed things up? Half the damn day was gone and her personnel record had yet to be transmitted from J Nine headquarters to his office. Hell, it would be faster to walk over to HQ and find it himself.

Alex drew in a slow breath and then released it. Earth gadgets didn't always function inside the Old City. For weeks, everything would go along fine, then, without warning, something would stop working. The techs never found any reason for the breakdowns. They'd still be scratching their heads when whatever had gone down resumed operating. Maybe there'd been a glitch somewhere and that's why he didn't have his info. Their communication systems always seemed to be questionable.

Of course, it was just as likely someone at HQ was sitting with his thumb up his ass. Jarved Nine might be light years away from Earth, but much to Alex's displeasure, the Western Alliance bureaucracy had survived the trip intact.

It was this same bullheaded bureaucracy that had led to the erection of prefab buildings inside the Old City. There were plenty of alien structures capable of housing the troops and providing office space, but McNamara had refused to consider it. The army had sent the prefab materials and they were using them, period. Alex frowned. The gray metal buildings were a blight on the beauty of the city. He looked around his office. Despite its awfulness, he hadn't bothered to pretty up the room. He had his desk, a few chairs and a computer. That was all he needed.

Leaning back in his seat, Alex closed his eyes and allowed himself a moment of quiet. Until he had that file, there was nothing he could do that wasn't already being done. His best personnel were investigating Hunter's death and he had MPs out looking for Captains Montgomery and Thomas.

Two hours of sleep on the cot in the small room behind his office hadn't been enough, especially after being grilled for half the night by Colonel McNamara. Alex rotated his shoulders, trying to relieve some of the tension. This was the first moment he'd had to simply be still since word of the murder had reached him yesterday evening, and he needed the respite badly. It didn't last long.

At the sound of a commotion in his outer office, Alex scowled and opened his eyes. A lone voice was raised— his aide's—and that meant only one thing. Spec Ops had arrived.

His aide became louder, more frantic, and with a sigh, Alex pushed to his feet. Time to rescue his desk jockey.

"Atten-shun!" the aide called, relief written all over his face.

"Colonel—"

"Not one word, Chief," Alex said quietly. Montgomery's team stood straighter. Good. They knew he was angry. "Sergeant Foster," he addressed his aide, "take your seat. I'll deal with these men."

"Yes, sir." The noncom headed back behind his desk as if it were a fortress that would protect him.

Alex circled the commandos, silently inspecting them until he felt their level of discomfort skyrocket. "I let my officers run their commands the way they see fit," he said at last. "Maybe I've made a mistake. Clearly, your captain doesn't enforce any standard." He moved closer, crowded the warrant officer. "Chief Cantore, your team is a disgrace."

"No, sir."

"No? Each one of you needs a shave. Only two have haircuts that meet regulations, and that's a near thing." Alex moved to the next soldier in line. He knew all his subordinates, not only his direct reports. "Most teams call their medic *Doc*. Maybe you acquired the handle *Gravedigger* because your appearance doesn't inspire confidence in your skills." He glared coldly at Digger and the man became more rigid. "Sergeant, you're wearing a ponytail. I want that hair cut and that's an order." He didn't wait for a response. "This team is going to pass *my* inspection, and I promise you, I run a tighter ship than your AWOL captain."

"With all due respect, Colonel, our captain is *not* AWOL," the chief said.

Alex ignored that. "Oh eight hundred tomorrow. Right here. And every single man better be spit shined." He continued down the line, eyeing each of them coldly, before returning to Cantore. "I came up through Spec Ops. I'm willing to allow some slack in discipline, but this team has abused the privilege."

He waited. No one said *yes, sir,* but no one was stupid enough to argue with him either. Alex was satisfied with that. "Chief, in my office. The rest of you find the barber. *Now.*"

The five men looked to Cantore and Alex shot them a glare that should have singed their eyebrows. Before he became really pissed off, the chief nodded, silently telling his men to comply. Alex didn't comment about the byplay, but tomorrow he would put Montgomery's men through more than a simple inspection.

After the team filed out, Alex looked at Cantore and pointed to his office. The chief, at least, did as he was told. "Sergeant Foster, find out where the hell that personnel file is. I've been waiting for four hours and this delay is unacceptable."

"Yes, sir."

With a nod, Alex went into his office, closing the door quietly behind him. Montgomery's XO stiffened at the soft snick and Alex left him at attention even after he was seated behind his desk. "Chief Cantore, I should be able to rely on you to keep control of the team even if your captain can't or won't. This breach goes beyond long hair and sloppy uniforms. I gave an order and your men hesitated. That's intolerable."

"Yes, sir," the chief said, "but . . ."

"No buts. I'm giving one warning and this is it. If anything like today happens again, I'll start disciplinary action. Am I clear?"

"Yes, sir."

For a long moment, Alex stared hard at Cantore. Satisfied that his point had been made, he settled back in his chair. Hoping to catch the man off guard, he asked quickly, "Why don't you think Montgomery is AWOL?"

The chief didn't blink at the rapid change in topic. "Word is out about Captain Hunter's murder, Colonel."

Of course it was. This was huge news and would have raged through the post like wildfire. "Why don't you think he's AWOL?" Alex repeated. He wanted more of an answer than he'd received.

"Marsh—Captain Montgomery is too responsible, sir, and he knew the briefing this morning concerned which teams were being sent back to Earth. He'd never deliberately miss it."

Alex was unhappy about the leak, but he didn't pursue it. Instead he weighed Cantore's assessment of his captain. He tended to agree that the kid was responsible, but even the best of them could think below the belt. "What if I told you that Captain Thomas is AWOL as well? Would your opinion change?"

Now Cantore reacted. "Kendall is missing too?" The chief returned to attention and added, "Sir."

"Puts a different spin on the situation, doesn't it?"

"No, sir."

With a frown, Alex stared at the man, but he didn't flinch or waver. "I want reasons, Chief Cantore. Tell me why I shouldn't believe those two are off somewhere having sex, completely oblivious to the repercussions of their actions."

Cantore nodded, relaxed a little bit, before straightening again. "At ease," Alex told him.

"I have a few reasons, Colonel," the man said as soon as

he'd switched stances. "First, Captain Thomas is compulsively responsible. Even if Marsh—uh, Captain Montgomery, was able to forget his duty, she wouldn't."

"And what makes you so sure?" Alex asked.

"From what I've heard, Kend—Captain Thomas had to take care of her family's obligations and finances even as a child. Responsibility is ingrained in her."

Alex nodded. That was something he wouldn't have gleaned from any personnel file, but it was an interesting piece of information. "So we have two usually reliable officers acting out of character. It happens, especially when sex is involved."

"Normally, sir, I'd agree with that—if it were two other people." Before Alex could interrupt, Cantore continued, "But it's more than personalities. Captain Montgomery was worried about Captain Thomas while we were out in the field. He told me something had her scared and that he'd asked Captain Hunter to watch out for her while we were gone."

Alex went still. "Did he tell you what had her alarmed?"

"Marsh didn't know, Colonel. That was part of what had him so antsy to get back to the city. Captain Thomas doesn't frighten easily. If something had her worried, it was big."

Instead of responding, Alex studied the man standing in front of his desk. Cantore needed a haircut and a shave too, but the fact that he was the chief warrant officer of a Special Forces team said a lot. And despite what Alex had said about the men being a disgrace, it was far from true. Montgomery had a topnotch group and their records were exemplary. The only point that had him hesitating was Cantore's obvious need to protect his captain. He might be exaggerating the situation.

"There's one more thing, Colonel."

Alex returned his attention to the chief and waited.

"Yesterday evening, I was sitting on Marsh's front porch.

As I was waiting to talk to him, I saw Captain Thomas hurry by and she was headed east. When I told my captain that, he muttered a curse and took off after her. I haven't seen him since then, and neither has anyone else we've asked."

With a scowl, Alex considered what the chief had said. First point was that Montgomery's team had been doing their own investigation into their captain's disappearance. He wasn't surprised by that—these men were obviously a close-knit group—but he didn't like it. The second thing undermined the chief's position, though he clearly didn't believe it would. Montgomery had taken off after Thomas and disappeared. It definitely sounded as if he'd hooked up with her and gotten lucky.

"Anything else to add, Chief Cantore?"

Alex didn't miss the way the man's jaw tightened. He'd figured out that his arguments hadn't swayed Alex's opinion. "No, sir," Cantore said brusquely.

"Then you can join your men at the barber. I want all of you in my anteroom at oh eight hundred; that hasn't changed."

"Yes, sir."

"Dismissed." The noncom saluted and pivoted to leave. "Chief, if you or your men find any evidence as to the whereabouts of either Captain Montgomery or Captain Thomas, I expect to be informed. Understood?"

"Yes, sir," the man gritted out tightly.

The door closed with a snap behind the chief, but not hard enough for Alex to take issue with it. His lips quirked. Expressing disapproval that subtly took skill.

A knock wiped the smirk off his face. "Enter."

Sergeant Foster walked in with a handheld computer. The tablet was wafer thin and lightweight but still a powerful machine. "Sir, HQ is having a tech glitch—they can't transmit. They had this tablet with Captain Thomas's file brought over for you."

"Thanks, Sergeant," Alex said, taking the computer

and placing it square on the blotter atop his desk. "That'll be all."

After his aide exited, Alex fired up the tablet. The first thing he saw as the screen lit up was an image of Thomas. His heart rate doubled.

"But sir, it's important."

Son of a bitch. Maybe it really had been important. She'd chased after him and hadn't backed down until he'd practically taken off her head. Now he had to give some credence to Cantore's insistence that the two captains weren't off screwing each other's brains out.

Alex pinched the bridge of his nose and stared at the girl's picture. Shit. He might have been the last person to see Captain Kendall Thomas before she disappeared.

Alex dragged his feet as he walked down the elaborate marble hallway. Even though he'd decided Brody was almost good enough for his sister, it went against the grain to consult with his brother-in-law about anything. Too bad he was the one person Alex trusted to be honest with him about Montgomery. He needed some answers before he decided how to approach the case. Brody was friendly enough with Montgomery to be able to give him some insight, but not so friendly that his opinion was suspect.

He scowled. It was late, he was tired and he hadn't been home since yesterday morning. He just wanted to call it a day and get some sleep. Instead, he'd been snarled at by his sister when she'd told him where to find her husband and now he had to chew the guy out for angering Ravyn.

Without knocking, Alex opened the door to the private sitting room. To his left was an enormous table surrounded by twenty intricately carved chairs. That side was empty. On his right was a sitting area with an overstuffed sofa, several matching seats and a low table. Alex spotted Brody lying on the floor next to his son. They were creating something with old-fashioned wooden blocks. He didn't doubt for a minute that his brother-in-law knew he was there, but the man kept his attention on what he was building with Cam. For a minute, Alex smiled fondly at his nephew. Ravyn and Brody had their hands full—the kid had a mind of his own—and Alex guessed it would only get worse as the boy got older.

A clumsy move by Cam toppled one of the blocks on the castle tower, sending it rolling across the floor. The boy's lower lip quivered, but only for an instant. Alex felt someone tapping into the planet's energy, directing it, then the block sailed through the air and settled back into its original position. *I did not see that. Cam did not telekinetically move anything.* "It's sleep deprivation," Alex muttered softly.

His nephew looked in his direction, and with a squeal, ran over to say hello. Alex picked the child up and got a grin, then a hug. Damn, he loved this kid—even if he was the spitting image of his dad.

Brody pushed to his feet at the same time Cam demanded, "Down!" Alex lowered the boy to the floor and the toddler hightailed it back to the blocks. For a two-year-old, he had an unusual level of intensity and focus, not to mention stubbornness. That last trait he'd gotten from Ravyn—no question about it.

Alex glared threateningly at Brody when his brother-in-law reached him. "What the hell did you do to piss off Ravyn?"

"I'm not the one she's mad at."

Something in the man's bland tone tipped off Alex. "Me? What did I do? I haven't seen her in at least three days."

"A few hours ago, Stacey came up to the house looking for you." Brody tucked his fingers in the front pockets of his jeans. "Did you forget she had a special dinner planned?"

For an instant, Alex was nonplussed; then he remembered. He'd promised Stacey he'd be there no matter what came up, and instead, he'd spaced out completely. "Oh, shit."

"Watch the language, Colonel," Brody warned him with a frown before glancing at his son.

Alex looked over too, but Cam was busy building a wall, oblivious to the conversation between them. "He's not paying attention to us; don't worry about it."

"You'd be surprised how much he hears. Ravyn doesn't want him to start swearing."

Shaking his head, Alex said, "That's an uphill battle. Not only is this an army post, but the kid has you for a father."

Brody grinned. "Hey, I'm doing my part. The bruises on my shins were incentive enough to watch what I said."

It was a struggle, but Alex kept from smiling. Damn, he didn't want to like Brody, but it was hard not to. All Alex had ever wanted was for Ravyn to be happy and treated well. Her husband filled both those requirements admirably. Hell, the man's whole world revolved around Ravyn and their son. "My stepsister has you wrapped around her little finger."

"If anyone would know that, it's you." Brody's grin broadened. "She had you wound there first."

"No, she had my father there first. I held out for a full day." Alex stopped fighting the smile. "Your wife is dangerous. You know that, right?"

"By the time I figured it out, it was way too late." But Brody didn't sound as if he minded. "What's up, Colonel?" he asked, sobering. "You didn't come here to talk about Ravyn."

Before he could answer, the door opened and his sister came in. She ignored him, which told Alex she was still angry. This was the biggest drawback to his relationship with Stacey. Ravyn and Stace were best friends and he usually took the heat on both fronts when he was in the doghouse with one of them.

"Time for bed, Cam," Ravyn said.

With perfect diction, his nephew replied, "Oh, shit."

Alex felt his face heat. This was not good.

Ravyn scooped up her son before turning and glaring. "Damon," she growled, voice low.

"Don't look at me, sweet pea." Brody held up both hands. "I'm innocent."

"Alex!" Ravyn stormed across the floor without jostling Cam even a bit. "Can't you control your mouth for five minutes?"

He considered telling her the same thing he'd told her husband—that if he were surrounded by soldiers it was merely a matter of time before the boy heard hard language—but when he saw the sparks jumping in his stepsister's eyes, he decided not to argue. If he used that as a defense, she'd clean his clock. "Sorry."

"Sorry," she muttered. "As if that's going to erase the word from his vocabulary. Thanks a lot." And with one last glower, Ravyn left, closing the door sharply behind her.

"You gave me up damn fast," Alex complained.

"Colonel, there was no way in he—heck I was taking the heat for your mistake, not when I sleep with her." Alex frowned, but Brody ignored it. "Look at it this way, Ravyn isn't half as mad as Stacey. You'll be facing much worse when you go home."

"Don't remind me." Stacey was slow to anger, but once her temper was ignited, it smoldered. He decided not to think about it until he had to. "I need to ask you a few questions."

Brody sobered. "Is this about the murder? I don't know anything, but I hope you find the son of a bitch soon."

"So do I." Alex rubbed his forehead for a second—fatigue was catching up with him. "I've put my best soldiers on the investigation—they haven't come up with much yet. But Hunter isn't who I wanted to ask you about."

"Who is?"

"Wyatt Montgomery."

"You think he's responsible? Not a chance in hell."

Alex was tempted to remind Brody about his language, but it wasn't worth it. "No, I don't think he killed Hunter, but he's missing. You know the kid, if he'd finally scored with the woman he'd been chasing for four months, would he go AWOL?"

"No."

Closing his eyes for a second, Alex took a deep breath before he pinned Brody with a hard look. "I need you to think about this carefully."

"It doesn't matter how long I think about it, Montgomery is levelheaded and responsible. He'd never go AWOL. Sorry if that's not what you wanted to hear, but you asked for my opinion. If you want your own ideas parroted back at you, there are plenty of ass-kissers around. Go find one of them."

Brody was right. "Shit," Alex said quietly. "This means I have two missing officers to find."

"Hunter and Montgomery went through Spec Ops school together—they were buddies."

"You're suggesting that Montgomery's disappearance might be linked to Hunter's death? I'm considering that. Especially with one of the pieces of information I was given today."

Hell, it had to be tied together. Montgomery asks Hunter to watch over Thomas. Hunter gets his throat slit and Thomas and Montgomery go missing. It had to center on the girl—on whatever had her scared. Alex wished to hell he hadn't blown her off. She'd wanted to tell him something, and maybe that something would have solved the murder.

And maybe prevented two other deaths.

Just because no one had found bodies, that didn't mean Montgomery and Thomas were alive. The Old City was huge. It was estimated that between twenty-five and fifty thousand people had lived here when the aliens had inhabited it. There were only six hundred Western Alliance troops present, leaving a lot of unoccupied ground—and a lot of places to hide a couple of corpses.

"Shit," he said again.

Brody knew better than to quiz him, and Alex didn't volunteer any info. When he met with McNamara tomorrow morning to give her an update on the situation, he'd have to mention that the problem might be bigger than one murder. The post commander had already given him hell over Hunter's death, and the last thing Alex wanted to tell her was that things might be worse than they'd thought. She'd really push him now.

"I'm going home. Try to sweeten Ravyn up, will you?"

A few moments later, Alex stopped right inside the door of the house he shared with Stacey and watched her. She sat at the table, picking at the edge of a sugar cookie. The plate was covered with small crumbs and he guessed she'd taken more than one apart.

For an instant, he thought about when he'd met her, the way she'd faced him down. Back then her hair had been strawberry blond, and long, flowing halfway down her back. Now it was auburn and cut to shoulder length. But the changes didn't matter to Alex. Stacey was special. With her, he didn't have to pretend to be someone he wasn't, he didn't have to watch every damn word he said, or blunt his personality. He didn't intimidate her in the slightest and that freed him. She chewed him out when he deserved it and hugged him when he needed someone to hold him. And she'd given him something he'd never had in his entire life—contentment.

She looked up, hazel eyes hot, and Alex almost smiled. He was going to catch hell, but that was okay.

"So you finally made it home."

"Stace, I'm sorry." He still hated apologizing, and the

words never came easily to him, but he'd learned how to say them in the three years they'd been together.

Standing, she tugged the belt of her pale green robe tighter and left her fingers tangled in the bow. "Answer one question for me. Did you miss dinner because of some breaking event in the murder investigation?"

Alex had always been honest with Stacey and he wasn't going to start lying to her now, not even to make things easier on himself. "No, there was nothing that couldn't have waited until tomorrow. I should have been here."

With a nod, she pivoted and left him standing flat-footed. He wasn't sure how to read her; this wasn't usual behavior for Stacey. Normally, she'd be ripping him up one side and down the other and he deserved it. Alex chased after her. He caught up with her as she stood in the doorway to their room. "Stace?"

"This house has four bedrooms. Use one of the others." She closed the door in his face.

Stacey stepped onto the back porch and set her teacup on the small table. She walked to the stone railing and looked out over the backyard. There was a patch of grass, some low bushes and flowering plants. The grounds weren't large, but they were beautifully landscaped and surrounded by a tall stone wall for privacy.

Even after living here for years, there were still times she looked at this perfection and was unnerved. Nothing ever needed to be trimmed or mowed. No dust ever settled and no bugs or animals made their way inside the city. Every building, every bench, every fountain remained as flawless as if they'd been created that very day. If she were on Earth, there would be birds singing and a breeze to ruffle her hair. Not here, though, and Stacey felt a pang at the absence—and a stronger ache as she realized, despite its oddness, she'd miss the Old City.

She ran her hands over the front of her khaki trousers

and returned to the table. Thinking about what she'd miss, who she'd miss, was a pointless endeavor. After adjusting her chair, Stacey rotated the teacup in its saucer so that it was at an exact right angle to her body. Normally, she wasn't this meticulous, but the precision was a way to hold herself together.

A way to keep the tears at bay.

It was over.

She couldn't do it anymore. Three years spent trying to break through the fortress surrounding Alex Sullivan was all she could take. Last night had merely been the last straw.

If he'd missed dinner because of something related to the murder, Stacey would have shrugged it aside—that would have been too important to put off. But when she'd asked him if that had been the reason, he'd said no. Maybe she should be grateful that he didn't lie to her. At the same time, though, she couldn't help wondering whether he'd told the truth because her response didn't matter to him. Maybe it was indifference, not respect.

The only place Stacey felt like she had Alex—really had him—was in bed. When they had sex, he didn't hold back much of himself, but that was the one time she didn't sense the distance he kept between himself and the rest of the world.

She bobbed the string from the tea bag slowly up and down, then pulled it out and let it rest on the side of the saucer. Her hands weren't entirely steady as she took a sip.

Herbal tea. For a coffee addict. It was a good thing Alex had cleared out before she'd woken up this morning.

Oh, she'd tell him about the baby. He deserved that and so did their child, but she wasn't sharing it with him now. After she returned to Earth and had her own home established—and her emotional equilibrium back—she'd give him the news.

It didn't take much thought to anticipate Alex's

reaction—he'd ask her to marry him. Too bad it would be for all the wrong reasons. She didn't want him this way. If he ever proposed, she needed it to be because he loved her. He might utter the words now, but they wouldn't be true. Alex was very goal-oriented; he'd do and say whatever he had to in order to bring her around to his way of thinking.

After taking another sip, Stacey replaced the cup on the saucer and stared into the garden. Life was a gamble, a risk. She'd taken her chances and she'd lost. Part of her felt as if it were dying, but better a fast death than the slow strangulation she'd been living with. It wasn't any surprise—she'd gone into this relationship with her eyes wide open. She'd known what Alex was like and there was no one to blame but herself for her broken heart. Her broken dreams.

This decision to leave him and return to Earth hadn't been made in the heat of the moment. For some time now, she'd been considering her options. Of course, getting pregnant hadn't been one of them, but sometimes the universe had a sense of humor.

A warped sense of humor.

She should have reminded Alex again that he needed to get the shot. The post doctor had been concerned about some indications she'd seen on Stacey's tests and wanted her off birth control for at least six months to see if the results normalized. Sullivan had been willing to take on the responsibility when she'd brought it up, but the one time she'd reminded him, he'd become short-tempered and told her he'd take care of it. Apparently, he hadn't.

Stacey used her index fingers to wipe the unshed tears from her eyes. She didn't regret the baby, but the timing couldn't be worse. Well, she'd handle it—women had been raising children alone since the dawn of time.

What she needed to do now was arrange to be on the

transport when it left Jarved Nine next week. She doubted that would be a problem, though. The only reason she was on this planet at all was because Alex had pulled strings and had CAT Command assign her to the Western Alliance project. The Colonization Assessment Team leaders would want her back if for no other reason than to cut the ties to the military. They didn't like the precedent it set.

Before she did that, though, she needed to pack. Although she hated putting her friend in the middle, she knew Ravyn would let her stay in her home until the transport left for Earth.

No matter what, Stacey wasn't spending another night under the same roof with Alex Sullivan.

Chapter Five

"Damn it, Wyatt, hold still!"

Wyatt swallowed a curse. "You need to hurry."

And she did. He'd been right—the room was airtight. Their breathing and pulse rates had increased and their coordination was off. With the army going into space, Wyatt had been trained to recognize the signs of oxygen deprivation, and they had all the symptoms. When the level fell a few percentage points lower, both of them would drop into unconsciousness without warning.

They'd spent hours and hours checking every portion of the walls they could reach from the floor and hadn't found a trigger. Now he had Kendall sitting up on his shoulders, letting her feel around in the area near the ceiling; it was a stretch for her. What worried him was they were already more than halfway through and had yet to find a way out. He stepped to his side.

"Wyatt!" she protested.

"We're running short on air."

"So you're saying we don't have time to do it right, but

we have time to do it over?" Bug barely paused. "Wait until I indicate that I'm ready before you move."

His hands tightened around her knees, but he didn't argue with her. She had a point. He didn't think they were going to have a chance to redo their search. The next stage in oxygen deficiency was nausea, maybe vomiting. They weren't to that level yet, but Wyatt didn't think they were far off. Kendall's leg pressed into him and he moved a few feet.

Since meeting her, he'd played out a lot of different scenarios on how their lives might go, but he'd never pictured it ending this soon. Four months. It was nowhere near long enough. He wanted to be able to kiss her, to pull her body against his and hold her without worrying about spooking her. Hell, he wanted to make love with her and wake up with her in his arms.

He'd lost count of how many times he'd pictured it, the number of ways he'd imagined loving her. Sure, he had memories of that other life, memories of when her name was Zolianna and his Berkant, memories of covering her with his body, of thrusting inside her until they both found pleasure, but they weren't those people anymore. And now that he knew her as Kendall, recalling the times with Zolianna weren't enough to satisfy him. She stretched higher and Wyatt swayed before he caught his balance.

Gripping Bug more firmly, he took a deep breath to steady himself. He'd been so smug, so certain that when he found her again, things would easily fall into place. Big miscalculation.

First off, Kendall hadn't recognized him as someone with whom she'd shared another life. Secondly, any advantage he thought he had since he did remember was soon proven to be nonexistent. Kendall's personality was radically different from Zolianna's. His Bug might be soft-spoken, but she didn't hesitate to raise hell when she deemed it necessary—the consequences be damned. As Zolianna she'd been more passive, preferring to ride the current rather than swim upstream. She signaled him again and he inched over carefully.

But it was the third factor, one that had nothing to do with any past life, that gave him the most grief. Bug's upbringing.

She'd shared enough for him to realize that her mother hadn't been much when it came to practical matters. Those had fallen to Kendall at a young age. On top of that, her childhood had been nomadic, and she'd never stayed in any place long enough to put down roots. Bug must have learned fast not to let anyone too close, that she'd only lose the friendship when she moved on, and she continued to hold people at a distance. Even him.

"Now he stands still." Kendall's voice jerked him from his thoughts.

"Sorry." Wyatt shifted. He'd missed her sign and he had to pay attention. If there was a chance in hell of preventing it, he wouldn't let her suffocate. Although as far as methods of dying went, this was a damn sight better than last time.

Deciding he didn't want to think about death, he let his thoughts return to loving Bug. He'd go slow, savor every second with her. Wyatt's eyes slid half shut as he envisioned lazily stripping her, letting his gaze, his hands, his mouth worship her long, lean body. He'd kiss her for hours, memorize her taste, before moving on to her breasts.

Hours. Right. As bad as he wanted her, he'd be lucky to hang on for minutes. Wyatt's lips curved. Hell with it. This was his fantasy; if he wanted to last hours, he could.

Okay, so he'd move to her breasts. He'd tease her with his fingertips first, make her nipples peak before—

"Wyatt, are you okay?"

The demand in her voice—and the thread of fear—puzzled him. "Yeah, why?"

"Because I signaled you to move, and you didn't. Again." Her hand cupped his cheek and he could feel her bend over, trying to see his face. The realignment of her weight threw his balance off and he staggered to keep them both from going down.

Maybe he wasn't okay. He was normally damn agile and he should have been able to make the correction without trouble. Wyatt stepped to his right when he regained his equilibrium. "Bug, maybe it would be best if you stayed as still as possible."

Her fingers tightened on his cheek, but she didn't say anything. Instead, she released him and he felt her reach above her head. Neither of them talked as she continued to pat the stone. Wyatt put aside his sexual daydreams and struggled to focus. His thoughts drifted from time to time, but he remained aware of Kendall; when she gave the indication he moved.

Without a watch, he didn't know how long it took, but it seemed like forever before they reached the corner. It was tempting to lean his shoulder into the stone, to let it help support him, but he couldn't. Not with Kendall perched up there.

Nausea had set in a while ago. He only hoped he didn't pass out before Bug had her feet on the floor.

"Talk to me right now! Damn it, Wyatt, do you hear me?"

Wyatt blinked. Shit, he'd been in a daze. It was clear that their time was running short. "What's up?" There was a hesitation and he expected Kendall to cross examine him.

Instead, she said, "I think I found something, but my fingertip only brushes it. I need to lift up a few more inches."

Her words didn't make sense—not immediately—then

it sank in. "Okay, let me brace myself. Can you raise high enough on your own if I hang on to you?"

There was about five seconds of silence, then, "Yeah, I think so, but you're going to have to remain steady." Kendall didn't sound too positive that he'd be able to do that.

Taking a deep breath, he shifted into a stronger position. "I'm set, but move slowly; no sudden jerks if you can help it."

As she began to stretch upward, she pressed more firmly against the back of his head, and Wyatt gripped her legs tightly. He felt her attempt to gain more height. In other circumstances, he might have suggested they try it with her kneeling on his shoulders, but not now. Not when he was barely keeping himself stable. The thought of Kendall taking a tumble from that stance to a solid marble floor was too frightening to contemplate.

"Can you step closer to the wall?" she asked.

He could, but not much. Bug made a noise he took to mean satisfaction and he leaned his forehead against the stone as he waited. She was having a lot less trouble—or appeared to be having less trouble—than he was with the lower levels of oxygen, but he wasn't sure why. Kendall was exerting herself as much as, if not more than, he was.

There was a light stroke on his cheek. "I need you to let me get down for a minute."

Shaking his head in the hope of clearing his thoughts, he loosened his hold and helped her slide from his shoulders. From her tone of voice, she'd made the request more than once and his lack of response was worrying her. The thing was, no matter how often he told himself to stay alert, he couldn't. She seemed to realize that he was struggling and she'd taken over. Wyatt managed to quirk his lips. He was okay with Bug in charge. Since she appeared to be thinking more clearly than he was, she was her own best hope of getting out of here alive.

Kendall went to her bag, dug in the side pocket and pulled something out. It wasn't until she returned that he saw she held a couple of hairpins. "Stay with me, okay? I think I can pull what I'm feeling with one of these things," she held up the hand with the pins, "but you have to hang in there."

"I'm trying, Bug." He wanted to kiss her, but instead he crouched down and let her climb back up on his shoulders. Wyatt swayed as he stood. It was the feel of Kendall clutching him that forced him to dig deeper, to find the balance needed to keep her steady. Without saying a word, he edged as close to the gray wall as he could and focused on her warm muscles to stay somewhat focused. Wyatt heard an occasional grunt, a couple of muttered curses, and watched a bent pin land at his feet.

"Ha! Got you." Kendall's center of gravity shifted as she yanked at something and he scrambled to keep from dropping her. He heard a rasping, grating sound and she whooped as she shook off his hold and slipped down to the floor again. Wyatt leaned forward, letting his head rest on the wall. There was a scraping against his brow, but he didn't move, just let the rock abrade his skin. Then Kendall's hands were on his arms, tugging him back from the stone. Only Wyatt didn't stop moving. He felt her try to prop him up, but he was too heavy for her. The best she managed was to slow his descent to the floor.

Bug was talking; he could make out her voice and the anxiety in it, but he couldn't hang on any longer. Wyatt tried one more time to concentrate, but the darkness was beckoning strongly, and he lost the battle to remain cognizant.

He stopped and stared. Heru, she was beautiful, and only grew more so each season. Over and over he told himself that he should stay away—it was best for them both—but his need for her overwhelmed good sense. There was no denying that Zolianna held his heart in her hands.

She was reading at her desk, head bent, and he shifted as he continued to drink in the sight of her. That slight movement was enough. Straightening, she turned in his direction. As she identified him, her expression changed, became softer, welcoming, and filled with love. In a trice, she was crossing the chamber and he met her midway, his arms going around her. Feeling her body against his soothed something inside him, something that ached whenever they were parted.

Contentment couldn't last, however. His hands found the fastening of her robes, and he pushed them from her shoulders, baring her to his hands, his gaze. Her own hands weren't idle and in moments he was as naked as she. The heat of her skin against his had him growing taut, and it made him recall how long he had been without her. Too long.

Cupping her breasts, he gently teased her with the pads of his thumbs. Her shiver of awareness, the way her nipples peaked, increased the heat he felt. Berkant disliked it when his job took him outside the city walls and away from her, but it wasn't as if he could refuse. She understood; the demands of her position and her responsibilities were every bit as great as his.

With a hunger he made no effort to hide, he took her mouth, kissing her almost savagely as the desire—the need—he'd kept pent up erupted from him. After a moment, he attempted to regain control, to adore her as she deserved, but she leaned into him and the fire raged free once more.

It didn't frighten her. Zolianna matched him kiss for kiss, caress for caress, her touch as eager as his. With little effort, she drove him to fever pitch. There'd be no lengthy bout of foreplay—not this time. He picked her up, placed her carefully atop the bed, and followed her down, lying at her side. Although he meant to slacken his pace, he couldn't, and instead, drew her against him for an-

other frenzied kiss. He needed badly to merge with her. Slipping his hand between her legs, he probed gently. He smiled as he felt how her body had dampened.

Without his being aware of it, their positions changed and he had his head in her lap as she leaned over him, her hand rubbing circles over his heart. He reached up, brought her mouth to his, and relished her soft moan as she hesitantly returned his kiss. Triumph surged through him as she opened her mouth and allowed him to deepen their contact. His erection throbbed, and he eased back until his lips but brushed hers. "Zolianna," he murmured.

She jerked away—

"Wyatt! Come on, Wyatt, look at me."

While he heard the worry—and insistence—in Bug's voice, he wasn't able to open his eyes. Not yet. Lethargy held him in its grip and it was too much effort to struggle through it. If they were in danger, he'd try anyway, but since he'd sort of regained consciousness, Wyatt guessed she'd gotten them some air.

Her fingers stroked his chest and he managed a faint smile. Until the caress stirred a vague memory. Shit, it hadn't been fantasy; he'd kissed her for real, and she was going to rabbit on him. Unless ... If Bug thought he didn't remember, she might not feel a need to pull away. It was worth a shot. His desire to assess the damage that kiss had done—and Bug's persistent voice—prompted Wyatt to work on surfacing. He forced his eyelids open.

"How are you feeling?" Kendall asked, voice subdued.

Blinking to clear his vision, Wyatt turned his head. "Ask me again in a few hours," he rasped.

Bug looked half panicked, he realized, and he blurted the first thing that came into his head. "How long was I out?"

"Completely out? Just a minute or two."

"How long was I drifting?" They had a safety margin before the smugglers returned to ensure they were dead, but he needed to know how much time they'd lost.

"Too long!" Bug grimaced, then shrugged. "Exact time? I'm guessing fifteen, maybe twenty minutes."

He bit back the curse. No wonder she'd demanded that he open his eyes. That must have scared the hell out of her. He considered Kendall, let his gaze roam over as much of her as he could see. "How're you feeling?"

Her agitation seemed to lessen with the prosaic nature of his questions. "I've got a headache, but other than that, I'm all right. You were affected more than I was."

"Yeah," he agreed unhappily. It was his job to take care of her, not the other way around, but as much as he hated to admit it, he wasn't running anywhere near full speed. Wyatt didn't even think he could sit up yet. From his position, he examined the area, but nothing seemed familiar. They weren't in the corridor they'd started from. That hall had been lined with a highly polished gray stone; this one was a sandy color with dark flecks scattered throughout the rock. "Where are we?"

"I suppose you'd call me a smart aleck if I said inside the pyramid?" She didn't wait for him to answer. "I can't be more specific than that, though. Wherever we are, the archeologists don't know about it. I've scrutinized everything on the temple; if they were aware of this secret passageway, I'd know too."

"It could be classified."

For a moment, there was only silence as Kendall studied him, then she repeated, "If the archeologists were aware of this secret passageway, I'd know too."

"Aw, geez, Bug." Wyatt closed his eyes for an instant. "I'm going to pretend I didn't hear that—my ears are ringing or something."

She must have hacked past computer security.

It didn't matter to him. What counted was that she trusted him and that was humbling. Kendall had difficulty putting her faith in others—probably because of the way she'd grown up—but she believed in him. There was a warmth in his chest that had nothing to do with the gentle stroke of her fingers—though that certainly heated his blood too.

"You sure you're okay?" he asked again. "You didn't strain yourself pulling me out of the room, did you?"

"I'm fine, really."

"Good," he said thickly. She seemed less nervous, and he decided that ignoring the kiss had been the right idea. What amazed him, though, was that Bug continued to pet him. It was driving him nuts. He guessed she was oblivious to her actions, but he wasn't. Wyatt decided he'd better sit up before she noticed exactly how attuned his body was to her touch. The movement made his head swim, but despite his dizziness, he didn't miss the color that flooded Kendall's cheeks or the way she curled her fingers into a fist.

Damn. If he didn't do more damage control—fast—she'd pull back on him, and that was the last thing he wanted. "I'm going to need your help to get us out of here. Can I rely on you?"

Kendall's attention was immediately redirected, and as her mouth firmed, she gave an emphatic nod. "You know you can."

"Good," he repeated, shifting till he could use the wall as support. His shoulder brushed hers. "Okay, here's the situation as I see it. We're completely on our own. If the archeologists aren't aware of this section of the pyramid, that means the MPs won't find us even if they do check the temple." Bug nodded and he continued, "We have to assume, though, that the smugglers *do* know about this corridor. It would be stupid not to since they've had an indefinite period of time to find it."

"Why would they look for a secret passageway?"

"Did you know about the room they locked us in?" He countered with a question of his own.

After a short pause, she said, "I get what you're saying.

If they could find that chamber with no reason to search for it, odds are good they found this section too." Kendall sighed. "When they find us gone, we're going to be hunted."

He risked sliding an arm around her shoulders and gave her a squeeze. She stiffened, but didn't pull away. "Yeah, we are."

"We can't go out the way we came in."

It wasn't a question, but Wyatt answered as if it were. "No. Easiest thing in the world is to put someone at the entrance to the pyramid and let him pick us off as soon as we step outside. We have to find another exit, and this is where I need intel from you. Is there a different way out?"

She leaned her head back and closed her eyes before she said, "Logically, a structure this size should have multiple entrances, but we've yet to find them. After what we've seen so far, I tend to believe they're here but well disguised."

If things were different, he'd mention that it made him hot when she went all intellectual on him, but he couldn't. It was too damn bad Kendall didn't have any recollection of their other life. She could lead them right out of here without a problem if she did.

Wyatt checked his wrist before he remembered he wasn't wearing his watch. "Let's go. Now that I can probably stand up, darlin', we need to move."

Cautiously, he pushed to his feet. The slowness didn't help, though, and he staggered. Almost before he could catch his balance, she had her arm around his waist, supporting him. "Are you all right?" she demanded.

"Just lightheaded. I'll be fine in a minute." But he slung his own arm over her shoulders, and as much as he hated to burden her, he let Bug take some of his weight. If he were steadier, Wyatt would have grinned about the way they fussed over each other—Kendall had asked after him almost as many times as he'd checked on her—and he'd been conscious a matter of minutes. Flare would be laughing his ass off if he were here to listen to this, but the hell with it. Nothing in the universe was more important to Wyatt than the woman he leaned against.

When his eyesight cleared, he looked around. "Where's your bag? Grab it and let's go."

"I must have left it in the room. I was more concerned with getting you some air than anything else."

The defensive tone made his lips twitch, but he managed to suppress the smile. Bug hated to be less than perfect at anything, and no doubt, she viewed this as a failure. "You don't need to persuade me. I'm glad I was your first priority."

"Sorry," she mumbled. Then she lifted her gaze to his and said more clearly, "I'm sorry about getting prickly."

"Don't worry on it. After the day you've had, you're entitled. Did the room close up after we left?"

"No, it was open the last time I saw it."

Wyatt thought about that, then made a decision. "We need to go back, get your bag, and shut that room again. I don't want to point the smugglers in our direction. With no indication which way we've gone, they'll have to cover every possibility, and this might spread them thin enough to give us a small advantage."

"Will the room be safe? It hasn't been that long since we escaped and I don't know about the oxygen levels."

"I'm going in and out, that's all."

"I should go. You can still barely walk." He scowled and watched Kendall smother a smile. "I'm concerned about you," she added, squeezing his waist.

His expression immediately softened. "I'm okay, I promise, but let's get moving. I want us to finish what we need to do and get far away from here before they come check on us."

As they walked down the hall, Wyatt became more surefooted and he leaned less on Kendall. They had to go farther, though, than he had expected. He cast her a sideways glance. This was a hell of a distance for her to have pulled him. Must have been adrenaline.

When they reached the room, Wyatt left Kendall in the hall and went in. As soon as he snagged her bag, he started to leave but stopped short when he spotted her discarded hair pins. He didn't want to leave *anything* behind. He bent to grab them and jammed them into his front pocket as he exited.

When he was back beside Bug, Wyatt put his hands on his hips and eyed the opening. He didn't immediately see another method to close it.

He was betting this room acted as some kind of buffer zone between sections of the pyramid. That meant finding a trigger to shut the door on this side of the wall should be easier. He just had to figure out where to look.

Kendall watched Wyatt walk away, and tucked her hands in her pockets as she waited. She could guess what he was doing.

She turned her head and stared at the wall herself, letting her eyes roam freely over the blocks of perfectly set stone. There were little inclusions in the highly polished marble. Pretty. Leaning against the opposite wall, she eyed the pattern and thought she saw the flecks start moving, and then they began streaming in a formation. Kendall found herself mesmerized.

The specks of color did a jig, seeming to leap out of the rock and perform for her in midair. A group of forest green motes chased the azure bits and Kendall smiled faintly at the antics. She heard Wyatt make a sound of satisfaction, but she kept her eyes on the flecks. They'd stopped playing tag and formed a kaleidoscope, segueing from one image to the next until they blended themselves into an arrow, and Kendall would swear the dots were looking at her. Before she could examine that thought, they rocketed from the hall into the secret room.

Straightening away from the wall, she waited for the specks to return. They didn't come back, and Kendall followed them.

As she stood in the opening to the chamber, they reappeared. They swarmed on the stone doorjamb, putting on an extra-energetic show and her smile broadened. The particles almost looked like men and women—partners in a dance.

Then, before she was ready for the waltz to end, they dove inside the stone and formed the outline of a hand. Bemused, she studied it. The inclusions pulsed, calling her forward. Slowly, Kendall raised her arm and pressed her palm inside the pattern.

There was a moment of relief, a moment when she could feel something inside her find peace. Before she could think about that, the stone started to vibrate, as if the temple itself were coming to life after a long sleep. The buzz traveled up her arm and filled her body. Kendall's eyes closed. It felt good.

As the sensation continued, the energy of the temple seemed to shift, although Kendall couldn't explain how, and there was a welcoming feeling that she'd never experienced before. In the past, she'd had a sense of possessiveness about the pyramid, but now, it seemed as if that claim were returned.

Wyatt glanced over at Kendall to share his success with her, but what he saw wiped the satisfaction off his face. Her back was toward the encroaching stone and she was standing directly in its path, her hand pressed against the side of the jamb.

"Bug, you need to move," he told her.

She didn't seem to hear him. He called her name a second time, but she remained oblivious. Wyatt eyed the distance between her and that enormously heavy rock; he started to run. If she didn't get out of the way, that thing would crush her.

The slab began to move faster.

Wyatt flat-out sprinted for her.

The instant he reached Bug, he grabbed her arm. She shook him off. That rock was almost on top of her.

He got himself a tighter hold and jerked her. Hard.

And with a dull thud, the rock shuddered closed.

Chapter Six

"For God's sake, Bug! What the fuck were you thinking?"

Kendall stared at him. Wyatt rarely cursed in front of her, so hearing him use that particular word shocked her. And shook her out of her fog. She looked at him, but couldn't make sense of anything. "What?"

"What do you mean, what? You were standing right in the path of that fu—fricking wall." The thickness of his drawl, and the fact that he'd nearly slipped a second time, told her how upset he was. "It was closing fast and it would have crushed you if I hadn't pulled you out of the way."

A muscle began to tic in his jaw, and with a sound she couldn't quite name, he hauled her against his chest and wrapped his arms around her. Fine tremors went through him and it left Kendall stunned. Wyatt was shaking?

After the kiss they'd shared, she knew it was the last thing she should do, but Kendall returned his hug anyway. She hadn't realized what was happening. Though she'd seen the wall moving, she hadn't felt any danger. A shiver went through her. That had been too close for comfort.

Kendall held him tighter as the knowledge sank in. The lower levels of oxygen must have caused her to hallucinate. She started to tell Wyatt what she'd thought she'd seen, but stopped before saying a word. He tended to be protective anyway, but if he believed she'd been out of it, he'd be watching her like a hawk. And he'd worry needlessly.

She turned her head on his shoulder and looked at the wall. The flecks seemed to wink at her, and that unnerved her enough to want to get out of here. Kendall pushed free of Wyatt's arms. "I think we need to get moving."

"Yeah, you're right," he agreed. While he looked around, Kendall glanced down at her still-pulsing hand. Although it was hard to be sure, she thought a slight pattern had been imprinted on the pad of each finger—it swirled like a paisley—but the exact style was lost amid her fingerprints. She blinked a couple of times, but when she looked again, the whorls remained. She curled her fingers, tucking the pattern against her palm.

"Let's head this way," Wyatt said, pointing to the right.

It was the opposite direction from the place where she'd dragged him, but Kendall didn't ask any questions. She simply walked with him.

Besides, she had plenty to think about. She ran her thumb across the tips of her fingers. Hallucinations didn't leave marks behind, so what had happened? Letting herself fall a few steps behind Wyatt, Kendall held her palms side by side. There were definitely new swirls on the pads of her right hand, not only the tips. Now she saw them on every swell of flesh.

"Bug, do you need me to slow down?"

Kendall stuck her hands behind her back before she realized that made her look guilty. "No, I'm okay," she assured him, moving her arms to her sides.

"Is something wrong with your hands?" Without waiting for a reply, Wyatt took her wrists and examined her palms. "I don't see any blood, cuts or punctures. Do they hurt?"

"No," she repeated. "Everything's fine."

He looked dubious, but Wyatt let go of her. "If you can't hold the pace I set, let me know. Until the smugglers are arrested, I don't want you even five feet away from me, got it?"

Soberly, Kendall nodded, but Wyatt wasn't done yet.

"If you injure yourself, I want to know. I don't care how small or insignificant you think the problem is. I can't make good decisions if you're hiding information from me."

In other circumstances, she might have teased him about the way he'd assumed command, but not now. Wyatt was Western Alliance Army Special Operations with plenty of field experience. She sat behind a desk and entered data on a computer. As far as she was concerned, he was in charge.

"Nothing's wrong," she reported. "I had a tingling sensation in my right hand, but it's dissipating. My biggest physical discomforts are hunger and thirst."

Wyatt reached for her right arm, and Kendall held it out for him, resigned. "Tell me if something hurts," he ordered, and then proceeded to press places on her hand and forearm. She stayed impassive as his fingers tested, but his touch affected her when she wanted to remain indifferent.

Finally, he released her. "I didn't feel anything out of place. Nothing bothered you when I pushed on it?" Kendall shook her head. "If anything changes, you let me know."

"I will."

Appearing satisfied with that, Wyatt nodded. "About your other complaints," he grinned, "we can't take time to eat now, but we can have water."

Without a word, Kendall opened the flap on her bag and pulled out the bottle. It was two-thirds full, and though he hadn't said anything while they'd been trapped in the room, she knew the small amount had him worried. The food situation wasn't any better. She had one sandwich, a kahloo fruit, and an oatmeal cookie—nothing else.

The grim look that settled on his face made her want to apologize for not grabbing more food and another bottle of water, but she'd never expected to need supplies beyond lunch. Wyatt gazed down at the water she held, then back at her. "We're going to ration everything to make it last as long as we can. It's critical since we're in a section of the pyramid that we're unfamiliar with. Take a small sip, no more."

Kendall nodded, and did just that. She passed it to him and watched him do the same, before he tightly screwed the cap back on. Carefully, she stowed it in her bag.

"Let's go," he said. "I want as much distance as possible between us and that room before your smugglers come back."

With a nod, she fell into step beside him. As they walked, Kendall found herself dwelling on the way she'd kissed Wyatt.

He'd surprised her when he tugged her down to him, but when she'd recovered, what did she do? Pull away? No, not her. She gave in to temptation and opened her mouth, let him explore as thoroughly as he wanted. The kiss had been so intense, they'd nearly been devouring each other. Maybe she'd been wondering for a while what Wyatt's lips would feel like against hers, but that didn't mean she wanted to jeopardize their friendship to find out. Thank God he didn't seem to remember what had happened.

They passed through an archway. There was a branch off the main corridor to the left, but Wyatt continued straight ahead. While he'd been unconscious, he must have been dreaming about some woman. Kendall fought the need to scowl, but lost.

Zolianna. The name sounded exotic, and mysterious—
two things she wasn't. How could she compete with this
woman?

Compete? What the hell was she thinking? Wyatt was
her best friend, not her lover, and she didn't want it any
other way.

But what did this Zolianna look like?

It wasn't as if she wanted to scope out a rival; she was
merely curious about what type of woman Wyatt found
attractive, that's all. There wasn't any Zolianna on J
Nine—it was an unusual enough name that she'd remember it—so it had to be someone back on Earth.

"Darlin', you're frowning something fierce," Wyatt
said. "What's on your mind?"

Kendall ignored the thrill that shot through her at the
endearment; he didn't mean anything by it. Then the question sank in and she felt the blood leave her face. She
couldn't tell him the truth—he might think she was jealous. Her brain raced until one thought settled. "The
thieves. They've been looting the Old City—the *temple*—
with impunity. We'll probably never recover most of trea-
sures they've stolen."

"That's true." He slipped a callused hand under her fall
of hair and massaged her neck. "But there's nothing we
can do right now. When we get out of here, you can raise
cain." Wyatt dropped his arm and chuckled. "Heck, we
both know you're going to give Sullivan an earful the instant you get him in your sights. I just hope I'm there
when you tear a strip off him."

"He's a superior officer and he's . . . intimidating."

Wyatt grinned. "Yeah, he is, but that's not going to stop
you, and neither will his rank. You'll be subtle enough
that he won't be able to threaten you with charges, but
you'll get your point across. And he should have antici-
pated smuggling, right?"

"Of course he should have!" she said heatedly, before

she noticed Wyatt's shoulders were shaking. Kendall glowered at him. "Bait me again, and I'll unload with a whole lecture about protecting the antiquities in this city."

"That's not much of a deterrent. I like it when you get all passionate on me." Wyatt winked at her.

Kendall jerked her attention forward. She knew her cheeks had scalded—she could feel their heat—but she couldn't help but wonder if he alluded to their kiss. Just what did he remember?

Kendall looked at Wyatt when he stopped short, and waited for him to explain why. They'd been traversing the corridors for hours. This inner section of the temple was a maze, and over and over, they'd run into dead ends or places where the halls forked into more branches. It had surprised her at first that he consulted her on which direction they should take, but she decided she liked it. This was what teamwork was about. But she didn't have a clue as to where they were and was trusting Wyatt to lead.

"What?" she prodded when he didn't say anything.

With a grimace, he said, "I think we made a circle."

She glanced around, but this marble passageway looked pretty much like all the others. "Why do you believe that?" No response. Kendall moved in front of him. "Wyatt?"

"This room?" He gestured to the open doorway to his right. "I think it's the one I told you not to explore."

Kendall blushed. They'd been walking for maybe half an hour when she'd spotted the first doorway. Her only thought had been to study the chamber, and when she'd looked inside, she'd completely forgotten about the smugglers. It had been spectacular, containing tapestries and statuettes that stole her breath. To her embarrassment, Wyatt had needed to wrap an arm around her waist to prevent her from entering.

He'd been right; they didn't have time for her to indulge her interest, and she'd dutifully walked past every other chamber they'd passed—even if she did stare longingly into them as she went by. After they escaped and sent up the alarm, she could come back and investigate to her heart's content.

"Why do you think we made a circle? Because of the mosaic of gems inlaid into the far wall of the room?"

"Yeah. Every room we've seen up till now has had a unique pattern of stones inside it," Wyatt said quietly. "Unless we hit our first repeat, we're almost back where we started."

Now she understood his grimness. "You haven't been marking our path in some top secret Spec Ops way?"

Wyatt started shaking his head before she finished. "I can't." He reached out and lightly clasped her shoulders. "We don't know who all is involved in this mess, and if someone on the teams is dirty, I'd be leading them right to us."

"Yeah." She almost leaned into him and Kendall stiffened her muscles to keep from giving in to the urge. For a similar reason, she clenched her hands into fists. She wanted to reach up to push his dark hair off his forehead, to feel it slide between her fingers, and that scared her. Usually, she didn't pay attention to how gorgeous Wyatt was, but right now it seemed to hit her like a sledgehammer. Even his stubble was sexy and her thinking this was *so* not good. "Right," she said, "we don't know who's involved." She took a step away, breaking his hold.

Kendall didn't miss the hurt that darted through his eyes, and she regretted causing it. The desire to close the distance between them and soothe him was so strong, she took another step back to resist temptation.

It was one kiss, nothing more, yet it seemed to have undermined her common sense. She knew better. Time after time, Kendall had let herself become attached to her mom's latest lover—had let herself wish they could be a family—only to have her hopes dashed. And when things fell apart, she was the one who consoled her mother. The breakups were the only times her mom drank, and at some point before she passed out, she'd slur out her regret that she'd taken John or Kent or Hank or whomever to her bed. Friendship, her mom had told her, was what lasted.

But that didn't stop Kendall from wanting Wyatt to kiss her again. She tightened her fists and reminded herself that while she'd been kissing him, *he'd* been kissing Zolianna.

"I . . ." She cleared her throat, tried again. "I don't know where we are. I'm sorry."

"Don't fret over it." Wyatt tucked his fingers in his front pockets. "Okay, here's what we're going to do. First, I'm taking a minute or two to think through the path we took and try to figure out where we went wrong. Then we're going to move and move fast. We lost our safety margin."

Kendall nodded. It didn't surprise her that he had some kind of mental map of their route, but the fact that they'd made a circle was proof that she wasn't the only one confused by the dozens of twists and turns they'd taken.

He stared down the corridor, his thoughts obviously focused inward. As she waited for him, Kendall started to lean against the wall, then stopped and eyed it warily, but the inclusions remained frozen in the stone. She breathed a little easier. This had to prove that her earlier hallucination had been brought on by the lack of oxygen. Nothing else. Relieved, she glanced around, but she couldn't see into the room and nothing else caught her interest. Except Wyatt.

She knew she should look away. Ogling him, even covertly, wasn't smart, yet she couldn't seem to tear her gaze from him. Wyatt was a big man, a couple of inches over six feet, and broad through the chest and shoulders. Her eyes slid lower, took in his narrow waist, his powerful thighs. His great ass. She thought about when they worked out together, how distracting he was in shorts, but sometimes he'd whip off his shirt and she'd be so busy trying not to gape that she'd forget what she was supposed to be doing. But a woman would have to be dead not to appreciate all those sexy muscles.

He put his hands on his hips and she shifted her stare. His long fingers hinted at an artistic side, but the calluses didn't belong to a dilettante. Kendall sighed. She didn't want to be attracted to him, didn't want to think about him using his hands on her, or what his palms would feel like caressing her bare skin—she couldn't risk their friendship. Not for a few weeks, or, if she were lucky, months of physical pleasure.

Propping her shoulders against the wall behind her, she closed her eyes, took a deep breath and struggled to extinguish her arousal. She didn't have much success until she pictured her life after Wyatt moved on, when she didn't have him to talk to or laugh with any longer. That hurt enough to dump a bucket of ice water over her desire. Sex was fleeting, she knew that.

Concentrate on something else, she told herself. Her brain skittered around before she thought about the gemstones she'd seen inlaid in the corridor walls. There was always a pattern at an intersection, and if there were a spoke of passageways, the design was even more detailed and elaborate. Wyatt had muttered the first time she'd stopped to record the image with her digicam so after that, she'd taken the pictures without slowing down. Some were blurry despite the camera's advanced stabilization features, but most had come out pretty well.

She wanted to study the patterns, learn from them. She was sure they were vitally important. Kendall bit her lip as she concentrated. Some of the stones were basic— sapphire, ruby, diamonds—but seeing selenite was a huge surprise.

It was a soft crystal, part of the gypsum family. She knew more about it than most other gems because her mom had collected wands made from the translucent rock. It was supposed to facilitate memory of past lives, which was why her mom surrounded herself with it, but it had other properties as well. She scrunched her eyes tightly as she tried to remember them.

"Bug, you okay?"

Reluctantly, Kendall looked at him. He stood close, concern etched on his face. "I'm fine," she assured him. "I was just resting my eyes for a minute."

"If we hadn't gone in a circle, we could stop for a while, but . . ." Wyatt's voice trailed off as he shook his head.

"I can keep up, Wy. Don't worry, okay?"

Wy? Where had that come from? Something flashed across his face, but it was gone before she could read it. Maybe it was the note of affection laced in the abbreviated name that startled him. God knew it had surprised the hell out of her. That was the kind of tone a lover used, not a friend.

He seemed to loom nearer, and every sense in her body sharpened. She could detect the slight citrus scent that seemed to cling to his skin, see the azure flecks in his navy eyes, and she could feel—Kendall stiffened before she swayed into him.

"We should go," she said, sidling carefully to the side. She couldn't risk touching him, not in the odd mood she was in. Not only didn't he move, but something in Wyatt's gaze made her uneasy. "Um, did you figure out where we went wrong?"

"Not for sure," he said at last, "but I have a few ideas."

But he continued to look at her oddly. The last thing she wanted was him asking questions. What could she say? That she couldn't help wanting him even though she knew better? Before she could think of some way to divert him, her stomach growled. Loudly. Kendall quickly moved her hand over it, trying to smother the noise, but she was too late. Wyatt's lips quirked, and she felt her cheeks heat again. "Sorry," she apologized.

"Nah, I'm the one who should be apologizing. If I was taking care of you right, I'd have fed you earlier. It'll have to wait, though. We're too close to where we started."

"I know." Kendall rested her hand over the flap of her messenger bag, fiddled with the ornamental buckle. *She* was the one who took care of things, not the one who was tended to, but Wyatt constantly watched out for her, and it always left her off balance. Uncomfortable. And with a strange warmth in her chest.

Before she realized what he was up to, Wyatt snagged her hand and drew her down the hall. The feel of his rough palm against hers ratcheted up her awareness of him. Damn.

She should pull her hand free, but Kendall didn't want to. Since she wouldn't let go, she needed to focus on something to distract herself. The smugglers. Yeah, she could think about them. Wyatt claimed they'd lost their safety margin, and she had no reason to doubt him. It was unnerving to know they'd be hunted, yet Kendall had faith in him.

But Dr. George was the leader of this band of thieves. Despite being warned not to underestimate him, Kendall still didn't think he was cunning enough to—She stopped short, and Wyatt gave her a tug to get her moving again.

What qualities did it take to lead a smuggling ring? Kendall thought about that, and tried to guess. Cleverness, for one, she decided, including an ability to strategize. Insight into personalities and who would be corruptible. Approach the wrong person to join the band and the gig was up. Logistics was a third quality. The relics had to be hidden, packed and shipped off the planet. Then there was coordinating with an accomplice on Earth, someone who could be trusted not to take the money and disappear. That had to be tempting with J Nine so far away, so loyalty would be a factor. The final attribute that came to mind was the knowledge of what could safely be stolen and yet still bring a good price on the black market.

Kendall gave low marks to George in all categories— okay, *almost* all categories. He would know what artifacts could be taken. That was his job. But George was a plodder. She didn't think he was shrewd enough to implement such an intricate scheme. She just couldn't picture it.

And loyalty? Kendall didn't know anyone who liked Dr. George; he'd managed to alienate at least half of the other archeologists, and nearly all the military personnel who had to deal with him loathed him. The kicker as far as she was concerned, though, was he was *not* a good judge of character. George was too self-involved to read people well. He looked down on pretty much the entire military contingent stationed here and barely tolerated some of the civilian experts. The ones he appeared to like were asskissers and suck-ups who, by their very natures, were generally untrustworthy.

Wyatt drew to a halt and Kendall put aside her thoughts to look around. She didn't see anything. "Why are we stopping?"

Rubbing the back of his neck with his free hand, Wyatt said, "I'm not a hundred percent sure which hall we chose our first run through, and I want a couple seconds to think about it. I believe we veered toward the left here, correct?"

Kendall pursed her lips as she studied the five spokes that split off the main corridor. "I think so," she said slowly, "but was it the far left, or second from the left?"

Shaking his head, Wyatt said, "I was hoping you'd remember." He smiled at her, and Kendall felt her heart rate pick up. "I'm leaning toward the hallway on the far left."

She studied it more intently, but there were no distinguishing characteristics. "I trust you."

His hand tightened around hers for a second, then relaxed. "Bug, your faith means a lot to me. I just hope it isn't misplaced." Before she could comment, he continued, "Okay, we'll head left, and take our chances."

"Does it matter?" she asked after they resumed walking. "I mean, one way is as good as another as we look for a door."

"Maybe, but I was having trouble keeping track of where we were. If this isn't the right hallway, then we're completely lost with no chance of finding our way back to where we started."

Kendall thought about that. "Are you saying that if our situation became desperate enough, we'd try to exit the way we came in? Despite the thieves watching for us at the entrance?"

He was dead serious when he looked at her. "We don't have much food, but what I'm concerned about is water. We can't last long without it, especially since we're moving. What do you think? Is there water in this section of the temple?"

Her first instinct was to say yes, but Kendall swallowed the word. "I don't know. There could be, I guess, but this part hasn't been mapped or explored."

"Yeah," Wyatt said grimly. "I'm aware of that."

They hadn't gone far before they reached a right angle in the hall. "I don't remember this our first time through," Kendall said quietly as they drew to a halt.

"I don't either. Fu—uh, dang."

Her lips twitched. "You don't have to watch your language. Don't you know by now that you can be yourself with me? If you want to curse, go ahead. I'm not going to be offended."

"I know you wouldn't be offended by swearing, but my mama told me not to cuss, and my dad said sometimes a man had to swear, but just be careful not to do it in front of a lady. I can't change twenty-five years of indoctrination."

Did he have to smile like that? So sweet and sexy? And did he have to talk about his mother and father with so much affection, so much respect? It made her melt every time he did either of those things, but both together, well, that was lethal. "Do we go back?" she asked before the silence dragged on too long.

"You know we have to."

Kendall nodded, but she didn't want to retrace her steps, even if Wyatt had that route more or less mentally mapped. When he started back the way they came, though, she followed. They reached the hub of halls and turned down the next passageway.

As they walked, an odor reached her. It wasn't a pleasant one, and it seemed out of place in the temple. Kendall lifted her nose, trying to get a better read on the scent. She thought maybe urine and feces, but there was something else, something that almost smelled metallic, something she couldn't name. The one thing she was certain of was that it was growing stronger. "What is that stench?" she asked.

"Nothing good." Wyatt appeared grim, and her throat went tight. He'd recognized the smell, she knew it. "When we get closer," he added, "you stay put and let me check it out."

Instead of asking him what they'd find, Kendall scowled. She didn't like the idea of Wyatt shielding her. On the other hand, while he'd always been protective, he'd never been unreasonable about it. If he didn't want her to see whatever this was, he probably had a good cause.

The odor was really strong now, and she put a hand over her nose, trying to block some of it. They slowed as they neared another intersection of halls, and she briefly glanced to her right.

Kendall froze midstep. She couldn't move, couldn't force herself to look away. From the corner of her eye, she saw Wyatt stop and follow her gaze. She heard him mutter a curse, but her feet were still glued to the floor.

Breathe, she thought, and gasped in a shaky breath. *Oh, my God. Oh, my God.* She felt her stomach heave, and she gagged. That broke her paralysis enough for her to close her eyes.

It didn't help. She couldn't block the image. One of George's stooges hung suspended, his body impaled by dozens of sharp metal spikes.

Chapter Seven

With a faint smile, Stacey gazed down at Cam. Her god-son slept like he did everything else—all out. She never would have believed a two-year-old could be capable of such determination, but that was before this boy had come along. Fortunately for everyone, Ravyn was accustomed to intense males and one more in her life didn't faze her.

Looking around the darkened room, Stacey found a chair and quietly pulled it closer to the bed before sitting. She rested her hand lightly over her abdomen and gave the baby cocooned there a small caress. What would her child be like? Would he be patient? Quiet? Focused? She stifled a laugh. Heaven help her if this baby took after Alex in that last regard.

Cam had taught her a lot about kids. If she'd had to guess, Stacey would have thought that babies developed an identity over time, but even as a newborn, Cam had been his own person. Sure, some of his traits must have come from his parents, but there were definitely things that hadn't. That made her wonder.

The little boy shifted restlessly, and she held her breath, hoping he wouldn't wake up. She'd volunteered to put Cam to bed, giving Ravyn the night off, but she'd had ulterior motives too. Stacey needed the peace this child gave her. There was nothing like a hug from him to put life in perspective and help her remember what was important.

He was a healthy, happy toddler, growing up secure in the knowledge that his mom and dad loved him. Heck, just plain growing up with both his parents around him every day. Something her own child wouldn't have. With a sigh, she slumped in the chair. She felt a clutching in her chest as she realized what a loss that would be for her son or daughter.

But Cam was also secure in the knowledge that his mom and dad loved and respected each other. She was doing the right thing for her baby; Stacey trusted that. What would she be teaching her son or daughter if she stayed with Alex? That love only had to go one way? That it was okay to settle for whatever affection was carelessly tossed out? Sometimes she felt like a dog waiting for scraps to fall her direction, and that was no way to live. She straightened. No child of hers was going to be raised to believe this inequity was acceptable in a relationship.

When Cam shifted again, Stacey knew it was time to leave and let him sleep without her hovering. It wasn't like she needed to avoid Ravyn. Her friend wouldn't ask any questions, not unless Stacey herself brought up Alex or why she'd left him.

Stacey closed the door to Cam's bedroom behind her and paused, trying to decide whether to find Ravyn or simply retire for the evening. As she stood there, she heard Ravyn talking to someone.

Alex.

Stacey grimaced. She should have guessed he'd show up. Forcing her feet to move, she headed down the hall. Ravyn shouldn't have to run interference for her. Sullivan deserved to be told face to face that it was over.

"For the last time," Alex said, "move out of my way."

Icicles dripped from his words and that told Stacey clearer than anything how angry he was. She'd learned quickly after meeting him that the colder he sounded, the more furious he was.

"No," Ravyn replied, her voice calm and almost as chilly as her brother's. "If you want to get past me, you're going to have to hurt me, and we both know you won't do that."

Stacey's lips curved before she could prevent it. Alex was tough as nails, deadly when he needed to be, and a complete marshmallow when it came to women—especially his sister and her.

As her friend's back came into view, Stacey stopped. She couldn't see Sullivan, but she could feel his intensity radiating down the hall, and her courage faltered. Ravyn had learned to deal with her brother a long time ago. Heat didn't win disputes with Alex. Once his opponent's temper became hot, Sullivan had the upper hand and the argument was all but over then. That was always Stacey's downfall—she couldn't stay cool like Ravyn did.

"Where the hell is Brody?" Sullivan demanded.

"You think Damon's going to back you up?" Ravyn sounded incredulous. "First, he's as big a teddy bear as you are, and second, he's always on my side."

Alex muttered something Stacey couldn't make out, then said, "Come on, Ravyn. Stace and I need to talk."

"If she wanted to see you, she would."

"Why do you have to be so damn stubborn?"

Stacey shook herself out of her daze. She couldn't stand here, out of view, and listen to them argue. "Ravyn's not being stubborn," she told Alex when she reached the other woman's side. "She's being a good friend. But it's okay." Stacey looked at Ravyn. "Alex and I do need to have a conversation."

"You don't have to do this," Ravyn said. "I can handle it."

"I know you can, but I *do* want to talk to him."

Ravyn studied her intently before reluctantly stepping back. "Just remember, I'm here if you need me." After giving her brother a last glare of warning, Ravyn withdrew to the master suite.

Reluctantly, Stacey turned back to Alex. She was an adult; she could deal with breaking up with the man she loved. If anything, his features had pulled tauter, and she swallowed a sigh. He was in a warrior frame of mind. Ravyn blocking his path had started it, but it was honed now and directed at her.

"Let's go home." Alex took her elbow and started to draw her toward the door.

Stacey dug in her heels and tugged her arm free. "No. We can talk here."

"I'm not having this discussion in the hallway." A thread of anger crept into his voice.

"Why don't we use one of the rooms off the main chamber? We'll have privacy there."

"Fine," Alex snapped, and taking her elbow again, he began to pull her across the large gathering room. Irritated with his high-handed behavior, Stacey tried to yank loose again, but she couldn't. Sullivan's grip wasn't painful, but he was hanging on tightly enough that she was stuck. She was staring at his hand, trying to figure out how he did that, when Alex stopped short.

Stacey looked up and saw Ravyn's husband blocking the path.

"Get the hell out of the way, Brody," Alex warned.

"Is everything all right, Stacey?" Damon asked pointedly.

"Thanks, Damon, but I'm fine. Really."

"Are you sure? You don't have to do anything you don't want to, you know. I'll make sure of that."

His concern touched her and Stacey had to blink a few times before she said, "You're a good friend, but honest, I need to talk with Alex. I'd just prefer," she glared at Sullivan, "he not tug me along like a dog on a leash."

Damon studied her for a moment, then looked at Alex. "You heard the lady, she doesn't want to be tugged."

Alex released her, but he growled, "This is between Stacey and me. Mind your own business."

"This is my business, Colonel. Stacey is my wife's best friend and a guest in our home. It's my responsibility to protect her when the need arises—even from you."

Stacey didn't need to be psychic to predict Alex's reaction to that statement. His jaw became so tense, a muscle started to tic in his cheek. "Brody," he growled, "if you thi—"

She jumped in quickly. "Alex, you know you'd do the same thing if the situation were reversed, so don't get indignant."

The two men hadn't gotten along when Ravyn had first fallen in love with Damon, but over the past three years, they'd made a lot of progress. In fact, they'd forged a tentative friendship, although she suspected both would deny that with their final breaths—at least for right now. After all that, the last thing Stacey wanted was to see it undone by one incident.

Alex grumbled, but he couldn't disagree. "Now that you're aware Stacey wants to talk with me, you can go away."

Damon seemed amused by Sullivan's bluntness, but his voice was serious when he told her, "If you need me, just holler."

The silence was absolute until Damon was gone, and then Sullivan demanded, "What did you say to them?"

"Nothing." She resumed her course for the room directly across from where they stood. Stacey ignored the cursing she heard behind her and took a seat in one of the overstuffed chairs, folding her hands demurely in her lap. Truthfully, she was nervous about this meeting. She loved Alex; what if she wasn't strong enough to stand her ground? Going back to him, living as they'd been living, would destroy her. She knew it. But her heart didn't seem to care. Even now, it was urging her to wrap her arms around her man and hold on to him no matter the cost.

Alex closed the door quietly behind him. "You must have said something," he said, picking up where he'd left off. "My sister and her husband are acting like I'm some dangerous felon."

"I didn't," she gritted out, "say one word to either of them about you." He was standing close enough to loom over her, his hands resting on his hips, and that irritated Stacey. Alex was always looking for an edge. He couldn't just sit down and have a discussion like a normal person. No, not Sullivan. He had to find a tactical advantage. "If they were concerned, it might be because when you're focused on something, your personality becomes extremely forceful. Maybe they think that I'm no match for you when you're in this state of mind."

"That's bullshit." Alex smiled. "No matter how strongly I come across, we both know who gets her way nearly every time."

Stacey opened her mouth to disagree, but shut it without speaking. Instead, she considered what he'd said—and realized it was largely true. If she didn't back down, eventually she did prevail unless her safety was involved. That was the only thing he never budged on. She needed to think about this some more, but not right now. Later, when she'd be left undisturbed.

"But Brody and Ravyn aren't important. Let's talk about why the hell you took your stuff and moved up here," he said firmly.

"Sit down, Alex," Stacey ordered, ignoring his question for the moment. "I'm not getting a crick in my neck because you're trying to intimidate me."

His face went red before he grabbed the chair next to hers and spun it around so he could look at her. "I wasn't trying to intimidate you." The growl held more frustration than it had earlier. "I wanted to see you while we talked."

She waved that aside. Maybe it was true, or maybe jockeying for position was so ingrained in him that he didn't even realize why he did things. It didn't really matter. What mattered was finishing this conversation without caving in.

"It was a surprise," Alex began, voice gentle, "to come home and find you—and all your things—gone." He paused to take her hand. "Don't you think you're overreacting? After all, it was only a missed dinner. I'll make it up to you."

The man was an idiot. He thought she'd moved out over one dinner? Stacey jerked her hand free and struggled to check her temper. "I am not overreacting," she said bitingly.

He nodded sagely, an understanding expression spreading across his face. She clenched her hand. Stacey just knew he was going to say something to infuriate her. She was right.

"PMS, huh?"

"PMS? PMS! Are you really that blind? It's not about a damn dinner; it's about our entire relationship!" Taking deep breaths, she tried to regain control. "Why is it that whenever a woman has a legitimate complaint, and a man doesn't get it, he chalks it up to hormones?" Alex started to reply and Stacey held up a hand to stop him. "That was a rhetorical question. You'll only dig yourself in deeper if you answer. We both know that."

He subsided, but he didn't look happy. "Okay, if it's not hormones, what is this all about?"

Stacey took another deep breath and tried to come up with a way to explain it so that he'd understand. It was about emotion, how she *felt,* and Alex had already proven himself unobservant on that score. Heck, she had tried to talk to him about this, over and over, but he'd never gotten it.

"I love you, Alex," she told him quietly. His expression didn't change, but Stacey could tell he was uncomfortable. "How many times have I told you that? A thousand? Ten thousand? But you've never said it in return, not even a 'me too.'"

If she didn't feel so much like crying, she might have laughed at the hint of terror that flew across his face. Alex Sullivan was a West Point graduate, he'd been a member of Special Operations for years, he'd fought in one of the ugliest wars in the history of Earth, and yet the idea of discussing his feelings sent him into a grade-A panic attack.

"I wouldn't need the words if I thought you loved me," Stacey continued, "but I don't think you do. I'm a convenience to you, someone to sate your physical needs with when the urge strikes, nothing more."

"You make it sound one-sided," he interrupted, "but you enjoy it too. I make sure of that."

"Yeah," she agreed thickly, "you make sure of it, except I need more from you than orgasms. You don't talk to me, not about anything really important. You don't contribute to holding our relationship together. I put in all the energy. The only time we're close is when we're having sex, and even then I feel like you're holding part of yourself back from me."

She dropped her gaze and blinked rapidly, not wanting him to see the tears. "At the beginning, I was willing to do most of the work. I knew you were closed off too much to reach out, but I expected at some point that you'd start making an effort. That never happened. I still do all the giving and you just take."

"Stace—"

Raising her head, she met his eyes squarely. "I'm not doing it anymore. I deserve a man who loves me, someone willing to put equal energy into our relationship. I'm not going to settle for less. We've drifted this way for far too long."

"And you're just saying something now?" he accused.

Fury roared through her, drying her tears. "You're a piece of work, Sullivan. I've tried to talk to you about this many times and always received one of two responses. Either you took me to bed and kept me there until I forgot about it, or you ran."

"Are you calling me a coward?" His voice was whisper soft.

"If the combat boot fits . . ." Stacey let her voice trail off when he surged to his feet and began stalking around the room. That was so atypical that she could only stare. Alex was always cool, no matter how tense the situation. No doubt he was upset about the challenge to his manhood, not about losing her.

"We've been through this before." He didn't look at her, but kept moving. "Three years ago, remember? I told you then that it was more than sex. Why in hell do we need to rehash it?"

Shakily, Stacey got to her feet. "Because you told me once, years ago, that it was *more than sex,* I should be happy with that and not expect more from you? Well, guess what? You were an emotional coward then and you're an emotional coward now."

Alex stopped short and glared at her. There was heat in his gaze now. "You're being unreasonable."

"Right. It's unreasonable to want the man I love to love me in return. What you're really saying is don't rock the boat. But while you might enjoy the status quo, it's ripping me up inside." She couldn't keep the tears at bay any longer, and they rolled down her cheeks. Impatiently,

Stacey wiped at them, but they were falling too fast. "It's killing my soul one piece at a time, and I can't afford to lose any more parts of me, not like this. So I'm doing what I have to do to save myself. I sent a message to CAT Command, requesting permission to board the next transport for Earth. Since they hate the fact that I'm here, I expect a prompt approval. It's over, Alex."

Pivoting blindly, Stacey hurried away.

Kendall stood in an ornate antechamber, amidst hundreds of women. The acolytes in their pale green robes led the slow procession into the chancel. Behind the novitiates stood the priestesses adorned in grass green robes, patiently waiting their turn. Although it was always a lengthy process when they gathered, no one dared speak, and the silence chafed her nerves.

Of all those present, only she stood without a robe. Instead, she was adorned in a close-fitting, sleeveless sheath. Kendall had nowhere to hide her hands and was forced to stand with absolute serenity. In truth, she felt anything but calm.

She didn't want this, had argued strenuously against it, but in the end, she'd had no choice. Linking her fingers at her waist, she glanced around. The white marble of the temple symbolized purity—and mocked her. Even now, Kendall had a pleasurable ache between her thighs, a reminder of the night spent with her lover. Neither of them had been able to sate themselves. Perhaps it was the knowledge that their future trysts might be much more difficult to arrange. It was challenge enough to meet him as a priestess, but after today . . .

The acolytes finished filing in and the priestesses began to follow. Did any of them regret their calling as she did? Kendall remembered pleading with the high priestess, begging to be released from her obligation. It had been her fifteenth birthday, the day all children were tested, and it had been her misfortune to score highly in the talents required by the temple.

She'd nearly confessed then that she'd already given her innocence to the boy she loved, but she hadn't quite been brave enough to do so. The disgrace wouldn't have belonged only to her, but it would have stained her entire family and his as well.

Now it was far too late to admit she'd repeatedly violated the most sacrosanct law of the temple. Her punishment would be severe, but her lover's would be even harsher.

Heru, she loved him. Had loved him with her whole heart for nearly twenty seasons, and she would do whatever was required to protect him. She'd made that decision long ago.

As the last of the women garbed in rich green disappeared from view, the temple sentinels moved into position. They were female, all priestesses, and trained as warriors. The city guard protected the exterior, but the interior of the temple was defended by these soldiers. They were allowed to wear trousers, and Kendall envied them the freedom.

Four members of the High Priestess's cortege formed a half circle around her. It was meant to offer support, but she saw it as a way to prevent her from running. She wouldn't do so and risk questions being asked, but the desire was there. Kendall could go to him seeking sanctuary; he wouldn't ask questions. Instead, he'd surround her with his muscular arms, hold her near, and kiss her with tenderness. She could relish his taste on her lips—and immerse herself in his love. Minutely, she shifted as the ache between her legs intensified. It was easy to remember him sheathed deep within her body, to recall the joy he gave her as he thrust into her.

She forced the memory aside and cast a quick glance to

either side. The women around her seemed oblivious to her distraction, and she thanked Heru for that.

Their robes were a deep emerald green denoting their station within the hierarchy of priestesses. Behind her, attended by the remaining five members of the cortege, was the High Priestess herself. Her clothing was the darkest of any, a forest green that seemed to shimmer in the light. Kendall had become all too familiar with this woman in the preceding weeks.

At last, it was her turn to enter, and on shaky legs, she stepped into the chamber. The chancel was by far the most ostentatious room inside the temple and it was cavernous, meant to hold every priestess and novitiate. Chanting began as she started down the aisle and a shiver coursed along her spine, leaving chill bumps on her bare arms. Without allowing her gaze to wander, Kendall walked sedately to the massive altar, her shaking knees hidden from view. Lifting her skirts, she ascended the white marble steps and stood before the second seat.

When Kendall was in place, the High Priestess made her own entrance. The remainder of the cortege came behind her, eyes downcast to show their respect for the woman they served. As the leader of the temple grew nearer, Kendall had to fight the need to flee. She would not be craven, would not risk her lover.

The ceremony wasn't overlong, or perhaps it merely seemed so to her. Before she was ready, she was summoned to the stone of wisdom. As she stood beside the High Priestess, the woman gazed deeply into her eyes. For a moment, Kendall feared she could see her transgressions, but the sense quickly passed.

As the High Priestess pressed her hand to the center of the marble, three attendants came forward and removed her robe, leaving her in a simple gown like the one Kendall herself wore. It was then that the woman chanted *the words that relinquished her power and position as leader of the temple. Though she would always bear the honorary title* pristinus *to signify her former rank, the decisions would no longer be hers to make.*

*The High Priestess stepped back, made a slight bow to the chancel full of women, then turned to Kendall. The woman took her successor's hand and drew her forward to the stone, then pressing Kendall's palm flat against the rock, she chanted four words—*To you I cede.

Beneath her fingers, Kendall felt the marble begin to pulse, as if the entire temple were aligning its vibration to hers. The buzzing sensation traveled up her arm, filled her body, and there was a sense of welcoming. She closed her eyes, embracing the gift being given to her. Something deep inside her, so deep she'd been unaware of its existence, sparked to life and grew until it permeated every cell of her being.

Recognition dawned. It was power. More power than she'd ever wielded before this day.

*The knowledge had barely made itself known when Kendall felt the robe of High Priestess being draped around her own shoulders. It was her turn to chant four words—*From you I accept.

The other woman removed her hand from atop Kendall's and the cortege began a chant of its own. It promised fealty to their new leader, but it was the stone that continued to hold her enthralled. Some type of energy was wending itself into her soul, becoming part of her. In a corner of her mind, she thought she should be frightened—and yet there was only rightness. This was meant to be, just as her predecessor had claimed.

When she opened her eyes again, the melding was complete. Kendall gathered her robes around her and stepped forward.

Raising her right hand, she telekinetically called the pink crystal staff to her. Once she held it, she raised the glow in the chancel, making the room almost painfully bright. There were a few gasps from the priestesses. The level of illumination was directly tied to how powerful the High Priestess was, and Kendall had raised the indicator to her left off the scale. This was the only time she would have to publicly exhibit her power.

Once the required demonstration of her strength was completed, she returned the chamber to its usual level of light. She conducted the rest of the ceremony, closed it, and granted permission for the priestesses and acolytes to depart.

It wasn't until much later, after the cortege closed the doors to her new chambers behind her that the euphoria she felt faded. Alone for the first time this day, Kendall slipped her robe off and draped it over a nearby chair. The letdown was sharp, and she paced until she saw the calling glass that her lover had given her the morning she'd been forced to enter the temple. None would recognize its function since it was unlike the usual stones used for communication, but it worked perfectly.

Sinking to the floor in front of it, she ran her finger over the top circle, picking up speed until she heard a soft hum, then she intoned the words that would connect her to him. His visage appeared almost immediately, telling her that he'd been sitting by his crystal. As she gazed at his dear face, her heart swelled with love until it ached. Her voice was choked as she whispered, "What are we going to do? Oh, my love!"

The man was Wyatt.

Kendall jerked awake and sat bolt upright.

"Bug, what's wrong?"

"Nothing. It was just a dream, that's all." Just a dream. That realization allowed her to take a deep breath and work on slowing her racing heart. Even as she closed her eyes and tried to fix the details in her mind, she felt the specifics fade. Kendall fought to hold on to them, but while she remained aware of major points, the little things were gone.

Wyatt put his arm over her shoulders and she went rigid before she could prevent it. Kendall fought the urge to pull away and forced some of the tension from her muscles. She'd already hurt him several times since they'd been imprisoned in the temple, and she'd try not to do it again. Reluctantly, she let him gather her close, but his nearness made her uncomfortable.

"That must have been some nightmare," he said quietly. "Was it about the body we found?"

Kendall fought off the image that immediately came to mind—she refused to think about it till they were safe— and shook her head. "It wasn't a nightmare, just a dream. But no, it wasn't about the stooge." She knew he was going to ask questions, so she added, "I don't want to talk about it." Especially not when her illicit lover had been Wyatt.

She itched to look up in her dream dictionary the elements she still remembered, but maybe she didn't need the book—the events had seemed more straightforward than symbolic. Dreaming about the temple made sense— she *was* trapped inside it—and the vibrating stone was logical too; she'd hallucinated that very thing because of her oxygen deprivation. Even the part about Wyatt fit. They had kissed today, and she'd been hot for him. And damn it, she was still a bit aroused.

Now that her dreams made sense, Kendall relaxed— straight into Wyatt's side. She stiffened again, then gave up. What the hell? It was just a kind of hug, something friends did all the time—right? Besides, his touch seemed to calm her, and at this moment, she needed that.

"Do you think they're still searching for us?" she asked. Instead of looking at Wyatt, Kendall stared straight ahead. They were in a room off the corridor, tucked out of sight from the doorway, and though the lighting was dim, she could clearly see the gems inlaid in the opposite wall. They seemed to sparkle, to call to her, and she fought the need to cross to them.

"Yeah, they're not going to give up even if they did lose a man, not when we can bring down their whole operation." Wyatt's voice almost made her start. "Are they searching for us right this minute?" He shrugged. "Who knows?"

Kendall nodded absently; she was attempting to identify the pale pink stone in the geometric design. It was the color of the scepter in her dream tonight and scattered throughout the temple and the city. She must have looked it up in her reference book dozens of times, but she couldn't remember what the book said. No doubt she should be concentrating on the smugglers and their close call instead of crystals—she knew how worried Wyatt was—but she felt more in control when it came to the rocks.

"Kunzite!" she blurted, identifying the jewel at last.

"I could make a really lame joke," Wyatt said, "but I won't. You can thank me later." She looked at him and he winked. "What the heck did you just say, though? Kunzite?"

"It's a stone, that light pink one." Kendall pointed to the mosaic. "I've been trying to place it since we came in here."

"You realize that this is an alien planet, right? That they might have pink stones here that we don't have on Earth?"

She wrinkled her nose at his tone. "Yes, I'm aware of that." But she knew she was right.

Kunzite. She wracked her memory for its properties. The gemstones had to be important to this society, and the information might help—somehow. A wisp came into her brain. The rock got rid of negative energy. And what else?

Stones always had multiple purposes. Wyatt hugged her tighter and another characteristic popped into her head. Love. This gemstone was largely centered on the heart chakra; it affected self-love, unconditional love, and—Kendall gulped—romantic love.

Then she almost laughed aloud over her own irrational fear. So what if a stone's energy worked on romantic love? It couldn't create what wasn't there, and she had free will—all humans did. She was getting a little freaked because of that kiss she'd shared with Wyatt, and her body's silly reaction.

"Bug," his drawl interrupted her thoughts, "there's something I better tell you."

"What's that?" she asked. The tone of his voice not only knocked thoughts of gems out of her head, it raised trepidation.

"You know how I grabbed your hand and we ran after I checked out that thief's body?"

Kendall shifted so she could see his face. It broke their embrace, and while part of her missed the closeness, a bigger part of her was grateful for an excuse to put distance between them. "Yeah, I remember that. So?"

"My plan was to take the route we'd already traveled. Not only did I have an idea where we were, but we'd likely avoid any hidden snares since we'd successfully traveled those hallways once." She thought she detected a slight flush on Wyatt's cheekbones. "Somewhere, though, I must have taken a wrong turn and when we kept running . . ."

He went quiet and Kendall leaned forward, urging him on. He couldn't mean they were—no, of course not. He was Spec Ops, and had been through training she probably didn't even know existed. "What are you saying?"

As he took her hand, he linked his fingers with hers. "We're lost, darlin'."

Chapter Eight

Wyatt sat with his back against the wall, his forearms resting atop his upraised knees, as he watched Kendall sleep. He had to get her out of here alive.

He really wished Bug remembered her last life right about now. Zolianna had been High Priestess of the temple; if she recalled that time, Bug could simply guide them to an alternate exit, and they'd be safe in their own beds by tonight.

But she didn't remember a damn thing. Not consciously.

He blew out a long breath. No sense dwelling on it. Most people didn't recall their past lives, and he shouldn't have expected Kendall to be any different. His awareness was a fluke, a cosmic joke. What else could it be when it had affected everything? When he couldn't tell anyone about it, not even Bug? Hell, how many times had he wished his memories were all some fantasy? But he'd known it was a past life—had always known—and he'd never had a choice except to believe it was true.

He'd always imagined that when he found the woman who'd been Zolianna, he'd finally have someone to share this with. But Bug got jittery and quickly changed the subject whenever he'd tried to discuss reincarnation.

Shaking his head, Wyatt forced himself to focus on their current reality.

They were stuck in a labyrinth with little food or water and were being hunted by smugglers who wanted them dead. And as an extra added layer of difficulty, the maze was booby trapped. The damn thing was that circumstances could be a lot worse. They could have been the ones to spring that snare.

God, the thought of Bug hanging there, a dozen metal spikes through her body, made his heart stop. Wyatt could still see the thief clearly. Kendall had turned away, but he'd needed to check things out. As horrible as the man had looked from a distance, that was nothing compared to up close. The worst of it was the spike that had gone through his skull and exited through his eye socket. Wyatt figured if they got out of this alive, he and Bug would be dealing with the aftermath for a while.

Examining the man, though, had revealed one thing. Despite the head wound, it was unlikely that he'd died instantly. Not judging by the amount of blood. How long had he been conscious? Seconds? Minutes? They'd heard nothing, and that worried Wyatt. If sound was dampened in here the way he was starting to fear, he and Bug could turn a corner, and without warning, walk right into the thieves. And the bad guys could be anywhere—in front of them, behind them, off to the side—he had no way to know.

The booby traps were problematic. Those things could be hidden anywhere, and he hadn't been able to figure out what had triggered the one that killed the thief. His best guess was some kind of pressure-sensitive plate, but it was a stab in the dark.

"You're frowning," Bug pointed out sleepily.

"Darlin', we're in a heap of trouble."

Sitting up, she shifted until she was next to him. "Probably worse than you've told me, right?"

"Maybe," he admitted.

"I thought so," Kendall said. "On a positive note, there's one less stooge looking for us."

Stooge? Wyatt didn't comment, but she'd used that nickname more than once and that made him believe Bug continued to underestimate the smugglers—not good. He needed her to be alert, and if she was writing them off as inept, she wouldn't be watchful enough. But that was a fight he'd have with her later.

"And on a negative note," he shot back, "we're just as susceptible to tripping those metal spikes."

Bug smiled at him. "On another positive note, now we know there are metal spikes to watch out for."

Reluctantly, Wyatt found his lips twitching. It was a silly game, but hell, they needed something to reduce the tension. "On a negative note," he said, "we don't know how to avoid them or what would signal the presence of a trap."

"On a positive note, with a smuggler missing too, Sullivan might discover something about him or the ring that would lead the cavalry to us."

"The negative is that they'd have to find us inside a maze filled with the alien equivalent of land mines."

"So much for looking on the bright side." She wrinkled her nose. "You must not be a morning person, Wy."

He let himself enjoy the way she shortened his name, then said, "It's not going to look better with more sleep and a cup of coffee. We're in a bad situation, Kendall. Really bad."

"I know." And surprising the hell out of him, she reached out and linked her fingers with his. It was a friendly gesture, not romantic, but she'd never before been the one who initiated touching. Wyatt savored the

warmth of her skin, the softness of it, just a bit more because of that.

Turning his head so he could see her better, he studied
her face. Her light brown hair obscured some of his view,
and carefully—slowly—he raised his free hand and
pushed it over her shoulder. There was wariness in her
gaze, and something else that he couldn't identify. Reluctantly, he lowered his arm.

Before he could tighten his hold, she slipped her hand
free and ran her palm over the thigh of her fatigues. Her
T-shirt had twisted so that the captain's insignia imprinted
on the left side of the chest was nearly at her shoulder.
The cotton was pulled taut over her breasts, and Wyatt
appreciated the sight until she tugged her shirt into place.

Reluctantly, he turned his thoughts to business. "Do
you mind if I catalog what you have in your bag? I need to
know what we've got available if I need something."

Without a word, Kendall turned, snagged the strap, and
pulled it over to him. He started with the side pockets. He
found hairpins, barrettes and a comb. Bug plucked the
last item from his hand and started to run it through her
snarls as he watched.

Shaking off his fascination with all things Kendall, Wyatt opened the bag's flap. There was a pocket on the inside, but it was empty. He moved to the main
compartment and pulled out a sheaf of papers. After un-
folding them and thumbing through them once, he started
to skim the first page.

"You don't have to read that, do you?"

"This is private? I'm sorry, darlin'." He handed the papers to her and she folded them in half again.

"Embarrassing, more than anything else," she said.

"Why? You write down some sexual fantasies?" Wyatt
wanted to kick himself as soon as the words left his
mouth, but luckily Bug didn't take his jest seriously.

"No, I put together a paper speculating what the aliens

believed about the crystals that are embedded in the walls all over the city. I was accused of writing New Age crap."

"Whoever told you that is an idiot," Wyatt growled. "It's clear that the stones had meaning to the inhabitants of the Old City. Just because we don't know what that is doesn't mean your ideas aren't valid." Bug just looked at him. "You're staring."

"I'm sorry; you surprised me, but I shouldn't have assumed."

Wyatt wanted to pursue this, but it was time they got moving again. He limited himself to saying, "Don't buy into that country-boy stereotype. I believe in all kinds of things that might shock you." He smiled. "But even if I didn't, I would never mock you for your beliefs." And with that, he went back to the contents of her bag.

In his peripheral vision, Wyatt saw her gape at him for a moment longer before she resumed combing her hair. The next thing he removed from her bag was a beat-up copy of Plato's *Republic*. A few sections had the page corners turned down. "A little light reading, Bug?" he teased.

She smiled. "I wanted to review the cave analogy."

Bug reached over, retrieved a barrette near his thigh and clipped her hair at her nape. He liked it loose—it sparked fantasies about her trailing it over his naked body—but he guessed it was easier for her fastened out of her way.

From the messenger bag, he dug out a digicam and a metal nail file with a pointed end. Flimsy, but he could cause some damage with it if the need arose. Reaching over, Kendall took the camera and snapped a shot of the gem mosaic. "There's something different about the way the stones are positioned in the temple. I want to study it in more detail."

Nodding, Wyatt returned to his search, but nothing else he discovered seemed helpful—just some personal hygiene items. He returned everything to where he'd found it, then slipped the nail file into a pocket of his pants.

"You didn't come up with much, did you?"

"No," he told her honestly, "but then I didn't expect you to be carrying around an arsenal, no matter how bad we need one."

"You only had one knife with you?"

"If I'd known what you were up to, I might have armed myself more heavily," Wyatt replied. "Dang it, why didn't you tell me about this? I knew something was eating at you."

Kendall bit her lower lip. "I wasn't sure enough to say anything then. What if I were wrong?"

"Then you'd be wrong." He knew her and knew what this was all about. "You don't have to be perfect." Wyatt reached out, gave her knee a squeeze, and left his hand there. "I could have helped you look into this." That reminded him of something. "I'm guessing you became more certain what was going on while I was outside the city. Did you say anything to Catfish?"

"I wanted to wait till you came back, but I was too scared." She admitted that as if it were a huge failing, and Wyatt wished he could have ten minutes alone with her mother. Bug shouldn't believe affection was dependent on being flawless, or that she couldn't be the one who needed help.

"I'm glad you told him." He was pissed enough at Kendall's mother that his voice came out choked. "And this helps us," Wyatt continued after he had cleared his throat. "Catfish will tell Sullivan what's up, and we both know once the Big Chill starts asking questions, things happen."

Bug frowned faintly. "I ran into the colonel on my way here. He blew me off and kept going."

"It doesn't matter. The minute Catfish learns we're missing, he'll track down Sullivan and sit on him if that's what it takes to get him to listen." Wyatt grinned at the picture that jumped into his head. Hunter might be quiet, but he got the job done no matter what. Of course, while it would help if the lieutenant colonel knew about the thieves, it didn't solve their problem. They couldn't count on anyone finding them, even if one of the smugglers was arrested and told security about this inner portion of the pyramid.

Bug shifted. Not far, but enough to dislodge his hand, and Wyatt bit back a sigh. Two steps forward, one step back. "We need to go." Wyatt hesitated, then added, "Our top priority is locating potable water. We can't last without it for long."

"Three to four days," Kendall agreed, tone matter-of-fact. "Wyatt? You don't think we'll find our way out that quickly?" Before he could answer, she added, "We have to. I don't care what we need to do, but we're getting out and we're warning the Brodys. I refuse to let those smugglers hurt that baby!" With a fierce glare, Bug swung the strap of her bag over her shoulder. "Let's go."

Alex paused in front of the home Kendall Thomas lived in and studied it. He found her choice telling. While those assigned here were restricted to houses within a certain zone, there was a wide variety from which to pick. Thomas had opted for something small. Not that she needed anything larger for a single person, but that hadn't stopped other officers from moving into mansions. McNamara, for example, believed that her rank had entitled her to stay in the so-called royal residence. She hadn't lasted there long, though, and by the time Ravyn and her husband had returned to J Nine, their home had been available for them.

That was just one grievance on a list of many that he had with the colonel. His latest complaint was how damn long it had taken her to grant permission for a search of Thomas and Montgomery's quarters. Alex didn't think he should have to ask for her okay. Shit, he was in charge of security; it was his job to make these decisions. McNamara thought otherwise, and since she had a bird on her shoulder, she got the final word.

He'd already gone through Montgomery's quarters and found nothing of any particular interest. The kid was reasonably neat, he liked suspense novels, and judging by the pictures scattered around, he was close to his family. Of course, for all Alex knew, Montgomery's team had already made a visit and sanitized the place. McNamara's damn delay might have cost him the opportunity to get to the bottom of this mess.

Shaking off his rising irritation, Alex climbed the stairs and reached for the knob. There were no locks in the Old City, so it surprised him that the door wouldn't open. He tried again, but it remained stubbornly closed. What were the odds Thomas had jammed it on the inside and used another exit?

Slim. He knew it, but the alternative . . .

After taking a careful look around, he shut his eyes and extended his senses. Alex hated this damn mumbo jumbo, but even though he wanted to, he couldn't deny the truth. He—the man with nicknames ranging from Colonel Control to Big Chill to that cold bastard—had psychic abilities. It had shocked him as much as anyone when they'd manifested three years ago. Stacey—

With a low snarl, Alex tried to push thoughts of her out of his head. If she wanted to leave, he was damned if he was going to stand in her way. He'd known from the beginning that it wouldn't last, that at some point she'd walk away just like almost everyone else had in his life. It wasn't the first time he'd been dumped, so it wasn't that big a deal, right? Besides, he had a task, one that needed all his focus.

He reached out with his senses again, and this time he read what he hadn't expected to find. Not really. Thomas had an energy shield surrounding her house.

To the best of his knowledge, only Stacey, Ravyn, Brody and he could erect one of these things, so how the hell had this girl managed it? And how had she known she had the ability? It wasn't something that the four of them talked about outside their circle. Alex's interest rose.

This field was an almost foolproof means to keep people out. Unlike locks, which could be picked or broken, no one could get through it who didn't know how to manipulate the energy of J Nine well beyond what it took to turn on the lights and water. If she were just a bit more skilled, no one at all—not even him—would be able to get around it. Thoughts racing, Alex homed in on the pattern Thomas had used, and lowered the protection.

He stepped inside and brought up the lights. After looking around, he toured the house, wanting to absorb the big picture before he began to explore more thoroughly. It didn't take long.

The thing that jumped out at him was the overwhelming perfection he saw everywhere he turned. While Montgomery had been neat, Thomas was obsessively so. In Alex's experience, people this anal never shirked responsibility—exactly what Chief Cantore had said. The last trace of doubt he'd had about whether the two captains had willingly gone AWOL disappeared.

Alex began his search in the bedroom. He expected to spend the majority of his time here, going through clothes and other personal items. But unlike Stacey and his sister, Thomas didn't have much, just her uniforms and the necessities. He found only three things that showed any hint the girl had a life outside the army.

One was a picture of her with Montgomery. Alex picked up the frame and studied the image more closely. The pose wasn't remotely romantic, but he could see an intimacy between them nonetheless. It was present in the way they were laughing, as if they shared a joke no one else understood.

The second picture was of a child, apparently Thomas, with a woman. Alex guessed it was her mother, although there was little physical resemblance between them. She looked about seven, maybe eight, in the photo, but her eyes were old. What had Cantore said? Something about Thomas having to assume responsibility at a young age? Alex was making a big assumption from a two-dimensional image, but the mother looked like she needed to be taken care of.

Next to the bed was a book titled *The Cultural Histories of Healing*. Alex fanned through it, looking for a scrap of paper or something jammed into the volume, but there was nothing there. Some of the pages had been dog-eared, so he skimmed them—and almost bored himself to death. The girl read *this* for pleasure?

Alex moved on to the bathroom. Everything he found was practical; there wasn't one item that could be labeled indulgent. Not like Stacey who enjoyed all kinds of lotions and oils. Shit, she'd almost taken over their counter with bottles and jars, and he'd lost count of how many times he'd ended up smelling like some damn flower or another froufrou scent because he'd joined her in the bath. More than once, Alex had intercepted questioning glances, but no one had dared to comment.

The smile disappeared when he remembered that he wouldn't have to worry about girly perfumes any longer. Stace had taken them when she'd left. Alex rubbed his chest just over his heart, but he'd almost become accustomed to the hollow feeling there.

How many times had he lain awake as a small child, listening to his parents argue and wishing they wouldn't fight? Then his father had left and the silence was worse than the bickering.

He'd been too young at the time to understand what was going on, but looking back, Alex could clearly see the way his mother had used him as a pawn in some unspoken war with his father. It had just about ripped out Alex's heart when his mother told him that his dad was gone because he didn't love them any longer. Nine years later, he'd discovered the truth—that his mother had done everything in her power to prevent his dad from exercising his custody rights. By then, though, the damage had been done.

Alex sighed, his hand going still. His mother had been a bitch, there was no question about that, and largely neglectful, but she'd been all he'd had. Until she'd met a rich man who wanted her but not another man's kid.

Concentrate, he told himself. Standing here thinking about events long past wasn't going to get him anywhere, and neither was mooning over Stacey. She was done with him—she couldn't make it any clearer—and he wouldn't beg. A man had his pride.

He moved to the gathering room, but there were even fewer personal possessions here. The only things that belonged to Thomas were some paperbacks—two anthropology texts, a book about the meaning of gemstones, and a dream dictionary. The latter items gave him pause, but he shrugged. It made her seem more human. Alex looked over the books and scowled. He hated it when people dog-eared corners, and it was apparently a habit of hers, since each of the titles was mutilated.

It wasn't until he checked the second bedroom that he hit pay dirt. She'd set it up as an office, and there were neat files full of papers. Alex groaned as he perused the first one. Shit, in her spare time she wrote tracts about the possible cultural meanings of artifacts in the Old City. "Thomas, what in the hell do you do for fun?" he muttered.

To Alex's great relief, the other folders held pictures, copies of e-mail, and her financial paperwork. He scoured those, looking for evidence—money always seemed to be at the root of every crime—but Thomas was frugal, and saved nearly her entire paycheck. Since arriving on J Nine, she'd spent nothing, not a cent. Of course, there was nothing to purchase here.

Closing the folder, he put it back and continued rifling through her possessions. Alex was pretty much resigned to coming up with nothing helpful when he found the computer tucked in a drawer. Carefully pulling it out, he set it on a table, and waited for it to boot up. Another interesting piece of info about Thomas. All officers were given the choice of a computer or a stipend to buy their own. Most opted for the cash. They'd add their own money to it and get something with more bells and whistles. Not this girl. She had the bulky, outmoded, Army-issued model. With a few enhancements.

Thomas was a geek. He recognized the signs of someone who knew far too much about computers—he was a closet geek himself. That was the only thing that enabled him to get past her security. The girl was good—he was better. Alex grinned. She had layers of defense, but he'd been using these things before she'd been born, and he was willing to bet he'd forgotten more about computers than she'd had time to learn. But he found himself enjoying the challenge.

It took him at least twenty minutes to reach her directory. Alex grimaced when he saw the number of files she had. He opened a few, discovered more anthropological data, and groaned. Shit. This was going to be a bitch to go through, and he'd have to page through each document in case something was tacked on at the end or hidden in the middle of unrelated data.

Halfheartedly, he opened another file, found more of the same, and decided he'd have to take the computer with him. The bad thing about that, though, was he'd need to fill out forms and give them to McNamara if he removed anything from her quarters. When he did that, word would leak out, and if Thomas were still alive, this could jeopardize her.

As he started to run through regulations that he might

be able to use to circumvent the paperwork involved, Alex continued to open documents. It was the one labeled *523-stc* that stopped his thoughts in their tracks. He only had to read a line or two to realize this wasn't related to anthropology.

He skimmed quickly, not expecting much. It was like a diary, although it was largely focused on her job rather than anything interesting. Might not hurt, though, to read through this when he got home. There was information here on how the department she worked in was run, and that could prove revealing.

Alex started reading when he saw two drawings side by side—sketches of a room that were identical except for one thing. Number two had a circle around an empty spot, but in number one, an artifact was there. He still wasn't reading as carefully as he could, but now it was because he wanted more info ASAP. A few screens later, he hit the bull's eye.

Son of a bitch. Thomas had documented a smuggling ring.

He kept going, found his own name, and scowled as he read that she thought he was intimidating. Thomas was certain he'd write off her suspicions if she only had circumstantial evidence, so she was determined to wait until she found conclusive proof because she didn't want him cutting her off at the knees. Alex muttered a string of obscenities.

The girl had tried to talk to him shortly before she'd disappeared, and he'd bet the bank that Thomas had come up with solid intel for him on the thieves.

He wanted to punch something. If he'd listened to her, she might not have gone missing. Montgomery either. And because Hunter's death was no doubt tied to the thefts, Alex might already have the man's killer locked up. He cursed again.

His single-mindedness had jeopardized the lives of those two kids, and if they were dead, he shared the blame.

Chapter Nine

Kendall leaned back against the wall, and stared at the viewer on her digicam, scrolling through the images of gem mosaics. The patterns of the stones reminded her of crop circles with their geometric complexity. Had the people of the Old City experienced the phenomena too, or was it simply a mathematical fluke?

She stopped at one shot that showed a hub of hallways. There were spokes going off in ten different directions with the mosaic covering the only large section of blank wall. The selenite was always arranged in a sort of line when it appeared, and in this image, it was at the seven o'clock position.

Its presence continued to nag at her. It was such a soft stone. All it took was a fingernail across the surface to cause splinters to come off the rock. Why use it?

Okay so this wasn't the most important thing to think about, but who cared? It beat wondering whether they'd get out of this pyramid alive. And it sure was better than trying to figure out who Zolianna was and what Wyatt felt for her. The more she thought about him with some exotic, beautiful woman, the angrier she became. Was it her fault she'd ended up looking so ordinary? Of course not. Since she didn't resemble her mother, the blame clearly belonged to her father—whoever he was.

And wasn't that a laugh? Her mom was a serial monogamist, but she couldn't remember who had fathered Kendall. Her mother couldn't even recall the names of the men she'd been involved with in that time frame. There were days it ate at Kendall, moments when she longed to know who he was. She had so many questions. Did she really resemble her dad? Would he like her if they met? Did she have brothers and sisters?

Wyatt knew her parents hadn't been married, but she had never told him her father was unknown. He came from an all-American family. Parents who'd gotten married before having children, and who were still together after more than thirty years; two older sisters who had also married before producing nieces and nephews for Wyatt to spoil; a real house near Fort Worth, Texas; he'd even grown up with a dog, for God's sake.

She bet Zolianna knew who her father was. Exotic or not, she'd probably been raised in a family as normal as Wyatt's. The kind of family Kendall herself had always longed for.

"You okay?" Wyatt asked.

With a sigh, she slipped the digicam in her pocket and turned her head toward him. "Yeah," she said slowly. "I was just thinking about my mom." And a few other things she wasn't going to mention.

"It's gonna be okay," he told her, sliding his arm around her shoulders and briefly hugging her. "I'll do everything in my power to get you out of this alive, I swear."

"Not just me," Kendall growled. "You better get yourself out of this alive too, or I'll hold a seance and kick your butt."

When he laughed, she dug her knuckles into his side and twisted. "Not funny, Wy. Whatever happens, we're together. That means either we both make it out, or I fight by your side until it's over. I won't run."

That sobered him. "If I order you to leave, you'll get yourself out of here, understand me?"

"No."

A flush tinged his cheeks. "You'll obey my orders, or I'll have you up on charges."

She smiled sweetly. "Nice try, but it won't work. First, we'd both have to get out alive for you to file paperwork against me. Second, you'd never press charges; I know that as sure as I know my name. Third, this isn't an assignment where you were designated mission leader, and I outrank you, so you can't accuse me of disobeying a lawful order."

For a moment, Wyatt stared at her, obviously stunned. Then, as the shock cleared, she saw anger take its place. "What the hell do you mean you outrank me? That's bullsh—" He swallowed the end of the word, but not quite fast enough.

"Nope, it's true. I made captain almost a full month ahead of you; that means I have rank. Seniority rules," Kendall told him gleefully, her grin widening. "I'm letting you lead because you have the experience and it's the smart thing to do, but don't try to pull rank again. It won't fly."

"Letting me?" he snarled. Wyatt went nose-to-nose with her. "I don't give a fu—damn if you do outrank me, you'll listen and you'll follow my orders. Both our lives might depend on it."

Kendall found herself staring at his lips, remembering how they felt against hers. She wanted to taste him again, to slide her tongue in his mouth and explore. And she wanted him to know he was kissing her, not that Zolianna woman. She began to close the space between them, but as her actions registered, Kendall jerked back, banging her head hard into the stone wall. The curse slipped out before she could stop it.

"Dang it, Bug! What did you do to yourself?"

"Nothing, I'm fine."

"Lean forward."

She started to argue, but at the look on his face, she decided it wasn't worth the fight. Kendall bent forward.

Wyatt unclipped her barrette and slid his hand into her hair to test the back of her head. She knew he was checking for bumps, but the feel of his fingers against her scalp sent shivers through her body. What was happening to her? He was her friend; she shouldn't be imagining his hands caressing other places, but still Kendall nearly protested when he lowered his arm.

"No lumps," he reported, "but if you become dizzy or nauseated or anything let me know."

"I will, but it's not that big a deal." Kendall knew she sounded subdued, but she was scared over her reactions to him. "How much longer are we going to stay here?"

Handing her the barrette, he sat back, and replied, "I want to take a full fifteen-minute rest."

Kendall sighed. They'd maybe been here five minutes, so she had a while longer to keep her thoughts controlled. She clipped her hair at her nape again and returned to studying the crystals.

Each chamber they'd passed in this section of the temple had a sameness to it that seemed wrong. Maybe because the rooms in the outer area were all different. Or maybe because the people of the Old City had demonstrated architectural creativity in every facet of the city. Even the houses, while similar in style, had something that set each apart.

But every room in this part of the temple had been the exact same size and shape—a squat rectangle. Every door was placed in the same spot; every room had gemstones in-

laid in the same location. Even the walls were the same
sandy-colored marble with darker flecks—although, thankfully, they hadn't danced again. She barely stopped herself
from glancing down at her hand. There was definitely a
pattern there that hadn't been present before her weird hallucination. Since she didn't want to think about what that
meant, Kendall returned her thoughts to the room.

Each chamber held a few statuettes, a couple of tapestries and some locked cabinets. Well, at least the ones she'd
been allowed near had been secured. Even the furnishings
were identical, right down to the color of the upholstery
covering the settees. The only differing feature in each room
was the pattern of the crystals, which reinforced Kendall's
belief that the gems were hugely important to the aliens.

Getting to her feet, she walked to the far wall. She felt
Wyatt's eyes on her, and knew he was watching out for her.
His protectiveness elicited contradictory emotions inside
her. Part of Kendall was irritated that he thought her inca-
pable of crossing the floor, while another part of her felt
warmed by his concern. People only worried that much
about those they cared for, she realized that. But even *that*
raised conflicting feelings. Kendall shook them off.

Hesitantly, she skimmed the fingers of her right hand
over the crystals. She felt the surge of energy through her
entire body, and it took all her self-command not to yank
away. If she did, Wyatt would be at her side in a heartbeat
and he'd be asking questions. She didn't want to try to explain things to him that she didn't understand herself.

Tucking her hands in the front pockets of her fatigue
pants, she leaned forward to study the gems. The overwhelming color here was green—peridot, tourmaline,
moldavite, and others she couldn't identify off the top of
her head.

What were the properties associated with these specific
crystals? She could only remember bits and pieces about a

few stones, notably the ones she'd looked up over and over the past eleven months, but nothing on these.

There were other colors besides the green, of course—a touch of blue, a scattering of pink kunzite and a bit of orange—but some instinct told her those weren't the key to this pattern.

As she stared, the throbbing began in her hand again, but this time, it seemed to be matched by a pulse in the stones. There was a rhythm that caught her attention, but it was so quick, Kendall was unable to read every shift. After a pause, it repeated and she tried to memorize it. Again and again, it ran through a cycle, until the sequence almost started to make sense.

"Bug, we need to go."

Kendall groaned, but didn't argue. She peered over her shoulder, but he didn't seem to have noticed anything about the gems. No way could she tell him what had happened; it would only concern him.

Pulling her hands out of her pockets, she rubbed her tingly palm over the hip of her pants. The soft abrasion of fabric against skin calmed her. The pulsing gems weren't a trick of her mind; she had to trust that. Besides, there was plenty of oxygen now and no reason to believe she'd suffered any brain damage earlier.

Before she turned to rejoin Wyatt, Kendall took one last glance at the mosaic, but the stones were quiet. When she reached him, she stopped to stare—and wondered if she knew him as well as she thought. Maybe it was nothing more than the stubble on his chin, but Wyatt appeared dangerous.

He didn't move; neither did she. Kendall was aware of the way his T-shirt pulled taut across his shoulders, the intensity in his navy eyes, and the fall of dark hair over his forehead. Another pulse went through her, but this one had nothing to do with gemstones and everything to do with desire. Before she could stop herself, she reached up and pushed his hair off his face. Something flared in his gaze, and she hurriedly withdrew. Kendall grabbed her bag, wanting to get out of here before Wyatt started asking questions, or she did something else stupid.

"I can carry that," he offered. "It's probably getting heavy for you after all this time."

"No, I'm okay. Besides, if we run into the other stooges, you need the freedom to fight them. I know who's got the better chance to win." With an overly bright smile, Kendall started to pivot, but Wyatt caught her arm.

"I've told you not to underestimate them." She opened her mouth to insist she wasn't doing that, but he cut her off. "No, I don't want to hear it. I don't care how big an idiot you think George is, this group has been successful for a while, and every time I hear you call them *stooges* with that derisive note in your voice, you scare the heck out of me. Maybe George is a fool—you know him better than I do—but if so, he's surrounded himself with people intelligent enough to get the job done."

The heat in his voice stopped her for a minute. "I'm sorry," Kendall said at last. "I do know how serious our situation is, and honestly, I'm not taking any of this lightly. If you're hearing derision when I talk about them, it's because they're thieves and I loathe that they're looting the Old City."

Wyatt's jaw went tight, and Kendall realized he still didn't quite believe her. She shrugged and changed the subject. "Do you think they came back and got the body of the thief or did they leave him there?"

Kendall had never seen anything like that impaled body, and she never wanted to see anything like it again. Although she'd been doing her best to repress her memories, they continually flooded back.

"I think they left him," he said after a brief pause.

Some of the tension had eased out of Wyatt, and he sounded resigned.

"But he was one of them."

He put his hands on her shoulders and leaned forward. Kendall found herself mesmerized. Wyatt had the sexiest eyes; why hadn't she noticed that before?

"You're too tenderhearted, and that's a good thing," he added, as if he expected her to be insulted by the remark. Then, before she was ready, he released her and stepped away. Nodding toward the doorway, he said, "Let's go."

As they headed cautiously down the passageway, Kendall did some thinking. *Was* she taking this lightly because Dr. George was running the show?

Wyatt slowed as they hit a fork in the hallway—the temple was riddled with them—and this one branched out in four different directions. "Well, darlin'," he asked with a subtle drawl, "which do you favor?"

"Since we don't know where we are and have no idea how to get out of here, one corridor is as good another."

He settled his hand on her nape and lightly squeezed. "You pick. Close your eyes and tell me which way feels right to you."

"What?" While she'd mentioned certain New Age ideas, she'd never let Wyatt know the depth of her belief. His suggestion led her to think, though, that she'd revealed more than she realized. "You heard me." He changed position until her back was against his chest and his hands rested on her hips. "Close your eyes," he said soothingly. "Come on, Kendall."

She decided to just do it. Obviously, it was too late to hide her unconventional life philosophy. After shutting her eyes she took a few deep breaths, but it didn't calm her, not with Wyatt's muscular chest and arms surrounding her.

"Think of water," he murmured softly against her left

ear. The gentle puff of warm air as he spoke sent a shiver through her, but it was his voice that made the muscles of her inner thighs clench. "Which way would you go to find water?"

Kendall was too steeped in Wyatt to even have a clue which direction to choose. But she didn't want him to know that. The left side just seemed better, so she raised her arm to point, shifting it until she felt comfortable.

Now that she'd picked, she should open her eyes, and step away from him—but she didn't want to. Involuntarily, Kendall leaned into him and deepened their embrace. He shifted, fitting her more snugly against him. His groin pressed into her bottom, and she felt Wyatt start to get hard. And still Kendall didn't break free.

She knew this was stupid, that she was jeopardizing their friendship. She didn't care. Not right now. Later, she'd torment herself about the repercussions.

Wyatt made a noise that sounded like a groan, and his hold tightened on her hips. For an endless moment, the possibilities hovered between them. Then he broke the mood. "No."

He put her away from him, and almost dazed, Kendall opened her eyes. Then the rejection registered. Hurriedly, she took another step away from him—and staggered to catch her balance. Her legs weren't entirely steady. The embarrassment was intense and she knew her face was red because it felt scalding hot.

Holding out his hand, Wyatt took a step toward her. "Bug—"

"No!" She backed up. "Let's just forget about it, okay?"

"You're thinking I—" He cut himself off. "Damn it! Come on." He grabbed her hand and tugged her down the second hall on their left. It was only then that she heard a light scraping sound. There was no indication that a human had made the noise, and no telling how distant the point of origin was, but they couldn't risk waiting around to see if it was the thieves.

Even as adrenaline spiked, Kendall considered it a reprieve. It was temporary, though. Wyatt would want to clear the air. He'd be nice about it, but he'd tell her that he didn't think of her like that. And she'd agree their friendship was important—which was true—and pretend what had happened was no big deal—which wasn't true. He released her and she breathed a sigh of relief. This whole thing had gotten so messed up. Why did he have to mistake her for Zolianna? If Wyatt hadn't kissed her, Kendall wouldn't be confused, wouldn't be wanting more of him.

They slowed when they reached a corner, and he checked it out before they took the turn. The memory of his erection pressing against her butt made Kendall's thoughts derail. If he didn't want her, why had he gotten hard?

Almost as soon as she asked the question, she had the answer. He was male, and men found her pretty—in a girl-next-door kind of way. Plus, she didn't think he'd had sex in the four months he'd been on J Nine. This post was so small that she'd have heard something if he had.

Kendall felt like screaming. Why was she thinking like this? She didn't want him to want her. Hell, *she* didn't want to want *him*. Nothing but hurt and heartache waited at the end of this path; she knew that better than anyone.

Time after time as she'd grown up, her mom would meet a man and announce that this was her soul mate, the person with whom she was meant to spend her life. Time after time, Kendall had let herself believe it, let herself dream of having a dad and a permanent home. And time after time, they'd packed up and moved on in mere months. Her mom was always in tears, swearing off men and wondering where her true soul mate was. And Kendall would be fighting her own need to cry. No matter how hard she'd tried to remain distant, she'd always ended up liking her *uncles*. Of course, her mom's celibacy never lasted—there was always another man who was meant for her—and the cycle would begin again.

Well, she wasn't going to be foolish like her mother. She wasn't going to risk her best friend for a quick roll in the sack—she wouldn't risk him even for a couple months' worth of pleasure. Wyatt meant too much to her to lose him. So she'd apologize for her lapse, blame it on the circumstances affecting her judgment and they'd move past it. She hoped.

Now that she had a plan, Kendall felt better. The most important thing, however, was that she maintain her control. She couldn't have another moment of weakness, not without ruining any chance she had of things returning to normal between them.

And it went beyond Wyatt. Because they spent so much time together, she'd become chummy with his team, and to a lesser degree, the rest of the guys in Spec Ops. If Wyatt pulled back, Kendall wouldn't just lose one friend, she'd lose dozens.

Wyatt was getting tense. Kendall was too damn quiet. He knew she was dwelling on what had happened between them. Shit, he shouldn't have pulled back, but he'd had no other choice given the situation. And he'd been right to play it safe. He couldn't say that noise he'd heard had been made by the smugglers, but since the pyramid was usually silent as a tomb—his lips quirked—he had to assume it was produced by a human.

If he'd been busy kissing Kendall, he never would have heard it. Hell, once he got his mouth on her, he wouldn't hear a fricking brass band come marching down the stone halls. So he'd pulled away before giving in to his need, and the look he'd seen on her face had him kicking himself six ways to Sunday. She'd taken his withdrawal all wrong.

He'd try to explain, of course, but Wyatt knew Kendall would pretend the moment had never happened, and she'd avoid any conversation about it. And like always, he'd back off to keep her from putting even more distance between them.

He was damn sick of that. Wasn't four months enough time to be patient? Wyatt grimaced. If he could keep from rushing her just a little while longer, he was going to get her, he was certain of that. Already the wall she'd placed between them was starting to disintegrate. She'd linked her fingers with his, and today she'd reached for him to brush back his hair. Then there was this corridor incident. Not only had Kendall leaned more firmly into him, she'd wiggled her butt against his hard-on. Oh, sure, it had been a minute motion, but he'd felt it in every cell of his body. Thank God she was unaware of what she'd done.

Forcing the memory out of his mind wasn't easy, but Wyatt did it anyway. There wasn't a damn thing he could do right now and he needed to remain alert. They were in a shitload of trouble, and thinking with his cock wasn't going to get them out of it. He'd failed Kendall the last time around, but in this life, things were going to be different.

Right now, his top priority had to be replenishing their water supply, not getting Bug into bed. Although it sure felt like he'd been waiting forever for her. Hell, according to his mother, his first word had been *Zo*. Someday he'd tell Bug that.

There was one thing he didn't ever intend to share with Kendall, and that was the fact that the women he'd been drawn to in the past had all reminded him of Zolianna in some way. Usually it was appearance, but with some it had been personality. Bug had been the first who hadn't fit the norm for him.

Wyatt smirked, amused at himself. He'd only been on the planet for two days, and because they'd still been wound tight as hell from three solid months in the field, he and his men had been hanging together, keeping to themselves. But that evening, a meeting with Sullivan had run late, and he'd ended up at the mess hall alone—behind Kendall. He'd found himself attracted to what he could see of her, which was basically her backside, and from time to time, her profile. She wasn't his usual type—too tall, too slender, hair too light—but they were stuck in a line that didn't seem to be moving, so he'd started a conversation.

The more they'd talked, the more interested he'd become. Then Kendall had turned to hand him a tray. At first, it had been her smile that hooked his attention, but slowly, Wyatt had raised his eyes to hers. And he'd known.

He'd tried to convince himself he was imagining things, that the odds of finding her again on a planet with so few people were slim, but he'd finagled an invitation to eat dinner with her anyway. And as the meal progressed, he'd become certain of her identity.

They'd talked until they'd been the last ones in the mess hall and the kitchen staff had kicked them out. Then he'd walked her home and sat on her porch talking with her some more.

A few subtle probes that first night had told him that not only didn't she recognize him, but that she didn't remember their past life. That had been unexpected, and disappointing. He'd always figured it would be like a love-at-first-sight thing, but that wasn't how it went. Not for her, and not for him either. It had been more like intrigued at first sight. His lips curved. Bug was so different from Zolianna—so much more than he'd expected.

And he was doing it again. He had to keep his mind on the situation—he couldn't let himself think about kissing Kendall or about the feel of her body against his. Yeah, the marble hallways were monotonous, but shit, he'd kept focus in tedious places in the past, and with Bug at risk, he should be more alert, not less. She was the most important person in his world. Hell, she *was* his world.

Despite his intentions, Wyatt found himself zoning out again, thinking about how much fun they'd had at the Peace Day picnic a few months ago. As soon as he realized that he was drifting once more, he snapped himself out of it, but it worried him. "Kendall." He saw her wince, but ignored it. "I'm having trouble paying attention. I need you to talk to me, and if I don't seem alert, nudge me or something, okay?"

Her reluctance immediately changed to concern. "This isn't like you. Is everything all right?"

"Yeah, but I can't seem to concentrate for long." Understatement. It only took seconds for his thoughts to wander to Bug.

She nodded, face serious, then asked, "What about the thieves? Won't my talking give away our position?"

"There's a dampening effect in the pyramid. If you keep your voice soft, we should be okay." There was a long silence. "Help me out here."

Kendall shrugged. "I'm not sure what to say."

"Anything. Tell me about the toughest field hockey match you played, or your favorite birthday. Heck, repeat the info you gave me on the smuggling ring. It doesn't matter."

There was another short pause, and then she started telling him about the temple. The longer she went on, the more enthusiastic she became and the more enthusiastic Bug got, the more his mood soured. Damn it, he'd competed with the fucking temple once before; did he have to do it again? How many times had Berkant asked Zolianna to run off with him? And each time, she'd stalled him. The excuses were always good ones, but what it really boiled down to was that she had ties to this pile of rock and wasn't willing to sever them. Sometimes he'd even wondered whether she loved the temple more than she'd loved him.

"Ow!" Wyatt rubbed his ribs. "Your elbow is sharp."

"You told me to make sure you paid attention." She didn't wait for him to respond. "Since you're not interested in the temple, I guess I better find another topic. Did you want to discuss the cave analogy in Plato's *Republic*?"

He groaned; he couldn't help it, and Kendall laughed. Some of the tension eased from him. If she was teasing, then she wasn't pulling back—his chief concern. "Why don't we try something less intellectual?"

Without missing a beat, Bug said, "How 'bout them Cowboys?"

"Low blow, darlin'. Even if you don't enjoy watching, football involves a lot of strategy."

"It's hard to notice that when there are so many penalties. Any sport that has cheating on every play isn't worth wasting time on. But baseball—now that's the thinking-person's game."

"We've argued this a few times already."

"For someone who said talk about anything, you're pretty picky." Bug shook her head. "We could discuss the inlay of crystals. One thing keeps bothering me. That pearly-looking stone? It's selenite."

"What's the big deal about selenite?"

"It's a really soft stone, like a two or so on the Mohs' Scale. To put it in perspective, diamonds are a ten, and talc is a one. If you were going to take the time to create mosaics from gems, wouldn't you go with the harder ones?"

Wyatt shrugged. "What do you think it means?"

"This has been nagging at me, but I finally remembered something interesting. Gypsum formation is tied to precipitation with a high saline content. I'm wondering if the aliens didn't use that association with rain to indicate where water was inside the temple. Like an arrow pointing thataway, you know?"

"Salt water isn't potable."

"Don't be so literal," Kendall said, then began explaining the properties of selenite and gypsum.

As she spoke, something flew past his head. Wyatt blinked as he looked around, trying to identify it. He didn't see anything, so he took another, more careful scan. Nothing. He glanced at Bug, but she seemed oblivious as she talked rocks.

Wyatt heard a noise and tuned her out as he tried to identify it. The buzzing had an inhuman quality to it, yet it sounded oddly familiar. He was still trying to figure out why when something hit his arm.

Almost dispassionately, he checked it out. A beetle about two inches long had landed on him, and Wyatt flicked it away. As he watched it hit the wall, he felt a sting on his nape, and reached back to brush his neck. Another large beetle fell at his feet. He stepped on it, making it crunch as he crushed it.

A third beetle flew at his head, and Wyatt swatted at it, trying to knock it down. He got it, but dozens of others swarmed at him. Kendall—how was she doing? He looked over at her, but none of the deep brown bugs were bothering her.

In the time it took to glance over, the number of flying insects had swollen to hundreds—shit, maybe thousands—and they were dive-bombing him. They seemed intent on finding bare skin, and when they landed, they bit. The wounds burned painfully, and Wyatt slapped at the beetles with less control. Kendall's voice sounded urgent, but he couldn't make out the words, and could only guess that the bugs were attacking her now too. He couldn't check on her, though, not while he was fighting his own battle.

They were going for his face, for his eyes. Wyatt's agitation increased, and his swipes became wilder. He crushed the ones that he sent to the floor, but no matter how many he killed, reinforcements arrived to take their places.

Hundreds of thousands of beetles flew and crawled and

scuttled through the hall. It would take a flame thrower to make a dent in their numbers, and each bite seemed to rip pain through his muscles, right down to the bones. He had to protect Kendall. Her skin was so soft, this must be complete agony for her.

"Wyatt!" Kendall sounded frantic, and he fought harder. He had to help her. Had to.

Something—someone—gripped him from behind, their arms imprisoning his own at his sides. He began to break the hold, to answer the threat, but thankfully, Wyatt recognized Kendall's touch a split second before he reacted.

"What's wrong with you?"

"The beetles," he said. But as he looked around, he realized they'd disappeared when Kendall had grabbed him.

"What beetles?"

"The ones that were attacking us."

She released her hold and moved so she stood in front of him. "Wy," Kendall said in a carefully neutral tone, "there were no beetles. You know there aren't any insects in the Old City."

Chapter Ten

Kendall enjoyed these quiet moments with her lover. They sat on the floor, his back against the sofa and her knees resting against his thigh as she was turned toward him. In the two seasons she'd been High Priestess, they'd found it easier to be together, not more difficult. Of course she had greater privacy now than she'd had earlier. But no matter how often they were with each other, it wasn't sufficient.

She studied Wyatt—his handsome face with the crooked smile; how his golden eyes shimmered with intelligence, and with love for her; the way his dark hair hung loosely, brushing his shoulders as he gestured. Wyatt didn't have golden eyes and she'd never seen his hair this long, though. A frisson of unease shuddered through her, but she pushed it aside. In her heart she felt this was Wyatt. Kendall smiled as her emotions welled. How she loved him! Had always loved him.

"What amuses you?" he asked.

"Nothing. I'm merely happy." She reached out, ran her fingers through his silky tresses, then closed the distance

between them to kiss him gently. Their lips clung for an instant as she eased away. She wished this was usual—sitting together and talking—but she didn't say it aloud. It was her fault they'd been unable to share a normal life.

"I saw you yesterday," Kendall told him. "You were handsome in your uniform, far superior to any other in the Guard."

He smiled. "You might be a bit biased."

"Perhaps," she allowed, returning his smile, "but that's my prerogative. You're the man I love."

When this kiss ended, Kendall rested her head on Wyatt's shoulder. The suite assigned to the High Priestess was feminine, yet her lover was just as comfortable here as he was in the masculine atmosphere of the City Guard. If it were up to her, there would be fewer frills, but she was no more than a temporary resident. At the end of her child-bearing years, she'd step aside for the next leader—and her obligation to the temple would be fulfilled. She held that in her thoughts, knowing that someday she'd be able to love him openly and live with him always.

With a sigh, she snuggled into Wyatt's side, relishing the strength of his arms as he held her. That day seemed a long distance off—too long when she remembered the nights without him or thought about the way they were forced to hide their feelings.

There were days when she wondered whether she was being fair to him. Days she wondered if perhaps she should free him, allow him to find another. She'd only seen her thirtieth season and could easily be tied to the temple for another fifteen or twenty. If he remained true to her, he would never have a child of his own. Kendall felt her chest ache at the thought of never carrying his babe, but her lot was cast; his was not. Wyatt could find another, mate with her, have children with her.

"What troubles you?" he asked, and she wasn't a bit surprised that he'd discerned her thoughts—from the time

they'd been small children, the two of them had been close enough to read each other's emotions.

Kendall didn't want to tell him why she was sad—not when it might lead to an argument. Instead, she chose a different concern. "I wish the temple had a better relationship with the lord and lady. Always we seem to be at odds, and yet we share a common goal, the welfare of our people."

"You've had another disagreement with our rulers?"

"When I saw you yesterday," Kendall said, "I was on my way to their residence for a meeting. Were you aware that Lord Kale and Lady Meriwa wish to build another community?"

Wyatt shook his head. "Why do that when we could double our population and yet live comfortably within the city?"

"My question exactly, and they had no good answer." She sat straighter, reluctantly moving from his embrace. "They maintain that by this time the other colonies had begun to erect a second city, and so must we. Yet we've adequate space inside our walls, and there is no need to build. Even their own estimates show that at our current birthrate, it is unnecessary to begin another compound for at least fifty seasons. They were unhappy when I said the temple would not grant blessing on this endeavor."

"I imagine not," Wyatt said. "Without your consecration, no one will agree to labor on the new city."

"The previous High Priestess had the same difficulty with them."

His arm went around her shoulders, and he gave her a brief hug.

"Why do they not listen to me when I only want what's best?"

Wyatt laughed. "They probably ask the same of you."

She grinned, not bothered by his statement. "That's different. How do you manage to get along so well with them?"

"Love, the Guard is under the command of the lord and lady. Besides, I don't deal with them directly."

Tilting her head slightly, she considered that. The city was divided into quadrants, and each section held troops led by a captain who reported to the Guard Commander. Wyatt was one of these captains—his quadrant contained the temple—and his high rank guaranteed he had more interaction with Lord Kale and Lady Meriwa than his answer suggested.

"You'll have to confer with them regularly when you're named Guard Commander," Kendall told him.

"That won't happen."

"How can you say that? You're the most skilled of the captains, and I'm not the only one who believes this."

Wyatt climbed to his feet and walked across the room. "You're aware the Guard is largely ceremonial, and skills in fighting are less important than appearance."

Kendall shifted to her knees in order to face him. "And even in that regard you're the natural choice. Gustus is aware of your talent for diplomacy, your tact, and your ability to defuse volatile situations. When he names his successor in a year or perhaps two, he will certainly choose you."

"He won't, but it's unimportant."

Her heart began to pound hard enough to make her chest hurt. "Why do you believe he won't name you?"

Shaking his head, Wyatt said, "It matters not."

Kendall stood, went to him. "Why?"

For a long moment, there was nothing save silence. Then he said quietly, "Gustus believes a man who has a mate is more stable, less likely to react rashly, than a man without."

His response wasn't unexpected, but Kendall had to bite her lip to keep from gasping. From the time they'd been children, Wyatt had wanted to be part of the City Guard, and luckily, his skill test had matched his interest.

As a young man, he'd spoken of his desire to one day be the commander, and yet he'd not achieve his goal—because of her. She wanted to cry at the unfairness. Not only had she lost her dream because of the temple, but now she was costing him his as well.

Reaching out, she clasped his hands with both of hers. "I love you," she told him, voice fierce. "I love you with all that I am, and I want you to have everything of which you've dreamed. If you found another, a woman free to be your mate, you could be Guard Commander." Tears started to roll down her cheeks, but she didn't release him to brush at them. "Find someone else you can love, take her as your mate, have children. You should be a father."

Unable to bear the thought, Kendall pivoted, her hands coming up to cover her face, but he stopped her, turned her until she met his gaze once more.

"You hold my heart, and I'll settle for no other." Wyatt pulled her against his chest, wrapped his arms around her, and, mouth against her ear, whispered, "I love you. I told you that before I took you as my mate—do you forget so easily?"

"I've forgotten nothing!" she insisted. "But our ceremony was not officiated by a priestess or attended by our families. As far as the world is concerned, we are not mated."

"Do you consider us mated?"

"That's neither here nor there."

"Do you consider us mated?"

There was no mistaking the demand; he wouldn't stop asking until she answered. For an instant, she considered lying—it was the only way he'd walk away from her—but Kendall couldn't do it. Never had she told him anything save the truth. "Yes."

The tension in him eased, and she could feel his muscles slacken even as he gathered her closer. "I feel the same."

"But we were children," she argued.

Putting her from him, he reached for her chin and tipped her face to his. *"I was old enough to be a member of the Guard. You were old enough to enter the temple the next day. We both knew what we were doing. I was aware that you'd be a priestess for thirty seasons or more. I wanted no other then, and I want no other now. I stood on that hillside beside you and took vows. I'll honor them until I die; don't ever think otherwise."*

"I want what's best for you."

"You're what's best for me." And he kissed her. It wasn't gentle, but hot, demanding—as if he were trying to impress upon her how much he desired her. How much he loved her.

He had her free of her garments in moments, and his own were shed just as quickly. Wyatt knew her body well after so many seasons, and knew what aroused her the fastest. He employed every bit of his knowledge, until her body writhed against his as she sought completion. *"Hurry,"* she whispered, *"join with me."*

"Not yet."

His hair hung damply, sweat covered his body, and his muscles quivered as he fought for control. She knew he wanted his completion every bit as much as she wanted hers. *"Why?"*

"Promise me something first."

As his tip nudged the center of her pleasure, she gasped, and arched her hips, inviting him to enter her. *"What?"* Kendall asked, but she was too busy trying to incite him past the limits of his self-command to hear his answer. *"What did you say?"*

"I said, come away with me." His voice was a growl, but she was unsure whether the frustration was sexual or because she hadn't been listening. *"We can live outside the city easily."*

"I cannot." He'd asked her so many times, in so many

different ways, but this was the first time he'd used her need for him as a weapon against her.

"Yes, you can—we both can." Wyatt moved his hips against hers, sliding his shaft against her cleft. The friction was delicious, and kept her on the edge, but it wasn't enough to push her over. "Leave with me."

"I have obligations. The temple—"

"Do you know how weary I am of hearing of the temple?" he snarled. "You always choose it over me." He rolled off her, and Kendall inhaled sharply as cool air hit her overheated body.

"I've never chosen the temple over you," she protested as she sat up. He still had his erection, and she knew that pulling away from her hadn't been easy for him.

"You think not?" He turned his head where it rested on the floor to give her a hard stare. "How many times have I asked you to leave with me? You always refuse."

"It's not that easy." Before he could prevent it, she straddled him and guided him inside her body. His hips arched as she sank down, and Kendall moaned softly— part arousal, part the sense of rightness she felt only when they were joined. "I took an oath the day I was brought into the temple as a novitiate." She undulated against him. "I took another oath when I became priestess and a third when I ascended to High Priestess."

"I took an oath too when I joined the Guard."

Kendall leaned forward to rub her breasts against the solid planes of his chest, to press kisses against his throat, his jaw, his lips. "A different vow." Her voice rose on the last word as he thrust upward.

His arms wrapped around her, and he rolled, putting her beneath him again. Wyatt stroked into her harder, and she savored each plunge. Closing her eyes as the sensations increased, Kendall wrapped her legs around his waist, allowing him to drive deeper. They both moaned, the conversation forgotten as they touched and tasted each other.

Finally, the arousal grew too intense, and Kendall opened her eyes so she could see him as she reached her peak. Although her rooms blocked all sound, she pressed her mouth against his shoulder to smother her cries. Wyatt was also quiet as he found his pleasure, and she gathered him close as he finished.

As she ran her hands across the damp flesh of her lover, Kendall considered their silence. No doubt it was habit now, a holdover from the many nights they'd coupled in secluded glens or other hidden places where a cry could bring discovery down upon them. Their society might be peaceful now, but in days long past, such hadn't been the case, and remnants of those less civilized times were still with them.

None outside of the temple were aware of this, but there were defenses built into the structure to protect the priestesses from harm. Long ago, so long ago that the ink had nearly faded in the tome, there had been wars. In those troubled times, the enemy had attempted to capture the priestesses, violate them, and the women could not trust the City Guard with their protection.

Kendall suspected that era was directly responsible for the proscribed punishments they had for the violation of their laws. Defiling a priestess would cause Wyatt severe repercussions. He'd told her many times that if the worst happened, she should claim he'd forced her, but she would never do that. Although she knew it wouldn't save him, she'd stand up and announce that she'd shared his bed willingly. Fortunately, they'd never been caught.

"Why?" he asked, raising himself to his elbows. "Why won't you leave with me? Why do you love the temple more?"

"I don't love the temp—"

"You do." His face appeared grim. *"Deny it all you wish, but it's true. A light comes into your eyes when you speak of it. Perhaps you had no great desire to be a priestess, but in the seasons since you entered, it's become important to you. I only wish you loved it less and me more."*

There was no heat in his voice, only resignation, and it cut Kendall to her soul. "I love you more than anyone or anything, never doubt it, but you know as well as I that running off isn't as easy as you make it sound. If we left the city, we could never reenter. What of our families? Your mother is ill; could you bear to walk away now and never know what happened to her?"

Wyatt sat up, his forearms resting on his upraised knees. Kendall immediately moved to kneel at his side. "There are stories in our history," she added quietly, "of the guards pursuing priestesses who've run off. There's no guarantee that they wouldn't track us, wouldn't find us. Then what?" He shook his head, clearly not having an answer. "And what of our survival? Yes, the planet is full of fruit and vegetables we could eat, and no, there aren't vicious animals, but you and I have never lived outside these walls. What of violent weather? What of accidents? I'm not a healer, and you can't raise your hands and stop the wind. We could die out there."

Studying her intently, he said, "Don't you know that I would never allow anything to happen to you? I love you, Zolianna."

Kendall woke up abruptly, but this time she had the presence of mind to remain still and not alert Wyatt that she'd had a disturbing dream. She didn't think he'd allow her to evade his questions a second time, and while she didn't want to lie to him, no way was she telling him about it. Not when she kept putting him in the role of lover. And not when she swore she could still feel him deep inside her. Damn it, she was aroused, her body aching for an orgasm. Aching for Wyatt.

The urge to squirm, to rock her hips, to do something nearly overwhelmed her. Never before had she experienced a dream that left her this hot. Heaven help her, if he reached for her right now, she'd probably spread her legs and beg him to take her.

But as alarming as that was, it was the last words that echoed through her head. *"I love you, Zolianna."*

She knew Wyatt hadn't really said them, that it was a product of her subconscious, nothing more, but they skewered her. As much as she wanted to deny it, she was jealous. She shouldn't be. Wyatt was her friend, and that's all she wanted. Honestly.

Okay, she was lying to herself. She wanted him. There, she'd admitted it. But she was stronger than her urges. She had to be, because if she wasn't, didn't that mean Kendall was just like her mother? Oh, God! She didn't want to end up alone, no better off than her mom was after her latest lover had moved on.

When Kendall had been nine, she'd taken paper and written down each of her uncles in chronological order. She'd had to because she was worried she'd start forgetting who they were, or mix them up—there'd been so many of them. Next to their names, she'd put information about them, like this uncle liked to paint or that uncle fished.

Even though her mom's relationships tended to end with fireworks, most of the men had kept in touch with Kendall. Sometimes it was only a message once a year to wish her happy birthday, but she'd worked to keep up the contact. It wasn't the same as having a dad, but knowing all these uncles cared enough about her to write meant a lot to her.

And it proved friendship lasted, like her mom had told her.

Kendall stared at Wyatt's back. He'd put her against the wall and slept in front of her as a shield. His protectiveness inflamed her hormones. Part of her longed to reach out, to stroke her hand over him, to press a kiss between his shoulders. That would wake him up, and when he turned to find out what she was doing, she'd bring his mouth to hers and kiss him better than that Zolianna ever had. The thought of any other woman with Wyatt tore at her. It was stupid, beyond stupid. He'd had a life before they met, and no doubt, if they were on Earth, he'd regularly be having sex with someone else. J Nine had fostered some weird intimacy, but it wasn't real. And Wyatt wasn't hers.

She tightened her inner muscles, but instead of relieving the feeling of emptiness, it exacerbated it. At least when a teenage boy had a wet dream, he got to come. It seemed unfair that she was left frenzied with no relief in sight. Wyatt's shoulders moved as he exhaled. Okay, so there was relief in sight, if he were willing to have sex with her.

And if she were willing to risk losing him forever.

Come on, Kendall, toughen up. It was just arousal, nothing more. If she had some privacy, she could take care of the ache in a few minutes, no big deal. All she needed to do was think of something else until she calmed down.

The dream. She could analyze it. Kendall frowned, trying to pin down details that were already fading. Wyatt had asked her to run off with him. Easy. They were trying to get out of the temple and he was leading them. Not quite exact, but close enough that it kind of made sense.

The part about letting Wyatt go to find another woman, well, she'd been oddly possessive since he'd kissed her, then murmured Zolianna's name. Obviously, her subconscious knew they were meant to be nothing more than friends and was telling her to stop being jealous.

What else? Disagreeing with the planet's rulers about building another city. Kendall considered that one for a while, but couldn't come up with an answer. She'd have to hope she could remember it and look it up in her dream dictionary later.

The I-love-you-Zolianna part was simple, however—her envy explained it. She didn't want to dwell on that, though, or the fact that she didn't want him to love another woman.

Instead, she moved on to Wyatt himself. He'd scared the crap out of her when he'd hallucinated. She hadn't known what was going on; she'd just seen him flailing his arms and stomping his feet. It had been one of the most frightening scenes she'd ever witnessed. And her fear had only increased when she'd tried to talk to him and he hadn't heard her.

It scared her even more to think what might have happened if she hadn't grabbed him when she had. He could have hurt himself. Or her. It would have been inadvertent, but Wyatt had been reacting to chimeras and wasn't thinking straight.

Kendall didn't believe the episode was a delayed reaction to the lack of oxygen. Any long-term problem would have manifested before today. But he'd been fine from the time he'd regained consciousness until the time he'd seen the beetles flying around.

So what had triggered his hallucination?

Wyatt was mentally stable; she'd take that to the bank. But if psychosis and oxygen deprivation were out, what was left?

"Bug, you okay?" Wyatt shifted onto his back.

"Yeah. How'd you know I was awake?"

"You were thinking so hard I could hear you in my sleep." He grinned at her, then sobered as he rolled on his side to face her. "What's bothering you, darlin'?"

More than she wanted him to know. "What isn't bothering me? Things just seem to keep getting worse for us."

"Yeah, but you can't let it cost you sleep. I know," Wyatt added, "it's not that easy. You remind me of my oldest sister. When something's eating at her, the insomnia hits right away. But lack of sleep makes problems seem insurmountable when they aren't. You need to rest."

He thought of her like his sister? *His sister?* That was worse than the girl next door. At least some guys went for her wholesome look, but no man was romantically interested in a woman he equated with an older sister. Instead of feeling relieved, Kendall wanted to cry.

Maybe it *was* lack of sleep. Maybe once they were out of here, had everything taken care of, and she'd spent about twelve hours unconscious in her own bed, she'd wonder why she'd ever fantasized about making love with Wyatt. Then they could go back to their friendship with minimal damage. Yeah, this was good.

But as she gazed into his eyes, she knew it was another lie. Things weren't going to return to normal, not for her—not when she longed to close the few inches between them and kiss him.

Cards on the table, Thomas. You wanted him before this imprisonment in the temple. God, she remembered the night they met in line at the mess hall as if it had just happened—the way his voice had made her tingle in places she didn't want to throb. She'd been afraid to look him in the eye, afraid he'd see what he was doing to her. Afraid it would kick her own need up a notch.

She'd been right to worry. When she'd turned to hand him a tray, and their gazes had finally met, the impact had been akin to taking a bullet in the chest. Or at least what she imagined that might feel like. Kendall hadn't been able to catch her breath, and for an endless moment, she could do nothing except stare at him.

Somehow, she'd managed to tamp down her attraction and talk normally when they'd eaten together. Or almost normally. She'd told him things about herself that she'd never shared, and if he hadn't come from some kind of *Father Knows Best* family, she might have told him even more. And at some point that evening, Kendall had managed to convince herself to keep him as a friend.

Now she wondered how she'd done it. And wondered if she could do it again. The longer she stared into his navy eyes, the more insistent the ache between her thighs became, and as that grew, the urge to pull him to her, to wrap her legs around him and kiss him senseless became overwhelming.

He knew what she was thinking.

Kendall saw the flare of awareness cross his face. He'd noticed that she wanted him and it scared her. She jerked her gaze away, closed her eyes, and took a deep breath.

It had to stop. She had to corral her desire.

"It's all right, darlin'," he told her, putting his hand on her shoulder. She jerked away and shook her head. It wasn't okay; didn't he get it? She was going to lose him and nothing would wound her more, nothing would leave her emptier than a life without Wyatt in it. Lovers parted ways. Always.

Friends were forever.

She repeated that like a mantra, and forced her eyes open. "I'm worried about you," she said, and while it was true, it was a feint. Kendall wanted his attention off her want of him.

He paused. "There's no need to be."

Something in his voice made her freeze. Frustration, resignation, irritation—she heard all that and more. Kendall didn't want to think about why he was feeling those things, so she ignored them. Just like she ignored the fact that her jerking away had hurt him again. Later, she'd feel bad about it, but right now she had to protect herself.

"You hallucinated! I've been trying to figure out what caused it because that's the only way to prevent it from happening again." He opened his mouth, but she kept talking, afraid of what he'd say if she gave him the chance. "I ruled out oxygen deprivation, and I know you're not prone to episodes. If you were, I'd be aware of it since we spend so much time together. I'm not sure what else it could be, tho—"

"It's not a big deal," he interrupted.

That stopped Kendall cold. "How can you say that? You weren't in your head at all! Marsh, you scared me."

"I'm sorry," he told her. She realized admitting fear was a huge mistake when he pulled her into his arms and rubbed his hand in circles over her back to soothe her.

Her mantra suddenly seemed a weak defense against her need for him. She should pull away, but she didn't want to. Kendall choked back a moan in time to make it sound like a hiccup. With his hard body pressed to hers, the desire to have him fill her roared stronger than ever. She moved her face closer to his throat, barely stopping herself from licking him.

"I think I know what caused my hallucination," Wyatt said, his mouth near her ear. She realized he was oblivious to her turmoil, and she sent up a silent thank-you.

Kendall struggled to regain her control, but she had to clear her throat before she could ask, "What?"

"The aliens believed in using the powers of their minds. Some of us can turn on the water and the lights here, but they could do more. Our scientists can't figure out what protects the shield around the Old City or how it keeps out dust and bugs and such. And there are dozens of other examples like that."

For a moment, she frowned, trying to connect what he was saying with what she'd asked. It was hard when all she could think about was him. Then it dawned on her what he was getting at and she pulled back so she could see his face.

"You're not saying . . ." Kendall stopped when she saw his expression. "You don't really think that you triggered some kind of alien mind trap, do you?"

Chapter Eleven

Alex glanced up from the computer screen, noticed dawn was breaking and muttered a curse. Leaning back in his chair, he rubbed his fingers over his eyes. He hadn't planned to stay up all night, but he'd been fascinated.

Thomas had documented this smuggling ring in excruciating detail. Not just dates, drawings and pictures, she'd commented on each step of her investigation—including when she'd become concerned enough that she couldn't wait for Montgomery to return from his mission outside the Old City. She'd gone to Hunter, told him her suspicions, and asked for his help.

And throughout the whole damn document, she'd repeatedly questioned whether she had enough to report it yet. Alex sighed heavily. Over and over, she'd worried about *his* reaction. Maybe his rep as a badass had reached a point where it was interfering with his ability to do his job. The girl sure as hell shouldn't have been more frightened of him than she was of the thieves, and clearly she had been. He only wished he knew why Hunter hadn't said something. No one in Spec Ops would be put off by him.

He thought about getting a cup of coffee—he was going to need the caffeine to stay awake all day—but Alex didn't feel like moving yet. According to what Thomas had typed, she hadn't known who was part of the ring, but she was sure the answer was in the computer files she worked with every day.

So if he were in the girl's place, what would he have done? Her notes said that Hunter told her to leave everything to him, but Thomas hadn't wanted to. She didn't come right out and say it, but it was clear she felt as if she had a better chance at coming up with answers than Catfish. Since she knew archeology and had a familiarity with the data and the systems used by the social scientists examining the Old City, she was probably right.

Alex tapped a finger against his handheld unit, and thought about the situation. Hunter was dead, Thomas and Montgomery were missing, and two more soldiers were AWOL. These men, however, had no ties to the three captains that he could identify.

McNamara was riding him about these events, and he was getting damn tired of it. Did she think he could rub a magic lamp and have the genie give him all the answers? At least he'd found a way around the regulation requiring he report removing the computer from Thomas's quarters. Instead of taking it, he'd downloaded the contents of the hard drive onto his PDA. Alex's lips turned up at the corners. The regs hadn't been updated recently, and since he wasn't taking any physical object out, he could skirt the issue. Of course, if the colonel ever found out, he'd have his ass in a sling ASAP.

With a grimace, Alex powered down the unit and unhooked it from the computer. In a matter of hours, he'd read a huge amount of info, and he needed to think, to connect the dots.

He'd password protected his handheld with layers and layers of security, but he wasn't taking any chances—Alex brought it into the bathroom with him while he showered. He'd sealed up Thomas's house again—no one was getting in and finding her computer—so the information was safe there too.

As he shaved, he thought some more about what he'd read. Thomas had updated her files every night, whether she'd found something new or not, so he was aware of exactly what she'd known until the day before she disappeared. What had happened that final day? What had the girl done? What had she discovered that had prompted her to chase after him that evening?

She was smart, she was thorough, she was tenacious and she was a computer geek—all things Alex appreciated. So what would someone with those qualities do? What would *he* have done in her place? The answer came as he was wiping the remnants of lather from his face. He would have continued to do the same things he'd been doing. They'd been bringing answers, so why quit?

Padding barefoot into the kitchen, Alex started the coffeepot. It was hooked up to a grid the Western Alliance had brought for power and didn't require any unusual knowledge to operate. Today, he appreciated that.

For a minute, he stopped, the silence of the house slamming into him the same way it had every other time he'd quit thinking about his job. So he missed Stacey, big deal. He'd get over it the same way he'd gotten over the other people who'd walked out on him. It would just take time, that's all.

He went into the bedroom and reached for a clean uniform. His heart lurched as he saw the emptiness of the closet. Alex pushed aside the pain and grabbed his clothes. When he was dressed, he hooked his PDA to his belt and headed for the coffee.

Mug in hand, he looked for somewhere to settle. The

house was full of memories of her, though. Absently rubbing his chest with his free hand, Alex headed for the front porch, a place without any ghosts. No privacy either.

"Chief Cantore." Alex switched the mug to his left hand so he could return the salute. "What are you doing here?"

"I wanted to talk to you, sir."

Alex had opened his mouth to send the man on his way, when he remembered Thomas. If he'd listened to her, how much different would things be right now?

"I want you to go into my house, grab yourself a cup and bring the coffeepot out here. If we're going to have a serious conversation at this hour, I'm going to need caffeine, and you look as if you could use some yourself."

"Thank you, sir," the man said, and Alex didn't miss the quirk of Cantore's lips before he went inside.

Did he need this? The noncom was going to be a pain in the ass, Alex knew it, but he couldn't fault the XO's loyalty to his commanding officer. With a sigh, he sat in the chair on the far side of the porch, closed his eyes and took his first sip of coffee. He wasn't sure how much he was going to say to Cantore. With no clue who was part of the smuggling ring, Alex had to be careful. Thomas had trusted Montgomery unequivocally—that was obvious in her notes—and she'd trusted Hunter because the kid had vouched for him, but she'd been wary of putting her faith in anyone else. Alex doubted that the XO was involved, but . . .

But someone had taken out a Spec Ops officer and who better than another Special Forces soldier?

When Cantore returned, Alex said, "Take a seat, Chief."

After putting the pot on the table, the man obeyed. For a moment, there was nothing but silence as they drank their coffee and enjoyed the quiet of early morning.

Alex wasn't going to let the silence last much longer; he

wanted answers from Cantore about why he was waiting. It was early, even by military standards, and if Alex had been following his usual schedule, the man would have had another hour to cool his heels. After pouring himself another cup, Alex said, "Okay, we've both had coffee; what can I do for you?"

There was a hesitation, and Alex tensed. "Colonel, we heard Edmonds and Wells went missing too."

"That doesn't surprise me." The post was too small for something like this to remain unknown. Cantore raised the mug to his lips, delaying again. "Have I ever given you the impression that all I want is to share my morning coffee with you?"

"No, sir."

"Then start talking."

Cantore put his mug on the table before saying, "Permission to speak freely, sir?"

It was tempting to tell him he could say whatever the hell he wanted as long as he did it soon, but Alex restrained himself. It wasn't the chief's fault that a sleepless night and a too-empty house had left his temper precarious. "Granted."

"Edmonds has a reputation for being a prick. Let me throw this out for a scenario," Cantore said. "Marsh was worried about Captain Thomas; something—or some*one*— had her scared. Now the two of them disappear and so does Edmonds. Edmonds has a history of frightening those he can. Want to bet, sir, that he's involved in some way with Marsh and Kendall going missing?"

Alex pinned him with a glare. "Do I look stupid?"

"No, sir."

"Then be quiet before I take offense." Cantore grinned and Alex ground his teeth. "I've been working under the assumption that Wells's and Edmonds's vanishing acts are related to Montgomery and Thomas's disappearances since I heard the news."

With a pleased look, the XO nodded. "The team and I, we've been working on potential scenarios to explain what's going on, and we decided that it's nearly a sure thing that Kendall stumbled across something illegal. We came up with about a dozen ideas. I wrote them down." Cantore's hand disappeared below the table and Alex tensed until it came out again with a slip of paper. Given the state of things, he didn't think he was overreacting. "Gambling is the most likely, but Kendall would just report it, so it has to be something much bigger than that."

When Cantore held out the paper, Alex took it and unfolded it. The team was inventive; he gave them that. Some of the options they'd come up with were pretty farfetched, but antiquity smuggling was near the top of the list. That wasn't good. They'd try to narrow this down, and in the process, they might inadvertently tip off the wrong people. If it leaked that he was investigating the theft of relics, the ring might decide it was best to get rid of anyone who could testify against them and murder Thomas and Montgomery—if they hadn't already.

On the other hand, letting it slip that he had everything Thomas had come up with might help keep them alive. The thieves would have to realize that killing those two captains wouldn't make a difference, not when security had the information.

Alex finished his coffee. He thought option number one was more likely than the second. If the thieves knew they were up to their asses in alligators, he was certain they'd eliminate as many threats as they could—just in case.

The only way he could keep Cantore and company from stumbling around on their own was to tell them what was going on. With a grimace, he put the cup back on the table and rubbed his hand over the back of his neck. It meant trusting the XO for sure and probably the rest of the team. And he couldn't put his faith in anyone right now.

Cantore was waiting patiently for him to say something

and Alex sighed. This was one of those damned if you do, damned if you don't situations. He was sure the team would try to ask their questions covertly, and they'd probably succeed to a large extent, but he couldn't chance them making a mistake. Shit, he couldn't risk the lives of those two kids.

Alex returned the paper and decided to go with his gut. "Gather your men and meet me at the firing range at the back of the royal residence in thirty minutes. Don't ask questions; just follow orders." It was the one place Alex knew they'd have complete privacy and he didn't want anyone to overhear this conversation.

After Cantore left, Alex slumped back in his chair. He hoped to God he hadn't just made an error in judgment. If even one of those men were involved . . .

Pushing abruptly to his feet, he gathered the two mugs and the pot. He wished Stacey were here. Alex rinsed out the dishes in the kitchen and sighed. She was good at reading people, good at knowing when he'd screwed up. He wanted to run this by her, to ask if she thought he was wrong. And he couldn't.

When had she pervaded every last corner of his life? When had he come to trust her so totally that he'd consult with her about decisions he made for his job? Shit, he knew not to let anyone that deep; he knew women left. She'd been insidious, flying under his radar so stealthily, that it was only now, when she was gone, that he realized what she'd done.

That ache in his chest intensified again, and he rubbed at it. Hearts didn't really break—he'd survived before, he'd survive again. He dried the clean mugs and returned them to their place, then turned to dry the pot.

You're a coward, Sullivan.

Alex froze, looked around, but Stacey wasn't there. He shook his head. Now he was imagining her voice. What next?

He checked his watch, decided he had enough time to grab a muffin from the mess hall before he had to meet Cantore and company. Alex patted his belt, verified the PDA was there and headed for the front door.

Coward!

"Shut up," he muttered, but he knew he was talking to his own mind—there was no one in the house but him.

If you love someone, you have to take the risk.

Great, now he was hearing his sister's voice. That was what she'd told him when he'd voiced his concern that Brody might break her heart someday. This time, he didn't bother looking around; he just walked out the front door.

But he couldn't help wondering if he *was* a coward. What if Stacey really did love him and he had hurt her through his own fears, his need to keep himself safe? Protecting himself was second nature, something he did as easily as breathing. It was more than his mother using him to control his father. It was more than her throwing him away when she'd met a man who wanted her but not another man's brat. And it was more than his father and stepmother dying, or Lara dumping him for someone else.

It was safer not to let anyone close. People died. People left. People said and did unforgivable things. Alex stopped short. Stacey might have left him, but *he* was the one who had said and done inexcusable things in order to protect himself.

Did he think by not telling her how he felt, by denying his feelings, that it would hurt less if things fell apart?

Maybe he had. Alex leaned against the building to his right and thought about it. He'd wounded Stacey. Repeatedly. Because he was too afraid to tell her how important she was to him. Too afraid to *show* her. She hadn't left because she didn't love him enough. Stacey had left because he'd hurt her so profoundly, she couldn't bear it anymore.

Alex looked squarely at his own behavior and realized it had been deplorable. If Brody had even once acted that way with Ravyn, he would have kicked his brother-in-law's ass from here to Earth and back again, yet Alex hadn't thought twice about doing it to Stacey. She'd deserved better. He knew how difficult he was, that living with him was a challenge, but she'd fought to hold things together. And he had taken that for granted until he'd come home to find her gone.

He resumed walking, shaking his head as he considered what an idiot he was. Too bad he hadn't realized just what he had until it was too late.

Was it too late? He stopped short again. What would happen if he fought for her? Tried to convince her to stay? What was the worst-case scenario? That she'd leave him? Shit, that had already occurred.

Alex thought about it. Would he walk away from a battle because he might get hurt? Hell, no. If the objective was to take the hill, he took the hill—no ifs, ands or buts.

Stacey might not believe it after years of his idiocy, but she meant everything to him. He couldn't allow her to simply stroll out of his life, because she'd take his heart—and a piece of his soul—with her. If she wanted to go, she'd have a fight on her hands. Alex Sullivan never quit, and no little five-foot-five redhead was going to make him wave the white flag. Not yet.

She said she loved him, and he was holding her to that. Until that damn transport lifted off Jarved Nine with her aboard, he was going to do everything in his power to convince her to stay. To quote an old movie, *"never give up, never surrender!"* Filled with determination, he headed off to meet his men.

Walking hand in hand with Kendall felt so damn right, Wyatt wished he could simply enjoy it without worrying over their situation. He was going to get his chance, he knew it—if they got out of this alive. Bug's wall was eroding. She was stubbornly resisting, but the more of her protection she lost, the faster the remaining fortress seemed to be coming down.

He knew better than to become overconfident, however. Once she realized just how vulnerable she was, Bug would pull back hard, try to restore a safe distance between them. Wyatt figured he had yet to fight the biggest battle in his war to win Kendall.

For now, though, her fingers were laced with his and she wasn't trying to get away. Maybe it was only coincidence, but he believed that it had been Kendall wrapping her arms around him that had ended the mind trap he'd been caught in. That was the reasoning he'd used when he'd suggested she hold on to him. Bug had appeared skeptical, but she hadn't argued.

Wyatt scowled. The idea that Zolianna's ties to the temple might have been reborn in Kendall concerned him. He had vague memories that didn't make sense, but they suggested there was some kind of unusual connection between High Priestess and pyramid. Berkant hadn't been able to tear Zolianna from this damn heap of rock and Wyatt refused to lose Bug the same way. His hand tightened around hers.

"Wy, are you drifting again?"

He heard the note of fear in her voice. "I'm okay, darlin', just thinking about things is all."

"So which thing had you frowning so fiercely?"

It didn't require much thought to come up with a substitute. "Water. It's been over twenty-four hours now since we ran out." It was rehashing ground they'd already covered, but it was critical.

"I've been thinking—" She stopped talking abruptly when they rounded a curve and faced another spoke of hallways.

"Which way?"

Kendall sighed and looked around. Wyatt knew she was tired of being asked, but what could he tell her? *Gee, dar-*

lin', you don't remember this, but three thousand years ago, you were High Priestess of this whole shooting match. I'm counting on you to have some kind of instinctual knowledge of the pyramid. Which of course, would lead her to ask why he thought this, and if he told her he knew because he'd been her lover, she'd break land-speed records trying to get away from him.

"Come here." She tugged him to the mosaic. His hand tingled where she touched it. "See this?" She pointed to an iridescent pearl-colored crystal. "It's selenite. Look how it forms a line at the ten o'clock position in this circle. Remember how I said the stone is formed from water? What if it was used to guide others to a source?"

"I don't see anything remotely resembling a line."

Kendall looked at him quizzically, then shrugged. "Sure, right here. See?" She ran her index finger along the wall.

"To call that a line," he told her, "is stretching the definition of the word to the breaking point."

"That stone isn't anywhere else in the inlay, just here." Kendall traced it again. "It's a line, like a hand on an antique clock, and it's aimed there." She gestured.

"That's dang farfetched."

She rolled her eyes. "You're a trial to me, Marsh," Bug told him with a smile. "You're the one who asked me which hall we should take, and I picked one. Besides it doesn't hurt anything to see if I'm right."

He nodded. She had a point. Wyatt headed in the direction Kendall wanted them to go, her hand still securely linked with his, and tried not to let the fact that she'd called him *Marsh* piss him off.

She only used his handle when she was trying to put distance between them, and he hated it.

"I've been thinking more about the smugglers," Kendall said suddenly. "What if Dr. George isn't the leader?"

"It's possible," Wyatt said slowly. "What makes you think it might be someone else?"

Bug was quiet for a moment, and Wyatt guessed she was organizing her thoughts. "George isn't smart enough to run this kind of operation," she said, "but he's too arrogant to take orders from just anyone. That rules out just about anyone in the military—even officers. He refers to us as simpletons."

"On the assumption that anyone who risks his life is too stupid to know better."

Bug nodded.

"Okay, so the boss is a civilian. Any thoughts on who?"

Kendall bit her lip, then shook her head. "Not really. At first I thought it must be another archeologist, but I decided that was unlikely. If the head thief was someone who already knew artifacts, they wouldn't need George."

"What if he caught them red-handed and the person brought him in to keep him silent? Or George could have discovered the thefts and blackmailed his way in."

They rounded a curve and hit another intersection of corridors. Wyatt felt that tingle again in Kendall's hand, and he looked at her, trying to read her reaction. The vibration increased as they closed the distance to the gem mosaic.

"This row of selenite points toward one o'clock."

"You still want to follow the rocks?" he asked.

"Yes. Give it a chance, Wy, you never know."

He nodded, unsure why he was resisting her idea. It wasn't like he had a better plan. She tugged him along.

"I suppose," Kendall said, returning to their topic, "that George could have caught on. He's nosy, so it is possible that he stumbled on the thieves."

Wyatt picked up on something in her tone. "But you don't think that's what happened, do you?"

"I'm not sure why, but that just doesn't feel right."

"If it wasn't another archeologist, that narrows the list some more. Any other people we can eliminate?"

"Yeah, anyone he considers beneath him, which would leave only the top level of civilian researchers."

That meant about fifty people, he estimated, maybe less, depending on how *top level* was defined. Wyatt didn't know most of them, though, and he doubted Bug did either. "Can we cross anyone else off the suspect list?"

Kendall shook her head. "I can't. The only group outside the military that I'm familiar with are the social scientists I work for. Not that it matters. We can't do anything right now, and once we're out of here, Sullivan will take over."

"Yeah, the Big Chill will take immediate control, but he'll listen to you and consider what you tell him; don't think he won't. And it *does* make a difference who's in charge," Wyatt told her. "The personality of the boss will affect what kind of orders our hunters have. If we can figure out who it is, and if we're lucky enough to know something about him, we might be able to predict what these underlings were told to do."

"Point taken."

He started thinking of the civilians he knew. Like Bug, he wasn't familiar with many. His list included the group he'd escorted outside the city walls, but even then, they'd segregated themselves, geologists in one group, Spec Ops in the other.

They came to a corner. Wyatt slowed, checked things over. They only went about a hundred yards before they hit another corner and he made sure that one was clear too. It was, and he and Kendall turned it before they stopped short.

A doorway to a chamber was on a sharp angle from where they stood. It was impossible to see much, but in the sliver of the room that he could view, there appeared to be a fountain.

Looked like Kendall had been right.

They'd found water. Maybe.

Chapter Twelve

The skin on Wyatt's nape prickled. They were exposed, vulnerable, and he drew back around the corner, tugging Kendall along with him. Leaning forward, his mouth next to her ear, Wyatt breathed one word. "Stay."

He didn't miss the way her lips tightened. She was not happy with the order, but Bug nodded once to indicate she understood and would follow his direction.

Leaving her where she stood, he slipped around the corner again to look at the fountain. There was no good way to do a sneak and peek, not with the layout of the area. Taking a few seconds to think things through, Wyatt evaluated his options, and chose the best of the few he had available.

Sticking close to the wall, he moved silently down the corridor away from the chamber. When he knew no one inside that room could see his position, he crossed to the other side, and, back against the stone, he eased toward the doorway.

He heard nothing, but that didn't mean much. When he

reached the entrance, he leaned over far enough to peer inside, and saw the tip of a boot. Shit. Just as he'd feared, they'd put at least one man in the room. Wyatt shifted back and waited, but he'd remained undetected.

Wyatt wanted a better look, but he wasn't going to get it, not without taking too large a gamble. If he were alone, he'd do things differently, but with Kendall involved, he was erring on the side of caution.

Okay, first he needed to move Bug farther away. If he failed, the guy would search the area, and Wyatt wanted to give her the best chance possible of getting out.

Following the same route, Wyatt returned to where he'd left her. Bug was tense, but she relaxed as soon as she saw him. He shook his head when she opened her mouth, then, hooking an arm around her waist, he steered her down the passageway and past the more distant corner.

When he felt they were safe, he embraced her loosely. Bug's hands went to his waist, and that momentarily derailed his thoughts. "Here's the scoop," he told her quietly. "There's one man in the room for sure. There may be more, but I couldn't see enough to be certain."

"What do you think the odds are that he's there alone?" she asked in a whisper.

"Fifty-fifty, darlin'. It could go either way."

She nodded. "What do you want me to do?"

Wyatt grinned. That was his Bug. No hemming and hawing. No discussing things to death. Just tell her what he needed, and she'd do it. Too bad she wasn't going to like his response. "I want you to stay here, and if things fall apart, run."

"No. I told you I wouldn't leave you, and I meant it."

With a sigh, he drew her nearer until her breasts pressed against his chest. She didn't break his hold, and her willingness to stay close got his heart thumping. "You can't come with me. I'm going to have a heck of a time sneaking up on the man or men on my own. Two people could never do it." Kendall still looked mulish. "You're a liability."

That deflated her, and his heart twisted. He didn't want to wound her. "Even if one of my men were with me," Wyatt explained, voice low, "I'd leave him behind. It's not a matter of skill; it's pure logistics."

For a long moment, she stared at him. He found his eyes glued to her mouth. Wyatt wanted to kiss her, and he wanted to be one hundred percent aware while he was doing it. Not like last time. Her tongue came out, moistened her lips, and he almost groaned. Damn, he wanted her.

"We'll do it your way," she said, and reluctantly he looked up to meet her gaze. "But you better not get hurt, understand?"

"Yes, ma'am." Kendall scowled at him, but he ignored it. "Here's how we're going to play it. You stay here. I'll take out the thief and come back for you. If things fall apart, you take off, *away* from the problem. The dampening effect of the pyramid might keep you from hearing if things go to hel—heck, but if I'm not back in say, fifteen minutes, you leave, got it?"

"I don't like it."

"I wasn't asking for your opinion. Do you understand what I want you to do?"

"Yes. I stay here, and if you're in trouble, I run like a coward instead of helping you."

"Exactly." Wyatt grinned again. "And no one is ever going to call you a coward. You're too gutsy for that."

She wrinkled her nose at him, and he almost bent down to kiss her. Shit, he had better get going before he did something that would scatter both their thoughts. "I need something from your bag," he said as he stepped away from her.

Bug adjusted the satchel till it was square in front of her, lifted the flap, and opened it. Wyatt dug around until he found her mirror. "Fifteen minutes," he reminded her. "No longer."

Her seemingly innocent smile made him hesitate, but he opted to say nothing. She'd already agreed to his plan. Wyatt tucked her mirror in the front pocket of his pants, and set off.

When he reached the second corner, the one nearest the room, he studied the sight lines and their relation to the light. Then he reached for Kendall's mirror, and angled it so it bounced a beam into the chamber. One flash, and he put his hand over it before ducking back behind the wall. Nothing.

He repeated the process. Even with the way sound was muted, he heard a voice ask, "What the hell was that?"

"Go check it out."

Two of them then. There could be more, but Wyatt didn't think so; it would be an unnecessary drain on manpower. He put the mirror away and shifted into position. If he screwed up, he'd lose the element of surprise. Right now, the guards might suspect the flash had something to do with their quarry, but they weren't sure. That gave him a small advantage.

The first thief made an appearance, pistol in hand. Wyatt recognized him—Lidge, a corporal attached to the security team. Grimly, he waited. The man looked around, but didn't head his direction the way Wyatt had hoped.

"Nothing," Lidge called.

"Look some more," the other one ordered.

Muttering his displeasure, Lidge went down the hall in the opposite the direction from where Wyatt was standing. The search was halfhearted at best, an indication that these men had been guarding the fountain for too long, and that complacency had set in. That gave Wyatt an edge—if that bastard would come this way.

Lidge headed back toward the room, and Wyatt frowned.

Another flash with the mirror would make those men too alert, but it looked as if he wasn't going to have a choice.

The corporal stopped, thought things over, then, shaking his head, wandered toward Wyatt. He slowed down as he neared, and it appeared as if he weren't going to cross the opening. *Come on, asshole,* Wyatt thought, *come on.*

As Lidge drew near, Wyatt plastered himself against the wall, and waited. From his position, he could see the corporal glance over, but the man kept moving. As soon as Lidge was past the archway, his back toward him, Wyatt attacked.

He didn't fuck around, and he didn't play nice. Wyatt grabbed the man and snapped the bastard's neck before Lidge could react or make a ruckus. With the corporal disabled, Wyatt choked off his air supply, asphyxiating him.

Unfortunately, the damn pistol clattered to the stone floor as the corporal's hand went limp, and it slid away from them.

Silently, Wyatt lowered Lidge's lifeless body to the ground. Maybe the other smuggler hadn't heard the noise the weapon made as it connected with marble, but he couldn't count on that. He eyed the distance to the pistol, knew he didn't have time to grab it, and cat-footed it toward the room.

He was two-thirds of the way there when the guy giving the orders appeared. The only point in Wyatt's favor was the split second of surprise. He used it.

Closing the remaining distance in a rush, Wyatt kicked the pistol out of the bastard's grip. This time he wanted the weapon to sail down the hallway and it did. Hand-to-hand.

Wyatt believed he had the odds in his favor even though the other man was about four inches taller and outweighed him by at least thirty pounds. Not waiting for the sergeant to land the first blow, Wyatt turned his fist and struck his opponent in the throat, then slammed his palms against the man's ears.

The son of a bitch was reeling, but it didn't stop him from throwing a punch. Wyatt dodged the one aimed at his face, but took a hammer fist in his kidney.

Intense pain shot through him, but he pushed it aside. He wasn't fighting only for himself, he was defending his woman too, and no way in hell was he letting Bug down. Hanging on to his adversary for leverage, Wyatt kicked him just below the knee, making the bastard's leg buckle. But before he could take him out, the man recovered, delivering a head butt to Wyatt's midsection hard enough to turn him around partway.

The man grabbed him from behind, and Wyatt countered with a sharp elbow jab to the side of his head. It wasn't enough to stun him, but it did back the sergeant off.

As they circled, Wyatt tried to find an opening to launch another assault. He wanted this over pronto. Just because he'd only seen two men, it didn't mean the temple wasn't filled with groups searching for Kendall and him, and it didn't mean one or more of those people wouldn't swing by this area at some point. He wanted to be far away before reinforcements arrived.

Wyatt saw it in the man's eyes the instant the bastard spotted his partner's body and figured out he was dead. His opponent had wanted to kill him before, but that was business. Now the sergeant knew it was kill or be killed.

The other man struck out. Wyatt blocked the blow with his forearm and grabbed the sergeant's other arm, swinging him face first into the wall. Before he could pin the bastard, he got free, going low, and caught Wyatt in the kidneys again.

Pissed off, Wyatt slammed the heel of his hand into the asshole's face. He was aiming for the nose, but the man ducked far enough that Wyatt got his forehead instead. It still would hurt and cause some disorientation, but it didn't have the full effect that Wyatt was hoping for.

They exchanged punches, both landing a series of

blows. The other man was skilled. He knew to go for soft areas, and he didn't talk. That was something for less experienced fighters, men who didn't know enough to realize someone with Wyatt's background couldn't be distracted that easily. It made him curious as to who this sergeant was, and what his duties were.

Wyatt grunted as the bastard connected with his kidney a third time. The son of bitch had a thing for that spot, and it irritated him. Grabbing the man's head, Wyatt jerked it down to meet his rising knee. He got him twice before the sergeant pulled away.

Blood ran from an obviously broken nose, and Wyatt saw the fury in the other man's eyes. Good. Emotion caused mistakes.

The sergeant rushed him, tried to tackle him, and Wyatt moved. He wasn't able to completely evade the assault, but the man didn't have a good grip, and he was able to spin loose. Wyatt linked his hands together and delivered a hard blow to the back of the bastard's neck.

The man lurched, but he didn't go down. Wyatt didn't give him a chance to recover. He kicked out, catching the sergeant in his ribs. The second kick only grazed the knee.

With a low growl, the man charged him. Wyatt spun out of the way, and swung his elbow back, catching his opponent in the face. While he was reeling, Wyatt caught his arm, and banged his head into the wall—repeatedly.

The sergeant pushed off, but he couldn't break Wyatt's hold. He could, however, find the same kidney he'd been pounding on, and his elbow connected solidly enough to make Wyatt groan.

Sweat dripped from him. Most fights were short, and this one had gone on long enough to leave both of them panting. But while the other man was fighting for his life, Wyatt had additional incentive. Bug.

He'd failed once before to keep her safe, but he wasn't letting it happen again in this life.

Digging deeper, he found strength, enough to get the asshole in a choke hold. Wyatt cut off his air, not loosening his grip even when he took another sharp blow to his left kidney.

The flailing arms were causing damage, but this tactic also used up oxygen, and the sergeant abandoned it. Instead, he tried to break the hold by putting his fingers between Wyatt's arm and his throat. That didn't work either. Wyatt held tight, cutting off his air until the man was dead.

He let the body fall face first on the floor, and leaned forward, gasping as if he'd been the one deprived of oxygen. Although Wyatt was positive he'd killed his opponent, he was unwilling to take any chances. Reaching out, he searched for a pulse. There wasn't one.

Wyatt remained bent over, and braced his hands on his thighs as he attempted to catch his breath. Mentally, he ran through his aches and pains, decided nothing would slow him down too much. He'd just have to make sure Kendall never saw the bruises, especially near his kidney.

Kendall. Shit, he had to go and get her. Adrenaline had a way of warping time, so he wasn't sure how close it was to the fifteen-minute mark, but he didn't want to leave her standing alone anyway. Not when they didn't know who was roaming about.

He eyed the two dead men and grimaced. Bug knew what he did, that he was Army Spec Ops, but he was sure she'd glossed it up in her mind. These bodies would show her exactly what he was capable of. He wasn't sure he wanted her to see this side of him, but there was no way to avoid it.

Swallowing a groan, Wyatt pushed himself upright. Although he doubted anyone else was around, he leaned into the room and did a fast visual sweep. He almost cursed when he saw a figure lying on the floor. It took an instant longer to realize that the man was dead, his body left where it had fallen, about half the distance into the chamber. Aside from the corpse, the room was clear, but he didn't like it. There was a lot of blood, and he'd bet big that there was some kind of alien snare involved.

He returned to the hall, patted down the second man, and found nothing. Wyatt rolled him to his back and unfastened his pistol belt before he realized it would take too long to open the clips on the holster. He needed to get Kendall first.

Quickly, he checked Lidge. The corporal had a knife tucked into his boot, and Wyatt helped himself to that. Next, he retrieved the pistols from the opposite sides of the hall, and shoved both into the waistband of his fatigues. Now at least he and Bug were armed.

With the important details taken care of, Wyatt went to get his woman. He wasn't entirely steady, but the farther he walked, the more surefooted he became, and by the time he rounded the final corner, he was almost normal.

Bug was pacing. He must have made a noise, because she pivoted fast, and her eyes ran over him, assessing him from head to toe. Before he realized what Kendall was up to, she threw herself into his arms. Her weight knocked him off balance, and he couldn't contain the grunt of pain, but that was the only sound he got out before her mouth was on his. For a moment, he was too stunned to react, and then Wyatt kissed her in return. Sweet Lord, he'd been waiting for this moment, wanting it for so long.

He pressed her back against the wall, unclipped the strap on one side of her bag, and let the damn thing fall to the floor. Once that satchel was out of his way, he tugged her closer.

Wyatt wanted to sink inside her. He wanted to savor the feel of her body clasping his, to thrust into her until they both climaxed. "Aw, damn, Bug," he murmured as he nipped her bottom lip. "I want you so bad."

Without waiting for her to respond, Wyatt took her mouth again, trying to show her with his actions alone how much he needed her, how deeply his feelings for her ran. Part of his brain told him to slow down, that he'd overwhelm her, but that voice was far away, and with adrenaline and desire rocketing through him, it was easy to ignore.

They shifted, moving with the familiarity of long-time lovers, and he rubbed his erection against her. She gasped, and he tightened his hold, bringing her lower body more firmly against his. Though he wasn't anywhere near ready to stop kissing her yet, Wyatt broke away to explore further. Nipping his way to her neck, he discovered her pulse hammering in the base of her throat, and lightly pinched the skin between his teeth before kissing and licking the spot.

Bug's moan was low, but the sound of her arousal was as potent as if she'd reached out and stroked him. He'd known it would be like this between them. God help him, he'd known.

The last thread of his restraint snapped. Wyatt tugged at her T-shirt, freeing it from her pants. He slipped his hand underneath it, stroked her stomach with his fingers. Impatience ate at him, and as much as he wanted to revel in every nuance of Kendall, he needed more. Now.

He moved his hand until he cupped her breast, but her bra prevented contact, and he growled his displeasure. Wyatt reached behind her, attempting to unhook the thing. His concentration, though, was centered on kissing Bug, and it seemed to take an eternity before he freed her.

His contentment was short-lived. Almost as soon as he got his hand on bare skin, Kendall pushed at his chest.

Reluctantly, he lifted his head. When he saw the expression on her face, he wanted to kick his own ass for being so stupid. Damn it, he'd known he had to take it slow.

"Sorry," he apologized, putting enough distance between them so that Kendall would relax. "Guess that adrenaline charge was stronger than I thought. I didn't mean to lose control."

That was an understatement, but once she'd put her lips on him, his cock had started doing the thinking. If he'd considered things for even a second, he would have realized not to take it further than a kiss.

With a jerky nod, she put her back to him, and attempted to fasten her bra. Bug was shaking so bad, though, that she wasn't having much luck. Again and again, she failed and finally he said quietly, "I'll close it for you. If you trust me."

Kendall froze, then slowly turned to look at him over her shoulder, her light brown hair falling wildly into her face. At some point, he realized, he'd removed her clip, and had put his hands in her hair. She looked sexy as hell like that, and his body twitched in appreciation.

For a long moment—an eternity—she sized him up. Just when he thought he'd really blown it, she nodded. "I trust you." Then she lowered her arms and gave him her back.

"I'm glad," Wyatt told her thickly. He closed the gap between them. "I need to lift your shirt, okay?" He waited for her nod before continuing. His own hands were unsteady, but he made sure he didn't fumble as he hooked her up. "There, done." Wyatt stepped away.

Facing him again, she looked around, then scooped up her barrette. Instead of putting it in her hair, she slipped it in her pocket, then retrieved her bag. It took her two tries to hook the strap back on the thing, then she slipped it over her head. "I'm ready."

Kendall's gaze skittered all over the place, but she wouldn't meet his eyes. Shit, he'd really screwed up and he didn't know how to fix it. He shifted, felt the weight in the small of his back, and reached for one of the pistols. "Here." He held the weapon out butt first.

"Don't you want to keep it?"

It took him a minute to realize that she didn't know there'd been two thieves. "I have another. This one's yours."

Bug took the pistol, discharged the clip, and pulled

back the slide. Satisfied that it was safe, she tested the balance, and aimed it down the hall to check out the sights. "If you can stomach dealing with some dead bodies," he said, "we can get a couple of holsters, more ammo, and their pistol belts. We can't hang around here long, though, so you'd have to help me."

For the first time, she looked directly at him. "I'll do whatever you need me to do."

Damn. No wonder he'd fallen in love with her all over again in this life.

Kendall tried to pretend that she wasn't mortified. She'd practically attacked Wyatt the minute he'd rounded the corner, and she had no explanation for it other than the fact that she'd been worried by his extended absence. Yeah, she'd still been aroused from that dream, but she'd been dealing with that. Now, though, the situation was much worse. She knew what it was like to feel Wyatt's hard body against hers, to have his hands stroke her, to feel the insistent press of his erection.

And she wanted more of him.

Nothing had ever felt so right as Wyatt's mouth on hers. He'd been kissing *her*, not Zolianna, and Kendall hadn't wanted him to stop. She'd been able to blithely ignore the ramifications of that, but not his warm palm teasing her breast. God, she'd wanted to strip him, to have him strip her and if—

"Bug, you okay?"

Blinking, Kendall looked over at him. Hell, he'd probably been talking to her for a while to look that concerned. "Sorry, I'm fine. Are you ready to go?"

He paused, and she tensed, waiting for him to question her, or worse yet, explain why that kiss was a mistake, and tell her that it could never happen again. She knew that, damn it, but she didn't want to discuss it. All Kendall wanted to do was pretend that nothing had happened.

To her great relief, he shrugged, and said, "We do need to move. It's dangerous to stay in this area too long."

Kendall nodded, and after another brief hesitation, Wyatt started down the hall. As she rounded the final corner, she stopped short, her heart catching in her throat before it started to race. Two men lay dead on the floor, but she didn't care about them. All she could think was that Wyatt could have died, that one of those bodies might have been his. She splayed her hand over the center of her chest, trying to massage away the ache. Just the thought was enough to rip her up inside.

Lost in what could have happened, it took Kendall a moment to realize Wyatt was watching her, his expression wary, guarded. What? Was he worried she was going to jump him again? "Are we working as a team or do we each take one man?" she asked quickly.

Wyatt stared at her, then he shook his head, appearing bemused. "You sure you're up to getting the belts off them?"

With a emphatic nod, Kendall walked to the closest henchman. "It's probably faster if we both do a man. Do you want me to take the big guy?"

"Yeah, why don't you. I already have his belt open, you just need to remove it."

Kendall nodded and knelt beside the body. After one short glance, she didn't look at his face again. She didn't know his name, but she'd seen him around the post. Maybe she should feel remorse over his death, but she didn't. If the choice was Wyatt's life or others', she'd always pick her friend. Always. But seeing these two men made her wonder how many people were part of the smuggling ring. Would there be someone she knew, someone she considered a friend involved in this mess?

Shaking her head sadly, Kendall reached for the nylon-webbed belt. The ammo pouch was held on with two clips, and she pulled the tab to unhook one, then the other. Once she had the pouch off, she went to the man's other side and pulled the belt out from underneath his body. Then, sitting cross-legged on the floor, she adjusted it until it would fit her. After checking to ensure the two clips were full, she reattached the ammo pouch. Satisfied that everything was to her liking, she stood, strapped it around her waist, and slid the weapon into the holster.

Wyatt was waiting nearby when she finished, but then the other guy was similar to him in build, and she doubted he'd needed to adjust the size of his belt. "We need to get that water and get out of here," he said. "Are you set, darlin'?"

This time the endearment made her uncomfortable. Before, she'd been able to write it off, but now, because of their kiss—because his hand had caressed her bare breast—the name felt, well, intimate. She couldn't stop her cheeks from heating, and Kendall had no doubt he'd seen it. Wyatt was too damn observant. "Yeah, I'm ready, Marsh." She forced herself to meet his eyes.

"Okay, stay behind me." He sounded irritated.

Kendall nodded. She guessed the tenuousness of their position was why he wasn't questioning her, but she knew that wouldn't last. At some point, he was going to insist they talk about it. Before then, she was going to have to come up with some plausible excuse for her behavior— one that wouldn't jeopardize their friendship. She couldn't lose him.

As she stepped into the room, the first thing she noted was the beauty of the stone fountain. It was plain compared to the often elaborate fountains centered in the various plazas of the Old City, but the simplicity gave it charm. The marble was a blush-brown and the middle had something that resembled an ancient Grecian column. Water flowed from the top and soundlessly cascaded down into the basin.

Gazing farther around the room, she saw a man's body

and gasped. He looked as if he'd just died moments earlier, but if what Wyatt had told her about the time of death being impossible to pin down was right, it meant the Old City preserved bodies. In that case, he could have been dead a long time. She didn't like it. It had to indicate this room was booby trapped.

Grimly, she studied the area more intently, looking for some sign of what had killed the man. That was when she noticed that the thieves had brought a couple of collapsible camp stools with them to make their stakeout more comfortable. They were positioned near the door, almost unseeable from the hallway.

"Looks like we hit the mother lode," Wyatt told her. He had a big grin on his face, and she found herself mesmerized for a moment before she could glance away. She knew he'd read the blank look on her face when he gestured toward two canteens.

Wyatt picked them up. "Nearly empty," he reported. "Those men must have been here for a while. We can fill them along with your bottle, and put them on the belts." Stuffing one under his arm, Wyatt bent down again, and checked out the tiny rucksack tucked between the two chairs. "The food's gone," he reported when he straightened. "Hand me your bottle."

"Maybe we should wait and get water somewhere else. I don't want you to get hurt." She cast a quick glance toward the body. "If we found one fountain, there must be more."

"There'll probably be some sort of snare around those too," he said, easily following her train of thought. "It's not going to be any safer somewhere else, and it's critical we have water."

Reluctantly, Kendall handed him her bottle. He was right. "What do you want me to do?"

"Stand guard," he told her. "The odds are slim that

we'll have company while we're here, but I don't want to be trapped unaware if someone does show up."

"Got it," she said, but her focus was more on Wyatt's rear end than the doorway to the room.

As she watched, her hand throbbed as some kind of energy swirled along the new grooves on her fingers and palm. Kendall made a fist, trying to stop the sensation. Instead, it seemed to intensify with each step Wyatt took toward the fountain. "Stop!"

He obeyed instantly. "What's wrong?"

"Don't move," she told him. "Whatever you do, don't move."

Chapter Thirteen

Kendall wasn't sure why she'd connected the tingle in her hand to Wyatt's progress, but she knew she was right—the intensity hadn't increased since he'd stopped moving. She turned her arm so she could see her palm. The paisleys had become much more pronounced, the grooves going deeper and elongating until some joined up with other swirls. She pondered over that for a moment, but she couldn't take the time now to think about it.

Letting her eyes go out of focus, Kendall lifted her gaze from her hand to the chamber. They were faint, but there were energy lines all through the room, intertwined with the intricacy of a spiderweb. And Wyatt stood right in the middle of them.

"Bug?"

She blinked and the web disappeared. "Just hang on, okay?"

Slowly, she allowed her vision to blur again, and studied the things. "Here's the situation, Wy," she told him when she thought she understood. "This room is riddled with energy lines. You're on the brink of the really heavy ones, and I think they'll trigger a trap. The fountain is like a hub that they come out of, but they're more dispersed farther from the center. The thing is, though, that they filled in behind you."

"What do you mean, energy lines?"

She shook her head, not sure what words to use. "They're lines and they glow faintly. I don't know how else to explain them, but they're real and they're dangerous."

The question was what kind of snare were they linked to—a mind trap or something physical like those spikes? He couldn't go forward, but he couldn't back up either since the lines had thickened behind him. How did she get Wyatt out of this mess?

"I can't see anything," he told her.

"They're there!" Did he think she was making this up?

"Darlin', I wasn't calling you a liar. I'm telling you that I can't see them. I need you to guide me clear."

"Sorry." Kendall dragged her left hand through her hair, embarrassed by her touchiness. "I'll try, but it might take a while to come up with a good way to get you out. You're surrounded, and every direction is heavy with them now."

From the start, he'd been worried that the smugglers would be watching for them by the water, so Kendall knew there wasn't time to waste. Wyatt had taken out two of the henchmen, but that didn't mean someone else wouldn't show up to relieve those guys.

The threads were almost nonexistent where she stood, and Kendall shifted to her left, hoping that a new angle would give her a different perspective. As she moved, she noticed something—the web around her disappeared. Freezing in place, she considered that. Maybe because they were so scant in this area, they were geared to disintegrate for anyone. After all, the two smugglers had been parked here for a while and hadn't set anything off. Except she didn't think that was the case.

Cautiously, Kendall eased forward, holding her hand out in front of her. The lines vanished, giving her a foot of clearance to her front and sides—and she'd bet behind her too.

"Any progress?" Wyatt asked.

"I'm on to something. Give me a couple more minutes to test it out, okay?"

After receiving Wyatt's agreement, she edged into the more densely lined area of the web. Same thing happened. Somehow, the strands reacted differently to her. Kendall didn't go any faster, and she carefully monitored her situation with every step she took, but she made her way closer to him.

"What are you doing?" Wyatt didn't move, but the snap in his voice suggested he had a good idea that she was near.

"Relax," Kendall told him. "I'm not doing anything stupid. The web collapses for me. It's allowing me enough clearance. If I wrap my arms around you, it should encompass both of us."

"It might not work with me in the mix."

"It'll work," she insisted. *Auric fields.* The words flashed through her brain, and she understood the message. Her energy should mingle with Wyatt's, and as they overlapped, the web would react as if his aura were hers. Of course, she didn't tell him this. While he claimed to be open-minded, she'd been ridiculed too many times for her beliefs to just casually toss the information out there and hope it was something he'd accept.

Kendall slowed even more as she neared him. She had to make sure the web came down; otherwise she might trigger the very thing she was trying to prevent. But nothing changed—the energy lines continued to vanish as she went forward.

She reached him, and before she could stop herself, Kendall ran her palm down his spine. He stiffened, but didn't move or speak. With a sigh of frustration over her strange behavior, she pulled her hand back, closed the remaining distance, and wrapped her arms around his waist. Glancing to each side, she saw exactly what she'd hoped—the web was gone. "Are you braced?"

"Yeah, why?"

"I want to check behind us, but I need to use you as an anchor. I'm going to turn as far to the left as I can without letting go," she explained. "Ready?"

"I'm set. Go ahead."

Keeping her movement as smooth as possible, Kendall twisted. As she'd suspected, the foot of clearance extended to their rear. "We're good behind us," she informed him, slowly shifting forward once more, "but I was thinking. We need water, and we've come this far already. If my hugging you clears the web in front too, we could go to the fountain and fill the canteens."

"Is it open in front?"

Clutching his middle, she went up on tiptoe, but Wyatt was eight inches taller than she was. Even balanced like this, she had a difficult time looking over his shoulder, and couldn't get much of a view. "I don't know. You're too big," she complained.

"So jump on my back, wrap your legs around my waist, and look over my head. Because of the canteens, I won't be able to hold you up, but you're athletic, so it shouldn't be a problem. If the path is as open as you hope, we can go to the fountain like this." He laughed. "Think of it as a piggyback ride."

Now she was even more befuddled. "A what?"

"You know, when you were a little girl and your dad let you hop up on his back while he pretended to be a horse."

Kendall went rigid. Her face was hot with mortification, but she was tired of pretending she'd had some normal life as she'd grown up. "I never met my dad," she confessed. Before he could comment, she added, "And none of my mom's boyfriends ever gave me a piggyback ride." There. She'd said it.

"I'm sorry," he said, "but don't worry, Bug, I'll help you make up for lost time. You can ride me whenever you like."

She knew a double entendre when she heard one. Wyatt might have had laughter in his voice, but he wasn't joking about the offer. It had to be because she'd kissed him in the hallway. Damn it, now he thought she wanted him. Okay, she *did* want him, but that didn't mean she was going to give in to the need. No way was she going to be a friend who offered *benefits*.

"Marsh, why don't you be quiet?" she suggested. "You're in a hell of a precarious position to be making risqué comments."

Wyatt sounded solemn when he told her, "I'm not worried. If there's one thing I know about you, it's that you're loyal. You'd never leave me enmeshed in a web of energy lines. I know it, and you know it. Now, why don't you hop up and take a look in front of us. I want that water if we can get it safely, and we've dawdled enough."

The idea of being predictable left her mildly unhappy, but he was right on both counts—she'd never abandon him, and they'd spent enough time here. "I'm going to use your shoulders to help me jump," Kendall told him, and pushed her messenger bag behind her back before she put her hands on him. "Are you ready?"

After he nodded, Kendall leaped, and even though she'd never done this before, getting into position was as easy as he'd claimed. She hooked her ankles in front of him, and wrapped her arms around him to help them both stay balanced. Once she felt steady, she rested her chin on his head and looked around.

"Well?" he prompted.

"It worked. The web is down for about a foot in front of us. Walk slowly. I'll keep a close eye on the lines, and if they're not disappearing, I'll tell you to stop."

Wyatt nodded, and moving at glacial speed, he edged toward the blush-marble fountain. The web, though, continued to dissolve, and they reached the water without incident.

"I think," he said, "our best option is to lower you to the ground again, and put you in front of me. I'll hold on to you while you fill the canteens. Then we get the heck out of here."

"Sounds good," she agreed. Kendall slipped to the ground, but never gave up contact with Wyatt as she moved in front of him and quickly filled the canteens.

"Take as much water as you want," Wyatt told her. "Then refill it and I'll do the same. I don't want to lower our supply of water before we have to, and we've got a large source right here."

With a nod, Kendall tipped the bottle back, drinking nearly the whole thing before she felt as if she'd had enough. She didn't worry about bacteria—this was the Old City—and she wasn't concerned that the thieves had poisoned the supply. The lines lacing the room wouldn't let anyone close to the fountain. She replenished the bottle and handed it to Wyatt.

As she watched him swallow, she became aware of a burning sensation in the hand she'd used to dip the containers. The water seemed to be interacting with the swirls, etching fire into the pattern. Kendall wiped her palm off on the seat of her pants, but the searing didn't stop.

Wyatt held out the empty bottle, and she stared blankly. "I'm good," he told her, and as it dawned on her what he was talking about, she took it from him.

This time as Kendall bent to dip the bottle into the water, she tried to keep her hand dry. Not that it mattered since the pain had never gone away, but she didn't want to make it worse.

As she leaned over, Kendall became aware of Wyatt's hands at her waist, the feel of his groin brushing her bot-

tom. She wanted to press backward, feel him grow hard
against her again, and she shook her head, denying the
idea. The instant the bottle was filled, she straightened,
and stowed it. Just as she closed the flap on her bag, she
heard a man shout outside the room.

"Move!" Wyatt didn't wait for her to comply, he tightened his hold around her, and half carried her as he ran
for the backside of the basin.

Someone fired a pistol, the shot sounding loud in the
stone chamber. The ricochet brought a curse from one of
the pursuers, but this voice was feminine. There was a
pair of them then, a man and a woman. Wyatt reached the
rear of the fountain and pushed her down behind it before
he dropped over her.

"I need to be on top!" she told him. Before he could disagree, Kendall rolled.

"Damn it, I have to be able to shoot."

"You can do that without lying over me." She understood why he was worried. The fountain was low and if
she raised her head, she'd become a target. Sure, they had
the marble basin between them and the doorway. It would
have to be a good shot, but it wasn't an impossible one. "I
was blocked down there," she explained. "The lines were
flowing back—if they touched you . . ."

Wyatt muttered a complaint as her voice trailed off. Before she could prevent it, he shifted their positions so that
he was kneeling, and she was shielded by him. They were
partly behind the column centered in the fountain now,
and that limited the shooting angles even more. He lifted
the flap on the holster and drew his pistol. "They're in the
hallway," he told her.

Almost as soon as he finished speaking, raised voices
drifted into the room. Kendall couldn't make out the
words, but their enemies were having a disagreement.

"What do you think they're going to do?" she asked
quietly.

"I don't know. I see three decent options. One, they wait us out. Two, they come in after us. But the best choice is to leave one person outside the room and send the other for help."

"They didn't have comm gear?"

"I didn't see any, and the men I killed didn't have it either. Western Alliance comm systems only work sporadically in the city, and the equipment has to be checked in and out, so unless they have a person in that unit, it isn't worth the risk to take something so noticeable."

The argument became more heated. "I don't think they're going to pick the best choice in your set of options. Neither one of them seems to want to give up the glory of capturing us."

"I hope you're right," Wyatt said without glancing away from the door. "A pair will be a lot easier to handle than an army."

As they waited, Kendall felt her nerves pulling tauter. She was behind Wyatt, and that made her more tense than anything else. She knew him. He'd protect her, no matter what—including taking a bullet.

Almost at the same instant Kendall noticed one of the thieves had stepped far enough into the door to be seen, Wyatt fired. The noise sounded as loud as a cannon. He didn't miss.

But while he'd definitely hit flesh, it was impossible to tell how badly the person had been hurt. There was no swearing, no moans, no vows to avenge the partner's death, and no return fire. The silence seemed downright eerie.

As tempting as it was to ask Wyatt, Kendall kept her mouth shut. He was too focused for her to risk distracting him.

They were out there, though, she knew it. If only they'd leave, so she and Wyatt could get out of here. The temple was filled with traps, some physical, some mental. Why couldn't those two run into something like that now when it would help? Maybe not beetles, maybe something scarier than what it had done to Wyatt, but Kendall wanted those smugglers gone.

Leaning forward to get a better view, she braced her hand on the basin of the fountain to keep her balance. The burning in her hand became almost unbearable. She bit back a gasp, knowing it would alarm Wyatt, but it hurt like hell. Kendall wanted to pull her arm back, but it was as if she were glued in place.

"Get it off me!"

Kendall forgot about her pain. The voice had been nearly frantic, and she wondered what was going on to upset the male thief so much. Then he screamed. She and Wyatt exchanged a glance, but he quickly returned his gaze to the doorway.

Biting her lip, she squeezed her hand more tightly around the marble. What was happening out there? A hallucination? Or something worse? And was it something that would impact on her and Wyatt too? Now the woman was screaming also, and Kendall felt a shiver go down her spine.

"What are you doing?" Wyatt asked, voice low.

"What do you mean? I'm just kneeling here."

Movement caught their attention, and Wyatt looked away from her. The man ran into the room, the female thief right on his heels. They were swatting at themselves, still screaming, and carrying on even worse than Wyatt had when he'd been hallucinating about the beetles.

"Stop!" Kendall shouted as the two raced deeper into the chamber, but the smugglers were beyond hearing her.

The energy lines flared, then something like the fine lines given off by a laser scalpel pierced through the space where the duo stood. Kendall closed her eyes and turned her face into Wyatt's shoulder the instant she saw what was happening.

Those laser beams were slicing through flesh, carving up the thieves like they were Thanksgiving Day turkeys.

If she thought their screams had been hideous before, that was nothing compared to the sounds escaping them now. Unfortunately, she couldn't plug her ears and block the sounds, not even the noises they made as they died.

Only when the room was absolutely calm again did the light dim to its previous level of brightness. Kendall didn't look over at the bodies, but she could remove her hand from the basin now, and she wrapped both arms around Wyatt. That could have been him. If she hadn't seen those lines, he would have died in agony, and there would have been nothing she could have done to save him. She held on more tightly.

"It's all right, darlin'," he said softly. He tucked his pistol back in the holster so he could return her hug.

"That could have been you," she said, still unable to get past the idea that she could have lost him.

"But it wasn't. You saved me." Wyatt lifted a hand to her face, brushed her hair off her cheek, and leaned down to kiss her. Kendall didn't demur; she met him halfway, immediately opening her mouth beneath his in invitation.

As his tongue played with hers, she felt her arousal deepen. Almost before she realized what she was doing, Kendall rubbed herself against his body. It wasn't enough, damn it, and she groaned her frustration.

She brought her hands up, cupped his face, and kissed him with all the pent-up desire she held for him. Her right hand felt scorching hot, but she ignored it.

"Ow!" Wyatt pulled back. "What the—" He took hold of her hand, and turned it so he could see the inside. She looked down when he did. There, deeply drawn into her palm, was the outline of a pyramid, and inside it were swirly symbols that Kendall couldn't identify. The lines weren't faint any longer, but thick and easily noticeable. "Son of a bitch," Wyatt cursed.

* * *

He was pissed as hell. The damn temple had claimed Bug.
She had the mark of High Priestess branded on her palm
just as Zolianna had after she'd ascended to the position.

"When did this show up?" he demanded.

For a second, he thought she was going to shut down
on him, and he was in no mood to tolerate it. Then, with a
shrug, Bug said, "It's hard to gauge time here, but it began
appearing the day the wall almost crushed me."

"You had your hand against the stone," he realized.

She nodded, but Wyatt wasn't looking for confirmation.
To go from kissing her—with her kissing him back just as
wildly—to this was like a fist in the gut. Taking a deep
breath, he forced the fury aside. He wasn't losing Kendall
to this pile of rock, and he'd fight however he needed to in
order to hold on to her.

With another deep breath or two, he calmed down
enough to realize this gave them a bit of an advantage.
The temple had laid claim to Kendall, but as High Priestess, she controlled a lot of things. He would bet a month's
worth of pay that Bug had caused whatever had made the
thieves scream in the hallway. "Turn off the trap in this
room," he said.

"What? How do I do that?"

Wyatt sighed silently. Her confusion was real, and it
went back to her not remembering any of her past lives.
"Picture it, okay? Maybe visualize flipping a switch, and
having all the energy lines in the room disappear." She
looked dubious and he smiled faintly at her reaction. "Just
try it."

She freed her hand, but he kept her body pressed
against his. It was this contact that let him feel her gathering power. Kendall might not consciously remember what
she was capable of, but she still had the talents.

"It worked." She sounded amazed. "The lines are
gone."

"Good job," he said, but Wyatt was less than happy even though she'd done as he'd asked. This was one more piece of evidence that she was connected to the temple. He debated whether to ask the next question, but decided Kendall would be quizzing him anyway from what he'd already said. "What were you thinking while those two were outside the room?"

"What do you mean?" Bug wouldn't meet his gaze.

Tightening his hold on her, he said, "Don't you dare do this to me, Kendall. Don't shut me out or lie to me." Her gaze flew to his, and she looked startled. "What were you thinking while those smugglers were outside?"

Kendall bit her bottom lip, then said, "I just wished that they'd trigger a mind trap the way you had, that's all."

Wyatt nodded, then reluctantly released her, so he could stand. Holding out a hand, he pulled Bug to her feet.

"What happened to them—it's my fault, isn't it?"

"No, of course not," he assured her.

"It is." She grabbed his arm, held on tightly. "I wanted them to run away from us, though, not into the chamber."

Gathering her close, he cuddled her against his chest. "You're not to blame, darlin'. They're the ones who chose to come in the room; you didn't force them." Kendall didn't argue with him, but he knew she didn't believe it. Wyatt didn't have time to talk to her about this right now. More members of the smuggling ring could show up; they weren't clear yet. "We need to get out of here," he told her. "Why don't you wait over by the door while I check out our uninvited guests?"

"I'll go with you," Kendall said. "I can handle it."

"There's no reason to. I already know you're tough enough to deal with it."

Bug *was* tough. She'd take on anything he asked of her, but there really was no benefit to her seeing the bodies up close. He knew this was going to be ugly, probably the worst thing he'd ever viewed. Unlike Kendall, he'd watched while the lights had sliced the pair to pieces. Wyatt had wanted to look away too, but he couldn't. He needed to know what they were up against, and burying his head in the sand wasn't going to keep them safe.

Taking a chance, he leaned forward and kissed her lightly, quickly. "I'll be fast, and you really don't need to see it."

With a jerky nod, Kendall agreed. He waited until she was halfway to the exit before he walked over to the corpses. Shit, they were a mess, pieces of them everywhere. He felt the water he'd had earlier come up on him, and Wyatt swallowed hard.

He considered taking their pistols, their ammo pouches and the canteens, but the items were saturated with blood. Not worth it, not when they'd remind Kendall what had occurred every time she looked at them. She already blamed herself; this would be like a thorn in her side, tormenting her continually.

Wyatt went over to the other body. This one had been pierced, probably by the same lasers, but not sliced. The only thing he could figure out was that this thief hadn't gone as deeply into the room, so the temple hadn't reacted as violently.

He left bloody boot prints in his wake as he rejoined Kendall. He grimaced, but there'd been no way to avoid it, not given the condition of the bodies. "Nothing salvageable," he reported when he drew beside her. She nodded. "When we leave the room, I want you to turn those energy lines back on again. They might take out a few more smugglers for us."

Bug paled, but she nodded, and the urge to kiss her hit him once more. Hell, he *always* wanted to kiss her, but this was specifically because she was showing her mettle. He appreciated her strength, her willingness to do what he needed even when it wasn't easy. Things were bad, but they could be a lot worse if Kendall wasn't as solid as she was. "Darlin', they'd do the same to us, or worse, if they had the chance."

"I realize that. You can count on me."

"Yeah, I know. Come on, let's get going. We need to put some distance between us and this fountain before we stop for the night."

Wyatt paused outside the room, waited for her nod indicating she'd rearmed the trap, then took her hand—the one on which the damn pyramid had carved its mark. He felt energy zipping between their palms, and ignored it. Kendall Thomas was his and he wasn't letting some fricking heap of rock scare him off.

Chapter Fourteen

Kendall battled to conceal her disappointment. She'd known when her attendant had informed her of Wyatt's arrival that it was official business, so there was no cause to feel disheartened at seeing his lieutenants at his sides. She herself had come with half her cortege and her personal guard. It was expected.

The men went down on one knee, her lover included, and bowed their heads. "My lady," he said.

She took a moment to study her visitors. "You've my leave to rise." At moments such as these, Kendall despised the formality to which they were forced to adhere. She wished to go to him, wrap her arms around his waist, and simply hold him while they discussed what was wrong. But they were surrounded by the entourages that came with their respective positions, and she could not.

Turning to her attendant, Kendall gave one regal nod. The young priestess stepped forward at once, and asked, "Would the gentlemen care for refreshments?"

"Thank you for your hospitality, senet," Wyatt said, "but we must decline."

"We shall be comfortable," Kendall pronounced, and with all the gracefulness she possessed, glided to the sofa. When she was seated, her cortege and guards in position, she indicated the opposite chair. It wasn't nearly as ornate or comfortable as her own, but since it was considered a great honor to be allowed to sit in her presence, that fact was usually overlooked.

Hands calmly folded in her lap, Kendall waited until Wyatt was settled to ask, "What news have you for the temple?"

"My lady, Guard Commander Gustus asked me to inform you of events which have taken place outside the walls of our city." He took a deep breath. "There's no easy way to impart this information. Thirty-two of our citizens were found murdered outside the city walls."

Kendall barely kept herself from gasping, but her young attendant was not so skilled at hiding her reaction. "Is the Guard certain it was murder?"

"Most assuredly," Wyatt said.

"Explain," she ordered.

"The details are gruesome, my lady."

After giving that a moment's worth of consideration, Kendall dismissed her attendant, then added, "All save my guard may leave if they wish to do so." Not one member of her cortege shifted. Kendall inclined her head toward Wyatt, and said, "Proceed."

There was a hesitation that Kendall ascribed to Wyatt's need to protect her. "My lady," he said at last, "the victims were mutilated—their eyes were missing from their sockets, their tongues gone as well, and their hearts torn from their chests."

Kendall clenched her hands tightly in her lap. The description itself was factual and held no unnecessary de-

tail, but she found it too easy to envision such horror. "Has the Guard discovered those responsible for such carnage?"

"No, my lady. The physical strength required to break through a person's rib cage is incredible. We've been unable to discover who could possess such power."

She asked more questions, but Wyatt had no answers. Perhaps that was not too surprising. The City Guard was ceremonial and unaccustomed to dealing with such matters. There were tales of violence in the ancient past of their home world, but they'd long since abandoned such uncivilized behavior. The Guard was at a loss as to what to do, that was obvious. By the time he and his men bowed before taking their leave, Kendall was concerned about how many more would die before this madman was apprehended.

Alex stared down at the paper lying on his desk blotter and scowled. It shouldn't be this difficult to come up with ideas to win Stacey. Hell, men wooed their women all the time.

He'd started with three items—flowers, candy, perfume. This was Jarved Nine, though, and any kind of candy was hard to come by. Everything they had that wasn't alien in origin had to be shipped from home, and space on the transport was too valuable to waste on chocolate. He'd crossed that off the list.

Giving her perfume ran into the same problem. Besides, Stace had so many damn bottles of the stuff, she hardly needed more. Alex had removed that item from his list as well.

Flowers were more viable since they grew everywhere in the Old City, but if he picked them, they'd look far from perfect. More likely, they'd resemble something Cam would gather for Ravyn, and Alex refused to hand something to Stacey that was less than what she deserved. That had taken care of his final idea.

Shit, it wasn't like he had time to sit and mull this over. Every damn time he turned around, it seemed as if more people went missing. Four more soldiers—three men and a woman—had been reported AWOL today. McNamara was riding his ass to come up with answers before, as she put it, "half the post vanished." Alex was working sixteen-hour days or longer, and so were his men.

Maybe he was foolish, playing this so close to the vest, but he'd told no one except Montgomery's team about the smuggling. Cantore and his men were investigating that angle, and Alex had everyone else working on pieces. He hadn't even informed the colonel about the antiquities thieves because she would jump the gun, and Alex refused to risk lives unnecessarily. The woman had always been too worried about how she appeared to the top brass.

It was a safe guess that most—if not all—of the missing were part of the smuggling ring. With the number of men and women involved, something must have leaked—that many people couldn't keep a secret—but no one had reported it. Not one damn soldier.

Tossing his pen down on top of the paper, Alex leaned back in his office chair and scrubbed his hands over his face. He was tired. Instead of spending his few off hours sleeping, he was spinning his wheels, trying to come up with a plan for his personal life. Why did Stacey have to throw down the gauntlet now? Why not six months ago or six months in the future?

He sighed. Women were a mystery to him. Alex knew better than to compare Stacey to his mother, but she was nothing like his stepsister or his stepmother, Marie, either.

How the hell had Brody wooed Ravyn?

Alex didn't have a clue. By the time he'd arrived on J Nine as part of a rescue team, the two of them were already committed to each other. He supposed he could ask, but he wasn't going to. Brody would have a good laugh, and Ravyn was too close to Stacey.

Leaning forward again, Alex picked up his pen and started doodling. With all the pairings that had happened on the planet, there must be dozens of examples to emulate, but after wracking his brain, he was forced to concede that he hadn't paid attention to the details, only the results.

If it wasn't for the damn situation going on around him, Alex could pull a quick covert op, kidnap Stacey and hold her in one of the buildings of the Old City until he got his point across—that she meant everything to him.

But it wasn't an option. Until Hunter's killer was identified and caught, until he'd located all the missing soldiers, Alex was stuck. He needed time.

If he'd had more warning, he could have out-maneuvered Stacey, made sure her request to return home was denied, but she'd blindsided him. It took more than a day and a half for messages to travel between the two planets and she'd already received approval before his communiqué had reached Earth.

He'd briefly considered asking McNamara to hold the transport on Jarved Nine until the murderer was apprehended, but he wouldn't. Those Spec Ops teams were needed back home and in position before war was formally declared with the coalition.

So that pretty much shot all his ideas to hell. Stacey would be leaving and his determination to win her was going to die on the drawing board. How pathetic was he?

He'd never given up easily. If Plan A didn't work, he used B, C, D or even Plan Z if that's what it took to get the job done. His persistence had distinguished him when he'd been part of Special Operations. So with his limited time and the obvious answers unworkable, he'd simply have to come up with another method to get his point across.

Alex dropped his pen and pushed his chair back. He had a couple of hours before he had to be back at his desk, and he was using them. Maybe he couldn't kidnap her indefinitely, but he could grab Stacey and talk to her.

"Sir?" his aide asked as Alex strode past him.

"I'll return for the twenty-three-hundred-hour briefing, Sergeant," Alex told him without slowing down.

When he reached his sister's home, though, he paused. Frontal assault or covert insertion? He opted for the first choice. His mood was fractious after the bitch of a day he'd had, and if Brody was stupid enough to get in his way, Alex could work out some of his frustrations.

It was almost anticlimatic to find the main gathering chamber empty. He proceeded down the hall, checked out the private rooms, and found those unoccupied as well. In fact, there was no one present—not Brody, not Ravyn or Cam, and not Stacey either. Where the hell were they?

Parking himself in the main room, he waited. Alex was fairly certain there were no events tonight, so they shouldn't be gone long, but he'd sit here all night if he needed to. With one person dead and eight more missing, he wasn't going anywhere until he knew his woman and his family were okay. If worse came to worst, he could hold the damn briefing here.

He should have brought some paperwork with him, Alex thought as his wait lengthened. So what if he'd been over the damn sheets a million times; maybe he'd spot something on the next read through. Since there was nothing here to keep him occupied, he began to pace, becoming edgier with each passing minute.

Alex was ready to start tearing the post apart looking for them, when he heard someone enter the house. He turned to light into whoever it was for taking off without telling him where they were going to be, but it wasn't a member of his family. "Sir," the private panted, "I've been searching for you everywhere."

"Well, you found me," he snapped. "What did you

want?" The gir—woman went white and Alex bit back a sigh. Moderating his voice, he tried again, "What did you need, Private?"

"Sir, Major Brody sent me to find you."

Alex felt his trepidation grow, and, not for the first time, he cursed the inconsistency of the Western Alliance comm systems within the Old City. "What's his message?"

"The major's son was hurt," she said, "and they're at the infirmary waiting for—"

He didn't hang around long enough for her to finish. Brushing past the woman, Alex was out of the house and headed for the infirmary at a pace just short of a run. If Brody had sent someone looking for him, Cam's injury was serious. It seemed to take forever to reach the prefab building, and he pushed through the door, his gaze immediately scanning.

Ravyn sat between Damon and Stacey, her hands linked with both of them. His sister was pale and tense. Her head came up the instant she heard him. What scared Alex shitless wasn't her wanness; it was the fact that her lower lip wobbled when their eyes met. Ravyn was as tough as they came, and seeing her on the verge of falling apart had panic bubbling inside him. "How is Cam?" Alex demanded of the room at large.

"The doctor hasn't come back yet," Brody reported.

"What happened?"

His sister did start crying then. She pushed to her feet and crossed the floor, putting her back to the room. Without saying a word, Brody followed. He wrapped his arms around his wife from behind, and Ravyn turned, burying her face against his throat. Alex looked away to give them privacy.

Heart heavy, he made his way over to Stacey, and sat beside her. "What happened?" he asked, keeping his voice quiet. He didn't want to upset Ravyn more than he had already, but damn it, he needed to know what was wrong with his nephew.

The silence lengthened, and he didn't think she was going to fill him in, but at last Stacey said, "Cam got hurt. We don't know how. Ravyn had put him to bed, but about an hour later she heard a noise, and when she went to check, she found him unconscious on his bedroom floor. God, Alex, his head was covered in blood."

Stacey suddenly seemed shaky herself, and Alex felt his own stomach heave. Not Cam. Shit, it would kill Ravyn— hell, it would kill *him*—if anything happened to that boy. "Head wounds bleed a lot," he offered thickly.

"I know." Stacey's voice was tremulous, and although he half expected to be rebuffed, Alex put his arm around her. It surprised him no small amount when she leaned into his side.

"Did the doctor say anything about his condition?"

Shaking her head, Stacey said, "Not a word. They just rushed him off. For a split second, I thought Ravyn was going to pass out." She turned her head so their eyes met. "I've never seen her like that. If Damon wasn't here for her, I don't know if she could have held it together."

Alex glanced over. Ravyn and her husband were clutching each other, sharing their strength as they waited for news of their son. At that same moment, Stacey stiffened, straightening away from him, and reluctantly, he pulled his arm back. "What about you?" he asked her quietly. "How are you holding up?"

"I'm okay, just worried. I wish that doctor would let us know how Cam's doing."

"They haven't even sent a nurse out with an update?" When Stacey shook her head, Alex decided there was something he could do besides sit here helplessly. "I'm going to find out what the hell that doctor is doing," Alex said, as he stood and headed for the back of the building.

Stacey caught him before he reached the hallway. "Oh, no, you don't. What if the doctor is in the middle of some intricate procedure? Do you think your bursting into the room and intimidating him is going to help Cam?"

"Someone has to get answers for Ravyn and Damon." His voice came out tight, but other than that, he sounded normal.

"You're not charging back there," Stacey told him again.

He stared at her, hands clenched at his sides as he struggled to hide his emotions. His whole life had been filled with people leaving, people *dying*. He couldn't lose Cam too; he refused, and he wouldn't allow his sister to lose her son. The problem was there wasn't anything he could do to make a difference. Not one damn thing.

Pivoting sharply, Alex walked outside. With his hands on his hips, he took a few deep breaths. Opening his heart had never brought him anything except pain. How many more times did he have to be taught this lesson before it finally sank in?

Slowly, deeply, Alex inhaled, then exhaled. He couldn't stay out here long. He had to go back inside, had to be there for Ravyn and Damon if they needed him. As much as this was hurting him, it would be a billion times worse for them.

Shit, maybe there was a reason he couldn't come up with a way to woo Stacey. Maybe it was because he was meant to spend his life alone. He should let her go, let her find someone who was easier to live with than he was. It was probably best for him too. After she left, his feelings would eventually fade, and Alex wouldn't allow another woman close. He'd do what he'd done before she'd swept into his life and turned it upside down—he'd take them to bed, enjoy them, and forget them. And if that existence seemed empty after three years with Stacey, well, he'd get over it. Someday.

"How long are you going to stay out here?" Stacey asked, her voice slicing through his thoughts.

"A few more minutes."

"Have you considered that you might be needed in there?"

Alex didn't say a word. Who needed him? His sister? She had her husband. Cam? He had his parents, and the doctor. Stacey? Sure, that's why she was getting on a shuttle bound for Earth. He was on the fringes, a fifth wheel—unnecessary.

The thought was enough to prompt him to try. "The house is empty without you."

"Right," Stacey said with heavy sarcasm. "I'm supposed to believe it's me you miss and not the sex."

"Sex?" Alex laughed derisively. "I'm damn near forty years old. Do you think with the kind of hours I've been putting in, and the situation I'm dealing with, that getting off is high on my priority list right now? I don't know whether to be flattered that you believe I'm that big a stud, or insulted you believe I'm always thinking with my—" he paused, decided Stacey didn't deserve crudeness, and substituted, "thinking below my belt."

"What am I supposed to believe? That you miss me?"

Carefully, slowly, he reached out and brushed a tress of her red hair off her cheek. When that didn't bring an adverse reaction, Alex cupped her face in his hand. "It's the truth."

For a split second, hope seeped into her hazel eyes, but with a blink, it was gone, and she jerked away from his touch. "Sure it is. You just hate to lose. You'll say or do anything in order to come out on top."

His temper spiked again, and Alex struggled to tamp it down. "So I'm damned if I do, damned if I don't? Nice." A sudden suspicion dawned on him. "Of course, maybe that's just an excuse. You want out of our relationship, and instead of telling me that, you list all my faults. Then, when I try to do something about my cited deficiencies, you accuse me of lying to get my way, so nothing I do will be good enough."

"That's not true!"

"Isn't it?" Alex jammed his hands in his pockets to keep from reaching for her. "You tell me, what can I do or say that you'll believe? Name one thing that you won't doubt me on."

Stacey's lips went tight and she wrapped her arms around her waist.

"Yeah," he said, "that's what I thought. As far as you're concerned, it's over, period, and I might as well save my breath because I'm screwed. Well, you know what, Stace? I'm not giving up on you—not because I have to win, but because you mean something to me—and if you board that shuttle to leave, we'll both know it's what *you* wanted."

"This is just like you to take your issues and turn them around onto me. Well, let me tell you—"

Alex leaned forward, got in her face. "Who are you trying to convince, Johnson? Me or yourself?"

He watched fury flame in her eyes and he bit back a smile. This was good. This level of anger meant there was still something between them. Maybe he'd hurt her feelings, and she was trying to save face. Maybe she really believed the bullshit she was spewing, but he knew better. His case wasn't lost yet.

"Now," Alex said, mood much improved, "why don't we head back inside and see how Cam is doing, or if Ravyn and Brody need us to do something for them."

"Alex Sullivan . . ." Her voice trailed off.

Raising an eyebrow in question, he waited.

"You are," she said, voice vibrating with fury, "a piece of work. Everything always has to be turned to your advantage. Let's say you 'win.' How long until things return to normal, and you're shutting me out again?"

Her question left him floundering for some kind of answer. "People don't change overnight," he finally offered.

With a growl, Stacey walked away from him, heading back toward the infirmary. Alex caught up with her, and using his hand to hold the door shut, he asked, "What?"

"What? What?" She yanked hard on the door handle, but he kept it closed. "I gave you three years! If I'd seen even the smallest indication that you were trying, we wouldn't be in this position today. But you never put out any effort at all. None. And I'm supposed to believe that suddenly you've seen the error of your ways? I might be from Iowa, but I'm not *that* gullible."

"All I'm asking," Alex said evenly, "is that you keep an open mind and give me a chance."

She jerked on the door again. He knew better than to push for a response, so Alex released his hold, brushed her hand out of the way and opened the door for her. With a last distrustful glare, Stacey entered the prefab building.

Alex stopped short to avoid plowing into Stacey. Following her gaze, he found out why she'd hung back. His sister and her husband were still the only two present, but something had clearly happened. Brody appeared murderous, and Ravyn was sobbing. His heart froze, air caught in his lungs, and he wondered whether it was worth breathing again if Cam was gone.

"What happened?" Stacey asked and Alex sucked in some badly needed oxygen. "Is Cam okay?"

Brody's arm went around Ravyn and he held her close as he said, "They want to keep him overnight for observation, but all of Cam's tests came back normal. He should be fine in a couple of days."

"What's the bad news?" And Alex knew there was some

of that. Brody tended to be even keeled, so it took a lot to piss him off, and even more to leave him looking violent.

"The bad news?" His brother-in-law's eyes were ice cold and promised hell. "The injury came from blunt-force trauma. Some bastard hit my son in the head."

Chapter Fifteen

Kendall wanted to look at the image on her palm, but Wyatt seemed disinclined to release her hand. Those faint paisleys morphing into deep, dark patterns had her a bit freaked out, but she was concealing that—she hoped.

The weird design made her anxious, but she didn't understand why Wyatt had become so furious. She doubted he would have gotten that pissed off just because he didn't like her leaving him uninformed. The anger had abated since yesterday, though, and Kendall had no desire to reignite it.

She looked around, trying to find something to take her mind off her hand. They'd been walking in these endless corridors for days, though, and there was nothing exciting here. Even the rooms they found had become monotonous because of the sameness. Of course, that didn't mean she didn't want to come back after they took care of the smugglers, but Kendall didn't find their surroundings much of a distraction right now.

She glanced at Wyatt, her most surefire diversion, and

wished she hadn't when her arousal intensified. She'd ached since the dream—it had never gone away—and Kendall wondered at it. On rare mornings, she'd wake up feeling a need, but it always been faint, and quickly gone. Not this time.

The worst part, however, wasn't the throbbing hunger. No, what made her heart race was the realization that the fever wasn't merely for sex, but for sex with Wyatt.

Her determination to resist him was wavering, and she'd begun to wonder if sleeping with him would be as destructive as she feared. What if she went into it with her eyes open—if they spelled out the ground rules up front? Then maybe their friendship could survive. If they knew from the start that it was temporary, how badly could it end? They'd simply wish each other well and resume a platonic relationship. It could work.

Yeah, right. Kendall bit back a sigh. She suspected it wouldn't be that easy. Not for her.

Besides, maybe Wyatt didn't want to risk their friendship either—but given the way he'd kissed her, she doubted it. Males thought differently from females. She'd seen a lot of types of men go through her mom's life—all socioeconomic classes, all races, all religions, all ages—and one thing was always the same: Men didn't view sex the same way women did. For them, it was more physical, less emotional. Kendall had absolutely no doubt that Wyatt could sleep with her, then treat her like his buddy again. But she wouldn't be able to keep their relationship separate like that. For her, it would become more.

She didn't want to think about this either; it sure wasn't conducive to a relaxed state of mind. What she needed was a good, strong dose of reality. "Marsh," she said quietly, "tell me some stories about your childhood."

"What for?"

To remind me how unalike we are, Kendall thought, but she didn't say that aloud. "To pass the time."

He looked at her hard, then shrugged. "I've told you plenty about how I grew up. Why don't you tell me about your childhood instead? That's something I've never heard much on."

Kendall's immediate reaction was to close down, but before she could give into it, she stopped. Why not tell him? Apparently, the interest was mutual, and although he'd pulled back the other day, she'd figured out that had more to do with their being pursued than the fact that he wasn't tempted. Heck, when they'd kissed yesterday, she'd felt proof of how much he did want her. If she threw caution to the wind and did something stupid, she wanted him to know her—really know her.

But what did she tell him? "I'm not very interesting."

Wyatt squeezed her hand. "There's no one I find more fascinating than you." Before she could truly register what he'd said, he continued, "What was it like moving from place to place like you did?"

"That's a broad question." Kendall sighed, and tried to think of what she wanted to share. "Always being in a new place made it tough to be part of the group. Sure, I made friends wherever I went, but they were superficial." Except for you, she thought, but swallowed the words. "With the way the army shifts us around, it's actually been good experience for adulthood."

He ignored her smile. "You don't keep in touch with anyone you knew while you were growing up?"

They reached another fork in the halls, and without him having to ask, Kendall pointed to the right. "Other kids I knew? No. I lost touch with them shortly after I stopped going to whatever school we all attended."

"And adults?"

She'd left herself wide open for that question, but since Kendall had already mentioned her mom's boyfriends, maybe this was a good time to tell the whole truth. "My mom had lovers—lots of them—and I keep in contact with most of them. Usually it's just a birthday wish, but I correspond with some regularly."

Tugging her hand to draw her to a stop, Wyatt asked, "Bug, did one of them hurt you? Is that why you shy away from men?"

It took a couple seconds for the ramifications of his questions to sink in. "No!" she said emphatically, trying to reassure him. "My mom may not have been good at making relationships work, but she always picked honorable men. No one even eyed me funny, I promise."

Wyatt studied her for a moment longer, then his lips quirked. "I'm glad, darlin'."

"My mom, well, she could have been a better parent in a lot of ways, but I always knew that if one of her boyfriends touched me, she'd go after him with a meat cleaver." Kendall smiled at the mental image. "She never had to, though. That's what made it so tough when she'd break up with whoever we were living with at the time. I liked these men, all of them, and there wasn't one I wouldn't have chosen to be my stepfather."

"So what happened?" Wyatt asked. He pulled her into motion.

"To prevent her from marrying one of them?" she asked for clarification. At his nod, she said, "I'm not completely sure. She'd tell me that the man who she believed to be her soul mate wasn't after all, and we'd move on searching for her *true* love."

"You sound awfully scornful. You don't believe in soul mates?" Wyatt's tone was casual, but there was something in his voice that had her hesitating.

"No. There's no such thing as one soul mate."

"You must not believe in reincarnation then."

Again, Kendall paused. Wyatt wasn't looking at her, but something was definitely going on. "I *do* believe in reincarnation," she admitted reluctantly.

"So do I. I told you not to make assumptions about

me," he said, and Kendall realized she must have looked as shocked as she felt. "But from the reading I've done on the subject, the consensus is that soul groups reincarnate together, that they even make plans before being born to meet in the upcoming life."

Kendall nodded, but while she did think there were soul groups, she didn't agree that there was only a single soul mate. The sparks, the fireworks her mom pursued were figments, there and gone in the blink of an eye. If her mom had understood that there wasn't a perfect love out there, maybe Kendall would have known her father—or at least had a stepfather.

"Bug?"

"Sorry." The determined expression he wore made something inside her flutter and Kendall jerked her gaze forward. "Just because we go through life after life with the same set of souls, doesn't mean there's only one soul mate. If you're going by that criteria, we have hundreds, even thousands of kindred spirits."

There was a long pause. "You don't recall your past lives."

Kendall felt her tension ease. This was less personal, and a lot more comfortable to talk about. It wasn't a question, but she answered as if it were. "No. A few times I thought about having a hypnotist regress me, but decided not to waste the money. If I was supposed to remember, I would."

He grunted, and Kendall wasn't sure how to take that. Making no attempt to hide her interest, she turned her head and tried to read his expression, but damn it, he was blank-faced. She hated when he went all enigmatic on her.

"Most people don't know anything." She heard the slight defensiveness in her voice, and took a deep breath before asking, "What about you, did you ever have a regression done?"

"No, I never felt the need to have someone else walk me back in time."

Again, Kendall picked up something in Wyatt's tone that she didn't understand. Of course, maybe she was assuming that because he believed in reincarnation he'd be open to being regressed. Some people simply weren't—she'd met more than a few. It might be safer to talk about something else.

"You know, I heard something when I was hiding from the thieves, but with all the . . ." Kendall made a helpless gesture with her free hand . . . "incidents since then, I forgot about it."

"What did you hear?" Wyatt sounded resigned, and Kendall scrutinized him again, looking for clues about what was going on with him, but he remained unreadable.

"Are you being sent home?" she blurted. When she realized how blunt she'd been, she added, "They said half the Spec Ops teams were being rotated back to Earth."

"The smugglers must have someone plugged into security." Wyatt shook his head, but he didn't seem surprised. "Yeah, it's true, half the teams are going back. Sullivan was supposed to issue the orders the morning after we were trapped in here."

Kendall fought off the sick feeling that was swirling in her stomach. She had to clear her throat before she could ask, "Do you think you'll be going?"

"I don't know, darlin'. I hope not."

Unsure of what to say, she nodded. If he was sent back to Earth, no doubt they'd drift apart as she'd done with her other friends. Even if he did send a note off now and then, they'd become less frequent as time passed until she'd be lucky to get a once a year happy birthday message like she did from most of her uncles.

They reached another spoke of hallways and Wyatt slowed, looking at her expectantly. Kendall studied the kunzite and peridot in the mosaic, but the stones gave no indication of an exit for the pyramid.

With a shrug, she pointed at a corridor slightly to the

left and Kendall mulled over what her life would be like without Wyatt.

Sleep with him.

She might lose him anyway, so why not? Her track record with long-distance friendships was abysmal, and at least if she let him take her to bed, she wouldn't spend the rest of her life wondering what if.

If she were going to do this, though, she'd need to make up her mind soon. Kendall knew the army. It wouldn't matter that they'd been trapped for days. If his orders were to be on the transport, he'd have to board it, even if it left ten minutes after they made it out of the temple.

Wyatt's thigh brushed against hers as they took a turn, and that one small thing was enough to make the ache between her thighs intensify again. Kendall felt as if she were burning up, like she'd die if she didn't feel him inside her, but she couldn't let this push her into something without thinking it through. Yet would it hurt any worse to watch him fly off if they'd been lovers? She'd miss him like hell either way.

And damn it, she couldn't believe she was waffling like this. Only yesterday, she'd vowed not to be a friend who offered benefits, and today she was trying to talk herself into that very thing. What was wrong with her?

"You're scowling," he observed.

"I know. Can we keep talking? It'll keep my mind off our situation." And maybe stop her from so much introspection.

"Okay, if we keep our voices low, it shouldn't be a problem. Tell me why you've never met your father."

Kendall felt her face go hot before the blood seemed to drain away. He'd asked that so abruptly, she hadn't had time to brace herself. Maybe she should have guessed that he'd remember what she'd said and bring it up when he had the chance. Kendall hadn't expected it now, but she was going to tell him and let the chips fall where they may.

"My mom," she said thickly, "never told him about me. I think she'd already moved on before she discovered she was pregnant. At least that's what she said, and by the time I was old enough to ask, she couldn't remember his name or even who she was involved with during that period of time." She cast a sideways glance at him. "I told you my mom had a lot of lovers."

Wyatt didn't say a word, and Kendall's heart started to pound. She shouldn't have said anything. His family was such a throwback to the traditional twentieth-century ideal that there was no way he could relate to the mess she considered normal.

"How could she not remember?" he finally asked. "How could she not realize you'd want that information, that it would be important to you? Even if she didn't consider it worth writing down, your mom should have known what it would mean to you."

Blinking rapidly to beat back the tears welling in her eyes, Kendall clasped his hand between both of hers, trying to tell him without words how much what he'd said meant to her. He was the first one to understand. Everyone else who knew had condemned her mom's promiscuity or how flighty she was not to recall the man's name, but Wyatt focused on *her*—what this meant to her.

"Aw, damn, Bug," he said, stopping to pull her into his arms. "I'm sorry. I didn't want to make you cry."

Which, of course, made the tears start in earnest. Wyatt practically wrapped himself around her, his hand rubbing her back as he murmured soothing noises near her ear. Despite her attempt to choke back the emotions, Kendall found herself sobbing out twenty-four years worth of pain as she held on to Wyatt.

When she finally calmed down, Kendall kept her face pressed against his chest, in no hurry to face him. How embarrassing. Displays like this weren't something she

did, not in front of other people. Ever. Wyatt must wish he
was anywhere but here.

Hell, Kendall wished she were anywhere but here.

He tried to gently move her away from his body, but she
clung tighter, not ready to look him in the eye. Wyatt
didn't allow that, however, and to retain her last trace of
dignity, Kendall loosened her hold. She was too close to
him to bring up her hands and wipe the tear tracks off her
cheeks, but she didn't have to. He did it for her, his
thumbs gentle.

"I'm sorry," he said quietly.

"No, don't apologize. No one else has ever recognized
how I felt about the whole thing. It means a lot to me that
you saw it." Her lips quirked. "I'm sorry that I cried all
over you."

Wyatt shook his head. "I didn't mind." And then he
leaned forward and brushed his mouth over hers. Their
lips lingered for a moment before he broke the kiss. "We
need to keep moving."

Kendall nodded, and wasn't at all surprised when he
took her hand again. The palm tingled briefly, but she
wasn't sure if it was a physical response to Wyatt or something with the temple.

They walked in silence for a few minutes before he said,
"If you want, we can do some investigating. Maybe we
could figure out who your father is, or at least narrow
down the choices."

"You'd do that for me?"

He looked at her, but didn't slow. "I'd do anything for
you, Kendall. *Anything.*"

Wyatt considered it a major victory that Bug only appeared to be a little panicked at his statement. A week
ago, she'd have looked like a deer in the headlights and
cut out on him so fast, she'd have left a vapor trail in her

wake. He fought the smile, afraid it would give away his satisfaction.

Over the past four months, he'd fielded all kinds of unsolicited advice about his pursuit of Kendall. Most of his friends had told him he was moving too slow, but Wyatt knew her better than they did. If he'd done something to spook Bug, odds were slim he'd have a second chance. The patience had paid off.

They'd come a long way. Not only wasn't she running, she'd actually trusted him enough to cry in front of him. Sweet lord, he'd been scared that he'd said something to cause her hurt, but instead it had been a release. He felt like fricking Superman because she'd allowed him hold her while she let loose. Wyatt struggled with the grin again. If Kendall saw it, he'd lose part of the ground he'd gained and he was damned if he'd give up so much as an inch if there was anything he could do to prevent it.

"Let me think about it," she said. "He might have a wife and other kids already." Kendall shrugged. "What if my father doesn't want to know about me?"

"Then he's an idiot. But keep this in mind; just because you find out who he is, doesn't mean you have to contact him."

From the surprise that flashed over her face, Wyatt guessed she hadn't considered that. Which told him something—Kendall wanted to meet her father. If she discovered who he was, she wouldn't be able to stop herself from communicating with him. He'd bet that the fear of rejection was what had kept her from doing a search on her own. Well, if they identified the man, he'd just have to make sure that he acted as intermediary. If her father was an idiot, Wyatt would do his best to shield her.

"Wy," she said, and he felt his heart clench at the endearment—because that's what it was. "Since we're talking so seriously, can we discuss something without you getting mad?"

Oh, shit, now what? This didn't sound good. "I won't get mad," he promised. "Say whatever you want."

Kendall nodded, but she didn't immediately speak. His pulse rate was astronomical before Bug said, "This pattern on my hand, it means something, doesn't it?"

Wyatt considered what to say. He didn't want to lie to her, but if he told her what he knew, he'd alarm her. "How could it not, darlin'?" An ambiguous enough answer.

"While you were looking for an alternate way to close that room up again," Kendall said, "I was studying the wall opposite me. It seemed as if the inclusions leapt from the stone and put on a show, before they disappeared inside the chamber. I had to follow them."

He caught the sideways glance. "Go on."

The more she explained, the more tense Wyatt became. He didn't like this.

"But what I have on my palm now, that didn't show up until right before you saw it." Kendall bit her lip, then said, "I think it happened when I got my hand wet. It felt like something was searing me, and then those symbols were there."

"How could the water do that?"

"I don't know." Bug shook her head. "Maybe I'm wrong and it wasn't the water, but the pattern wasn't there until after I felt the burning, and that didn't start till my hand got wet."

"Okay, that makes sense." He kept his voice neutral, but he felt grim. Kendall had the mark of High Priestess, but she didn't have the knowledge that went with her powers and she needed it. Not for the first time, Wyatt cursed Zolianna's secrets. She'd shared almost nothing with Berkant about the temple, and most of what he did know were things he'd figured out from observation and inference.

"This thing on my hand, I'm sure it's why I could see the energy web yesterday."

"I agree."

"But how did you know that I could turn the lines off and back on again? And why did you get mad enough to swear in front of me when you saw my palm?"

Damn, he'd known those questions were coming, but he hadn't thought up any good answers. "If you saw something etched deeply onto my hand that didn't belong there, wouldn't you be upset?"

"Yeah, it would scare me." Kendall smiled, but there wasn't any lightness in it. "I'm scared now. This isn't normal."

"I wish I could tell you there was nothing to be frightened of, but I don't think I'd come across too convincing since I'm worried about it myself." No shit he was worried. The temple wanted a High Priestess, but he wasn't letting it have Kendall.

"You never answered one of my questions. How did you know I could manipulate the energy around the fountain?"

Wyatt frowned. Bug wasn't going to let him off the hook. "You had a pyramid on your hand. I figured it had to do with *this* pyramid, so it seemed logical you could control things in here." There, that sounded good.

"I wouldn't have guessed, and you knew that I'd done something to send the thieves running into the room. There was no reason you should have assumed that," she accused.

"If you weren't emotional about the pattern," he told her, "I think you would have come up with the same answer. You know how to turn on the lights and water here, and you were talking about some way to use energy to lock up the houses. All you need to do is extrapolate those talents to things inside the pyramid."

Bug nodded and he breathed a silent sigh of relief. It was a bit hard to tell how much time had passed since they'd been trapped, but Wyatt estimated they'd been on the run for three days. And in all that time, Bug had managed to do what a unit of hostile coalition forces hadn't—

she was making him sweat. Wyatt wasn't lying—not exactly—but if she ever remembered their last life, and if she discovered he'd always known of it, she'd have his ass. And not in a good way.

"I wonder what else I can do?" Kendall smiled up at him and Wyatt wanted to kiss her so damn bad, he nearly bent over to do just that. Shit, he had to keep his mind on getting out of here.

"The possibilities are endless." He settled for returning her smile. "If I think up any suggestions, I'll mention them."

She laughed, her green eyes twinkling, and Wyatt stopped fighting it. He kissed her. Immediately, Kendall kissed him back, and he thought again about how far they'd come in only a few days. If they got out of this alive, then getting trapped in the pyramid was the best thing that ever could have happened.

He had her pressed against the wall, his tongue in her mouth, before he remembered they couldn't risk being unaware of what was going on around them. With a groan, he broke off, but rested his forehead against hers. "I want you, Bug," Wyatt told her. "Don't ever doubt it, but our first time isn't going to be up against a wall, especially when we've got bad guys hunting us."

Kendall flushed red, and he kissed her again before she could get more embarrassed. She wasn't ready to admit they were heading toward becoming lovers, but that was okay. Wyatt knew it was true. "Let's go, darlin'," he ordered.

It didn't take much thinking to realize he couldn't let her stew in silence. Kendall would spook herself, and he wasn't taking any chances, so he searched for some topic to keep her occupied. It wasn't too surprising that the first thing that came to him was the future. "So where do you see yourself ten years from now?" At her sharp glance, he continued, "Will you be finished with school?"

"I should be. I still owe the army two more years, and I'd have to save up a lot more money to do grad school without taking breaks to just work for a while, but even if I did have to stop a few times, I can't see not being done."

"When you have that Ph.D., are you going to teach?"

"I hope not!" she said emphatically, then moderated her tone. "Not that there's anything wrong with being a college professor, but that's not what I want to do."

"Are there any jobs that don't involve teaching?" He knew more about anthropology than he had before meeting Kendall, but it had never been something they'd spent a lot of time on.

"Yeah, there are. More and more nonprofits are hiring their own anthropologists to better serve their constituents, and there are also positions working for the government or even the military. As we go deeper into space, the Western Alliance is going to continue to run into evidence of alien civilizations. Actually, I'd love to have a job like the social scientists stationed here have." Kendall's eyes were filled with passion. "How great would it be to work all around the galaxy studying cultures no one has ever seen before?"

She clasped his hand tightly for a minute, then relaxed her hold, but there was so much excitement on her face that Wyatt wouldn't have been shocked if she shook free and did a little twirl. He didn't share her enthusiasm. "What about friends? What about your mother? And what about getting married and having children of your own? That'll be awfully hard to do if you're flitting around the universe."

Kendall looked at him as if he were speaking Swahili. "My mom hasn't missed a beat since I've been on J Nine, but if she got ill, of course I'd return to Earth for as long as I was needed. As for the rest, well, I've always made friends wherever I've gone, and I'm sure I always will."

"You left out having a family." It was all Wyatt could do to keep his tone even.

"Marriage and two point five children, huh?" Bug rolled her eyes. "I'm not much for living a traditional life. What about you, where do you see yourself in ten years? Still in the army?"

"Yeah," Wyatt said, voice flat, "still in the army. I haven't found anything else I want to do more. My next promotion will take me out of the field, and I'm not thrilled about that."

"Since you just made captain before coming to J Nine, you have a lot of time before that's something to worry about."

He nodded. She was right about that. Wyatt decided to lay a few things on the line. Bug would completely miss what he was really saying—her blinders were firmly in place—but whether she realized it or not, he was stating his intentions. "Unlike you, I do see myself married. Sooner rather than later," he told her. "To a woman I love more than anyone or anything, a woman I would kill for if that's what it took to protect her. And I want kids too, but not right away. First, I want years alone with her, time to simply enjoy my woman."

"You've already met her, haven't you?" Kendall asked, sounding subdued.

Wyatt paused, shocked. Yeah, he'd been kissing her whenever he could, but he hadn't expected her to get it. Maybe it was a sign that they'd come further than he knew. "Yes, I've met her."

"It's Zolianna, right?"

For an instant, he could do nothing but gape at her. Furious, he demanded, "Where the hell did you hear that name?"

Chapter Sixteen

"You're squeezing my hand," Bug complained, and Wyatt relaxed his grip at once.

"Sorry," he apologized, and made an effort to sound more moderate. "You took me by surprise, is all. Where did you come up with the name Zolianna?"

She looked at him oddly. "You said it."

Oh, no, he hadn't. He'd been damn careful not to use it from the instant he'd realized Kendall had no memory of that life. "I don't think so, darlin'. I never bring her up."

"But you did. When you were starting to come around after the oxygen deprivation thing, you said her name."

Wyatt stared at her blankly, then memory hit home. Either right before he'd kissed Kendall for the first time or right after, he must have slipped. Shit, maybe he'd thought he was dreaming, and that he was Berkant. It had happened often enough in his teens, but the timing was terrible, close enough to his kiss with Bug that she would have been hurt by it.

"I'm sorry." Damn, how many more times was he going to need to apologize to her today? "I didn't remember."

Kendall shrugged one shoulder. "That's okay. You were mostly unconscious. But that's why I knew about Zolianna and guessed that she's the woman you love."

"You're wrong. *I* don't love Zolianna." He stressed the *I* as hard as he dared. "She'd make me insane pretty dang fast. She was too passive, didn't stand up when she needed to, but drifted along with events." Wyatt gauged Bug's reaction, and decided to continue. "I want a woman with more fire. A woman who'll fight when something's important to her."

"Who is it then," she asked slowly, "if it's not Zolianna?"

"When you figure it out, we'll talk. Now let's get moving." Wyatt looked over at Bug for a moment and had to press his lips together to keep from growling at her. It irritated the hell out of him that she believed he could kiss her with the intention of having sex and be in love with another woman. The only thing that prevented him from being royally pissed was that he knew her attitude had nothing to do with him personally.

He was still aggravated when they rounded a corner about ten minutes later and hit another dead end. Wyatt did snarl then because he had an excuse, then wished he hadn't when Kendall apologized for making another mistake. "Darlin', don't worry about it, okay? I'm not mad at you, just the situation."

"Maybe you should pick the hallway when we reach a spoke. I still haven't figured out which stones will lead us to an exit."

He was staring at the pattern of concentric circles made from a rainbow of colored gems when her words turned on a light bulb in his brain. "Am I remembering wrong, or have we only hit a wall coming out of a hub of corridors?"

Kendall appeared thoughtful for a moment, then said, "I think you're right. You think this is a key to the maze?"

"Maybe." He shrugged. "It won't help much, though, since we could still pick the wrong hallway." Wyatt lifted her hand. "It's also interesting that your palm buzzes when we see gems on the walls."

"I know." Kendall sounded glum. "I don't understand why."

"Me either, but it's something to think on since there's gotta be a reason."

"I have been thinking about it."

Wyatt started back down the corridor, but he had to tug Kendall to get her moving. "Reach any conclusions?" he asked when she was at his side again.

"Not yet, but you never give me enough time to study the mosaics. Like now, you just pulled me away."

"For a damn good reason—we're being hunted. What do you think our chances would be if we're trapped in a dead end?"

Bug sighed loudly enough for him to hear. "I know, but I'm curious, and the pics on the digicam aren't good enough. It's frustrating not to have time to figure it out."

He understood frustration; he'd been living with it for four solid months. "We'll be stopping for the night soon, and you can study the wall in whatever room we hole up in."

"It won't help," she said. "These corridor patterns are different from what we find in the rooms."

If anyone would know, it would be Kendall, but damn, he hated her ties to the temple. "Once the smugglers are caught, I'll personally escort you back here, and you can study it to your heart's content. Deal?"

With a faint smile, Bug said, "Deal."

* * *

Kendall paced her chambers impatiently. Where was he? Surely, her lover should be here by now.

With a sigh, she slowed. Things hadn't been the same since the first murders outside the walls of their city.

It was unsafe to leave the fortification, but simply being near the walls could be dangerous. And as fear ran rampant, the Guard's lack of progress had led to unrest among the citizens. The people wanted results, wanted to return to their serene existence. But Kendall didn't know whether such was possible even once the murderer was captured. Too much innocence had been lost.

This should make her own situation seem negligible. Truly.

But what would Wyatt say when she told him?

Fear rose, one that had little basis in reality. He'd loved her for decades, just as she loved him. Never would he abandon her, and most certainly not when she needed him most. But even should he stand with her, her situation— their situation—would be difficult. This she knew with certainty.

And it wasn't just this that made her uneasy. Her powers were gone. She had no more ability than the average citizen. Because of her connection to the temple, these ordinary skills had been enough to perform her daily duties, and she'd managed to conceal her loss from others, but it terrified her. Was this why priestesses were supposed to remain chaste? Would her powers return or had she lost them forever?

Nerves drove her to the mirror, and Kendall smoothed her hands down the front of her robe before she froze in place. It was her—she knew it was her—and yet she looked nothing like herself. She leaned forward, but the image reflected wasn't hers. This woman was shorter than she was, and she had much darker, much longer hair.

Dreaming. She was dreaming.

The realization took her partially out of the scene. While most of her remained in front of the mirror, studying her appearance, some of her consciousness played observer, standing at a distance.

Her alter ego resumed pacing, and she felt more of her awareness return to the woman. Perhaps she should contact him again, make certain that he understood she needed him. Kendall paused in front of the calling glass, but surprise held her in place. The piece closely resembled her wind chime. How could that be?

Dreaming. Yes, this was all imaginary. She was creating her reality, so certainly she'd add things that meant something to her like her chime.

She decided not to bother him again. He'd come when he could, she knew that with her entire being. Wyatt had never let her down, and he'd not do so now.

With a sigh, she walked to a wall in her bedchamber. The inlaid gems formed patterns across the stone, and she pressed her hand against a triangle that fit perfectly within the pyramid on her palm. The rock became transparent, allowing her to gaze upon the city she loved. Her temple stood taller than any other building, and she could see all the way to the outside walls.

She lowered her hand to her side and examined what lay before her. In the heart of town, lights blazed, illuminating the night, but near the outskirts—the area closest to the fortification—there was darkness.

It frightened her to the depths of her soul to realize that the guardsmen were continually at risk. They were the ones required to step outside the city to recover the bodies. They were the ones who patrolled the edges of the town, trying to prevent the foolish from lingering. And they were the ones who responded to reports of the killer.

If anything happened to her love, a piece of her would die with him. He was her heart, her very soul.

Kendall pressed her hand against the wall once more and it returned to its usual opacity. She felt his presence then. Turning, she found Wyatt standing there, watching her. Again, she paused. This was Wyatt, she knew that beyond doubt, and yet he too, looked quite different from his usual self. Like her, he was shorter, and his hair brushed his shoulders. His eyes weren't their navy color, either, but a yellow that seemed more catlike than human. She remembered her puzzlement at his appearance in an earlier dream as well.

Dreaming, she reminded herself. Just go with it.

His lips turned up in a smile as he caught her gaze, but she could read the weariness on his face, and she hurried to him. As Kendall put her arms around him, she feared the burden her news would add. Already he was exhausted; could she lay one more problem at his feet? And yet what other choice did she have? He would be angered if she did not share this with him.

Slowly, gently, he kissed her, then simply put his arms around her. "I'm glad you called me," he told her. "I'd have stayed away, kept working, but simply holding you brings me a peace I've not had in far too long."

"It's been almost a full lunar cycle since we were last together, my love." She stroked his back. "I have fruit in the outer chamber. Do you hunger?"

"No, I've eaten. What I need is to hold you." Wyatt eased away far enough to see her face.

"Whatever you need, I freely give to you. I love you." Stepping free of his embrace, Kendall took his hand and led him to the settee. When he was settled, she seated herself beside him, nestling close to his side. She rested her head upon his chest, and her marked hand on his waist, but she didn't truly become comfortable until his arms surrounded her.

For a long time, neither spoke. She had no need to

bombard him with questions; the guard commander regularly updated her. Nor had she a need to fill the silence with idle chatter.

Her fingers flexed at his waist. She was in no hurry to tell him. Closing her eyes, she luxuriated in his closeness. From the warmth of his body, she gleaned strength, contentment, and a simple, basic joy.

"I love you," she told him again, voice barely above a whisper. She needed him to know how dear he was to her.

"As I love you."

Kendall turned her head to meet his lips. Their kiss was slow, soft, an expression of all they felt for each other.

At its end, she snuggled into him once more. The backs of his fingers stroked her cheek, but before she could become too comfortable, Wyatt asked, "You had need to tell me something?"

Relaxation left her in a rush. She knew he was aware of her reaction, that he could feel it in the sudden tension of her muscles, and his own body became taut. Kendall regretted that more than she could say. "Yes, but perhaps it can wait."

"It's bad news?" He put her from him, in order to see her.

She smiled wanly. "I know not; it will depend on how you view it. Even if you do not find it to be unwelcome, it brings with it a set of problems that will not be easy to overcome."

He took both her hands in his. "Tell me."

Gazing down at their linked fingers, Kendall considered her words. While she was pacing, perhaps she should have mulled over the best way to present what she had to say. Instead, she was at a loss for how to broach the subject.

Wyatt squeezed her, and she glanced up at him. "Straight out, my love," he said. "That's the best way."

With a nod, she gathered her courage. "I'm with child." Stunned didn't begin to describe his expression.

Kendall tried to find more words, but her mind went blank. She could do nothing save stare at him expectantly. He wouldn't abandon her. If she had faith in nothing else, she had faith in that.

Perhaps some small part of her, however, had hoped he would be elated at the news. Perhaps that part was mourning that he did not share the happiness that had grown in her since she'd first learned of her condition. Perhaps she had fantasized that he'd draw her near, excitement in his voice as he expressed his pleasure at becoming a father. She could not blame him for his reaction; she could only castigate herself for expecting more.

His hands tightened around hers once more. "You're certain?" Kendall nodded. "How is it possible?" He shook his head before she could speak. "I know you've taken precautions so this would not happen."

Heart in her throat, she explained, "The healer who provided me with the powder died. Natural causes," Kendall added what once would not have needed to be spoken. "I had to be careful whom I approached next, lest our secret be revealed. The time without the elixir was but days. We should have been safe."

"How far along are you?"

Wyatt's countenance had become unreadable, his voice flat, and Kendall had to struggle for an even tone. "Two lunar cycles. I believe I conceived the night of the Covenant Circle."

He nodded jerkily. Covenant Circle was one of the holiest of days. That night he'd come to her chambers and had reached for her over and over, unable to slake his need. It was only later he'd admitted he'd been part of the patrol that had found the bodies of the missing children—thirteen of them, all brutally slain.

Abruptly, Wyatt surged to his feet, striding back and forth across her bedchamber. Kendall wrapped her arms around her waist, hugging herself against the pain wash-

ing through her. He'd never spoken of wanting children. Always, she'd assumed it was because she couldn't give them to him, but that might have been an incorrect belief.

"The timing is not good," he told her.

"I know, but there is no good time for a High Priestess to become pregnant."

He crouched before her, cupping her face between his hands. "I'm aware of that. I meant that the timing isn't good because we cannot leave the city now, not when everyone who does meets their death. Were circumstances different, we could run off tonight and raise our child in the wilderness."

Hope crept into her heart. "You want our babe?"

Fiercely scowling, he told her, "Of course I do. You doubted that I would?"

Leaning forward to close the distance between them, Kendall said, "I thought that you would be happy, but when you acted as you did, I was uncertain."

"My love, how many times have I pleaded with you to leave with me, to live outside the city?"

"Many."

"If my reaction was not what you wished for, I apologize. My unhappiness isn't that we'll have a child; nothing could bring me more joy. The difficulty is this killer." Wyatt released her and returned to the settee, then gathered her on his lap. "We cannot leave the city; we'd be dead in short order."

Kendall nodded.

"And yet we cannot allow anyone to discover your pregnancy. The proscribed punishment for an unchaste priestess is banishment, and at this moment, that means certain death."

It meant more than that. Their book of laws set out that the man who defiled a priestess be flogged in addition to being banished. Given the situation, they could ill afford Wyatt to be incapacitated. Not that anyone, even the brawniest of men, had survived the killer outside their walls.

She wanted to tell him of her loss of power, but Kendall could not. She had already broken her vow of chastity; she would not break the one of secrecy as well. "I can hide my condition for a time. My robes are loose-fitting."

"What of your attendant?" He rested his hand on her belly, his fingers circling over where their child lay.

"I rarely allow her to dress me. If I were careful to always be robed when she arrived, it might work."

After a slow kiss, Wyatt said, "If you could conceal the babe until the murderer is caught, we can leave the city once it's safe. I identified a spot that offers fresh water, plentiful food, and is protected from the worst of the elements."

That gave Kendall pause. "You chose this spot cycles ago, did you not?" she said slowly. "Before you asked me to leave the city with you for the first time."

She didn't need his nod to know she was correct. If only she'd gone with him then, how different things might be. Except if she'd done this, they might have been the first victims of the fiend hunting their people.

"We're agreed then?" he asked. "We're leaving as soon as the killer is caught?"

"Yes," she assured him, settling her head on his chest. "And I'll make certain no one discovers I carry your child."

"It won't be for long. With the entire City Guard working to capture him, surely it will be less than another lunar cycle."

Kendall nodded, believing in his judgment. "I trust you, and I love you with all my heart. Never doubt it."

For the first time since shortly after his arrival, Wyatt smiled; she felt his lips curve against her temple. "I don't. And don't doubt that I love you, as well as our babe. I promise to care for you and our child, to do whatever I must to ensure you're both safe—always."

* * *

Kendall intercepted another glance from Wyatt and sighed. He'd been checking on her throughout the day, but so far he hadn't asked about her preoccupation. She had a lot to think over. That dream had left her unsettled. Embarrassed.

They'd discussed spouses and children yesterday, so it wasn't a huge stretch to explain why she'd dreamt about carrying his baby. But good reason or not, just thinking of it was enough to make her face go hot. Her only consolation was that he couldn't read her mind, because if Wyatt ever found out, she'd die of mortification.

Logic, however, didn't account for everything, and that's what left her uneasy.

Lucid dreaming.

She'd heard the term, but she'd never before experienced it. How cool was it to recognize that she was dreaming while it was occurring? Yet it was so eerie to remember nearly every word, every action, every emotion in last night's episode.

There were a few other things that left her nervous. For one, Kendall now realized that she'd been this other woman in every dream she'd had since they'd been trapped inside the temple. She hadn't noticed at the time, but the certainty was deep inside her. It had been the same with the man who was Wyatt, yet didn't look like him—he'd been in all but one vignette with her as well. These dreams were clearly more than some kind of nighttime entertainment.

Her palm started to tingle, and Kendall guessed they were approaching a spoke of hallways. As they turned the corner, she discovered she was right.

"Which way?" Wyatt asked.

Kendall grinned up at him, amused that he'd asked her despite her record of choosing dead-ends. "I like the corridor at the one o'clock position, so we should probably pick any other hall."

Wyatt returned her smile and said, "You definitely have a point. Eleven o'clock?"

"Sounds good."

Once they'd gone far enough that her palm stopped buzzing, she returned to her thoughts. What if her dreams were a spontaneous regression to a past life? Maybe she was only thinking that because they'd discussed it so recently, but it made sense.

How many times did a person pick up the same dream at a later point? She'd bet almost never. Yet Kendall had gone through incidents in this woman's life as if she were hitting the highlights—sort of an abridged biography.

It also explained why she'd looked different, even though she knew it was her. Past lives, different bodies—it made sense. The very thought was enough to give her heart palpitations. Kendall didn't want this to be a past life. If it was, it meant that Wyatt had been her lover then, and the argument could be made that he was her soul mate. She cringed away from the thought. It wasn't true. It couldn't be.

The notion of a soul mate was a bunch of bull, some fairy tale that ruined lives. The pursuit of a soul mate meant losing her latest uncle. It meant watching her mom cry, and listening to her warnings never to fall in love. It meant moving, a new school and new friends.

Almost everything she dreamt could be explained from the events going on around them now, and if she had her dream dictionary with her, Kendall would bet that the elements she didn't have reasons for would be cleared up as well. She was simply being fanciful. Nothing more.

With determination, she forced the dreams from her thoughts. She needed to keep her mind on practical matters like what to say when they got out of here and approached Sullivan. Since the colonel would be leery if they came across like a pair of raving lunatics, she'd have to remember to stay calm while she made her report. Kendall couldn't afford to be rattled, not by events and not by the man himself. The Big Chill. Yeah, the name fit Sullivan perfectly.

If she didn't want to think that far ahead, there were other sensible things to consider. Food, for instance. They'd had little to eat for six days, and absolutely nothing for the past two. The body could go a surprisingly long time before things became critical, but she knew her own strength and stamina had begun to diminish.

Kendall had her hair clipped back so it didn't touch her face, but she hated that it was so stringy and greasy. Both her body and her uniform stank. Her only consolation was that she'd spent the money to have some of her body hair permanently removed, and she didn't have to worry about stubble anywhere.

Of course, Wyatt wasn't any better off than she was, but he still looked good with a bristly beard and dirty hair.

At least she'd had a few hygiene items in her bag. They'd been able to brush their teeth, although the intimacy of sharing a toothbrush with Wyatt was enough to make her squirm.

To be honest, though, she'd been squirming since that one dream. Kendall didn't know how it was possible she could be this aroused days afterward, but she was. Maybe nothing would put out the fire except an orgasm. And she knew just who she wanted to provide it. Her eyes cut over to Wyatt. The warmth of his hand caused a different kind of tingling in her palm. And elsewhere.

How could she be thinking about sex with him now? Bad enough that they were on the run, but she'd just finished wishing for a shower. She wouldn't want him to touch her while she was this icky. Would she?

"Okay, Bug, what's going on with you?"

Kendall gulped, the sound audible. "What do you mean?"

"The absolute silence is bad enough, but you've been looking at me odd all day. What's the deal?"

Playing dumb wasn't going to work. Wyatt would just keep asking until he got an answer, but she wasn't going to tell him anything she didn't want him to know. "I'm just a little, I don't know, down maybe." It wasn't exactly a lie. "And feeling sorry for myself. You don't want to hear me whine about how I want a cheeseburger with a side of fries or that I want to take a shower so bad I can almost feel the water on my skin."

He eyed her for a moment, but before she could worry that he'd seen through her, Wyatt said, "You haven't complained once during this whole mess. If you want to do it now, I don't mind."

"Maybe you don't, but I do. This thing is my fault anyway, not yours. If anyone has the right to complain, it's you."

That got her one of his slow, sexy smiles. "If I whine, will you kiss me until I feel better?"

Kendall gaped at him. On the surface, what he'd said wasn't that big a deal, but it was the way he'd said it. His manner had been teasing, the sexual undercurrents swirling beneath the words.

"It depends where you want me to kiss you." What kind of imp had grabbed control of her and spoken? Kendall knew *she* would never say anything like that, certainly not in a tone of voice that suggested she'd be happy to drop to her knees and do more than kiss him.

Wyatt's eyes immediately went hot, and she found it hard to breathe. He didn't slow down, but Kendall had this sudden feeling that he was thinking about taking her down to the stone floor. The scary thing was that she wouldn't protest.

Frantically, her gaze darted around, looking for something, anything to say that would take their minds off sex. "Intersection," she reported, voice thick.

For a moment, she thought he was going to ignore her warning, but Wyatt shook his head and took in their surroundings. "We'll keep going straight," he said, and he sounded more choked than she had. Before she could breathe easy again, he added, "Don't think I won't remember what you said." His free hand came up to tip her face to his. "Don't tease, Kendall, because if you offer, I'm not saying no. Got it?"

Before she could do more than wonder over a side of Wyatt that she'd never seen till now, they reached the point where the hallways crossed, and out of habit, Kendall glanced both ways. She didn't know who was more surprised, the two men coming down the hall to her right, or her and Wyatt.

He didn't have to tug her; she was running a split second after spotting the thieves. One of the idiots fired, and she could hear the other berate him before they were out of earshot.

They ran past an open chamber door and around a corner. Kendall could feel herself becoming winded already. Damn. Had to be the lack of food.

She knew the temple dampened sound, but she could swear she heard the sound of the men running after them. "Faster, Bug," Wyatt said, and she dug for more speed. Her small burst lasted until they reached a fork in the hallway. They didn't pause for even a nanosecond before he pulled her to the left.

A stitch started in her side as they ran around a large curve in the hall. Her body didn't appreciate her pushing it harder when it was sorely lacking in resources. Their pursuers were still behind them, and she strained to hear where they were. She couldn't pick up anything, not over her own harsh breathing.

They neared another corner, rounded it, and stopped short.

There, not twenty feet in front of them, gaily decorated in gemstones, was another dead end.

Chapter Seventeen

Kendall saw Wyatt eye the way they'd come, but the fork they'd gone by was too far back—the smugglers had to be past it already—and the last chamber they'd seen was even farther away.

"Get against the wall," he ordered grimly. "In the corner." Drawing his knife, Wyatt positioned himself in front of her, blade in one hand, pistol in the other.

Kendall did as ordered, but wasn't happy about him acting as her shield. As she tried to catch her breath, she looked around wildly for some escape, something they'd missed. She couldn't let Wyatt die, not because of her.

Those men had to be close, had to be, and she wished for some sound cue to let her know how near they were.

She was getting ready to draw her own pistol, to fight beside Wyatt, when she spotted a triangle pattern of stones near her elbow that looked familiar. In her dream, she'd put her hand on this identical thing and the wall had become transparent.

Without hesitating, she laid her marked palm over the

gems. The vibration increased instantly, filling her body with enough energy to make her blood feel as bubbly as champagne.

The wall opened fast, silently.

"Wyatt," she whispered fiercely, "come on!"

He glanced over his shoulder, saw the open wall, but he didn't move. Kendall grabbed him by the waistband of his pants and gave a yank. One tug was all it took to prod him into action, and she released him, darting into the opening. There were no lights burning inside, but she didn't turn them on. Illumination from the hall revealed a matching triangle on the inside, and as soon as Wyatt was in, she put her hand over it.

The wall seemed to be closing much slower than it had opened. Surely, the thieves would reach them before the damn thing shut. She willed it to move faster.

Wyatt stood facing the gap, pistol drawn, prepared to fire if the wall didn't shut in time, and Kendall stared past his shoulder. Her eyes were glued on the corner, waiting for those smugglers to round it. *Hurry, hurry, hurry,* she urged.

The gap continued to narrow, and Wyatt shifted, keeping his weapon trained into the hall until, with an nearly inaudible scraping sound, they were entombed. No sooner did she breathe a sigh of relief when she heard the smugglers outside the wall.

"Where the fuck did they go?" The voice was muffled.

Reaching past her, Wyatt took her wrist and gently removed her hand from the stones. In the darkness, she couldn't see a thing, but he'd remained oriented enough to know where she was.

"They gotta be hiding around here somewhere," the other man said. "We'll find them."

Her adrenaline began to ebb, and Kendall swayed as lightheadedness replaced it. Before she could catch her balance, Wyatt's arms were around her and he held her against him. For some stupid reason, she felt emotion slam into her. He always took care of her, protected her. He'd been willing to stand in front of her and shield her from the bullets as long as he could.

She reached out and hugged him back. One or both of them could have died—her mind circled back to that fact repeatedly. She might have gone to her grave without feeling his body over hers, inside hers, and that loss suddenly was more than she could bear. The reasons to sleep with him were legion, the reasons to play coward seemed as insubstantial as cotton candy. Men like Wyatt Montgomery didn't come around often. He was one in a million and she'd have to be a fool to keep running from him.

"Keep looking," voice number two ordered, but he sounded farther away from the wall now.

Kendall leaned forward, resting her cheek against Wyatt's heart. It was pounding rapidly, showing that for all his outward cool, Wyatt had experienced an adrenaline surge himself. There was something reassuring about that, and she held him tighter.

They didn't move. Of course, since it was dark and she'd been focused on the threat coming toward them, Kendall hadn't looked around before the wall had shut. They could be standing in a room or a corridor—she had no clue—but she wasn't going to turn on any lights. What if the glow somehow seeped into the corridor and alerted the thieves to their presence? Unlikely? Yes. Impossible? No. She was erring on the side of caution.

Holding Wyatt in such absolute darkness made her other senses sharpen. There was the gentle stroke of his fingers running up and down her back, the soft sound of his respiration, and the way her body seemed to fit against his just right. His heat seeped into her and settled between her thighs. God, she wanted him, and she was tired of denying it.

They continued to wait, to listen. The henchmen didn't

give up easily, continuing to search the area for quite some time. And while the two men looked, she and Wyatt waited. Kendall wanted to sit down, but she didn't move, even after it grew quiet. She flexed her fingers against Wyatt's back and indulged herself in a few fantasies while they bided their time.

It had been silent outside for a long while before Wyatt said, "Turn up the lights, Bug, and let's see where we are."

Kendall obeyed immediately, then gasped. She pulled away from him and turned slowly, gaping at the sheer magnificence of her surroundings. White polished marble with the softest dove gray inclusions lined the corridor as far as the eye could see—floors, ceilings, walls, everywhere. About twenty feet away was a pillar so beautifully carved, it was a work of art.

Almost in a daze, Kendall walked forward, her right hand outstretched until it rested against the cool stone of the column. Carefully, she traced the fingers of her other hand along one of the ridges in the pattern and felt herself calm. "Home," she murmured, the word escaping without her consent.

"Let's go." Wyatt's voice was hard.

Shaking off the trance, Kendall looked at him. His face was blank, but something told her he was pissed off. Deciding to ignore his mood, she pointed to the bejeweled wall through which they'd entered. "You don't mean go back out there, do you?"

He scowled. "No. I reckon we have a whole new section of pyramid to explore. Let's see if we can't find an exit in here."

Wyatt took her hand, linking their fingers and drawing her close against his side. There was something possessive about the gesture, and if there'd been another man present, Kendall would have thought he was wordlessly staking his claim to her.

His pace was faster than she would have liked. She

wanted to look around, to absorb every detail, but he
wasn't allowing that. This time, reminding herself that she
could come back later didn't make it easier to walk past
statues and mosaics of gems. Everything here was more
beautiful, more elegant, more perfect than anything she'd
seen before in the temple.

Thank God the thieves hadn't been able to gain access.
She had no proof of this, just instinct, but Kendall would
bet every last dollar in her grad school fund that those
bastards hadn't looted this area of the pyramid. Somehow,
some way, that pattern on her hand was the key into the
inner sanctum, and no one else had it except her. Her lips
curved with satisfaction. She would protect this section
from anyone and everyone—even the Western Alliance
and their social scientists.

No one was desecrating this sacred place.

Wyatt kept his jaw clamped shut so he wouldn't say anything that would either piss Kendall off or ignite her suspicions. The damn temple was calling to her like a siren
song, and though he'd fight for her, how the hell did a
man battle against a pyramid? And she was so blissful to
be here again. Shit.

Berkant had been willing to settle for half of Zolianna,
but Wyatt wasn't that magnanimous—he wouldn't share
Kendall. This life, he was going for broke. He'd either
have everything he always wanted with her or he'd have
nothing.

Already, Wyatt felt her reluctance to pick up her pace.
He never thought it would come to this, not again. Last
time—He gave Kendall a gentle tug to pull her away from
a statue that looked like a lion. Last time, they'd both lost.
Not again.

They reached a large open area. She stopped, and so
did he. There was light coming in, and yet if one looked at
it from the outside, the pyramid was one hundred percent

solid stone. Wyatt put his hands on his hips and leaned back, but it was impossible to identify what produced the fake sunlight. Lowering his gaze, he looked around, taking in as much of the vicinity as he could see.

The atrium had plenty of greenery. The aliens had brought a lot of the outdoors into this building, but only in a controlled, manicured way. For Wyatt, the beauty of nature was untamed, not landscaped, and though he'd been fretting over Kendall the entire time he'd been outside the walls, he'd liked being away from the artificialness of the Old City.

"Come on," Bug said, and this time she tugged him.

For a moment, Wyatt resisted, then decided to see where she was leading him. It wasn't far. Toward the center of the atrium, there was a collection of platforms arranged in an arc. He counted eight that he could see and assumed that the arc was part of a circle and there'd be just as many on the opposite side. Kendall stepped up on one and he followed.

Almost instantly, a stone balustrade rose from the floor and surrounded the edge of the raised dais. When it was at waist height, it stopped, and the whole platform began to rise. Wyatt was ready to grab Bug and leap before they went too high to get off without injuring themselves, but then he realized she was doing it. He could feel her directing the energy, using the same power that operated the lights and water within the Old City.

Elevator. They were on the alien version of an elevator. Curious about how it was engineered, Wyatt leaned over, trying to get a better look below them. They came to a halt, and Bug grabbed his arm. "Don't do that. It's not safe," she told him.

Reluctantly, he stepped back from the railing, and as soon as he was balanced, they resumed moving. Wyatt fought the need to scowl. Kendall hadn't remembered much of anything out in the middle section of the pyramid, but here it seemed to be a different story. There was no way in hell she could have taken one look at the collection of daises and thought elevator.

Bug brought them to a smooth landing and the front banister came down. He was scoping out the place when she exited the platform and moved down the hall. Wyatt scrambled to catch up with her. "Damn it, don't walk off on me like that!"

"Okay," she agreed easily.

Given her absolute calmness, Wyatt felt a bit foolish for getting upset. "Sorry. We need to stick together."

She nodded, but Kendall was already looking past his shoulder, trying to see beyond him, and Wyatt felt his heart skip a few beats. No way was he losing her. He held out his left hand and waited until she finally took it. "Now we can go."

Her palm vibrated continually, but she didn't seem to notice and that bothered him. He didn't want all this strangeness to be so ordinary to her. He didn't want her to slide further into the world of the temple, to discover she liked having powers, and that she wanted them as much—or maybe even more—than she wanted him.

Then she looked at him, gave him a grin that made her eyes light up, and said, "Come on, Wy!"

Damn, Bug was going to make him insane. From time to time, he'd wondered how Berkant could have allowed Zolianna to string him along the way she had—he had an inkling now. Hope. He'd felt it when Kendall had smiled at him and used that endearment. Had his alter ego felt that too? Had Berkant believed that if he just hung in there, he'd win his woman?

Berkant, for a brief moment, had felt satisfaction. Zolianna had agreed to leave the temple and live with him. Wyatt, though, saw it as a hollow victory. It hadn't been love that convinced her to leave; it had been her pregnancy.

They walked past door after door, and Kendall showed

no interest in checking out what lay behind any of them.
She wasn't allowing herself to be sidetracked from some
destination. As much as he hated this newfound confidence, Wyatt knew she had to get them out of the temple.
He'd lost track of the days, but he was sure they were running out of time to warn Major Brody and his family.

Kendall turned right when they reached an intersection,
and quickened her pace down the long hallway. At the end
was a set of double doors.

When she reached them, Bug pulled her hand free and
pushed them open. Then, before he could do more than
grasp the fact that they stood in front of a massive indoor
garden, Kendall grinned at him. "Dinner is served," she
told him, then darted inside the chamber.

He followed slowly. Wyatt almost laughed as she
shifted from foot to foot, clearly wanting him to hurry. As
soon as he reached her side, she tried to skip off, but he
snagged her elbow and drew her back. "Hang on, darlin',
don't be so dang eager."

Her stomach growled, and he did laugh then. Kendall
wrinkled her nose at him. "I'm hungry."

"Me too, but I want to look around."

From his vantage point, it seemed as if this indoor farm
stretched across the entire side of the pyramid. The doors
they'd entered through appeared to be directly in the center. To the left was an orchard filled with different kinds
of Jarved Nine fruit trees. To his right were rows of crops.
In front of him was a large fountain that had a smaller
version of the temple at its midpoint. Water flowed down
from the capstone. All around it was a smooth stone shelf
that matched the ivory marble of the fountain. It was the
perfect place to sit and relax.

Kendall's stomach growled again, and he nodded. She
took off into the orchard and he followed, making sure he
kept her in sight. She picked a variety of fruit, and when

she had her hands full, she handed him her haul. Wyatt had his own arms loaded before she was satisfied.

They returned to the fountain. Kendall set down the fruit she held, then shrugged off her bag and left it on the floor. "You know," he said when he sat near her, "we haven't had food in days. We can't eat too much too fast or else we'll get sick."

"I know." She bent forward and opened the flap on her messenger bag and started stowing some of the harvest inside. "I picked enough to take with us if we want more later."

As they ate, Wyatt tried to figure out how this whole indoor garden was possible. Given the way the Old City took care of itself, he had no problem with the idea of crops growing indoors, but he wondered at their cycles. Shouldn't there have been fruit and vegetables that had ripened over the last three thousand years? Shouldn't they have fallen to the ground and formed some kind of mulch? And yet there was no sign of this. It was as if everything had simply waited to be picked, held in some kind of weird suspended animation. It left him unnerved.

Not Kendall, however. She lay back on the bench, knees bent, feet near his thigh, and happily munched on a purple kahloo as the fingers of her left hand played in the water.

Watching her eat aroused him. She was just messy enough that he wanted to lean over her body and lick the juice from her lips. When their gazes met, she smiled, and Wyatt felt it deep inside his heart. Yeah, she was going to drive him plumb loco, there wasn't a doubt about it.

Kendall finished eating, but she didn't get up, and he was content to watch her. For the first time in days, Wyatt was able to relax. They were safe here; he knew it even if he couldn't recall any details about this section of the temple from his other life.

His body clock told him it was late afternoon already,

and if they stuck to their usual schedule, they'd be stopping for the day soon anyway. Wyatt had plans in mind for the night, plans that involved staking his own claim on Bug—if she were willing.

She plucked her hand from the water. "You're staring."

"Just enjoying the view. You're beautiful, darlin'."

Some of her easiness left her face, and Kendall sat up. "Yeah, right. My hair is beyond gross, my face will probably break out after not being washed for so many days, my clothes are limp and they reek. I'm sure I'm downright gorgeous."

He stood, grabbed the straps of her bag, and held out a hand to help Bug to her feet. "I'll carry this; it's heavy," he told her. "And you are beautiful even when you're a mess. Heck, I'm no better off than you are when it comes to being clean."

"It doesn't bother you, though, the way it bothers me."

"I'm used to it." Wyatt shrugged. "I was out in the field for three months before I came to J Nine. There were no regular showers and no chances to shave or change clothes."

She didn't reply, and Wyatt followed Kendall's lead again. They went past the lift they'd used earlier into a tighter circle of platforms. There were only a handful of the things here. He and Bug were in the very center of the pyramid now, he was certain of it. He stepped on the dais with her and glanced around as she took them to a higher level.

They walked down a hallway, past a series of doors spaced a fair distance apart, then up a flight of stairs. There was another wall covered with gemstones and it was extraordinary—by far the most elaborate, richest-looking inlay he'd ever seen.

Bug looked it over, found the symbol she wanted and opened the wall. As he trailed her inside the room, Wyatt struggled to hide his reaction. He remembered this place from a thousand dreams. They were in Zolianna's suite.

"Let's spend the night here," Kendall suggested.

"Sounds good to me." But his mind wasn't on the question. He was flashing through dozens and dozens of memories, recalling the eternity of nights he'd loved her here.

Taking the bag from his grip, she set it on the low table in the seating area and wandered away. He followed her, coming to a dead stop in the bedroom. There, in the corner, was the calling glass that Berkant had given Zolianna just before she'd entered the temple. Had Bug seen it? Did she notice how closely it resembled that wind chime she had hanging outside her home?

Kendall returned before long, but she seemed oblivious to the textured pieces of glass. "I found the bathroom," she told him with a grin. "I'm going to take a shower, okay?"

"Yeah," Wyatt said thickly, still affected by his thoughts. He cleared his throat. "I want a shower too."

"Why don't you use one of those rooms on the floor below this one? Each has its own bath, and that way you won't have to wait for me. I plan to camp out in there for a while." Kendall smiled at him. "You don't need this," she showed him her right palm, "to enter any of those chambers."

"Makes sense," he agreed, but only because he was positive they were completely safe here.

"Good. I'll leave the hall door open so whenever you're done you can come back inside my rooms."

Kendall danced away, humming under her breath, but Wyatt didn't move until he heard a door deeper inside close. Damn it to hell, this suite belonged to Zolianna, not Bug, and he didn't like that she called this place hers.

* * *

There was one thing Stacey hadn't taken into account when she'd decided to stay with Ravyn and her husband, but she should have thought of it—Alex was as welcome in their home as she was. Agitated, she paced from one side of her room to the other. Oh, sure, Ravyn and Damon tried to run interference for her, but they hadn't told Alex not to stop by and she couldn't ask them to. Because of this, she never knew when she was going to step outside her bedroom and find him around somewhere.

She didn't know how he managed it, since there was no question about the amount of time he was pouring into his job. If he'd been working sixteen-hour days before Cam was hurt, he must be putting in twenty hours or more now. Yet he still had time to stalk her. Alex called it courting—an oddly old-fashioned word—but Stacey thought it more closely resembled a siege.

This bedchamber was her one refuge, but she knew if Alex decided to come in here, nothing would stop him. She supposed she should be grateful he'd allowed her this much space, since it showed respect—if not for her, then at least for his sister and her husband—but Stacey had a feeling that this sanctuary might not last indefinitely. Sullivan played to win, period, and if he had to breach her room to achieve his goal, he'd do it without hesitating. And without caring about the consequences.

He honestly amazed her. Cam had been hurt less than forty-eight hours ago, and it hadn't even been a day before she'd begun to feel like prey. Alex always had a good excuse for his presence. He needed to investigate the crime scene. He needed to ask Ravyn some questions. He needed to talk with Cam. But no matter what he said or did, his focus—his intensity—was squarely on her. It was unnerving, to say the least.

Bemused, Stacey walked to the window, leaned her shoulder against the wall, and gazed outside, but the view didn't hold her attention long—she'd seen the square in front of the so-called royal residence too many times—and her thoughts returned to one of her chief concerns. Who had hurt Cam and why? He was practically a baby, for God's sake! Luckily, there'd been no permanent damage, but a blow to the head could have killed him.

Damon was livid, and whoever had hurt Cam better hope he was arrested—by someone other than Alex—before the boy's father got his hands on him. Or his mother. Ravyn was just as furious.

And Stacey understood that desire to protect, to defend, in a way she never had before. This amazed her too. She hadn't expected to feel so fiercely maternal so quickly, but it was there. She was outraged at what had been done to the toddler, but she knew if it had been her baby, she would be beyond infuriated.

Her stomach growled, and Stacey sighed. She was going to have to risk running into Alex if she wanted dinner. When she realized that she was actually considering skipping a meal to avoid him, she frowned. She wouldn't let him affect her like this; it gave him too much power over her. Straightening her shoulders, she strode from the room.

And lucky her, Alex was camped out in the main gathering chamber. Her heart leapt at the sight of him, and Stacey silently berated herself. She wasn't going to moon over him; she refused. Time after time she'd reached for him emotionally, and he'd never cared enough to reach back. Not even once.

The instant he saw her, he put aside the papers he'd been reading, and stood. "You're ready to go to dinner?" he asked.

Stacey narrowed her eyes. "If you think you're accompanying me, you better think again, Sullivan."

"We can do this the easy way, or the hard way, it doesn't matter to me. You want me to question you here about the night Cam was injured, that's fine. Although as late as it is, the mess hall will probably be closed by the time we're finished."

"Talk about a bunch of cow manure," Stacey accused. "You don't need to talk to me; I didn't even pick up the noise Ravyn heard. You're maneuvering so that I have to eat with you."

Alex's lips quirked up. "Now you can hardly blame me for this turn of events. If you'd come out of your room earlier, I could have questioned you, and there still would have been time for you to go to dinner. This is your own fault."

That smirk ignited her temper, and Stacey struggled to rein it in. If she'd appeared at the very start of the dinner hour, he'd simply have come up with something else. She'd lived with him for three years and knew how fast he thought on his feet.

Right now, he'd narrowed her choices to two: eat dinner with him or face his version of the inquisition and miss the meal. If she tried to push back, he'd counter with something like, didn't she want to help find who'd attacked Cam? Stacey would end up on the defensive and Alex—damn him—would move in slick as spit. Her stomach growled again, loud enough for him to hear. His smirk deepened, and Stacey saw red. "You think this is funny?"

"No, ma'am," he said, looking as serious as if he were at a funeral. Too bad the gleam in his brown eyes gave him away.

She took a deep breath, and counted to ten. It didn't help, but she did reach a decision. "Okay, you want to eat with me, fine, but you better not utter one word that doesn't have to do with Cam, do you understand me?"

"Yes, ma'am."

Stacey wanted to hurt him. No one had ever been able to make her mad faster than Alexander Sullivan, and there were times she knew he relished that ability. But if they fought now, he'd realize how deeply she still loved him and she was darned if she'd give him that satisfaction. Without saying a word, she pivoted and headed for the door. If he wanted to eat with her, he was going to have to keep up.

As they walked across the plaza, Alex said, "I hear you received approval to return to Earth."

"Yes." She left it at that. No doubt he'd seen the entire message, and knew that while CAT Command had granted her request, they weren't thrilled with it. They had, in fact, actually left it up to her whether to come back. *If your professional assessment indicates that the Colonization Assessment Team has no need of representation on Jarved Nine during the military study of the planet, you have permission to return to Earth on the next available transport.*

Obviously, the new director of CAT had a different view of the situation than the previous head. When Alex had first pulled some strings to get her here, Command hadn't been happy because they didn't want ties to the military or their operation. Now, apparently, the new head wanted someone from CAT here and knew the army would never give the okay for Stacey to be replaced. It was clear to her that if she returned to Earth her career would go nowhere fast. It was something she'd have to live with.

Alex held the door of the mess hall for her. As his hand rested on the small of her back, Stacey felt a shiver course through her and sighed silently. Would he always have the power to affect her so strongly? Despite knowing better, she didn't move away from his touch.

"So," Alex said, his voice low, almost seductive, "you didn't hear anything the night Cam was hurt?"

Dazed, she shook her head. Then realizing she was falling under his spell, she cleared her throat. "Ravyn heard something and asked me what that noise was. I told her that I didn't hear anything, but she looked troubled. Then she decided to go check on Cam, just to make sure everything was okay. Which you know since Ravyn told you all this."

"Go on." His face didn't give anything away.

"I stayed in the room, reading, until I heard Ravyn yell. Then I ran to check on what was wrong. That's when I saw Cam on the floor, his head covered with blood."

The line inched forward and Stacey wished it would move faster. She wanted something to do other than stand so close to Alex that she could feel his body heat seeping into her. Stacey edged away from him, but he shifted, and she was right back in the same position she'd been in before.

"What happened next?"

"You know what happened." He stared at her, face impassive, until she said, "Fine, whatever. Ravyn must have used her mental link to talk to her husband because Damon showed up with a team from the infirmary. He didn't want his son moved without being immobilized first. As soon as Cam was secure, they brought him to the doctor to be checked out."

"When you were in the room, did you see anything?"

"Like a fleeing man?" Stacey asked sarcastically, then ditched the attitude, and added, "Sorry. No, I didn't see anything, but I wasn't looking either. My focus was on Cam."

From outside the mess hall came the sound of running feet. Lots of them. Conversations stopped, and about half the people present tensed as the door burst open. Five young women came in, looked around, and one said, "Good, we made it!"

Stacey started to relax, until she identified a member of the group. Tami with an i. The young woman had been a patient at the infirmary the day Stacey had found out she was pregnant. Immediately, Stacey faced forward, hoping to go unrecognized, or at least unnoticed, but she and Alex were at the end of the line and the newcomers were directly behind them. Tami's smile of recognition made

Stacey's heart pound, but it dimmed when the young woman glanced at Alex, and she turned to her friends.

The door to the mess hall opened again, much more sedately, but Alex's reaction was every bit as noticeable as when the women had exploded into the building. When the man came up to them, she figured out why. "Excuse me, Colonel, but I need a word with you. Sorry, ma'am," he apologized.

"Important?" Alex asked.

"Not earth-shaking, sir, but important enough to interrupt."

Alex nodded. "I'll be right back," he told her, and the pair walked about twenty feet away.

"Hi Stacey," Tami chirped the instant Alex was gone.

Stacey nodded, but she didn't want to encourage her. Although he was carrying on his own quiet dialogue, Stacey didn't have a doubt in her mind that Sullivan could hear Tami. When he wanted to, he could follow a good half dozen simultaneous conversations. Of course, he could also tune out anything he didn't want to hear.

"I'm glad you and the colonel are back together! It's like I told Gin, here," Tami pointed to another of the latecomers, "you two just needed to talk in order to work it all out."

Stacey cast a quick glance toward Alex, and almost groaned. Not only did he seem more alert than he had a moment ago, he'd half turned to face her. "How's your burn?" she asked quickly, hoping to change the subject and keep it changed. Tami had bumped into her at the infirmary, scattering the test results she'd been clutching, and Stacey had been slow to react, still in shock from the news. That's when things had gone south.

Stacey hadn't been fast enough to prevent the girl from bending to pick up the papers, or to stop Tami from reading them. Accidentally, she claimed, but it didn't matter. What mattered was Tami knew something Stacey didn't

want her to know. She'd made the young woman promise
not to tell anyone, and Tami had sworn up and down she
could keep a secret, but it appeared she'd discussed this
with her friends. Great. At least it hadn't gone any
further—yet. If it had, Sullivan would have heard something and he wouldn't have calmly escorted her to dinner.
Nope, he would have shown up breathing fire.

"Oh, much better. See?" The girl held out her hand
palm up and pointed to the red mark on her inner forearm. "The blister is gone. But to get back to you guys,
it's—"

Stacey asked the next question that popped into her
head. "Did the doctor think it would scar?"

The woman switched topics without a hitch. "Nah, he
said the discoloration would fade in time, but if I wanted,
we could do a permanent scar-removal thing. Those can
be kind of painful, though, so I'll wait and see if it goes
away on its own."

Finally, the line moved forward, and Stacey all but
lunged for a tray. If she could just fill the thing and get to
a table, she'd be safe.

Tami, though, didn't give up easily. "Gin and I were
talking after we heard you and the colonel broke up. She
thought it was over, but I told her men need a little time to
get used—"

"Vitamin E," Stacey all but squeaked.

"What?"

"Break open a capsule of Vitamin E and rub it on the
burn mark. That's supposed to reduce scarring."

Stacey hadn't realized Alex had finished his discussion
with the other man, and she nearly gasped when he came
up beside her. He looked suspicious, and she guessed it
was because he'd overheard the way she'd continually interrupted Tami.

"Men need a little time to get used to what?" he asked.
Tami was reaching for trays and passing them to her

friends. The young woman was distracted, and from her relaxed manner, Stacey guessed the girl was completely oblivious to who'd asked the question.

Without bothering to glance over, Tami said, "The idea of being a daddy, of course."

Chapter Eighteen

Kendall stared at her reflection in the bathroom mirror. She'd towel-dried her hair, then combed it smooth. Lotions found in a cabinet had a light, spicy scent and made her skin feel silky. In a closet, she'd come upon a skimpy, sexy sapphire-colored nightgown, and it had taken only a second's worth of consideration to decide to wear it. Because she was taller than the original owner, it was barely decent, just covering the essentials, but she didn't care.

It was her eyes, though, that caught and held her attention. Her pupils were dilated, her irises barely more than a ring of green. It didn't surprise her, not when she felt like she was burning up. Even her skin was hot to the touch.

Her plan to relieve her sexual frustration had backfired. The quick orgasm she'd given herself in the shower had left her aching in a way she never had before, and longing for more.

Longing for Wyatt.

Every inch of her felt hypersensitive. Beneath the shimmery fabric, her nipples were peaked, more physical proof of how aroused she was. Kendall pressed her thighs together, trying to find relief, but instead of helping, the pressure made it worse.

Wyatt was out there. She wouldn't have to make the first move; he'd need only a glance to see how fevered she was. All she had to do was walk out of this room, and he'd take over.

It was an irrevocable step, one that would change things between them forever. And one that put their friendship at risk. The reminder did nothing to cool her need. This was what she wanted. Heart thundering, Kendall opened the door.

He was across the room, wearing nothing but a towel around his waist. As she entered, he looked up from the clothes he was folding, then did a double take. Wyatt met her halfway, and she was mesmerized by the fire in his eyes.

Uneasy, Kendall dropped her gaze, and gasped. On his side, near his waist, was a big, ugly bruise. It was a deep purple color and it had to be painful. Kidneys, she realized belatedly. One of those bastard thieves had done this to him! "Wyatt?" she asked, and gently brushed the back of her fingers over the spot.

"I'm okay," he told her, capturing her hand. "I'm more interested in this." He indicated the nightgown. "Are you sure?"

"Yes." She held out her arms in invitation and closed the distance between them.

The feel of his body against hers made her moan. She pulled his head down to hers, and took his mouth. Their kiss was wild, verging on the edge of control, and it wasn't enough. Kendall writhed against him, seeking relief, but Wyatt tightened his grip on her hips to keep her in place. Frustrated, she muttered a complaint against his lips; he ignored it.

She explored the warm skin of his back, ran her fingers over his hard muscles. Part of her couldn't believe she was doing this with her best friend. Another part of her couldn't believe she'd waited this long. Nothing had ever felt so right in her life. She sighed with pleasure as their tongues dueled.

No matter how much they touched each other, it wasn't enough. Desperate for him, Kendall reached for the knot at his waist, undid it, and pushed the towel to the floor.

Wyatt stiffened in surprise, and much to her dismay, lifted his head from hers. "Kendall?"

"You're moving too damn slow."

"I wanna make sure you enjoy it too, darlin'," he said, drawl thicker than she'd ever heard it before.

"Wy, look at my eyes. Do you see how hot I am?" He nodded, the movement jerky. "I don't need a lot of foreplay." Kendall reached out, and curled her hand around his shaft. "I need this. I need *you.*" She stroked him until his hand covered hers, stopping the movement. "Are you going to stare at me, or are you going to get me naked and make me scream?"

He smiled, and his hands slid down her hips, under the night slip. When he discovered she wasn't wearing anything beneath the tiny scrap of material, his grin became feral. He reached for the hem and lifted the garment over her head. As soon as her arms were clear, she took a step forward to close the gap again, but he shook his head. "No, don't move. I wanna look at you."

For the first time, Kendall felt self-conscious. She was athletic, not curvy, and she worried he'd be disappointed. But she didn't have to wonder long; the expression on Wyatt's face reassured her. He liked what he saw. A lot.

With the relief came her own curiosity. She allowed her eyes to roam. His chest and shoulders were broad, muscular, sexy as hell, and so were his arms. He didn't have much chest hair, but it gave her a better view of his gorgeous pecs. His dog tags rested against his sternum, and Kendall became aware of her own tags hanging between her breasts. Nervously, she started to reach for them, but forced herself to keep her hand at her side. In order to forget she was standing there naked, she focused on him again. Wyatt's waist was narrow, the muscles of his abs perfectly delineated. Her gaze drifted lower, and she found herself staring at his erection.

His whole body was beautiful, but that part of him was a work of art. He was big, thick. She lost her breath at the sight, and became even wetter at the realization that she was going to have Wyatt deep within her. Soon.

"If you want to look at me some more, could you do it later?" Kendall reached for his hand, pulled him toward the bed. He didn't protest. When the backs of her legs hit the edge, she released him and scooted over to the middle.

He joined her and the mattress gave slightly under his weight. When they lay torso to torso, she reached for him again, but Wyatt caught her hand. "No. You're not rushing me. I have things I wanna do."

As he kissed her, she could feel his shaft pressing into her belly, feel the moistness at its head. Since he held her wrists captive, she shimmied, caressing him with her body. Groaning, he moved his mouth to her throat, bit the pulse point, and licked at the spot as she gasped. His whiskers were rough against her skin, but she didn't say anything. He'd stop if she did.

As she breathed in sharply, her fingers dug into his back. The smell of soap teased her, but beneath it was Wyatt's scent. Wyatt. Her chest ached from the sheer joy of lying with him. It was so much more than she'd expected.

"Dang, Kendall, you're gorgeous. I shoulda told you that." Wyatt took a nipple into his mouth, teased it with his teeth and tongue until she wriggled, then he moved to the other. He had her moaning before he raised his head and hovered over her, face intense. "I'll never get enough of you, enough of this."

He kissed her mouth, her throat, ran his tongue around

her navel, and worked his way lower. His fingers separated her folds, and Kendall raised herself up on her elbows to watch Wyatt stare at her. As if feeling her gaze, he looked up and licked his lips. She moaned softly with arousal before it dawned on her how exposed she was. Immediately, she tried to close her legs, but his shoulders were in the way, keeping her open. Another moan escaped, this one from embarrassment, but it quickly changed as he dropped his head and began to tease her with his mouth.

Her first orgasm slammed into her. Wyatt held her hips steady, but he didn't stop. She felt his tongue delve deeper, tasting her, and Kendall whimpered.

She buried her hands in his hair, holding him to her. The second time she came was every bit as intense as the first. She sobbed his name as she arched, but it wasn't enough, damn it, no matter how good he was, his mouth wasn't enough.

"No more," she begged.

He shifted his body over hers, his hips moving between her splayed thighs. The feel of his erection pressing against her brought another whimper.

As he kissed her, she could taste herself on his lips, his tongue. "No more foreplay, Marsh. I need you now."

Wyatt froze, raised his head, and the expression on his face was far from loverlike. "My men call me Marsh," he told her harshly. "You don't, especially when we're in bed. Got it?"

Kendall nodded.

"What do you want?" he asked.

"You."

"Try again." He nudged her with his tip, and she sucked in a sharp breath as sensation careened through her.

"Wyatt. I want you, Wy."

Satisfaction eased the tension in his face, and he reached between their bodies, guiding himself to her entrance. Kendall held her breath as his broad crown started to penetrate her. Her head fell back, her eyes slid half shut, but she couldn't stop looking at Wyatt as he entered her.

He moved slowly, and Kendall savored every centimeter. When he was about three quarters of the way, she raised her legs, and wrapped them around his waist to let him drive deeper. She wanted all of him, as far as he could go. More than want, it was need, yearning. It was as if he were part of her, a part that had been missing for too long, and at last she was whole again.

Wyatt slid completely into her, then went still. His navy eyes shone with an intensity she couldn't remember seeing from him before. This was more than sex, she realized, but before she could think about it, he grinned.

Kendall's breath caught. Wyatt Montgomery was beautiful when he smiled. "Why are you waiting?" she asked.

"I haven't had sex in more than seven months. I don't want to come too soon."

"If you're too fast," she told him, winding her arms around his neck, "you'll just have to do me again."

His first thrust was almost hesitant, but the second was hard, and Kendall groaned her appreciation. That's all it took to incite him and she lifted her hips to meet his. As primed as she was, it didn't take her long. With a keening moan, she came before he did. Wyatt pushed into her faster, and then he was coming too, prolonging her own orgasm.

It seemed to take forever before she could surface from the oblivion that followed the ecstasy. Wyatt lay atop her, but she found the weight of his body welcome. Kendall lightly stroked his back and shoulders.

For the first time in days, she was at peace, her arousal quenched. But it was more than the physical satisfaction. It was being with Wyatt this way—the man she laughed and played with, the man she could share anything with. Her best friend.

Bracing himself on his elbows, he kissed her slow and deep. With obvious reluctance, he pulled out and rolled to her side, his arm going around her waist to keep her close. As she lay there, cuddling with him, Kendall realized something. Her heart stopped, and when it resumed beating, it had lodged itself in her throat. "Wy, we didn't use birth control."

Wyatt heard the panic in Bug's voice, and tightened his hold before she could leap out of bed. For a moment, she struggled, then collapsed against him. "Shh, darlin', it's all right."

"How can you say that? Damn, I don't have my calendar in my bag, but the timing can't be as bad as I think. It can't be!"

Reaching up, he lightly pinched her chin between his thumb and forefinger, raising her face till their gazes met. "Kendall, do you think I'd risk you? I had the shot; we're clear."

Bug blinked and he saw some of the fear leave her eyes. "You had the male birth control shot?"

"Yep." Wyatt almost grinned over her need for absolute clarity, but knew she wouldn't appreciate it, not when she was barely calming down. Part of her terror over a pregnancy was based in their last life; he understood that even if she didn't.

She clutched at his shoulder. "When? When did you get it?"

"The morning after I met you." Let her deal with that bit of truth. "It's good for another two months, so you've got nothing to fret over."

Kendall sagged against him, and Wyatt gathered her close. "Thank God," she muttered against his chest.

"I know you want to go to grad school; I want that for you too, and I'd never do anything to mess it up. Got that?"

"Yeah, I got it." She eased back, and smiled at him. "Thanks, Wy. I wasn't thinking, not until it was too late. I'm glad you were on top of things."

Wyatt looked down to hide the laughter in his eyes over her unintentional double entendre and found himself fascinated by the contrast between his tanned chest and the paleness of her breasts. Damn, he and Bug looked good together. It still seemed beyond comprehension that he was finally with her this way. He was half afraid he'd wake up and discover it was nothing more than another dream.

When he raised his eyes again, he said, "You don't need to thank me. If I was lucky enough to get you in bed, I didn't want you changing your mind because we didn't have something handy to prevent conception."

Her smile dimmed, and she cleared her throat. "You really wanted to have sex with me for the last four months?"

"No," he corrected, "I wanted to *make love* with you for the last four months."

It was no surprise to see her nerves return, but Wyatt had the urge to curse anyway. Kendall didn't want to hear this, but he wasn't backing off this time. Of course, he wasn't going to push either. Not yet. They'd come a long way in a few days, and Bug needed time to assimilate the changes. He'd give it to her.

"You know what I was thinking earlier when I was cleaning up?" she asked, and from her tone of voice, she was done being serious.

"What?" he replied, going along with the change in topic.

"That it would be fun to get wet with you. Interested in joining me in the shower?"

"Lead the way, darlin'."

She rolled out of bed, and he followed. Wyatt loved the fact that Bug showed no sign of self-consciousness as they wandered naked into the bathroom. That said something to him because he knew she was pretty modest.

Trust. Sweet lord, the kind of trust this took for her humbled him.

He let out a low whistle when he saw the chamber. "This is a palace, not a bathroom," he told her.

"It is something, isn't it?" Kendall grinned. "You should see the shower. It's big enough for an orgy."

As he looked around, memories of Zolianna poured back. He forced them aside. He was Wyatt now, and this was Kendall. Those other two people had no place here, not anymore.

Bug came over, and leaned into his side. "I've never seen marble this color before, not anywhere."

"Me either," he said thickly, but he didn't give a rip about some stone, not when he had Kendall's body pressed to his.

"You're not interested at all, are you?"

"Whatever gave you that idea?" he teased, knowing full well that she'd noticed his erection.

She laughed, and said, "Let me get us some fresh towels. Then I'll take care of this for you." Bug gave his cock a quick stroke, spun away, and headed for one of the walls. He watched her press her palm against it, saw the stone around her hand light up, and a door slide open. When Kendall bent over, he forgot all about hidden doors and the imprint on her palm.

When she turned back and saw his condition, she teased, "Gee, soldier, it really has been a long time for you."

"You don't know the half of it. You gonna keep lolly-gagging or are you gonna offer a little aid and comfort?"

Putting the towels down on a nearby chair, she sashayed toward him and Wyatt had to swallow a groan. He never would have guessed Bug would be such a tease. She didn't stop until her breasts pushed firmly into his chest and her arms were wound around his neck. Her kiss was openmouthed and hot.

"What do you say," she punctuated each word with a short kiss, "to a quickie before we get in the shower?"

Wyatt had hold of her hips, and he pulled her closer as he ground himself against her. "Darlin', I say I'm one lucky son of a gun." They didn't stop kissing. "What would you say if I asked you to brace yourself on the vanity?"

For an instant, she froze, and he wondered if he'd pushed her too far; he knew she didn't have much experience. Before he could get too worried, Bug stepped away, and leaned forward, arms supporting her body on the countertop, her feet shoulder-width apart. "Like this?" she asked, looking back at him.

"Yeah, just like that." He wasn't going to last much longer now than he had in bed with her. "How much foreplay are you needing this time?"

Kendall laughed, and tried to push her hair off her face. It fell back where it had been. Giving up on that, she said, "None. Seeing you naked got me raring to go."

"Definitely a lucky son of gun." Wyatt came up behind her and entered her slowly, unwilling to take a chance on hurting her. She hadn't been lying, though; she was ready for him. Taking hold of her hips, he began moving in and out of her.

He could see her face in the mirror, and Wyatt watched Kendall as he thrust and withdrew, memorizing every expression. As revved up as he was, one thought never left his mind—he was making love to the woman he planned to spend the rest of his life with. Hell, he planned to spend all his lives with her.

That idea was every bit as arousing as Bug's small gasps and moans. Damn, he really wasn't going to last long. He slid his hand between her legs, and found where her pleasure was centered. She arched her neck as he caressed her. Wyatt knew from the look on Kendall's face that she was coming before he felt her squeeze him and that was all it took to push him over the edge.

Wyatt poured himself into her, his body shuddering. Kendall, he thought, this is Kendall. And then he couldn't think at all as sensation overwhelmed intellect.

When he regained awareness, he realized he was leaning over Bug, his hands barely keeping his weight off of her. He looked up and noticed she was watching him in the mirror, much as he'd observed her. Their eyes met. "You're sexy when you come," she said, one side of her mouth quirked up.

He grinned, then leaned forward to press a kiss to her shoulder. "Hand to God, as soon as I can find some self-command, I'll make love to you the way you deserve."

"There's nothing wrong with the out-of-control version—it's damn good. But do you think you could let me up? This position isn't all that comfortable."

"Sorry," he apologized. He straightened and stepped back, but not far. If Kendall needed help, he'd be there to provide it. She pushed herself upright using the vanity for leverage, turned to him, and brushed her hair out of her face. For a moment, they stared at each other: a communion of souls. It was only then that it dawned on him that the hole he'd felt inside him his entire life was filled. Awed by that realization, he started to tell her.

"Ready for that shower?" she asked, before he could get a word out. Without giving him a chance to answer, she tugged him along, and Wyatt wanted to groan. Damn it, after all this, she was still pulling back when things turned emotionally intimate. If she wouldn't let him tell her, he'd have to demonstrate.

As the water sluiced over them, Wyatt reached for her. "No," Kendall said, "it's my turn. I've hardly been given the chance to touch you. Now you stand still and let me explore."

There was a decanter filled with soap. Bug rubbed her

hands together until it foamed, then ran her palms over his body. She stroked him everywhere, his back, his chest, his thighs. He wondered whether she realized how revealing her gentle touches were.

He had an erection—again—long before she found her way to his cock. She made a little hum of pleasure, and he jerked in reaction.

Kendall grinned and dropped to her knees in front of him. When she looked up, his legs buckled and he had to lock them to keep from hitting the floor. Her expression made his heart clench. His Bug, his woman, his love. Before he could savor the emotion, she used her soapy hands to stroke him, and then let the water rinse the suds away.

She didn't stand. And as he gazed down at Bug, her mouth level with his hard-on, Wyatt didn't know whether to pray she took him between her lips or hope to hell she didn't. As he tried to decide what to do, she leaned forward and pressed a kiss on his tip. He was sunk, Wyatt knew it. Fists knotted at his sides, he struggled to hold on to his control. If Bug wanted to explore him, he'd let her—even if it killed him.

Kendall ran her tongue around his crown, then licked her way down his shaft. He groaned as she went lower. Wyatt would bet the bank that she'd never done this before, but he didn't care because it was Bug. She laved her way back to his tip.

"Stop teasing," he growled, unable to prevent the words from escaping. She froze, and it took him a minute to realize that she wasn't entirely sure what he meant. He could read it on her face. "Take me in your mouth. Suck me. Please."

Without a bit of finesse, she did, but Wyatt wouldn't trade her inexpert attentions for the best blow job he'd ever received. The sight of Kendall's mouth wrapped around him drove him wild, and it didn't take long to smash his control. Again. "Darlin', I'm gonna come," he warned.

She didn't back off. Kendall stayed on him, her mouth and hand moving until he finished.

"Damn, Bug, I'm sorry."

"Why?"

And as she looked up at him, honestly bewildered by his apology, something dawned on him. She'd swallowed.

His legs did give out then. Kneeling in front of her on the floor of the shower, Wyatt gathered her to him, and held her close. "I'll explain it to you later," he promised. "Right now, it's my turn to touch you, and I can probably last longer than about two minutes." He smiled. "I hope."

Pulling her to her feet, Wyatt mentally turned off the water and helped Bug out of the shower. Her legs were shaking so badly, he didn't know whether she could stand on her own, but she rallied quickly, and they dried each other, using the towels as weapons in their war to arouse the other. And they laughed. That was the best part as far as Wyatt was concerned.

Kendall challenged him to a race. She beat him to the door, nudging him aside with her hip, but he had longer legs, and got to the bed first. Together, they yanked the blankets back, and dove beneath them. Still laughing, he kissed her, then pulled back. "This time," he said quietly, "I'm going to do you right."

He went slowly, adoring her, worshiping her with his hands, mouth, lips, and teeth. Kendall. His woman.

She didn't try to rush him or take charge. Instead, she gave herself over to him, and Wyatt felt his heart clench. This required even more trust than displaying her body.

Later, after they were both sated, he cuddled her close. As they exchanged kisses and gentle caresses, Bug spoke and drove a blade into his heart. "That woman you love is lucky."

Pain shot through him, followed by an anger deeper than anything he'd ever experienced. She was deliberately blind, and he was fucking sick of it. "You haven't figured it out yet, despite everything we've done? You know me; I would never screw around on someone I loved." He leaned over her, so livid, his eyes were no doubt shooting flames. *"You're* the woman. I love you, Kendall."

Chapter Nineteen

The pathways were filled with citizens going about their business, but the energy of the city was far from idyllic. Kendall had never before felt such mental chaos, such terror from the residents. Yet at the same time, she viewed everything with a level of disassociation that left her wondering until she realized she was dreaming again. With a shrug, she let herself be sucked back into this other reality.

In certain quarters of the city, there had been riots, fistfights, and the Guard found its time splintered between trying to find the murderer and keeping peace among their own population.

As she strolled through the plazas and streets, she studied her people. She was without her personal guard or cortege. Kendall felt little unease despite the high tension and flaring tempers.

She'd frequently made this journey between the temple and Kale and Meriwa's residence. Always there were meetings. She'd seen more of the lord and lady in the last five lunar cycles than she had since becoming High Priest-

ess. She consulted with them, their guardians, their advisors, and the Guard Commander. Yet everything they'd tried had failed to end the killings.

This day, she'd made a suggestion that had shocked all present into silence. Kendall had recommended that the lord and lady send the citizens back to their home world.

Never before in the history of their people had a colony returned to its planet of origin. Kendall, however, did not see how they had any choice. How many more must die? They would all have to give up the only home they'd ever known, but they would be alive. After the murderer was captured and dealt with, they could come back.

Kale and Meriwa had been incensed. They'd learned that the killer was an alien stranded on this planet by his own people because he'd repeatedly committed mass murder. The lord and lady had also discovered that the killer believed he was honoring his goddess with the sacrifice of sentient beings.

Kendall tried to comprehend such thinking, but could not.

As she entered the square at the rear of the temple, her eyes naturally strayed to the Guard headquarters for the quadrant. She drew to a halt as she spotted Wyatt standing at the front of the building, talking to a handful of his men. How handsome he was, and how she loved him. Their babe kicked, as if realizing his father stood near, and it was all Kendall could do to prevent herself from rubbing her belly in response.

Her pregnancy was advanced, and her robes would be unable to conceal her state much longer. Were she and Wyatt to be expelled from the city, they—and their babe— would die. There would be no leniency from the lord and lady, and two against this killer—

Someone bumped into her, causing Kendall to lose her balance. The man put an arm around her to prevent her from falling, apologizing profusely for his inattention.

When he went still, she knew he'd felt the swell of her child.

"My lady?" he asked, voice incredulous. And as he turned her to face him, she saw confusion, agitation, disbelief, and other emotions she couldn't identify. Before she could find words to diffuse the situation, anger—nay, fury—mottled his complexion. Roughly, he tore open her robe. The clothes she wore beneath did nothing to hide her pregnancy.

"This," he called to those around them, "is what has caused our curse!" Anger radiated from him. "Our High Priestess has sinned against Heru, and he is punishing us for her wickedness!"

Disbelief held her in place. Their religion did not teach such doctrine, yet clearly this man's words had found resonance with the people. They instantly clustered around her.

"That is not true," she called, speaking loudly to be heard above the angry murmurs. "Heru is love, not vindictiveness. He does not punish—"

"Silence, harlot!" a woman shouted.

"You are not fit to speak the name of Heru," a man accused.

Another man pushed her, and she stumbled into someone behind her, who pushed her back toward the center. Zolianna—Kendall realized in this life she was called Zolianna—tried to find words to calm the men and women before the situation became even more unstable. "Please," she said, wishing desperately for her powers back. "Do not take action which will shame you and our people."

"You're the one who's shamed us," another woman shouted, "and brought this evil down upon our heads!"

Zolianna found herself fending off slaps and punches. When a rock hit her, she froze, almost unable to fathom such behavior. The second stone nearly hit her abdomen and she fought harder. She could not allow them to kill her babe, she couldn't!

Then she saw him, her love, shoving his way through the mob. "No," she called. "Do not!" But either Wyatt— no, his name was Berkant—did not hear her or he chose not to heed her warning.

He put himself in front of her, shielding her as best he could with his body. "Desist," he ordered. "Leave this woman be. Hurting her will not stop the murders."

A roar of outrage rose from the throng. "This whore has sinned, and brought the scourge upon us. Stand aside, guardsman, and let us end this abomination."

Zolianna knew not who had spoken, only that the voice was male. They were going to kill her, and they'd kill Berkant as well if he did not stand aside. "Leave me," she told him. She could not bear the thought of him dying with her.

"Never," he told her. "I promised I would always protect you and our babe, and so I shall."

What was he thinking? Frantically, she looked past him, skimming her gaze over the people standing nearby. As she'd feared, his claim of fathering her child had not gone unheard; word spread in an angry buzz, and the mob became frenzied.

Zolianna could not begin to guess where they'd found so many stones, but the supply seemed nearly endless as they were hurled at them. She was hit time after time, as was Berkant. He continued to shove at the masses, as if trying to clear a path through the crowd that would allow them to retreat.

If she didn't need all her strength to remain on her feet, she would have told him it was pointless, that there would be no escape. These once-peaceful men and women would either kill them or drive them out of the city to be killed by the murderer. They would not be allowed to slip away.

The mob grew. She saw Berkant stagger, saw the blood running from multiple places on his head, from his body, and wanted to cry. This was her fault, her fault! If only she'd stood up at fifteen seasons and told the High Priestess that she was not innocent, the ostracism would have been a small price to pay to avoid this moment.

Sunlight bouncing off the temple's capstone blinded Zolianna, but before she could raise a hand to shade her eyes, pain shot through her abdomen, and she doubled over. There was a gush of moisture, and she looked down to see her skirts sodden with blood. Her baby! Berkant's baby!

The sight of her child's life flowing from her body impelled the crowd to a new level of madness. It was impossible to fight, impossible to protect herself or Berkant.

He fell, and she caught him, clutched him as she sank to her knees. She was reeling, her own blood streaming into her face. Zolianna blinked to clear her vision and looked into his eyes. She saw Berkant's soul leaving his body. "No!" she cried. "No."

Blood. There was so much blood. It soaked her clothes, pooled around them. Not just her baby's blood, but Berkant's and her own.

"I love you, Zolianna. Through all eternity."

"And I love you, always. Always," she added in a whisper as his body went lax in her arms.

She wanted to cry, wanted to wail over the loss of her child, the loss of her love, but she had no tears. Zolianna bent her head to his and waited for the mob to close in, waited for her own death. With everything she loved gone, she had no more will to struggle against them.

It didn't take long before the crowd surged forward. Zolianna barely felt the blows—her body, her very soul, had become numb. And as her own spirit started to leave her physical self, she murmured one word. "Berkant."

* * *

Kendall awoke with a sob. Damn him!

"Bug," Wyatt said, without a trace of sleepiness in his voice, "what's wrong?"

"What were you thinking?" she demanded. "There was nothing you could do to stop them! Why did you push your way into the middle of that mob and try to protect me?"

"You'd have me stand back and watch them kill you?"

"Yes! At least then you would have been alive." Kendall got out of bed and paced the room a few times, trying to force the shakiness, the absolute terror, from her body.

Wyatt caught her on a pivot, holding her arms as he glared down at her. "I'd vowed to protect you, to protect our child. I could no more idly stand by and allow them to stone you to death than you could have let them do the same to me."

"There were too many of them. You had no chance!"

"I was a member of the Guard, trained in negotiation."

Kendall shook her head emphatically. "You can't negotiate with a mob."

"No, but we came from a culture unaccustomed to violence. It shouldn't have escalated to murder. Their actions should have shocked them back to reason."

"You're talking in circles," she accused. "First you say you couldn't let them stone me to death, then you say the horde should have seen sense. Which was it, Wyatt? What were you really thinking to put your life at risk?"

His eyes were molten with his anger. "I wasn't thinking beyond you. I loved you more than anything or anyone else in the world, and I would dare anything to keep you safe—then and now."

"You died in my arms," Kendall accused. "Our child was already lost, and I held you as you died. Did you have any idea what that did to me? To know I was to blame?"

"You weren't at fault."

"I was! If my pregnancy hadn't been discovered—"

"The mob killed us—you, me, our baby—you were not responsible, they were."

Kendall opened her mouth to rebut, then felt the blood drain from her face as their argument registered. She'd never told Wyatt about her dreams, had never mentioned her suspicion that she was regressing to a past life. He should be confused, wondering why she was mad at him when he hadn't done anything. "How the hell do you know what I'm talking about?" she challenged.

The expression that crossed his face told her clearer than words that she'd caught him. "How long?" Kendall asked. He released her, took a step back, but she followed.

"Now, Bug—" Wyatt said, trying to calm her, but she interrupted him before he could continue.

"How long have you known about Zolianna and Berkant?"

He grimaced.

"Wyatt?"

"All my life," he admitted, voice quiet.

For a moment, Kendall could only stare at him. He'd always known about that past existence. She wasn't sure she wanted to ask this next question, but at the same time, she had to know. "And when did you realize that I'd been Zolianna?"

After a pause, he said, "The night we met."

Kendall felt a pain start in her chest, and for the first time, she realized that she was naked, that he was too. Moving past him, she grabbed the nightgown from the floor and pulled it over her head. She couldn't bear being vulnerable in front of him, not any longer, not when he didn't care about her, Kendall. He wanted Zolianna.

A gasp escaped as she recalled he'd even referred to her as Zolianna the first time he'd kissed her. He'd been half conscious, but it hadn't been her he desired. No, he'd called for her alter ego, someone she hadn't been in thousands of years.

Taking a deep breath, she tried not to think about the fact that she was wearing Zolianna's clothes, that the priestess had donned this very garment to drive Berkant wild. As she'd regressed to—and relived—her death, Kendall had gained full memory of that other life.

Slowly, reluctantly, she turned back to Wyatt. "I am not," she enunciated every word carefully, "Zolianna."

"I know that."

"Do you?" Kendall asked coldly, but then ice was freezing her from the inside out. "You only became my friend because of who I'd been. Were you ever interested in *me?*"

"Damn it, Bug, I love you."

"You love Zolianna. I just happen to be her reincarnation."

Kendall saw the heat flare in his eyes. "Wrong. *Berkant* loved Zolianna. I, Wyatt Montgomery, love you, Kendall Thomas."

"Sure," she scoffed. "Tell me something. Would you have invited yourself to eat with me, would you have included me in so many of the things you did, if you didn't know who I'd been?"

He hesitated, and that was all the answer Kendall needed. Whirling away, she tried to escape him, but Wyatt caught her by the arm. "I was hopped up from three months in the field, and I wasn't fit company for anyone," he explained. "That's why my men and I weren't socializing right then. So yeah, maybe I wouldn't have moved that fast if I didn't recognize you, but I would have gotten around to it eventually. I was attracted before I had a clue what kind of connection we had."

"Why should I believe you?"

"Because I've never lied to you."

Her voice was low, intense, nearly shaking as she told him, "You lied to me every day, every single time we were together, and you didn't mention that we'd shared a past life."

"What the hell was I supposed to say? You didn't remember a fricking thing!" Wyatt tugged her closer, scowled at her. "And it didn't take me long to figure out the surest way to scare you off was to mention we were lovers in another life." He gentled his tone. "I didn't want to lose you."

Kendall shrugged off his hold and turned. Something, though, caught her eye, and she slowly walked toward it. A round piece of crystal held strings of colored rectangles as they flowed downward. She laughed, not an amused sound, but one of bitter recognition. This calling glass had been a gift from Berkant, and it closely resembled her wind chime.

Although it had been years, Kendall still recalled how excited she'd been to see it in the store window. Since each piece of the chime was handcrafted, the price had been exorbitant. She'd certainly never spent that much money for one item in her entire life, yet she'd begged the reluctant store owner to hold it for her. As soon as she'd gotten a grudging agreement, Kendall had raced to her bank and raided her savings account.

Not once had she regretted the purchase. It had been her dearest possession, the only thing she owned that meant anything to her. Now she knew why.

"You recognize this, don't you?" she asked Wyatt, swiveling her head to look at him over her shoulder.

"Yeah."

"How much do you remember?"

He closed the distance between them again, but she didn't move. Kendall refused to run like a frightened rabbit. His hands closed gently over her shoulders, his naked groin nestled against her bottom, and just that fast, her desire for him surged back. She wanted to curse. How could she still need him?

"On a percentage basis," he said, his mouth next to her ear, "I probably recall as much from that life as I do from this one."

Her nipples peaked from the feel of his warm breath against her skin, and damn him, she knew he'd noticed. Using her elbow to nudge him back, Kendall started to pivot away, but froze as another realization crashed into her consciousness.

"What is it?" Wyatt asked, his hands stroking down her sides to comfort her.

"I've been dreaming about our deaths off and on since the night I met you. I couldn't remember anything about the nightmares, though, except for the blood, and that flash off the capstone." Kendall shook her head. "It explains why the fear I woke with didn't go away until I saw you."

His hands tightened at her waist. "Those would be the mornings you showed up at my house and invited me to breakfast?" Kendall nodded. "Figures," he muttered, sounding unhappy.

She stepped away from him, breaking his hold, and put the room between them. "That was a hell of a secret to keep," Kendall accused. "It gave you an unfair advantage over me."

"How much do you remember now?" he asked.

"On a percentage basis," Kendall said, echoing him, but with a hint of sarcasm, "probably about the same amount you do."

"Then you should realize that knowing you were Zolianna gave me no advantage at all." Wyatt crossed his arms over his chest, obviously unconcerned about his nudity. "You're nothing like her, Kendall. You don't think like her, you don't act like her."

"Yet you fell for her the instant you looked into my eyes."

"That's complete bullsh—crap, and you know it," Wyatt said, heatedly. "All you have to do is think back over the time we spent together, and be honest about it. Yeah, I was interested from the get-go, but I had to get to know you, I had to fall in love with *you* the same way any man falls for any woman. I didn't take one look and skip over the important stuff."

"Right."

"Damn it." He strode across the floor and went toe-to-toe with her. "I knew you'd be looking for excuses to run after what happened tonight, but can't you at least admit that you're using this to put distance between us because you're scared? Can you be that honest with yourself?"

"You're lecturing me about honesty, Mr. Lie of Omission?" Before he could argue with her any more, Kendall shook her head and asked, "Do you know what day it is?"

For a minute, she thought he'd ignore the question, but roughly he said, "Not for sure, no. I lost track in here."

"So did I. I remember how to get out of the temple, though. We better not wait till morning to send up the warning. I'll just take a shower, and then we can go."

Wyatt jerked on his clothes, uncaring about the stench. Bug hadn't said it, but she wanted the shower to wash away what had happened between them, and the realization ripped out his heart.

He'd known. From the minute he touched her, he'd known she'd pull back on him, and she'd do it hard. He thought he'd been prepared for how deeply Bug would hurt him, but he hadn't been. Maybe it was because he hadn't expected her to hit him from the angle she had, but how the hell could he have guessed that she'd suddenly remember her life as Zolianna? For four months, she hadn't recalled a damn thing.

Grabbing his boots, he sat down on the bed to lace them up. From the corner of his eye, he could see the sheets and blankets, and Wyatt felt the heat build as he thought back to how they'd messed them up. Nothing in his life had ever felt as good as being inside Kendall. No way in hell was he giving up on her. He might be pulling back now, but it was a strategic retreat.

Sheer willpower got him moving again, and once he had his boots on, he worked on emptying the fruit from her bag. Bug wouldn't leave it behind, but if she knew how to get out of the pyramid, they wouldn't need the extra food.

Wyatt strapped on his pistol belt, checked the weapon, the clips, and slid the knife into position. Then he waited. Kendall, it seemed, was in no hurry.

Her attack wasn't personal—even if it sure seemed that way. He knew it was fear that caused her to lash out at him. This was probably the final battle in the war, and if he could win it, Bug would be his. But he had to put aside his hurt feelings and dig in.

The door opened, and Kendall came into the room dressed in her dirty clothes. He'd been right; she had wanted the shower to wash him away. "You ready?"

"Yeah. Where's my—" He held out her messenger bag. "Thank you," Bug said so impersonally, Wyatt ground his teeth.

She led him to an odd little nook in the far corner of the room and pressed her hand on a stone to the right of it. When they were through the hidden exit, she closed the wall again, and brought him to a balustrade. Another alien elevator, Wyatt realized, as she raised it to their level.

He followed her and stood patiently as they went down to the base of the pyramid. This was how Berkant had sneaked in to visit Zolianna. Wyatt knew it, although he hadn't remembered the doorway or the lift until now. It made sense, though, that the High Priestess would have a way in and out of the temple that no one else knew about.

As soon as they came to a complete stop, Bug was off, moving through the maze with certainty. She stopped and waited until he drew even with her.

"I know you're mad at me." She grimaced. "I'm mad at you too, but will you do me a favor?"

"What?" he asked warily.

"Don't say anything about the temple's inner sanctum," Kendall said in a rush. "Please?"

"You want me to lie?" Wyatt waited for her to say something about him being good at lies of omission—he'd given her the perfect opening—but she didn't, and he knew why. She wanted his promise more than she wanted to fight with him. Bug needed to protect this pile of rock from the Alliance, and she couldn't do that without his cooperation.

"Not lie," she said at last. "Just maybe don't mention it, you know? I mean, they'll be elated enough over the middle with all its corridors and hidden traps and such. No one really needs to know about this innermost part."

Wyatt didn't care if the army tore this pyramid apart stone by stone, and he almost said that. But Kendall did care about her precious temple, and he loved her enough to do just about anything for her. That included an outright lie to his superiors, though he didn't think it would come to that. He wasn't letting her off scot-free though. "If I keep quiet, you'll owe me," he told her.

Bug nodded eagerly. "Anything, I promise."

"We have a deal, then." Wyatt held out his hand, and hesitantly, Kendall shook to seal their bargain.

They rounded one more corner, and fifty feet ahead of them was a blank wall. When they reached it, Kendall pressed her hand to the side at waist level, and the door opened. As soon as they were through, she carefully sealed it up again.

"Where are we?" he asked, voice lower than a whisper.

"In an outbuilding near the temple." Kendall raised the lights far enough for them to wend their way through the room.

Wyatt led the way up the stairs. He turned down the lights, and as he waited for his eyes to adjust to the lower level of brightness, he listened—there were no sounds emanating from the other side of the wooden door. Slowly, he opened it, but everything remained still.

There was enough moonlight streaming in the windows for Wyatt to clearly see the cluttered room. Everywhere he looked there were tables filled with aromatic herbs, and sheaves of dried plants hung from the rafters. It took some searching to find the door amid this disorder, but he bet it was deliberate. When he located it, he reached back and took Kendall's hand.

Ducking and twisting to avoid low-hanging herbs, he moved toward the exit. Although they were out of the temple, Bug's palm continued to tingle, sending wave after wave of energy to him. He scowled, then pushed the irritation aside.

"This herb house is on the far side of the pyramid," Bug explained. "To reach Sullivan and security headquarters, we'll have to walk around nearly half of the temple."

That just figured. Given the size of the pyramid, they were going to be exposed for longer than he'd like. The alternative—to take a roundabout path—didn't sit well with him either.

It was night, but what time was anyone's guess. He didn't know what kind of shifts the thieves were working or when they came and went from the temple. They would be watching one spot, though. "Where are we in relation to the main temple entrance?"

"The opposite side."

He nodded to let her know he'd heard her. That was good news. Depending on how big the ring was, the smugglers might only have one person on the outside of the temple. Wyatt weighed the factors and reached a decision.

"Hang close to me. We're going to head for Sullivan's home. We know at least one person's dirty at security HQ, but the Big Chill is incorruptible. Ready?" When he saw Kendall's nod, he eased the door open.

Wyatt took the path with the most cover, but even with his caution, there were times when they were completely visible.

The night stayed quiet, but he knew that didn't mean anything except that they hadn't run into trouble yet. Wyatt stopped and swallowed a curse. He'd forgotten about this big square. Going around it would be worse than crossing it. Either way, they'd be exposed, but at least if they went through it, they could use the shadows of the temple itself.

He looked back at Kendall, and she nodded once. The show of support should have lightened his mood, except he couldn't stop remembering. This wasn't the same plaza that Berkant and Zolianna had died in—that was on the other side of the temple—but it was similar enough that he couldn't put that mob scene out of his head.

Maybe that was why his nerves were so taut. Wyatt studied the area more carefully, but he didn't see or hear anything that gave him reason to hesitate. His sixth sense, though, said something was off. It was a judgment call. While this area was a hot zone, he didn't see any advantages to wandering the city on a convoluted path to elude the smugglers. The quicker they reached Sullivan, the quicker Bug would be safe. He tugged Kendall's hand, signaling her to move.

The darkness at the pyramid's base wasn't as deep as he would have liked, but they went unchallenged, and once they were clear of the ceremonial plaza, they'd have a lot more cover.

Although he never paused, Wyatt moved cautiously. The hair on his nape prickled, but their path remained unblocked.

By the time they neared the corner of the pyramid, he had a route through the city and several alternates picked out—just in case. Wyatt slowed their pace. This was the one place where there was a chance for an ambush. He wasn't taking any chances.

Wyatt pulled his hand free of Kendall's and began to scope out the angle. But before he could do much more than take a quick glance, three smugglers came around the corner, pistols drawn.

If he tried to reach for his own weapon, they'd shoot, and he had to make sure they didn't hurt Bug. Damn it, he wouldn't fail this time. Berkant hadn't been able to protect Zolianna, but he was saving Kendall—no matter what it took.

Chapter Twenty

Kendall took in the situation in the blink of an eye. Calling on Zoli—*her* powers, she heated the smugglers' pistols. The plastic pieces melted instantly, and it took only a fraction of a second longer before the metal became so hot the three thieves were forced to drop their weapons. As soon as they clattered to the stones, Wyatt launched himself at the men.

His action caught her flatfooted. Last time, Zolianna had stood by and watched them kill her love. But Kendall wasn't heavily pregnant, and unlike her life as High Priestess, this time she'd been trained to fight. She ran after Wyatt.

Choosing the smallest man, Kendall landed a kick to the back of his knee. His leg buckled, but he didn't go down, and with a growl of anger, he turned to face her.

She wanted him away from Wyatt, so she eased back. Using her forearm, she blocked his first strike. Then Kendall grabbed hold of the man and brought up her knee. He twisted out of the way, so that she hit his hip, not his groin.

They broke away from each other and circled. His eyes glittered in the moonlight, making him appear inhuman, or at least evil. She heard a groan, and her gaze flew to Wyatt.

The distraction cost her. The jerk grabbed her from behind. Lifting her right leg, Kendall kicked his shin as hard as she could, and at the same time, jabbed him with her elbow and gave him a head butt.

His hold slackened. She broke free, and clasping her hands together, brought them down on the back of his neck with enough force to drive him to the ground. She hesitated; the man was reeling, struggling to regain his feet.

Then she heard Wyatt groan again, and Kendall found her killer instinct. She wouldn't let him die for her. With a silent apology, she kicked the thief in the head. This time, he stayed down.

Wyatt. Spinning around, she raced for him.

One of the two men had his arms pinned behind his back, while the other pummeled him. Kendall snarled low in her throat. Those bastards. There was a scuffle, and the two men blocked her view. She didn't know what they were doing to Wyatt.

Almost there. She was almost close enough to help.

When she could see again, Kendall spotted the glint of a knife, and she called on the energy. The blade melted, dripping molten steel onto the henchman's hand. His scream echoed.

Wyatt twisted free from his captor, and as he struck out, Kendall noted his holster was empty. Scanning the area, she looked for his pistol. She found it near the smuggler who'd been wielding the knife. Using telekinesis, she sent the weapon sailing out of his reach. They both chased after it.

Kendall reached it first and the thief tried to grab her. Before he could touch her, though, Wyatt had him, and with a violent twist, he broke the bastard's neck.

As Wyatt dropped the man he'd just killed to the ground, Kendall looked for the guy Wyatt had been fighting. She found him motionless on the plaza.

With all their attackers accounted for, she went and retrieved the pistol. Her legs were shaking, but her hands were steady enough as she returned the weapon to Wyatt. "Thanks, darlin'," he said as he holstered it.

"Someone had to save that gorgeous ass of yours." Kendall's eyes widened when she realized what had come out of her mouth, and, embarrassed, she hurried away.

"You like my backside?" Wyatt teased as he caught up with her. "That wasn't what you kept reaching for in bed, you know."

Kendall's cheeks went so hot, she figured they must be scarlet. "Sorry, I don't know why I said that. My brain is all jumbled up or something."

"It's okay," he told her, his arm going around her waist. "It's the adrenaline. Try not to crash on me, though, because we are a long way from safe, and I need you alert."

She took a deep breath. "I'll give it a shot."

"Good. Now let's get out of here and find Sullivan. I want this over ASAP. Then, Bug, you and I can have a talk."

Wyatt took his arm from around her, and snagged her hand instead. Kendall looked at him, but the expression on his face was resolute. That hadn't been a threat, but a promise.

Alex sat unmoving on his front porch, the shadows hiding him from view. It was after midnight, and he'd been camped here for hours, out of touch for the first time since Hunter's body had been discovered. He needed the time alone.

Never before in his life had he been as furious at another human being as he'd been at Stacey. It had taken all his self-command to remain silent in the mess hall. He knew anything he said would be inflammatory. Besides, he refused to air their problems in front of an audience. God knew, the gossipmongers on the post would have a field day if he did.

Shit, part of him still couldn't believe it. The woman he'd lived with for three years, the woman who'd claimed to love him, had been prepared to walk out without telling him about the baby.

Maybe she was getting even with him. After all, it was his fault she was pregnant since he'd promised to take over the responsibility for birth control. She'd even reminded him, but before he could get to the infirmary, that bout of food poisoning had laid low more than half his personnel, and he'd had forty-eight hellish hours trying to find ways to cover the security responsibilities of J Nine. Even after some of his people started coming back, they'd been weakened, and his juggling act had continued for another ten days. By the time the crisis was over, he'd forgotten about his promise.

Honesty forced Alex to discard the idea that this was some kind of revenge for his lapse. Stace was too straightforward for that kind of shit, and she'd be more likely to rip his head off than anything else. Why the hell then had she kept this secret?

His stomach clenched. Maybe she'd decided he'd make a lousy father and she didn't want him messing up their kid.

Alex couldn't blame her for that. He'd never had a really good role model when it came to parenting. His mother had been a selfish bitch who'd considered him nothing more than a pawn in some bizarre war with his father. And God knew while his dad had tried, he hadn't been the best parent either. First and foremost, he'd been a soldier. Sure, when he was home, he tried to make up for his absences, but he'd been gone more than he was present. Besides, Alex hadn't seen his dad from age five to fifteen, and a lot of damage had been done by then.

He sighed silently. No doubt about it, he was a bad bet to raise a child, but Stacey should have told him about the baby anyway. Then, after he knew, she could have let him know she didn't want him near their son or daughter. It would have hurt, but not half as much as her concealing the information had.

They needed to talk, but Alex didn't think he was capable of having a conversation yet—at least not a constructive one. He was still too pissed.

When he spoke to her, he'd have to be cool. Maybe Stacey didn't want him to help raise their child, but for damn sure he was getting some visitation. He would never walk away from his kid; Alex knew what it was like to grow up thinking his father didn't care, and no child of his was going to experience that pain. His child would know a father's love—even if Alex only visited on holidays and the occasional weekend.

When he realized he was strangling the arms of his chair, Alex forced himself to release his grip. He had to get a hold on his temper, so he could discuss this with her before she left on the transport tomorrow. Unease filled him, and he pushed it aside. He'd been in tough situations before, and he'd do whatever he needed to do. No way was he letting his kid down.

Maybe Stacey's pride had prevented her from telling him about the baby. She was aware that he'd ask her to marry him the instant he knew, and she wouldn't want him to feel obligated. But even before she'd walked out on him, he'd planned to spend the rest of his life with her. The baby just would have sped up his proposal. He'd have gotten around to it on his own—eventually.

The sound of people running jerked him out of his thoughts.

Alex watched as two people turned onto his sidewalk and hurried up the steps to his front entrance. A woman pounded on the door. "For heaven's sake, Bug, softer. The colonel will hear you without half the danged neighborhood being alerted too."

As if suddenly sensing Alex's presence, Montgomery stiffened and glanced around. His captain's razor-sharp instincts brought Alex an odd pride. As their eyes met and the kid ID'd him, his body relaxed.

He captured the woman's fist before she could knock again, and said, "Come on, darlin'."

Alex recognized Kendall Thomas, as he returned his captains' salutes. Both looked exhausted and had obviously lost weight, but they were healthy enough, thank God.

"At ease," Alex said softly. "I'm assuming you're not here to turn yourselves in for being AWOL."

Montgomery remained impassive, but the girl looked like she wanted to go for his throat. For the first time in a long while, Alex felt like smiling.

"No, sir," Montgomery said. "We're here to report a smuggling ring on Jarved Nine."

"I know about it." That shocked them. "Captain Thomas, have you considered a career in investigation? I have MPs who aren't half as good as you are at following trails. The level of detail in your notes was impressive and very helpful."

"Thank you, sir." She sounded distracted, barely pausing before asking, "Has the transport left yet?"

The non sequitur had him stiffening. "It's scheduled to take off in about ten hours or so."

The girl turned to Montgomery. "We might still have time!"

"Start talking, Thomas," Alex ordered. He wanted answers now.

"Sir—" Montgomery started.

"Is your name Thomas?" He didn't have to say another

word to shut the kid up. Alex turned to the girl, and she immediately launched into a condensed, need-to-know report.

"The smugglers are planning to steal the obelisks from your sister's house—the ones in her bedroom. They're supposed to be on this transport because they have a really important buyer waiting, which means they'll have to break in and take them tonight. Sir, their orders are to get those crystals no matter what they have to do or who they have to hurt!"

She said it all without drawing a breath, so it took a second for the words to make sense. When they did, his blood turned to ice, and his heart spasmed. Not only was his family at risk, but Stacey too. Alex jerked to his feet, struggling for composure. "Montgomery, are you capable of acting as my backup?"

"Yes, sir," he said.

"Thomas, I want you to go to security headquarters and send reinforcements to the royal residence."

"With all due respect, Colonel," Montgomery said, "there's no way in hell I'm letting Captain Thomas out of my sight. Every member of that smuggling ring is looking for her, and if they spot her, she's dead."

Alex started to point out that the silver oak leaf he wore beat a couple of bars, but he swallowed the words. If he dragged Montgomery with him, and all he did was worry about Thomas, the kid would be worse than useless. A distracted man in a life-or-death situation was a danger to himself and others.

He dismissed the idea of letting Thomas come with them. She didn't have the training or experience to be any help, and Montgomery would be so busy watching out for her that he could jeopardize Stacey or Ravyn or Cam. Alex thought about suggesting Thomas seal herself inside his house, but guessed the kid would still have his attention divided. That left only one option.

"Okay, let's try this then. You stick with her and you both find me some backup—send them to the royal residence ASAP. Tell them I'll be inside when they arrive. I'm not waiting."

The kid nodded. "Major Brody will be able to help you out until the troops get there, sir."

"McNamara assigned him to night duty a few days ago. That makes it critical that you don't waste time, understood?" Alex all but growled the words, but his impatience level was rising.

"Understood, Colonel."

Before Alex could reach the stairs, his unease became full-out terror. Ravyn. Since she'd been five years old, he'd known when his sister was in trouble. He recognized the feeling instantly. Something was seriously wrong.

"Move it!" he ordered. And Alex started running.

Stacey couldn't sleep. No matter how hard she tried, she couldn't rid her mind of the expression on Alex's face when he'd found out about the baby. It had only been there for an instant, then rage had replaced it, but she hadn't needed more time in order to recognize it. Pain. A pain so deep, there weren't words to quantify it. Her keeping this secret had hurt him badly.

She hadn't expected such a strong reaction.

Turning from her side to her back, Stacey draped an arm across her eyes. He hadn't said more than a handful of words to her after Tami had dropped the bombshell, but she knew better than to believe that would last. Either he was formulating a strategy or trying to calm down enough to talk to her without losing his self-command. Sullivan hated being out of control.

A soft moan escaped as she realized Alex probably considered her secrecy to be on par with the manipulative tricks his mother had used against his father. His parents, both of them, had left Alex with a lot of baggage. Too much. The only thing that had saved him was his mother sending him to his dad when he was fifteen. And even then, Stacey thought Ravyn was the one that had given him a ray of light, not Gil or Marie, his stepmother.

Ravyn had helped Alex open his heart again. She'd needed someone to watch out for her, and her new step-brother had taken on the role of guardian without hesitation. This was partly why he'd had such trouble standing aside for Damon. Sullivan needed to be needed, and with Ravyn married, he'd lost the one thing that made him feel worthwhile.

With a groan of frustration, Stacey pushed aside the blankets and got up. She wasn't going to sleep, not before the transport left Jarved Nine. The clothes she'd worn earlier were on a nearby chair, and she pulled them on. Maybe she'd talk to Alex, have it out with him. Meet the enemy on your terms, wasn't that what he always said? It was time to put his advice to work.

But as she strode into the darkened gathering chamber, her uneasiness surged into outright terror. She was trying to figure out why when she heard Cam call, "Mommy!" He must have had a nightmare; he sounded frightened.

"No! Mommy!"

Stacey hesitated. Where was Ravyn?

"Mommy!" Cam sounded mad, and Stacey almost laughed. She'd better see what had him up in the middle of the night.

She was past the first door to Ravyn and Damon's suite when she heard a sob from the sitting room. Reversing her steps, she walked inside, and stopped short.

A man dressed in dark clothing held a struggling, almost-hysterical Cam. The boy was alternating between trying to fight the thug and trying to get away from him. Cam saw her then, and went still. "Mommy!" he shrieked, pointing.

For the first time, Stacey saw the body. Ravyn was lying on her stomach. *Please, God, don't let her be dead!*

She had to do something. She had to rescue Cam.

Stacey rushed the guy restraining the little boy, but she was grabbed from behind before she took more than a few steps.

Fighting with all her strength, Stacey tried to get free, tried to put into practice the different defensive moves Alex had taught her, but she was no match for the jerk. Then Cam's crying stopped with a suddenness that made her freeze.

"Here's the deal, lady. You behave, the kid remains healthy. You kick up a fuss, and he gets hurt. Simple enough?" the guy pinning her arms behind her back asked.

"Yes," she whispered.

"Good. You stay quiet and cooperative, and everything will be fine. We'll do what we came here for, then get out."

"Uncover his face," Stacey said, nodding toward the man who had one big hand blocking Cam's nose and mouth. "I'll cooperate if you stop smothering him."

"He's making too much noise," the thug holding the boy said.

"Cam, sweetie, you need to stay quiet, okay?" The word he said was muffled, but Stacey understood. "We'll check on your mommy soon, but can you be quiet for me?"

He nodded the best he was able.

"Now take your hand off his face," she told the guy.

The man lowered his arm slowly, ready to cover Cam's mouth again in an instant if he cried. The boy, though, kept his promise. With her godson able to breathe again, Stacey moved on to her next worry—getting them out of here alive. She didn't care what these men said; she and Cam had seen their faces, and there was no way on earth they were letting them live. Where could the thieves hide? J Nine had only a small contingent of people, and everyone was confined within the walls of the city. Once she identified them, they'd be arrested immediately.

No, she and Cam were a vulnerability these men couldn't afford, and they'd already proven they weren't averse to violence. Her eyes strayed to her friend's procumbent form. Stacey refused to believe Ravyn was dead; she couldn't be. That meant she had two helpless people to rescue tonight. The question was how.

"You hang on to the brat," thug number one said, thrusting Cam at her. She read the heat in the boy's eyes and quickly made a shushing noise to calm him. She needed Cam to stay quiet. If they became too much trouble, the creeps would either kill them right away, knock them out, or tie them up, and none of those scenarios were helpful.

"Watch those two while I get to work," the first man told the other one.

The second guy complained, but Stacey ignored it. Cam had started crying, big tears silently running down his face, and she was busy trying to soothe him before he became louder.

"Find something to tie them up with then if you don't want to keep an eye on them." And the first thug left. Stacey saw him enter the bedroom, and turned her head slightly to look at their captor. He was smaller than the first guy, but she knew firsthand how strong and quick he was.

What were her options? Think! she exhorted herself when nothing came to mind.

She couldn't take on both men by herself. Handling one was probably beyond her. How could they get help? There was a comm unit in the house, tucked in one of the rooms off the main gathering chamber, but at night there was only a ten- to fifteen-percent chance it would actually work.

Stacey didn't like those odds.

Damn it, why did the Old City have to mess with all their electronic equipment? Cam snuggled his face against her throat, and she felt the wetness of his tears against her neck. She stroked his scalp gently and wished she could cry herself.

The royal residence sat on the busiest square in the city, but at this time of the night, chances were good that there wouldn't be anyone outside for her to flag down. She didn't think she could get away from the thief, and even if she did, he'd catch her before she could find help. Then there was Cam. He was trusting her to get him and his mom out of this mess. How could she leave him?

"Great," thug two muttered. "I'm baby-sitting a woman and a kid." Stacey stayed silent, unsure what to say. "Come on." He gave her a push. "I want you farther away from the door."

Since it was in her best interest to comply, Stacey followed orders. What would Alex do in this situation? But as soon as she asked the question, she knew she couldn't hope to emulate him. Knowing Sullivan, he probably would have realized there was trouble and entered the room covertly, taking out both men before they even realized he was there. Unfortunately, not only was it too late to sneak in, she didn't have his training or strength.

So the question was what did Stacey Johnson, pregnant woman with minimal self-defense skills, do in this situation?

Her answer—wait for Alex to come to the rescue—didn't work. He was furious, and he was hurt. If he showed up at all, it would be in the morning, and that would be too late.

She forced herself to face a few hard truths. She couldn't get them all out of this. Stacey blinked hard to keep from crying. She might be able to save Cam, but she couldn't save Ravyn too. The idea of sacrificing her best friend left her feeling as if someone had driven a stake through her heart, but Stacey knew Ravyn would want her to get Cam out of here.

If she ran, the jerk would chase her. Stacey knew it was

unlikely she'd get far, but that wasn't the aim—the purpose was to ensure Cam had a few seconds to run in another direction and find somewhere to hide. These men couldn't afford to waste time looking for him, not for more than a few minutes, and he'd be safe. It wasn't a great scheme, but she was desperate and it was all she had.

She shifted the boy, and the creep glared at her. "Sorry," she apologized, "he's heavy."

The man grunted. She waited a couple more minutes, then switched Cam to her other arm. Lifting his head, the boy looked at her, and Stacey kissed his chubby cheek. He lowered his face again, snuggling against her, and she knew he was trusting her, relying on her to take care of him.

From the bedroom, she heard a loud thud and a curse. The second guy tensed. "What's going on?" he called.

"These sons of bitches don't want to come down. It's like they're fastened in somehow, but I don't see an anchor."

When he moved toward the bedroom door to offer advice to his partner in crime, Stacey lowered her mouth next to Cam's ear and murmured, "We're going to play hide and seek. I'll hide first, and when the bad man runs after me, then you run and hide and be as quiet as you can, okay?" She cast a glance at the thief, but he was still talking to the other man. "Don't come out until I come for you, got it?"

Bless him, Cam was wise enough to keep his voice soft. "Mommy?" he asked, and looked over his shoulder at Ravyn.

Stacey wasn't sure what to say. There was nothing either of them could do to get Ravyn out of here. The first man cursed again, and Stacey said, "You know your mommy would want you to listen to me." Cam nodded. "Then you'll do as I say, right?"

There was a hesitation, then Cam nodded again reluctantly. She switched him to her other arm and the thug looked back at her. "Shit, put him down already," he groused.

That was just the invitation Stacey was waiting for. Slowly, she lowered Cam to the ground. He clung to her, and she gently put him from her and gazed into his solemn eyes. "Remember, hide and seek," she whispered. When he released her, she straightened, and prepared to take action.

Another thud came. Her guard was only half in the bedroom, and distracted. There wouldn't be a better time.

Stacey bolted for the door.

Chapter Twenty-one

Alex swept his gaze over Ravyn's home, instinct warring with intellect. One side of him wanted to charge in and protect the people he loved. Years of training, though, insisted that he reconnoiter first, that rushing in blindly was stupid. Before he could make a choice, Brody rounded the corner at a full-out run.

Quickly, he moved to intercept his brother-in-law. The man heard him and whirled, pistol drawn. Alex froze in place and held both hands up, but it only took a second for Brody to ID him and stand down. Lowering his arms, Alex closed the distance.

"There's trouble," Brody said. His voice was tight, and he almost hummed with barely contained adrenaline. "Let's go."

Alex grabbed Damon's arm to keep him from racing inside. "We have to play this smart or we risk everyone. You know that."

Brody cursed a word he rarely used, but Alex saw him struggle to take it down a notch. "My family's in there."

"So's mine," he countered. "What's going on? Do you know?" Alex might have an empathic connection with Ravyn—one that had been eerily quiet for some time now—but she shared something more with Damon, and he wanted to know what Brody knew.

"I haven't been able to hear Ravyn for a while. Too long. Something's happened to her."

The fear in his brother-in-law's eyes worried Alex. Damon didn't frighten easily. "Even more reason to play it smart," he said, but he wanted to get inside as badly as Brody did. "Did Ravyn tell you anything before the link was severed?"

"All she said was *men,* then she went silent. I don't know how many. She was scared, though, I felt that plainly."

So had Alex. "I sent for backup."

"I'm not waiting for them to show," Brody said, pulling free of Alex's grip.

"Neither am I, but we'll go in there as a team. I don't need you acting like some cowboy, understood?"

"I got it." And when Brody looked at him, Alex noticed his brother-in-law had his control back. Good.

They entered the house slowly and cautiously. Both of them were ex-Special Forces, and the training allowed them to operate smoothly although they'd never worked a mission together.

The main gathering chamber was empty, but the lights blazed. That wasn't normal for this time of night; Alex exchanged a glance with Brody. Through the archway was the hallway that led to the bedrooms, and to the private suite that his sister and her husband used. They'd need to go down the corridor, however, chamber by chamber; it was too risky to do anything else.

Before Alex could gesture, a child started to wail.

His heart stopped, only to restart in double time. Alex lunged, and caught Damon before he could rush down the hall. "Damn it, Brody, you're more experienced than this."

"That's Cam. He doesn't cry like that."

"You're not going to help him if you go off half-cocked. You know that." Alex didn't know how he managed to keep his voice even; he was every bit as tense as his brother-in-law.

When the crying stopped abruptly, Alex firmed his grip. Damon's muscles tensed, but he didn't try to break loose. "If anything happens to Ravyn or Cam, I'm killing those bastards."

Brody was deadly serious, and Alex nodded. "If anything happens," he said, "I'll help you."

They were at the far end of the room from the corridor. They needed to figure out where Stacey, Ravyn and Cam were located and how many bogeys they had to deal with.

The crying started again, louder and more frantic, derailing his plans. A man shouted. There were the sounds of what could only be a scuffle. Shit, all hell was breaking loose. He didn't even try to hold back Damon this time.

They had the archway covered from two different angles when Stacey appeared. She didn't make it far; an arm went around her throat and held her in place.

Alex had to dig deep to find his self-command. The rage was rocketing through him, demanding he take action. Demanding he hurt the bastard hurting Stacey.

The man had a pistol to her head, and Alex flexed his hand around the butt of his own weapon. Seeing her in danger brought his instinctive need to defend to the fore, but it also returned his control as easily as flipping a switch.

"Drop your weapons," the man ordered.

Alex ignored the demand, and kept his pistol trained on the intruder's head.

"I'll shoot her," the smuggler threatened.

"The hell you will." Alex's voice came out as cold as winter. "You do, you'll be dead a second later. Bank on it."

Standoff.

The son of a bitch tightened his hold on Stacey's neck. He looked edgy, and that wasn't good. Alex couldn't charge forward—it was too easy to squeeze the trigger in reflex if not on purpose. If anything happened to Stace—

Her eyes met his. She was tense, afraid, but there was also faith there. Despite everything, she trusted him to get her out of this. And he would, no matter what it took.

He began drawing power from the planet and reached out for Stacey. Although they hadn't done this in three years, not since Ravyn and Damon had faced the alien, she helped him blend the energy and create a protective field. Once he had her wrapped in it, he allowed it to flow around him and Brody as well.

Even though Stacey wouldn't be hurt now, he had no clue where Ravyn or Cam were, and he couldn't risk rushing the guy. He'd have to negotiate instead. Alex took a deep breath. Trying to sound nonthreatening, he said, "Let's talk about this."

"Shut up!" The asshole's eyes were frantic, wild, and Alex felt his heart jump into his throat.

"Why don't you use me as your hostage?" he offered.

"Alex—" Stacey began, but the thief choked her, cutting off the protest.

"I said be quiet!"

He ignored that. "I'm a better choice. The army would protect a lieutenant colonel; they'll agree to whatever you want to keep me healthy."

"Do you think I'm stupid?" the man asked.

The answer was yes, but Alex didn't say it. Only an idiot would believe there was a way out of this situation. Jarved Nine had no place to disappear, and the son of a bitch was only making things worse for himself by taking a hostage.

There was another shout from down the corridor, and Alex tensed. This wasn't good.

The man holding Stacey twisted, pulling her with him as he sidled into the room, his back against the wall.

"No!" Stacey cried. "Cam!"

Cam was being chased by another man. Alex tried to direct the protective energy field around the boy, but no matter how hard he and Stacey worked, it wouldn't enfold him.

Brody rushed forward, and Alex was only a split second behind. The bastard grabbed Cam when he reached the archway, and the boy kicked at him. As Alex watched, the asshole lifted the struggling child, and he didn't do it gently.

Shit, they weren't going to be in time. Damon couldn't get to his son quickly enough, and Alex couldn't help both Stace and his nephew. If Brody would head for Stacey . . . But a glance told Alex that Damon was focused only on Cam.

There was no choice. The boy was helpless, and in immediate danger. Stacey was protected.

He ran to his nephew's aid and prayed.

Kendall paced around the living room of the house Wyatt's team shared. The men had left to back up Sullivan, but she and Wyatt had remained behind.

It was the first time she'd ever seen the team in action, and they'd deployed fast. Incredibly fast. It was also the first time she'd really seen Wyatt in his role as their leader, and he'd amazed her too. Wy hadn't been his usual easygoing self, but someone much more intense.

Maybe she'd seen some of this in the temple—after all, he had killed those men—but he'd morphed back into her friend so quickly that she hadn't given it much thought. But now, well, there was nothing to do but think.

"Bug, you want to sit down? You're walking in front of those dang windows over and over and it's making me nuts."

Reluctantly, she plopped onto the sofa.

"Do you think the smugglers will try for the obelisks, or do you think they decided to call it off since they've lost so many men?"

"I don't know." Wyatt sat beside her on the couch, not too closely, but near enough. "It hinges on how brazen they are."

"What do you think's happening at the house?"

He leaned back, slouching in his seat, but despite his position, she could feel how alert he was. "It depends on the situation they find. Best course of action is to get the civilians clear, then lie in wait for the thieves."

"Assuming they haven't been there already."

"Yeah, assuming that."

She leaned back too. "I'm sorry you're stuck with me," she apologized softly. "I know you'd rather be with your team backing up Sullivan."

"Nothing is more important than keeping you safe." He was silent for a moment. "You're not being distant and formal with me anymore. Does this mean we're friends again?"

"We've always been friends," Kendall told him.

Wyatt sighed. "You know what I'm asking."

Yes, she did. Grudgingly, unwillingly, she said, "I'm sorry I accused you of confusing me with Zolianna. It isn't true, I know that. I just needed time to remember."

"I'm glad you figured it out. You really are nothing like her. If you were, you'd have abdicated this whole mess to security the instant you suspected something." Wyatt turned his head to look at her. His face was unreadable, and his eyes glittered with an emotion she couldn't name. "But Kendall, you have a quiet strength that awes me at times. When you feel you have to do something, you do it. No announcements, no hesitation. You charge forward, ready for battle."

"I'm not sure you're complimenting me."

"It is a compliment, but I swear to God, you've taken years off my life since I've known you. Why can't you ask for help?"

"Because no one has ever been around who I could ask." She bit her lip. Damn, that was too revealing.

"Me. You can ask me."

She'd known that she could go to Wyatt for anything, and it scared her to think how easily she could begin to rely on him. She'd always been alone. Always. At first, when she'd been a child, she'd allowed herself to turn to the parade of uncles for support, but they'd never been around long. Until she'd learned that she could only depend on herself, their departures felt as if she'd had the rug pulled out from under her time after time. Her mother had never been there for her. She was too busy searching for her true soul mate, the next relationship that would give her excitement and make her heart flutter—

Kendall stopped short as realization dawned. Why had she never seen this before? Her mom had constantly been looking for fireworks, but that was sexual attraction, not love. Sure, the two went together, and should go together, but when the heat wore off, there had to be more there. Her mom had never taken the time to build that base. Kendall already had it.

Wyatt was her best friend, and when the fire between them was banked, he'd still be her best friend. But he'd be more too. Or he could be if she were brave enough to reach out.

He said he loved her. *Her,* not Zolianna. And although it scared her, she believed him. He'd told her to remember their time together, to realize that he hadn't simply looked at her once and fallen in love, that they'd taken it step by step. What he meant was that they'd carefully created a foundation between them, one firmly anchored in *this* life, in who they were now. They had a solid footing on which to build if they wanted.

But what if it ended? So many couples broke up, and they weren't on good terms after that happened.

Kendall gulped. It might be too late anyway. Could they go back to being nothing more than friends after what they'd already shared with each other? She swore she could still feel Wyatt deep inside her, and she wanted him again so badly she ached.

She couldn't think about this, not now. Not with him sitting right beside her. It would be too easy to let desire sway her actions, too easy to turn to him, to kiss him. Too easy to go further, and forget that while she still wasn't sure about things between them, Wyatt was. If she touched him, he'd read more into it than she meant, and he deserved better than that.

It was definitely safer to focus on the obelisks.

"Too bad Major Brody has night duty. I hate to think of the colonel taking on those smugglers alone."

Wyatt looked at her and sighed. "Nothing might be happening, you know that."

"True," she conceded. But it was strange. Brody was loosely connected with one of the archeological teams. Like some kind of consultant, she'd been told. Although she'd done some investigating, she hadn't been able to figure out what, exactly, he was doing. If she was scorned with an undergraduate degree in anthropology, his degree in history should absolutely leave him excluded. Yet it hadn't.

Wait a second. The social scientists kept regular day shift hours. None of them willingly worked at night, not without it being a huge production. "Sullivan said that McNamara assigned the major to night duty a few days ago, right?"

"Yeah, so?"

"That means it began shortly after we were sealed in the temple, shortly after I heard Dr. George assign his two henchmen to steal the stones. The archeologists don't work at night, not without a lot of bitching, and Brody is supposed to be working with them, so why would he be put on nights?"

"Aw, geez." Wyatt groaned and closed his eyes. "Darlin', please tell me you're not saying that you think the colonel is the head of the smuggling ring."

"It makes sense," she told him. "McNamara is the one person who gives orders that George the Jerk always listens to."

He turned and looked at her. "She's the post commander; why would she do it?"

"Are any of us overpaid?"

Wyatt got up, and this time, he was the one who paced. "Sullivan is going to go berserk when you tell him this. He and McNamara have never gotten along, and if he investigates her, there are going to be accusations that he's on some vendetta."

"Sullivan? Berserk?" Kendall shook her head, unable to imagine it. "I hope I'm wrong about the colonel; I respect her. She's had to work hard to get where she is because she didn't go to the Point. You know the army likes to put their ring knockers in positions of power, and McNamara went to OCS."

"There are plenty of people in high places who came in through Officer Candidate School," Wyatt argued. "And for God's sake, don't say ring knockers in front of Sullivan. He attended West Point."

Kendall couldn't stop a smile. "I know, Wy. Don't worry, I only used the term because I'm talking with you."

He shook his head and kept pacing. When Kendall had first been told to report to J Nine and Colonel McNamara, she'd done some research, and a stray memory was teasing her brain. She frowned as she tried to grab it. Then it came to her, and with a gasp, she jumped to her feet. "We have to get to the transport!"

She knew Wyatt would be pissed, but she ran out of the house anyway. He caught up with her before she'd made it fifty feet, and she twisted out of his reach when he made a grab for her arm.

"Damn it, Kendall, what the hell are you doing? You know we're being hunted, and you're too smart not to realize that bolting out of the fu—fricking house this way is stupid."

"If you think I'm sitting there doing nothing while the thieves loot the Old City one last time, you better think again."

Wyatt actually growled before he said, "Start explaining."

"The thieves probably already have most of the artifacts stowed on the transport. You know, the ones we saw in the hidden room before they used the popper," Kendall added. "Now they know the gig is up, or at least they have a good idea."

"How do you figure that?"

"The men we left unconscious outside the temple must have come to by now, and you can bet they mentioned that we're loose. The big shots have to realize we've reported what's going on. But if they can make it to the transport, and return to Earth, they'll probably get away. It's easy for this type of vehicle to evade an intercept mission; they could land and disappear long before anyone found the transport."

"Yeah, but someone would have to know how to fly that thing. It's not like anyone could just sit down and figure it out."

Kendall turned her head so she could meet Wyatt's eyes. "Colonel McNamara started her career as a transport pilot."

Chapter Twenty-two

Stacey watched both Damon and Alex come to a screeching halt, and despite the grip the goon had on her, she tried to peer over to learn why. When she saw the gun pointed at Cam's head, she gasped. Drawing more energy from J Nine, she tried again to wrap the protective field around her godson, but even though Alex worked with her, they still couldn't do it.

There were no guarantees that the shield would stop a bullet anyhow. They'd never tested it out against conventional Western Alliance weapons.

"Here's how we're going to play it," the thief holding Cam said. "I'm going to walk out of here with this kid, and if you want to keep him alive, no one will stop me. Got it?"

"Leaving here," Sullivan said, voice reasonable, "gains you nothing. Where can you go? Even if you make it outside the city walls, do you plan to spend the rest of your life alone in the planet's wilderness?"

The thug ignored Alex. "We'll shift positions slowly. The two of you on this side, and me and my partner by the door. Then we'll leave. You'll stay here for no less than half an hour; after that, you can do what you want."

"What about the woman and the boy?" Sullivan asked.

While the first thief was talking, the one who'd grabbed Stacey had slackened his hold. Not a great deal, but she suspected if she wanted to, she'd be able to get herself free. With the guy holding a gun on Cam, though, she couldn't do anything without endangering him.

"When we're safe, we'll turn them loose," the hood said.

"There's no way in hell you're taking my son out of here," Damon snarled.

Cam struggled then—and went still with a whimper as the creep tightened his hold on him. Damon looked murderous, but he didn't move and he remained silent.

The standoff couldn't last indefinitely, and as these jerks became more desperate, there was no telling what might happen. If only she and Sullivan had the telepathic link that Ravyn had with her husband, then she'd be able to ask him how she could help. Or if Ravyn were here and conscious, she and Damon could do their thing. Stacey grimaced. While she was wishing, why didn't she just dream the whole night had never happened?

"Let's try this again," the lead thug said. "I'm going to move over there with my partner, and you're going to stay out of my way and be statue-still, got it?"

"No," Damon said without elaboration.

"I'm the one in control. If you want your kid to stay healthy, you get the fuck out of my way."

"I said this to your buddy," Alex told the thief, "and now I'll say it to you—you kill that boy, you lose your shield. The instant you're unprotected, you're dead. Simple as that."

Stacey tried to keep her breathing deep and regular. She wanted to seem calm. What would the guy do since Alex and Damon had left him no options? She had to trust they knew what they were doing, but in her experience, when you cornered an animal, it attacked.

Something had to give, and it was Damon who knocked over the house of cards. "Where's Ravyn?" he asked.

"Mommy!" Stacey saw Cam's lip wobble, but he firmed it before he cried.

Damon took a step forward, the hand not holding his pistol clenched at his side, but he stopped short when the thug pressed the gun firmly against Cam's temple.

Someone was drawing energy from Jarved Nine, and Stacey tensed.

Then music blared. Lights flashed.

She jerked in reaction, and so did the man restraining her. The thief using Cam as a hostage took the gun away from the boy's head and pointed it toward the room as he searched, looking for whoever was playing with the lights.

Damon and Alex launched themselves toward the head creep, and Stacey used the distraction to slide her hand between her throat and her thug's arm. Bending forward, she brought her elbow back hard into his stomach.

Immediately, she turned and chopped her fist down on his arm. The gun fell to the floor, and she kicked it away.

Her captor made a run for the door, but Stacey didn't attempt to stop him. Instead, she turned the other direction, ready to help save her godson. She laughed shakily when she saw things were under control. Alex had the thug facedown on the floor, and Damon had his son wrapped securely in his arms. She walked over to them.

"Creating that diversion was smart thinking," Alex told her.

"I didn't do anything."

"It was Cam," Damon said, raising his head from his son's. "Instead of crying when he was a baby and he needed us, he'd play with the lights or the entertainment system. Ravyn had to—" He stopped short. "Where is she?"

Before Stacey could answer, Damon thrust Cam at her

and put both of them behind his back as he aimed his gun at the archway where the thief had disappeared. Only then did she see movement.

"You officers misplace this guy?" a blond man dressed in combat gear asked as he entered the room. He was dragging her goon by the arm. Five other men, all similarly dressed, came in behind him.

Stacey didn't relax until Damon lowered his weapon. "Thanks, Chief," he said. "That one got away from us."

"Any more bogeys or did we miss all the fun?"

Alex and Damon both looked at her. "I only saw two," Stacey said, and stroked her hand over Cam's dark hair.

"Mommy's hurt," the boy piped up.

Damon's whole body went tense. Holstering his gun, he demanded, "Where's Ravyn?"

"In your sitting room, but . . ." Stacey let her voice trail off. Damon was off like a shot. Before she could tighten her hold on him, Cam wriggled and dropped to the floor. He was almost as fast as his father when he headed down the hall.

One of the men broke off from the group and handed Alex a set of restraints. After securing the goon's wrists behind his back, Sullivan hauled him to his feet, then handed him off to the soldier. Once he was free, Alex stood next to her, putting his arm around her shoulders as he gave orders. She nearly let herself rest against his side, but stopped in time. Maybe she wasn't strong enough to step away from his hold completely, but she wasn't going to lean on him either.

Damon strode back into the room, face ashen, and Stacey saw he had Ravyn slung over one shoulder in a fireman's carry. Cam was tucked securely against his left side.

"Is she—" Sullivan started, but stopped short.

"I got a pulse, but I can't rouse her. I'm taking her to the infirmary." Damon barely paused.

Cam was safe. Her baby was safe. Alex and Damon

were safe. The bad guys were caught. Now all she needed was to hear Ravyn was okay, and everything would be perfect. Stacey began shaking as reaction set in, and Alex hugged her more tightly.

"Is the comm gear working, Cantore?" he asked.

"No, sir. That would be too convenient."

"Yeah. Here's what we're going to do. I want your men to sweep the house, every room. If there's another thief here, I want him found. Once I'm confident the building is clear, we'll pick up your captain and Thomas, then take everyone to security headquarters and start asking some questions."

Sullivan said more, but Stacey stopped listening. She could have died tonight. An innocent child could have died tonight. And Ravyn— She cut that thought short.

But Alex had shown up. Despite everything that had happened between them, despite his anger, he'd come to her rescue. He would have sacrificed his life for hers, even if she wasn't pregnant. Stacey needed to sit down.

Wyatt dragged Kendall to a stop. Before she could complain, he said quietly, "We're doing this the smart way, Bug, and that doesn't mean charging out of the city with righteous indignation."

She nodded. "Just tell me how we're handling it."

He drew her to the side of a nearby building, hiding them in the shadows. "The only gate that hasn't been sealed off is guarded. If you're right, and McNamara is involved, she could order the men to let her pass." Wyatt scowled. "They can tell us if anyone exited, and one of them can back us up—provided they aren't dirty themselves."

"That makes sense," she said slowly, "but why are we stopping here?"

"Because we need to check out the gate carefully from hiding before we approach."

They must be closer to the wall than she thought. "Okay."

Her easy agreement took some of the steam out of Wyatt, and Kendall had to bite her lip to keep from smiling. He'd been all geared up to argue with her, but she'd surprised him.

"Stay close to me," Wyatt ordered, and after she nodded, he began to wend his way through the buildings. When he stopped again, they were hidden behind the side of a shop, and had a clear view of the wall.

"Where are the guards?" she whispered.

Wyatt shook his head, silently telling her he didn't know.

Either the soldiers were part of the smuggling ring, or something had happened to them. Or maybe they just headed into some nearby building to play poker or something.

Except Kendall had a bad feeling about this.

After they'd waited and watched for a while, Wyatt said, "I'm going to reconnoiter the area near the gate. Stay here."

Before she could protest, he was gone. Even though Kendall kept her eyes glued on the portal out of the city, she never saw Wyatt. She was getting scared that something had happened to him, when he slipped up beside her. He looked grim.

"What happened? Did you find them?"

"Yeah, I found them, darlin'. Their throats were slit. That means mission scrubbed." Kendall started to protest, but he shook his head sharply. "No. One person couldn't take out both men, so if it was McNamara, she's not alone. It's too risky for either one of us to go out there, not without backup. What we are going to do is head—"

Kendall reached out and put two fingers over Wyatt's lips. She'd seen movement over his shoulder. Using her chin, she gestured toward the indistinct shapes behind him. It looked like two people, but she couldn't be entirely certain.

"Stay here," he whispered in her ear.

Kendall told him softly, "I won't let you go alone, not a second time. You need someone to watch your back."

For an instant, she read the conflict in his eyes. Special Operations were trained to work in teams. On the other hand, she knew he didn't want her in danger, and there was no telling who was skulking around or how violent they'd be. With a grimace, he signaled her to move.

He remained in the shadows, the only concealment they had, and she stayed with him.

As they neared the people, Wyatt silently signaled, indicating what position he wanted her to take. Kendall nodded, shifting so she flanked the duo. It took her farther from him than she felt comfortable with; she wanted to be able to help him if he needed it.

The figures were armed—she saw one of them was wearing a pistol belt—and she pulled energy, ready to wield it instantly if they drew their weapons.

They managed to remain undetected until Wyatt aimed his pistol at them, and hollered, "Freeze."

Of course, the pair didn't do that. Even as they reached for their pistols, Kendall started directing the power, melting the plastic pieces and heating the metal. They weren't able to hold on to their weapons long.

She hurried to close the distance. Anyone who knew Wyatt knew he wouldn't shoot an unarmed person, and these two were not going to cede quietly. Dismay filled her as she grew close enough to ID the duo—George and Mc-Namara. She'd really wanted the colonel to be innocent.

Kendall didn't have time to think about it before the fight broke out. Without hesitating, she dove in, taking on McNamara. She knew the colonel would be the more formidable opponent, but Wyatt might pull his punches if he had to go head-to-head with a woman, and she didn't want anything to happen to him.

McNamara was a street fighter, and Kendall found herself in a no-holds-barred brawl. Blocking a blow with her forearm, Kendall landed a thigh kick. Some of the neighborhoods she'd lived in weren't pretty, and this was the type of free-for-all that she was most comfortable with.

The colonel made a lunge for Kendall's holster, but she turned her hip, and went for the woman's eyes. McNamara barely twisted away in time to avoid Kendall's fingers.

Ignoring the glare, Kendall looked for vulnerabilities. McNamara struck out at her, and she was able to grab the woman's arm. Kendall spun her into the side of a building, but before she could smash her into the stone, the colonel ducked away.

A quick glance to her right showed her that Wyatt was still tied up with George the Jerk. It surprised her, and she stared a second too long. Her inattention cost her. McNamara grabbed Kendall's hair and pulled until tears came to her eyes.

"You fight like a girl," she told the colonel, trying to enrage her. But even as she derided her, Kendall dug her own fingers into the woman's short hair, and pulled every bit as hard. Maybe they looked like a pair of fifth-grade schoolgirls, but this was causing some pain.

Kendall leaned away as McNamara tried to bite her. Finally, she hooked a foot behind the colonel's leg, and pushed her hard enough to make her fall to the walkway. Unfortunately, Kendall was pulled down with her.

They rolled on the ground. The colonel was in her midforties; Kendall was twenty-four. She had youth and stamina on her side, and she used them. As she gained the top position, McNamara sank her teeth into her left hand.

Pain roared through her; so did anger. Kendall slammed the colonel's head into the stone-paved street until McNamara released her. She thunked the woman's head back one more time for good measure.

McNamara wasn't out cold, but she was stunned. Kendall used the moment to flip her on her belly and pull her arm up between her shoulder blades. Only then did she look around for Wyatt. He was standing, arms folded over his chest, watching. "You could have helped," she complained mildly.

"Darlin', I was looking for a way to join the fight, but the way you two were rolling around, I didn't have an opening." He grinned. "Remind me never to bite you."

"Mar—" she cut herself off as she recalled he hated it when she used his handle. "Wy, I'm okay with *you* biting me—in fact, I have a few places in mind." When she heard what she'd said, Kendall gulped. To pull his attention away from that, she held up her injured hand. Blood dripped down her palm. "I need to swing by the infirmary and get a rabies shot," she joked.

McNamara didn't like that comment, and she struggled. Kendall pulled her arm harder, and the woman gasped before she subsided. "He's out?" she asked, nodding toward Dr. George.

"Yeah. For a rich puke, he put up a heck of a fight."

Before she could ask anything else, Wyatt tensed, and turned, aiming his pistol even as he shifted to her back to protect her. She heard a whistle in some strange cadence, then Wy said, "It's okay. It's my team."

"What took you guys so long?" he asked. Kendall looked over her shoulder to see an army. Not only were Wyatt's men there, but so were Sullivan and at least three other Spec Ops teams.

"Sorry, Marsh," Flare said, deadpan. "We didn't think Kendall needed any help since you were standing around watching her fight."

Wyatt growled and she laughed.

"Stand down, Captain," Flare said, coming up beside her. "I'll take your prisoner."

When she was on her feet, Wyatt put his arm around her shoulders and steered her over to Sullivan. She listened, her mood souring, as he gave his report. Two privates were dead for no reason other than they'd drawn guard duty on the wrong night.

Sullivan began issuing orders. Wyatt left to help his men secure the prisoners, and Kendall found herself on the edge of the group, forgotten. The bite hurt, and she pressed her hand against her thigh, trying to make it feel better. It didn't help.

Wyatt and his team escorted McNamara and George away, and the other teams prepared to head out to the transport. She wanted to join them, but knew she'd be a hindrance. All she could do was hope that nothing happened to the men or the relics.

"Captain Thomas."

"Sir?" Kendall came to attention.

"At ease," Sullivan told her. "I just wanted to tell you that you've done a good job."

Kendall gaped at him; she couldn't help it. "Thanks, sir."

"I wasn't joking earlier tonight when I suggested you think about a career in security. Your files on the smuggling ring are going to go a long way toward convicting the participants."

She thanked him again, bemused by all the compliments.

"But you should have come to me with what you knew."

"I did try to talk to you, Colonel." Kendall refused to let him cow her. "You told me to make an appointment."

"There was a good reason for that, but I meant that you should have come to me the minute you suspected something was happening. I'm here for a reason," he added, voice hard.

"Next time, sir, your office is my first stop."

Sullivan shook his head. "I think I liked it better when I intimidated you. Go catch up with Montgomery. The kid is going to give himself whiplash if he keeps looking over here. I'll meet you at the infirmary when things are wrapped up."

"Yes, sir." Kendall saluted and hurried to close the gap.

Wrapped up. After weeks of stress and days of being hunted, things were almost finished. They'd done it. They'd taken down the smuggling ring. Kendall started shaking as it sank in that at last she and Wyatt were safe.

Chapter Twenty-three

Alex looked up at the royal residence and sighed. He was exhausted and felt about a million years old, give or take a millennium, but he'd accomplished something worthwhile tonight.

Wearily, he climbed the steep, narrow stone steps to his sister's home and went looking for Stacey. He found her in the main gathering chamber, curled up in the corner of the sofa with her feet tucked beneath her. Wordlessly, she watched him cross the room and sit beside her. Alex leaned back, resting his head against the couch, and stared up at the ceiling.

"Ravyn's okay," he said quietly. "Doc said she caught a blast from a popper, but she should be raring to go in a matter of hours. Brody and Cam are sacked out at the infirmary with her."

He could sense the tension leaching from Stacey's muscles. "Thank God. What else happened? I know something did."

"One of the men we captured here told us that there

were plans for the big players in the smuggling ring to take the transport and leave. We got there in time to catch about a dozen of them all together, including Colonel McNamara."

"Bet you enjoyed reeling her in," Stacey said after a moment. "The two of you have been at each other's throats for nearly three years."

Alex shook his head. "I wish I had been the one to arrest her, but I wasn't. Captain Kendall Thomas wrestled the colonel to the ground and sat on her until we arrived." A smile crept across his face. "Stace, you should have seen it. McNamara was belly down on the street, her arm twisted up high behind her back, and she was pissed as hell. So was Thomas. The girl kept muttering about how no one would get away with looting the Old City as long as she was breathing."

Alex saw Stacey's lips twitch, but she said, "You shouldn't call her a girl. It's sexist."

"Bullshit. I'm not referring to her as a girl because she's female; I call her a girl because she isn't even twenty-five years old yet. When did these officers get so young?"

Stacey's grin widened, and she shifted, lowering her feet to the floor. "The better question might be when did you get old."

Alex blew out a long, slow breath. "Yeah. The thing is, in my head, *I'm* still twenty-four. But then I'm surrounded by these kids, and I feel like Methuselah."

"Do you think it might seem that way because you'll be forty on your next birthday?"

"Maybe," he admitted. Alex didn't say anything else for a moment. Stacey wasn't being short with him. Granted, her tone was fairly impersonal, but it was an improvement over how their conversations had gone recently. "You don't have to worry about being on the transport this morning," he said. "We're holding it for a thorough search. It'll be two or three days minimum."

"Did you—" Stacey started heatedly.

"It has nothing to do with you," Alex interrupted. "We have to pull that thing apart looking for contraband. If you have a problem, I suggest you discuss it with Captain Thomas. I had to listen to her lecture me for nearly half an hour, and I'm not going through that again—not even for you." He shook his head. "She's passionate about protecting the antiquities here."

"I wish I'd been there to see you chastised. I'm surprised you didn't bring her to heel before a half hour was up, though."

"Bring her to heel? Ha! I could have been a four-star general, and I wouldn't have been able to stop that girl from giving me an earful. And Montgomery—the other missing captain—was sitting there smirking the whole time. I'd still be trapped while she told me how I'd failed in my duty as head of security if she hadn't caught the kid chuckling. I snuck out of the infirmary while she was chewing him out."

Stacey didn't reply, and the silence lengthened. Alex liked sitting with her, just being. It had been too long since he'd had this, but he had more he wanted to tell her. "I think we got Hunter's murderer—his team's warrant officer, John Dye. Catfish would have trusted him and let him get close. We don't have evidence yet, and Dye hasn't confessed, but I'm sure we'll find what we need to convict him, now that we know where to look." He hesitated, unsure Stace would care, but he needed to say this too. "I didn't brief Montgomery about the murder. The kid will find out soon enough and blame himself. He's the one who asked Hunter to watch out for Captain Thomas."

"Why are you telling me this?" she asked. There was curiosity in her voice, nothing harsher.

"Because you're the only person I can share things with, the only person I trust with my guard down." Alex sat up and shifted until he faced her. "Can we talk? Without anger and hurt? Just have an honest, open discussion about us?"

"Without emotion, you mean?"

"That's not possible." Alex ran his hand over the top of his hair. "We've got too much between us not to have emotion. I'm not great with words, at least not to express how I feel, and whenever I try, you hop off the train before I can hook up all my cars. What I'm asking is that you don't jump to conclusions, don't make accusations, don't storm out of the room. Let me have the time I need to find what I want to say, or if I screw up and say it wrong, give me the chance to explain what I meant. Can you do that?"

"Are you implying this is all my fault?"

Alex gnashed his teeth. "That's not what I'm saying, but this is the kind of comment that derails me. Why do you have to look for hidden meanings? Can't we talk honestly without one of us struggling for an advantage over the other?"

"What's the point in talking now?" she asked.

He took a breath and pushed the frustration aside. "The point is us. We have three years together. That's a lot to throw away without trying till the end."

"You didn't mention the baby."

"That's part two of the discussion. You and I are part one." And how the second half of the conversation went would depend in large measure on what happened in the first, but he wasn't stupid enough to tell her that.

"Okay," Stacey said slowly. "I guess we can try."

Maybe he couldn't change her mind, but he'd had a few epiphanies tonight, and he was imparting them. She gazed at him expectantly, but he found himself at a loss for words—again. Why was he always much smoother in his head than when it came down to crunch time? Whenever he tried to talk about feelings, he was about as articulate as a wart.

"Well?" she prompted. There was no impatience, more of a resignation, as if she'd expected nothing else.

Running through a variety of different potential starting points, Alex decided on the most salient. "I love you, Stacey."

She stiffened. "No, you don't."

Irritation rose, and he struggled to control it. "Do you think I'm just saying it? I've never spoken those words, not even to my sister or nephew."

"I think you're claiming to love me because I'm pregnant, and you want to do the right thing. We both know about your unbending sense of honor." Stacey got up and walked away, but at least she didn't leave the room.

"You're wrong," Alex told her quietly. "I've never lied to you. Not even to make things easier on myself. Remember the night you kicked me out of our bedroom? We both know I could have claimed to be looking at info on the murder, and I would have been out of the doghouse. I didn't do that; you know why?" He stood and crossed the floor until he stood behind her. "Because I love you. A man doesn't lie to the people who are important to him."

Stacey shook her head, but she didn't turn to look at him or comment on what he'd said. Alex was okay with that. Her silence gave him time to find the words he needed.

"You say you're the one who did all the work to hold us together, and you're right about that, I know it. You've said I'm an emotional coward. You're right about that too. I could tell you horror stories about my childhood, but in the end, they're not important. I'm an adult, and I repeatedly made the decision to protect myself. It wasn't until I saw that bastard grab you tonight that I realized what an idiot I'd been."

He reached out, his hand not entirely steady, and lightly ran it down her hair before jerking his arm back. She glanced at him over her shoulder, her face impassive.

"You could have died, Stace." Alex had to clear his throat. "You could have died believing that you didn't mean a whole lot to me, but the truth is, you mean too damn much. I never wanted to love anyone as deeply as I love you. It scares the shit out of me, and that's putting it mildly. I honest to God don't know how Ravyn found the courage to throw herself into her relationship with Brody. She must be stronger than I am."

"Ravyn," Stacey said, shifting around, "had you to protect her. She had you to turn to when she needed someone in her corner. Who did you have, Alex?"

He started to shrug that off, to deny it meant anything, but that was the old Alex, and he'd sworn that man wasn't going to get in his way. "Ravyn was there for me too."

"No, she wasn't. Not in the way I'm talking about, and not in the way you were there for her. She couldn't be, not with a ten-year gap between your ages. For much of her life, she was simply too young to offer the support you needed, and by the time she was old enough, the pattern of your relationship was set."

Alex stared at Stacey. She was defending him? "I had to be strong for her, especially after her mother and my father died. She was reeling." He grimaced as he recalled a conversation he'd had with Stacey years ago. "So was I, but I was twenty-four, and a man. She was barely into her teens."

Stacey turned to face him, her arms hugging her waist. "Over the last three years, you could have reached for me."

There was only a hint of accusation in her voice, and Alex guessed she'd struggled hard for that evenness. With a faint smile, he said, "I was thirty-six when we met, and by then my defenses were firmly entrenched. It took seeing a gun at your head to shake me up."

"And I'm supposed to believe that in a matter of seconds, you changed completely and irrevocably."

"Sarcasm," Alex pointed out mildly, and watched her

blush. "And no, we both know it won't be that easy. I'm going to have to work on it every day for years before it becomes ingrained. You'll just have to call me on it when I backslide, and we both know I will. Not much of a bargain for you, but there'll never be another man who loves you more than I do, even when I forget to tell you." He shrugged, trying to disguise his discomfort.

"I wish I could believe you," Stacey said, "but we've been through too much. I can't spend the rest of my life fighting with you, trying to get you to change."

His heart had settled somewhere around his boots. This wasn't going well, and he couldn't blame her. He'd blown opportunity after opportunity in their time together, held on to his pride at the expense of their relationship. It would serve him right if he had only his dignity to keep him warm, but he had to believe he still had a chance, had to believe she still loved him. Emotions didn't turn on and off so easily.

"You have no reason to trust that things will be different," he said, "but I swear they will. This time I *want* to change, and that distinction makes all the difference in success."

She shook her head, but he saw the tears pooling in her eyes. Fear—all right, terror—surged through him. God, he couldn't lose her, not now. Not when he finally understood.

"You want me to beg? I will." Alex dropped to his knees. "I love you, Stace. Don't leave me. Please."

"Get up," she told him.

He didn't. Instead, he reached for her hand. Voice thick, Alex told her, "I'm not a prize, but I'm not without pluses. I've never lied to you or cheated on you, and I never will. I'll always treat you with respect. I don't forget birthdays or anniversaries, and you'll never have to worry about hunting me down at some bar. I don't gamble, and I don't spend more money than I have."

"I know this," Stacey said, and she was crying in earnest.

Alex panicked. If she knew his good points, and those weren't enough, what did he have left? Not a thing. He could see a wasteland laid out in front of him—spending his life alone, seeing his kid on holidays and occasional weekends, burying himself in work to fill his emptiness. No Stacey.

"Tell me what you need me to say, what you need me to do, and I swear to God, I'll say and do it." He wanted to tell her that without her, he'd die inside, but that wasn't fair. "You want me to crawl across the plaza? Shout from the rooftops that I love you? Serenade you from the street? Tattoo your name on my ass? I'll do all of those things if that's what it takes to prove how much you mean to me. Give me a chance to show you that I want to change—that I can change. There'll always be another transport back to Earth if I fail miserably."

"Damn you, Alex. You're such a bastard."

"I know." And he did know that, had prided himself on it.

Slowly, she sank down until she was knee to knee with him. "Why did you have to do this now—when I finally had the strength to walk away from you?"

He shook his head. There was no answer he could give her, and Alex settled for gently wiping away the tears rolling down her cheeks. "Just a chance," he pleaded. "I love you, Stace."

More tears fell, and he brushed those away too. When the sob escaped, Alex gathered her close, snuggling her against his chest. She didn't pull away, and for the first time since he'd walked into the room, he felt a speck of optimism.

Stacey's arms went around him, and she held on tightly while she cried. He'd caused this pain, had wounded her this deeply, and Alex apologized in whispers against her hair as he rubbed circles on her back. It took her a long time to calm down, and by then, he was sitting against the wall, with Stacey on his lap.

As the silence lengthened, he felt more hopeful. She wasn't moving off him, wasn't telling him to get lost. He kissed the crown of her head and waited.

"You're a bad bet, Sullivan," Stacey said a long time later.

"I know. You can do much better than me." And she could.

Lifting her head, she looked down into his eyes. "You swear you're not saying these things because of the baby?"

"Word of honor. I've never lied to you," he repeated, "and I never will. You have my word on that too."

She was measuring him, and his heart thundered in his chest. What if he didn't look sincere? What if he got a tic in his eye and she thought it was because he was lying? What if—

"One last chance. If I don't see you making an effort, that will be it."

Moisture welled in his eyes, and he had to blink rapidly to keep from looking like a sissy. "Thanks," he said, his voice nearly unintelligible. "You won't regret it."

"I better not," she warned, but ruined the effect by leaning forward to kiss him. "I love you, Alex—don't break my heart again." And mimicking him perfectly, she added, "Are we clear?"

"Yes, ma'am." This kiss was longer, and when she settled against his chest, Alex went for broke. "Marry me, Stace."

She shook her head. "No, not yet. Not until I can trust that you're for real."

"Fair enough," he conceded. He had Stacey in his arms, and back in his life. Alex had what mattered.

* * *

Wyatt sat on his front steps, his forearms resting on his knees, and watched faint fingers of light begin to touch the horizon. It was difficult for him to see much through the reddish glow of the city's force field, and he realized he missed viewing the sunrise.

He should be in bed, but he couldn't sleep. Too many thoughts whirled through his head, distracting him every time he closed his eyes, and not even a warm shower had calmed him.

Bug hadn't needed stitches in her hand, but it had been a near thing. McNamara had really chomped down. He hadn't realized just how bad the bite was until he'd seen it in good light at the infirmary. Shit, he should have taken on the colonel, not Kendall, but she'd jumped right in.

It was easy to guess why. She knew he'd feel bad afterward if he fought a woman, but he could live with it—he wasn't such a gentleman that he couldn't clock a female if the need arose. Kendall hadn't given him the option.

Kendall. She'd been furious, lashing out while they'd been in the temple, yet before they'd gone to the gate, she'd seemed to be over it. He wasn't sure if the last personal exchange they'd had was a good sign or not. She'd changed the subject after he'd told her she could rely on him. On the other hand, she hadn't told him she didn't want his help.

They needed to talk. He'd wanted to do it tonight, but Bug had nearly been asleep on her feet as he'd walked her home, and she wasn't up to the kind of discussion they had to have.

Shifting his gaze, he stared at the capstone of the pyramid. It seemed to be glowing faintly. He might never know a fraction of all the secrets the temple held. If it weren't for Bug, he wouldn't want to know, but if the fricking thing were trying to claim her, he had to learn as much as he could in order to fight it.

Wyatt heard a sound, and looked to his right. For a

minute, he thought he was imagining things—conjuring images of Kendall out of thin air and wishful thinking—but when she sat beside him, her hip warm against his, he knew it was no dream.

"How's the hand?" he asked quietly.

"Throbbing," she told him just as softly, "but that isn't what kept me awake."

"Why couldn't you sleep?"

She shrugged. "I had a lot to think about."

The possibilities were endless, but there was one topic that was the most likely. "You fretting about the smuggling ring?"

"Not right now."

Silence. Wyatt wasn't sure how to broach what he wanted to talk about, and Kendall didn't seem to be in a rush. Taking a deep breath, he decided the ball was in her court. She'd sought him out, and she'd get around to why in her own time. Hell, maybe she simply wanted to be with him. He was good with that.

But as she grew more tense, he knew she hadn't come to just sit quietly, and her stress made his own nerves pull taut. Bug meant everything to him—everything—and he was scared of what would happen if he pushed. But he'd never avoided the tough stuff, and so he said thickly, "Straight out, Bug, that's the best way."

"Easier said than done."

Wyatt rested his palm on her thigh, just above her knee. Like him, she'd changed into fresh clothes, and her camo fatigue pants were crisp to the touch.

About the time he feared he'd lose his mind, she said, "Wy?"

"Yeah, darlin'?"

"I love you." She blurted the words fast, and before he could reply, Bug added, "More than that, I'm *in* love with you."

Almost afraid to believe his ears, he turned his head to

meet her gaze. As terrified as she looked, Wyatt knew he'd heard her exactly right. "I love you too, Kendall."

"I know. I worked out a few things, that's why I couldn't sleep." Her smile was sickly. "The thought of losing you leaves me petrified, but I can't play it safe and go back to being just friends after we've been more. So I guess I'm on this ride for as long as it lasts." Her voice petered out, and she shrugged.

Wyatt about whooped, but then what she'd said sunk in. "What the hell do you mean, *as long as it lasts?* I'm in this forever, and I expect the same commitment from you."

"Don't worry, I intend to give our relationship everything I have, but things will change when we have to leave J Nine."

Taking a deep breath, he forced himself to listen to what she was trying to say, to read between the lines. He knew Kendall; she would give it her all. So what had her nervous? "Yeah," he told her, "things will change when we get back to Earth, but we'll deal with them as they arise. I'm not looking for an off-world fling; I'm planning to marry you."

So many expressions flew across her face so fast that Wyatt had no hope of reading them. "I think," Kendall said at last, "that we should wait on that. You'll change your mind."

Anger burned, but he forced it down. This wasn't about him. "Why do you think that?" he asked with hard-won neutrality. She looked uncomfortable and Wyatt wanted to cuddle her, but he couldn't. Not until after they'd hashed this out.

"Relationships don't last." He tried to interrupt, but she talked over him. "Your parents are the exception to the rule."

"You're not your mother," he told her.

"I know that, but it's not only her." She rested her hand

over his. "No one stays together forever anymore. Ten years, fifteen, and they're on to the next person."

Wyatt snorted. "That's not us. You and I are willing to do the hard work, to ride through the storms without bailing out. Dang, darlin', we're both so stubborn, the more difficult things get, the deeper we'll dig in—together."

"Yeah," she conceded. "And you grew up with an example of how to do it, while I was raised learning what not to do."

"The most important thing we know is that forever isn't easy. It's compromise and discussion and going toe-to-toe when it's necessary. We already do that," he reminded her.

"We do," Kendall agreed. "But there are other challenges. When we're back home, you'll be in the field a lot, especially since we're on the verge of another war, and in two more years, I'll be out of the army. I don't want to give up grad school."

"I don't want you to give up school either. Is there some reason why you couldn't pick a college near where I'm stationed?"

"The army moves people around all the time. If I move with you, then I'll continually have to start over in a new program, but if I don't move with you, what happens to us?"

Wyatt gave her thigh a squeeze. "That's easy." He grinned. "Most of Spec Ops is stationed at Fort Honore in California. The odds are slim that I'll be sent to any other post." He sobered. "I will be out in the field a lot, though, you're right about that, but you're strong. You can take care of anything that comes up while I'm on a mission. I'll miss you like heck while I'm gone, but I won't have to worry that you can't cope alone."

"Do you have an answer for everything?"

"Pretty much. I checked into it, and once we're married, the army will make sure we're stationed at the same post." Wyatt turned his hand to hold hers. "The other benefit to making it official is that you'll be protected if anything happens to me."

"Nothing better happen to you," Bug growled.

"As much as I'd like to promise you that, I can't." He swallowed hard, almost afraid to ask. "Can you handle the fact that when I leave on a mission, I might not come back?"

Kendall stared off into the night—right at the top of the pyramid—but he didn't say anything. If she needed to think about this, he had to give her time. They'd both need to make concessions for each other, and hers would be the more difficult. Wyatt liked his job—most of the time—and he was good at it. He didn't consider himself an adrenaline junkie, but he was already regretting the day he'd be pulled out of the field. His next promotion, though, was at least six years away. In his mind, it wasn't long enough, but for a woman wondering whether her man was going to make it home, that was an eternity of uncertainty.

Her sigh sounded loud in the predawn silence. "Yeah," Bug said at last, "I can live with it, but I won't like it."

"If our situations were reversed, I'd feel the same way." His good mood evaporated as he realized she hadn't stopped staring at the capstone. "Damn it, Kendall, is that fricking pyramid going to come between us in this life too?"

"The temple didn't come between Zolianna and Berkant," she disagreed.

"The hell it didn't. She loved that thing more than she loved him."

Kendall finally looked at him, her gaze heated. "You're wrong," she said quietly. "You need to consider how her behavior fit into *their* culture."

"He asked her time after time to leave with him. She wouldn't. I think that speaks for itself."

He heard Kendall blow out a long, harsh breath. "Zolianna—and Berkant, for that matter—were raised to follow the rules. The aliens didn't prize rebellion. Yet you expected her to toss aside a lifetime of conditioning and run off with him."

"Why not? He was willing to go against expectations."

"Not at first he wasn't, not when she could have left the temple easily. If he'd suggested it before she entered as a novitiate, she would have said yes. If he'd asked her before she took her final vows, she would have said yes. Hell, if he'd bothered to bring it up the first few years she was a priestess, Zolianna would have left with him immediately, but he didn't. Berkant waited until she'd been part of the temple for almost fifteen years. He waited till after she'd been proclaimed successor to the High Priestess, and her sense of responsibility wouldn't allow her to leave. Think about that, Wy."

He frowned. "You have a point," he admitted grudgingly. "Berkant did wait a long time, but that doesn't change things for us. I'm not playing second fiddle to that pyramid."

"Did I ask you to?"

"No, but you've spent more time since you arrived staring at it than looking at me." And damn it, that hurt.

Kendall glanced down at her hands, then back at him. "Because I'm a coward, okay? Because I'm afraid to look at you, and talk about how I feel. Not because you mean less to me."

"Aw, darlin'." He put his arm around her shoulders and pulled her to his side. "I'm not scary."

"No, but what you make me feel is. I've never been in love with anyone. I never wanted to be, but you snuck up on me."

"It's all the training I've had in covert operations," he teased, and was rewarded when Kendall gave him a weak smile.

Since she was already frightened, he decided not to

bring up marriage again. That could wait till she got used to the idea of being a couple. Hell, now that they were headed the same direction, he'd wait dang near forever for her to catch up with him.

"I heard you at the infirmary when you asked Sullivan if your team was staying on J Nine. I'm glad you are."

"Me too." Damn glad. Kendall loved him, but if he returned to Earth right now, she might convince herself they'd never last. It wasn't true, but he needed the time to help her trust that.

"There's one more thing I want to say."

"What's that?" Wyatt asked. Bug sounded serious.

"Remember that pink stone in the temple? The kunzite? I wondered why it was all over the place, but now I know. It was there to remind the priestesses that when in doubt, they should follow their hearts, not their heads. That the heart always knows the truth." She edged closer. "When I listened to my heart," Kendall put her uninjured hand over the center of her chest, "I knew we belonged together. It's still scary, but I'm not going to run from what we have, I promise."

"I know. Once you commit, it's full steam ahead." He grinned, then closed the gap between them to kiss her. It was long, and slow as he tried to show her how much he loved her. Kendall was his heart, part of his soul, and his whole world.

"Wy?"

"Yeah?" he murmured, then nipped her earlobe.

"Why don't we go to bed, and see if a little physical exertion won't help us sleep?"

He grinned. "Darlin', you read my mind."

Epilogue

It was nearly nine when Stacey heard Alex come in. Emma had been changed, fed, and burped, but she'd stubbornly refused to fall asleep. "Daddy's home," she said quietly, and she would swear she saw her baby's eyes light up.

Before she could do more than wonder whether it was imagination, Alex entered the room looking tired. "Hey, Stace." She lifted her face for his kiss. He lingered long enough for Emma to squawk. Easing away, Alex bent down, and pressed a loud smooch on Em's forehead. "I didn't forget you, munchkin."

Emma reached for Alex, and Stacey handed her over. She was used to this. Em was definitely a daddy's girl. It never ceased to bring a lump to her throat when she saw Alex cuddling his daughter. With care, he settled in the second rocker, and began to slowly move. "The private came by and told you I'd be late, right?" he asked keeping his voice low.

"Yes, he did." Alex had developed a habit of making

sure she knew when he wouldn't be home on time. "Is there something going on? Or can't you talk about it?"

With a huge yawn, Emma snuggled closer to Alex. "It wasn't anything important. Noguchi wanted to meet with me and my three Spec Ops captains, so we could brief her on what we do."

Stacey nodded. Alex had been running things, but last month Colonel Sakura Noguchi, the new post commander, had arrived and he'd resumed his usual duties. "What do you think of her?"

Alex didn't speak for a moment, simply rocked and rubbed Emma's back. The baby, Stacey noticed, was mostly asleep, and she couldn't help wondering whether Em had deliberately remained awake until her dad came home.

"Noguchi is a hard ass," he said at last.

Something in his voice tipped her off. "You like her."

"Yeah, I do," he admitted reluctantly. "She's a straight shooter, and diplomatic enough to take over command without stepping on anyone's toes. Not an easy feat with all these civilian consultants running their little fiefdoms."

And not easy because she was taking over for the disgraced Colonel McNamara. Alex had spent months rooting out the members of the smuggling ring. It had helped that many of those caught had been eager to turn evidence, but he'd been meticulous—Stacey hid a smile. He'd had to be. Captain Kendall Thomas had made herself part of the investigation, combing through the files when she was off duty until Alex had officially drafted her. Stacey liked the young captain, but to say she was zealous about protecting the antiquities on J Nine was understating the matter.

"Noguchi invited us to dinner next week. Think you're ready to leave the munchkin with a sitter?"

Stacey smiled. "The question is whether a sitter will be prepared to deal with Emma. She's a little spoiled, thanks to her daddy."

"Hey," Alex said, returning her grin, "I have to get on her good side while I can. We both know that when she's a teenager, Emma and I will be butting heads."

"Because you're overprotective."

"Damn straight. It's a dangerous world out there. I shielded Ravyn; I'll shield my daughter too."

Stacey shook her head. Em was only a few months old, but she already displayed a tenacity that was daunting. It was easy to imagine the battles her willful daughter would be having with her father in about thirteen years, and Stacey decided she'd better enjoy the relative peace while she could.

She didn't say any of that, though. Alex knew. He'd been through the war once when he'd raised his sister, and he wouldn't flinch at any weapon Emma brought to the battle.

"She's asleep," Stacey told him instead.

Alex checked, decided she was right, and stood to gently lower Emma into her crib. He gazed down at her for a minute, and Stacey joined him. "She's beautiful," Alex said softly.

"Yes, she is," she agreed. Little Emma with her cinnamon hair and big brown eyes was going to break hearts one day. If her daddy let a boy near enough to ask her out.

"She's already grown so much since she was born. Before we know it, she'll be walking." Alex was silent for a moment. "I hope Noguchi doesn't call many of these after-duty-shift meetings. I don't want to miss out on more than I have to."

Emma stirred then, and Stacey tugged him out of the room before the baby woke up. When she had the lights lowered and the door partially closed, she asked, "Did you eat?"

"Yeah, the colonel had them bring mess to us."

She nodded. "Do you want to sit outside for a while?"

Without a word, he led her out to the back porch. Alex

had set up a bench swing next to Emma's window, and
that's where they settled. They sat side by side, Alex's arm
around her shoulders, and idly swayed. She could feel
him winding down, sense the tension leaving his muscles,
but he remained silent. "You're pretty quiet tonight,"
Stacey said.

"Just thinking." For a minute, she thought she'd have
to prod him to get him to talk, but Alex asked, "Do you
have regrets? About staying on J Nine, having Emma,
marrying me?"

Stacey's heart leapt into her throat. They'd only been
married a month, he couldn't be sorry already—could he?
"No," she said thickly, "I don't regret any of it. Why do
you ask?"

He pulled his eyes from the yard to meet her gaze. "A year
ago today you told me to find somewhere else to sleep."

The military operated on Earth time as much as they
could, but it didn't match up with Jarved Nine's cycles,
and Stacey frequently lost track. Then it occurred to her
that Alex had marked the date, remembered it, and was
brooding over it. "You're still rough around the edges,
Sullivan, but you're getting there."

Smiling faintly, he said, "You're sure? You really don't
regret staying with me, giving me that last chance?"

"I really don't. When you put your mind to something,
there's no stopping you. You decided to change, to open
yourself, and while you have your days, they're becoming
rarer. Staying with you was the best decision I ever made.
I love you, Alex." Stacey felt his whole body relax.

"I love you too, Stace, for keeps."

Wyatt heard the sound of the wind chimes as he turned
onto the street. Kendall. His heart beat a little faster, and
he picked up his pace. He found her sitting on the
balustrade of their front porch, a boot propped on the rail.

"Hey, darlin'," he said, and cupped her head so he could kiss her the way he'd been hankering to all day.

Before he could really sink into her, though, Bug eased away, and stood, her body pressing into his. They both froze as sensation rocketed through them—he knew she felt it as strongly as he did—and Wyatt pulled her more tightly against him. They'd been living together for nearly a year now, and they still had the fireworks she'd mentioned. He leaned down to kiss her again.

"Hold that thought," Kendall said, stepping back. Before he could object, she took his hand, and said, "Come on."

Reluctantly, he went along with her. Although he was curious, Wyatt didn't ask questions—at least not until he saw the direction they were headed. "Are we going to the temple?"

"Yes." When he balked, she added, "Please, Wy."

With a scowl, he capitulated. They had one point of serious friction between them—the fricking pyramid. In the beginning, she'd talked about her trips there and what she'd discovered, but that hadn't lasted long. It was his own damn fault. He never could manage to hide his anger when she mentioned the temple, and after a while, Bug had stopped sharing anything about it. Wyatt was sure she hadn't quit visiting it, she'd just quit telling him about those forays. That ate at him.

And it was starting to drive a wedge between them.

He knew it was happening, and yet he couldn't change how he felt; he was jealous of a damn pile of rock. The temple had become the elephant in the living room, the thing they were both aware of, yet pretending to ignore.

Apparently, Kendall had decided it was time to deal with it.

She led him through the herb house, into the secret passage, and onto the lift. Instead of taking him to the High Priestess's chambers, however, she stopped at a lower level, and walked until they stood in the doorway of a cavernous room.

"This is the chancel," Bug said. "You can't enter, but you can see everything from here."

Without waiting for him to reply, she slipped inside the room and strolled to the raised altar. Wyatt felt uneasy, and that grew as Kendall donned the forest green robe that she'd worn as Zolianna. He tried to take a step forward, but some unseen field held him at bay. A growl of frustration escaped, and that intensified when she started chanting in an unknown language.

Fear. He'd faced down armed enemy soldiers without feeling as terrified as he was at this moment. "No!" he called, but Kendall either didn't hear or she ignored him.

Part of him wanted to walk away and not see this, but another part of him couldn't leave. Wyatt had to know if he'd lost Kendall for good. He clenched his hands into fists to try to control the trembling and watched her move to a large, flat stone. Her intonation sounded more staccato, as if she'd reached an important point. Then he saw Bug put her palm down.

A glow formed around her. Wyatt's throat felt thick, and his stomach was turning barrel rolls. "Kendall," he said, but his voice came out a whisper.

Gradually, the light around her dimmed, and Bug stood back. Even from where he stood, he could see she was unsteady as she shrugged out of the robe, and carefully folded it. Slowly, she descended the stairs, and walked up the aisle to return to him.

When she stood before him, Wyatt demanded, "What the hell did you just do?"

Kendall smiled tiredly. "I know how you feel about the temple, and it's caused tension between us for much too long." She put her arms around his neck. "I understand why, but I'm not Zolianna. I don't love this place. Yeah, I'm fascinated by it, but I love *you*. I did what I had to do so you'd know you're first with me, and you always will be."

Wyatt's stomach steadied, and he felt hope spark. "What did you do? I couldn't understand any of it."

"Zolianna died unexpectedly, without passing on her powers to a successor. There's a rite for that situation, but her people abandoned the planet before it was performed. I'll translate for you the diary I found, but the gist of it is the lord, lady and their guardians planned to remain here, imprison the killer, and then the people would return. Since the priestesses expected to be gone only a short time, the cortege decided they'd wait to transition the powers to a new leader. They also left the temple online, so to speak. Only they never came back." Kendall shrugged. "My guess is the plan to capture the murderer was unsuccessful."

His hands tightened at her waist, then relaxed. "The temple took you when we entered the middle portion of the pyramid."

"It recognized me," Bug corrected. "As long as the temple is active, it needs a High Priestess, but the only way to get rid of the powers is to transfer them. I don't trust anyone else. Not with what I can do." She pulled herself closer. "So I did the next best thing. I made the temple dormant."

"What exactly does that mean?"

"It means the pyramid will continue to perform the vital functions it must do to help the city run, but no more than that. I've turned off its links to the planet and the universe. Bottom line, I gave up my connection to the temple."

For a moment, all he did was stare at her, then he said, "You didn't have to do that."

"Yes, I did. I want forever with you, Wyatt Montgomery, and I wasn't losing you because of some fricking pile of rock."

He grinned at her attempt to imitate his drawl. Hell, he grinned just because he was happy. Tipping her face up to his, he kissed her long and slow. He had to convey to her how much this meant to him. Bug loved him. She loved him enough to walk away from everything the pyramid had to offer.

Wyatt broke the kiss. "I love you, Kendall, and I swear to God you won't regret doing this."

She leaned back, and gave him a nervous smile. "So you love me; I love you. What do you say we get married?"

With a whoop, he spun Bug in a circle. He must have asked her two dozen times, but the answer had always been *let's wait.* "Darlin', I say heck yeah! The sooner the better."

Kendall arched her neck to allow him access as he kissed his way down her jaw. "You don't want to wait till we're back on Earth," she asked breathlessly, "and your family can be there?"

Nipping her throat one last time, Wyatt raised his head. "I love my family, you know that, but I'm not giving you a chance to change your mind. As soon as I can get you in front of the chaplain, I'm putting a ring on your finger. Okay?"

"Okay," Kendall agreed, and pulled his head back to hers so she could kiss him senseless.

"What do you say," Wyatt murmured when he came up for air, "we find somewhere to celebrate?" Since he had her bra unhooked, and his hand under her T-shirt, cupping her bare breast, he was pretty confident she knew what he had in mind.

Bug shook her head. "Do me here."

"In the hall?"

"Zolianna and Berkant hid their trysts under cover of night. He snuck into her rooms, and out again, but this is the main corridor of the inner sanctum. Maybe it's silly, but if we make love here, it'll be like erasing all the furtiveness of their relationship, and starting with a clean slate."

Smiling slowly, Wyatt said, "Yeah, I get it. We'll be exorcising a few ghosts." He raised her shirt over her head, and dropped it to the floor. The bra followed. "Kendall? Next life, it's your turn to chase me."

"Only if you promise to let me catch you."

Wyatt froze as she opened his pants and stroked him. His voice came out choked when he said, "Deal."

Patti O'Shea
THE POWER OF TWO

The U. C. E.: In the 21st and 22nd centuries, the United States changed and grew. Now the "United Colonies of Earth" dominate the globe. But a mysterious voice is broadcasting treason, inciting revolution and referring to an enigmatic figure named Banzai Maguire.

To find Banzai, the U.C.E. assigns Cai, whose neural implants allow her to sit back in a control chair and feed information to her partner, the dark-souled Jacob Tucker. He's as rigid as he is deadly…or handsome. But this time, Cai needs Jake to trust her completely. Whether he likes it or not, she can't sit back while he fights the bad guys. Wherever this mission takes her, Cai is gonna be the one kicking a little tail.

CRIMSON CITY

Don't miss any of this fabulous series!